Queen

A collection o
the world's lea

International
bestselling author

ANNE
MATHER

has written more than 150 books,
appeared on the New York Times bestseller
list, and sold more than 40 million copies
of her novels.

"Anne Mather shows herself equally
adept at taking on a foreign drug
cartel or the sensual beast within, both
of which add up to pleasure for her
readers."
—*Romantic Times*

"Anne Mather pens a wonderful hero
and a passionate, dramatic storyline."
—*Romantic Times*

Available in the
Queens of Romance
collection

17th March 2006

7th April 2006

21st April 2006

5th May 2006

Collect all 4 superb books!

ANNE MATHER

Innocence Betrayed

Containing

Her Guilty Secret
Innocent Sins

M&B™ and M&B™ with the Rose Device
are trademarks of the publisher.
Harlequin Mills & Boon Limited, Eton House,
18-24 Paradise Road,
Richmond, Surrey TW9 1SR

Innocence Betrayed © by Harlequin Books S.A. 2006

Her Guilty Secret and *Innocent Sins* were
first published in Great Britain by Harlequin Mills & Boon
Limited in separate, single volumes.

Her Guilty Secret © Anne Mather 1999
Innocent Sins © Anne Mather 2000

ISBN 0 263 85042 0

062-0506

Printed and bound in Spain
by Litografia Rosés S.A., Barcelona

Her Guilty Secret

ANNE MATHER

Anne Mather has written since she was seven, but it was only when her first child was born that she fulfilled her dream of becoming a writer. Her first book, CAROLINE, appeared in 1966. It met with immediate success and, since then, Anne has written more than 150 novels, reaching a readership which spans the world. Born and raised in the north of England, Anne still makes her home there with her husband, two children and, now, grandchildren. Asked if she finds writing a lonely occupation, she replies that her characters always keep her company. In fact, she is so busy sorting out their lives that she often doesn't have time for her own! An avid reader herself, she devours everything from sagas and romances to mainstream fiction and suspense.

CHAPTER ONE

THE man sitting at the other side of the desk cleared his throat. 'You are familiar with this kind of thing, aren't you?' he asked, glancing doubtfully about the office. Kate guessed that her addition of some pot plants and a parlour palm had caught his eye. Perhaps they didn't look very professional, she thought defensively, but they brightened up what was otherwise a rather gloomy room.

'Perfectly familiar,' she answered him now, shuffling the papers in front of her as if each and every one of them was a case pending her attention. In fact, since her father's death, the cases had been few and far between. Not everyone was prepared to trust their secrets to a woman who looked considerably younger than her thirty-two years. And the name on the door said William Ross, Private Investigator, which meant they were already disappointed when they encountered a woman instead. 'Just give me the details of the last time you saw your wife, and I'll do my best to get you a satisfactory result.'

The man hesitated, evidently still not convinced she could handle the matter, and Kate fought back the urge to scream. For heaven's sake, she thought, what was so difficult about finding a missing spouse? Her father used to practically survive on such cases, usually finding the runaway in some other man's bed.

'You do understand this must be dealt with in the strictest confidence?' he persisted, and Kate gave him her most convincing look. But she couldn't help the thought that he was not the most appealing of clients. He was wearing a worn jacket and trousers and grubby trainers, and she had to wonder if he could afford her services.

5

'Any information you give me is totally confidential,' she assured him firmly, aware of a certain reluctance to take on this case. But beggars can't be choosers, she reminded herself dryly, and her mother wouldn't be very pleased if she started turning clients away.

'The charges,' he said now, as if putting off the moment when he had to give her his wife's details. 'Are they negotiable?'

'I'm afraid not.' Kate always hated this part of the business. 'It's a hundred pounds a day, plus expenses. And I'm afraid I have to ask for payment in advance.'

'In advance?' His rather close-set eyes widened in a face that was neither distinguished nor memorable. Kate imagined he was in his late forties, but the downward curve of his mouth added at least half a dozen more years.

'It's customary,' she said, endeavouring to sound professional. 'After all, if I have no luck in finding your wife, you might object to paying then. Besides—' she forced a smile '—naturally there are expenses. But I'll keep a record of what I spend on a day-to-day basis.'

'Hmm.' The man considered her explanation with a drawn brow, and Kate began to feel uncomfortable. If she'd had only herself to care about, she'd have been quite happy to send him on his way. To some other agency, with a man to attend to his needs.

But she wasn't a free agent. And, despite the law degree that she'd spent more years than she cared to remember getting, this was the only job she had. Of course, if she'd been prepared to move to London, she might have been able to find some solicitor willing to give her a chance. But in a small town like King's Montford there were too many articled clerks already waiting for dead men's shoes.

The man was fumbling in his jacket pocket now, pulling out an envelope that looked surprisingly thick. Opening the flap, he threw a wad of notes on the desk in front of her. 'Will that do to be going on with?' he asked. 'There's a couple of thousand there.'

Kate tried not to look as shocked as she felt. Most of the clients she'd had recently had been prepared to put up a couple of days' expenses and nothing more. What couldn't she do with two thousand pounds? she thought weakly. She could pay the rent, for one thing, and give Joanne the money she needed for that school skiing trip.

'I—that's fine,' she said now, inadequately, though she held back from picking up the notes. Her father's training was warning her to find out what the job entailed before she committed herself. Even if she couldn't see any immediate problem in attempting to locate his wife.

'Good.' The man, who had been resting one foot on his knee, now dropped it to the floor and leaned forward in his chair. 'I expect you want to know her name, don't you?' he said. 'And the last time I saw her.'

'It would help,' said Kate whimsically, but then, seeing no answering humour in his expression, she quickly sobered. She mustn't let him know that this contribution to her finances had brought her such a sense of relief. And she hadn't decided to take the job yet, she reminded herself. What had her father always told her? Make sure it was legal first.

'All right.' The man nodded. 'Her name's Sawyer; Alicia Sawyer.'

'Alicia—Sawyer.' Kate grabbed a clean pad and wrote the woman's name at the top. But Alicia, she thought ruefully. Somehow that name didn't go with the rather shifty individual sitting opposite. Still—

'She hasn't been seen for a couple of months,' he added, rather curiously, Kate thought. Had he waited two months before deciding to report her missing? Or had the police been dealing with the matter up till now?

'And your name, Mr Sawyer?' she ventured, deciding to take things in order. 'Your first name, that is,' she appended, arching her dark brows. 'Just for my records, of course.'

He frowned. 'Is that necessary?'

'If you don't mind.'

He waited a beat. 'It's—Henry,' he said at last. 'Henry Sawyer,' he repeated, with a sniff. 'Can we get on?'

Kate wrote his name beside that of his wife and then looked up. 'Of course,' she said pleasantly. 'Perhaps you'd better start by giving me her description. Or do you have a photograph?'

'What? Oh—yeah.' He rifled his pockets again and came up with a two-by-four-inch snapshot. 'That do?' he asked, hunching his shoulders with obvious irritation.

Kate looked at the photograph. She saw a blonde-haired woman with a well-developed figure. The photograph was slightly smudged so the finer details were not clearly defined. 'Um—how old is Mrs Sawyer?' she asked, frowning, surprised at how attractive the woman was.

'I—' He hesitated and then blew out a breath. 'Thirty-nine,' he volunteered shortly. 'Yeah, that's right. Thirty-nine.'

Kate nodded and added that detail to her pad. 'I assume you reported her disappearance to the police?'

He looked down at his hands. 'Yeah, yeah,' he said. 'Of course I told the police my suspicions. But you know what?' He looked up. 'They didn't want to know.'

Kate stared at him. 'I find that hard to believe.'

'Oh, they went through the motions,' he muttered harshly. 'But I didn't have any real evidence. That was when I knew that finding her was up to me.'

Kate was confused. 'You say you reported your wife's disappearance to the police and they did nothing about it?'

He shrugged. 'Sort of.' And then, seeing her incredulity, he said, 'That's right.'

'But—'

'See, she wasn't living with me when she disappeared,' he added abruptly, and Kate began to get the feeling that he was just wasting her time.

'Not living with you?'

'No.' Sawyer flashed her a look of dislike. 'She walked

out six months ago. Women!' He scowled. 'The bitch didn't even leave me a note.'

The bitch!

Kate made another note on her pad and then slid another sheet of paper over it. She didn't want him to see what she'd written down. 'If your wife left you six months ago—'

'She did.'

'Then surely her whereabouts are not your problem. If she doesn't want you to know where she is, Mr Sawyer—'

'I know where she went,' he broke in savagely, and Kate felt an uneasy twinge of alarm. She was alone in the building, the other office workers having left for home over an hour ago. She'd even let Susie go, assuring her she could manage on her own. She'd only hung on because Sawyer had asked her to. He'd maintained he couldn't make it before six o'clock.

'If you know—' she began faintly, remembering that her father's old revolver was still in the bottom drawer of the desk. If he made a move on her, she could always threaten to use it. She didn't know if it was loaded, of course, but he wouldn't know that.

'Until she disappeared, I knew exactly where she was living,' he informed her impatiently, but at least he seemed less aggressive than before. 'But, like I said, no one's seen her recently, and I want to know where she is, all right?'

'All right.' Kate sighed, wondering how to broach her next question. 'Would you like to tell me why she—walked out?'

'Why d'you think? That bastard seduced her into leaving me, didn't he?' His jaw compressed. 'He stole my wife, Mrs Ross. And now she's disappeared, and he won't say where she's gone.'

Kate didn't correct him. Although her name wasn't Ross, it was sometimes easier to let people think it was. It gave a certain anonymity to her private life, and enabled her to use her own name when she didn't want to advertise her occupation.

She frowned. It was all becoming abundantly clear. This

woman, his wife, Alicia Sawyer—that name still stuck in her throat—had run off with a man her husband knew. A friend of his, perhaps? But no longer, obviously. If that was the case, she saw no reason why she shouldn't take it on.

'The other man,' she ventured now. 'You know him?'

'Oh, yeah, I know him,' he snarled, baring nicotine-stained teeth. 'His name's Kellerman; Alex Kellerman. Have you heard of him? He owns that big property just off the Bath Road.'

Kate felt her jaw drop and quickly rescued it. It wouldn't do to let her client see how shocked she was. But Alex Kellerman, she thought incredulously. She couldn't believe it. What would a man like Kellerman want with Henry Sawyer's wife?

But she had no right to think that way, she chided herself severely. If her photograph was anything to go by, Alicia Sawyer was a beautiful woman, and any man would be proud to be seen with her. Just because Alex Kellerman had had his own problems, that did not mean he was immune to sexual attraction. Life was full of surprises. She should know; her own life hadn't exactly gone to plan.

'I—know who Mr Kellerman is,' she said now. And then, just in case he took her words literally, she added, 'I mean, I've heard of him, of course.' She tapped her pen against the pad in front of her, suddenly aware of the ramifications. 'The Kellerman stables are well known in King's Montford.' She took a breath. 'Um—how did your wife meet Mr Kellerman? Do you know?'

Sawyer gave her another scornful stare. 'Of course I know!' he exclaimed, as if it should have been obvious to her as well. 'She worked for him, didn't she?'

'Did she?' Kate's dark brows ascended again, but she refused to be intimidated this time. 'Well…' She made another note on her pad. 'That explains a lot. In what capacity was she employed?'

Sawyer regarded her sourly. 'You mean what was the job he offered her, don't you?' Kate nodded and he rubbed his nose with a grimy finger. 'Some kind of office work, I think. That's what she told me, anyway.'

'Right.' Kate added that piece of information to her list. 'Did she work there long?'

'Long enough.' Sawyer was bitter. 'Long enough to persuade her to leave me. We were happy enough until she went to work at Jamaica Hill.'

'And where did she go when she left you?' Kate thought she could see where this was going, but she wanted him to lay it out.

'To Jamaica Hill, of course. She went to live with Kellerman. She moved in there about six months ago.'

'Ah.' Kate rolled her lips inward. 'And you believe they were having an affair?'

'I don't just believe it. I know it.' He grimaced. 'She left me, didn't she? Why else would she do that?'

Kate could think of several reasons but she didn't voice them. 'And now you say she's not there any more.'

'She's gone missing,' he corrected her, his tone sour. 'I— I loved the silly bitch, didn't I? I've kept tabs on her ever since she left.'

Kate wondered if that constituted stalking, and then put the thought out of her head. It wasn't up to her to question his motives. If his wife had disappeared, it surely couldn't be too difficult to find out where she'd gone.

'So—you'd like to know where she's working now,' she said carefully, refusing to give any credit to a more sinister solution. He was jealous and resentful. That was normal. It was quite a relief to understand where he was coming from.

'If she is working somewhere else,' he put in grimly, and she couldn't quite suppress the unease that his words aroused inside her. 'See, she disappeared more than eight weeks ago. And no one seems to have heard from her since.'

Kate swallowed. 'She's probably left King's Montford,' she said, ignoring her misgivings. 'Perhaps she doesn't want—anyone—to know where she's gone.'

'I don't believe that,' he contradicted her harshly. 'That

bastard's hiding something. And I guess you remember what happened to Kellerman's wife.'

Kate sucked in a breath. 'You're not seriously suggesting—'

'That he killed her?' interrupted Sawyer disparagingly. 'Why not? He got away with it before, didn't he?'

Kate gasped. 'Mrs Kellerman's death was accidental.'

'Was it?'

'Of course.' But she could feel herself trembling, even so. 'Besides,' she persevered, 'Mrs Sawyer was an employee. If he'd wanted to get rid of her, he only had to fire her.'

Sawyer could see her indecision. 'And what if Alicia refused to go quietly? Who knows what kind of scandal that would have caused? She was a sucker for a clever line, but she could be awkward, if it suited her. I doubt if Kellerman's business could have survived any more bad publicity.'

Kate shook her head. What had begun—in her eyes, at least—as a simple inquiry had suddenly assumed the proportions of a major investigation. Or it had if she gave any credence to what he was implying. For God's sake, was he mad? Alex Kellerman was not a monster. His wife had died in suspicious circumstances, but he'd been absolved of any blame.

And yet…

She didn't want to consider it, but she couldn't help remembering the torrid headlines a couple of years ago when Pamela Kellerman had broken her neck. She'd apparently been riding a horse that her husband knew to be dangerous, the tabloids had reported. At a time when she was three months pregnant with the couple's second child.

There'd been a lot of speculation, she recalled reluctantly. Despite Pamela Kellerman's pregnancy, it had been common knowledge that Alex Kellerman and his wife were having marital problems. It had been mooted that it was only because of their daughter, who had been two years old at the time, that they'd stayed together. It had even been hinted that the child she'd been carrying when she fell to her death wasn't her husband's. That she'd been having an affair and that was why her husband had snapped.

Of course, it had all been speculation. And the newspapers had been careful not to print anything that might give Alex Kellerman a reason to sue. But the fact remained that Pamela Kellerman should not have been riding that particular horse, and no one had ever satisfactorily explained why two horses with similar markings—but very dissimilar temperaments—should have been put into opposite stalls.

The inquest had proved to be quite a drama, with Pamela's father accusing his son-in-law in court. He had had to be led away by his solicitor, she remembered. Alex Kellerman had been cold and tight-lipped throughout the whole proceedings, but there'd been no evidence to implicate him. Pamela's death had been judged accidental, and although the rumours had persisted for some time they'd eventually died away.

Recalling Alex Kellerman's hard, yet compelling features—as portrayed in the newspaper reports at the time—Kate couldn't dispel a shiver of apprehension. But she couldn't allow Sawyer to go around making accusations he couldn't prove. 'Mrs Kellerman's death was an accident,' she insisted firmly. 'I'm not surprised the police didn't take you seriously if you made unsubstantiated allegations like that.'

'You said anything I told you would be treated as confidential,' he reminded her sharply. 'Now, do you want the job or not? I don't have time to f—to mess around.'

Kate made a pretence of studying her notes to give herself time to consider. Were her rent and Joanne's school trip really worth the hassle of taking this case? So far all she'd handled were divorce and insurance investigations. She was making a living, but only just.

And, if she ignored her client's surely exaggerated insinuations, it should be a fairly straightforward inquiry. Alicia Sawyer had worked for Alex Kellerman for some time so there would obviously be people at the stables who remembered her. It ought to be easy enough to find out why she'd left and where she'd gone. If they'd known who Sawyer was—and that seemed likely—they'd probably been reluctant to divulge any information to him.

'I'll need a few more details,' she said at last, hoping she wasn't going to regret her decision. 'When did you first suspect that Alex Kellerman was interested in your wife? Have you spoken to her since she left? And did she take all her belongings with her?'

It was after eight o'clock when Kate let herself into the apartment she shared with her mother and daughter in Milner Court. It had been dark and cold as she drove her father's old Vauxhall through the empty streets of King's Montford, but the apartment was warm and welcoming, and the living room, where her mother and twelve-year-old Joanne were watching television, was cosy in the lamplight.

'You're late!' exclaimed her mother at once, getting to her feet and coming across the room to meet her. 'I put your supper in the oven a couple of hours ago, so I doubt if it's very palatable now.'

'Don't worry. I had a sandwich in lieu of lunch at about three o'clock so I'm not particularly hungry,' replied Kate, smiling as her daughter raised a languid hand in her direction. 'Hi, darling,' she added. 'I hope you did your homework before you started watching the box.'

'I did,' said Joanne placidly, and her grandmother confirmed it with a nod.

'She did it before supper. When you said you'd be late, we hung on for you. For a while, anyway. I didn't think you meant half-past eight.'

'I didn't,' admitted Kate ruefully, taking off her overcoat. 'But my client was late, and after he'd gone I called into the *Herald's* office to do some initial checking into the facts of the case. I should have rung, I know, but I didn't expect to take so long. I'm sorry if you've been worried.'

'So you should be,' agreed her mother wryly, removing Kate's overcoat from the back of the chair where she'd deposited it and folding it over her arm to hang away. 'I assume Susie was with you, was she?'

'Well, no.' Kate was contrite. 'She had a hot date tonight, so I said she could go.' Besides, Susie was a teenager. She answered phones and did some necessary typing, but that was all.

Mrs Ross shook her head. 'Well, I think you're very foolish. You know how I feel about you seeing clients after hours. Your father was a man. He could look after himself.'

'I can look after myself, too,' Kate insisted, pulling a face. 'Honestly, Mum, you're so sexist at times.'

'But realistic,' remarked Joanne, turning from the soap she was watching to give her mother a warning look. 'Come on, Mum, we both know your martial arts training wouldn't be much good against a knife. Get real! You're no match for a serious villain.'

'I don't deal with serious villains,' retorted her mother impatiently, her eyes darting a silent plea for restraint. Joanne knew how her grandmother worried. Didn't she have any more sense than to suggest she was running a risk? 'You've been watching too much television,' she added. 'My cases are very ordinary, as you know.'

'So far,' said Joanne, ignoring her mother's expression and determined to have the last word. 'So who is this man you had to see after hours? Was he ordinary, too?'

Kate thought guiltily of the two thousands pounds residing in her shoulder bag and then pushed the memory aside. 'Very ordinary,' she said determinedly. 'And you know I never discuss my cases with you.'

It wasn't until she was safely in bed that Kate allowed herself to think about the case again. She was still not at all sure she had made the right decision in accepting it, and she tucked the covers beneath her chin as if to ward off the sudden sense of chill that invaded her bones.

Yet, she had only Henry Sawyer's word that Alicia Sawyer had disappeared, and the idea that there might be something suspicious about it if she had was purely supposition. Her client hardly inspired confidence, and with a husband like him Alicia might just be keeping out of his way.

She'd probably moved on, got another job, decided not to let her husband know where she was going. Kate didn't believe for a moment that Alex Kellerman was involved in her disappearance. It was far too melodramatic and smacked of a desire for revenge rather than justice.

If—and she had no real proof of this yet—if Alicia had had a relationship with Alex Kellerman, what of it? There was no law that said a man shouldn't have an affair with an employee. The only unpleasant aspect of the situation was that he'd taken another woman to live in the house which he'd shared with Pamela. He must have known it would cause gossip—or didn't he care?

The Kellermans had only been married for three years when she'd fallen to her death. Kate had discovered that that evening during the time she'd spent going over the old news reports. She'd also learned that his daughter had only narrowly avoided witnessing the accident. Kate's heart ached for the little girl and the trauma she must have suffered since.

She sighed. Not for the first time, she wished her father was still alive so that she could have discussed her thoughts with him. She'd have welcomed his advice. His experience had meant a lot. The tragedy was, they'd only worked together for a few months before he'd had the heart attack that had killed him. A heart attack, her mother was convinced, which had been brought on by the strains of the job.

But she'd have been grateful for his wisdom now, thought Kate ruefully. The wisdom of any man, she conceded, aware that her own life was sadly lacking in that department. But since Sean had been killed she'd shied away from any serious attachment, and despite the fact that it was over ten years since his death she rarely admitted a man into her life.

In the beginning, she'd made Joanne the excuse, and it was true that immediately after the accident she had clung to her small daughter. She'd been bitter then, and hurt. She'd given up so much for Sean Hughes, and, however devastated she'd felt when he was killed, he had let her down.

Her parents had been marvellous, of course. Despite the fact that they'd never approved of her relationship with Sean, they'd been there when she needed them. They'd given her and Joanne a home when the house she'd shared with Sean had had to be sold, and they'd supported her until she could get a job and get back on her feet.

She punched her pillow, trying to get comfortable, but thoughts of her husband's betrayal only added to the restlessness she was feeling tonight. It was listening to Henry Sawyer describe his wife's infidelities. It had reminded her of so much she wanted to forget...

She'd been in her freshman year at university when she'd first met Sean. She'd been working at the supermarket during the Easter holidays, stacking shelves, trying to make some money to supplement her grant, when he'd started taking an interest in her. It had been such a thrill, she remembered unwillingly. All the other girls had been fascinated by the handsome young under-manager and she wouldn't have been human if she hadn't been flattered by his attention.

They'd started a relationship: a light-hearted one to begin with, but by Christmas it was getting really heavy. He'd wanted her to stay in King's Montford, not to go back to Warwick in January, to move in with him instead. He was crazy about her, he'd told her, and he didn't know what he'd do if she left him now.

What he'd really meant, Kate had realised, was that if she went back to university he wouldn't wait for her. There'd be some other woman by the time she came back in the summer. And, because she'd thought she was in love with him, she'd abandoned her law degree, marrying him instead and moving into the tiny house he owned in Queen Street, and staying on at the supermarket full-time.

They'd been happy, for a while anyway. Even her parents, who had been so disappointed by her decision to give up her university place, had swallowed their pride and helped them to buy a car. When Joanne had come along, they'd been delighted to welcome their granddaughter, even if they would have preferred for Kate and Sean to have saved some money before they'd brought a baby into the world.

Then, a few days before Joanne's second birthday, Kate's world had fallen apart. Sean had told Kate he was going to Bristol on business, but when the police had come to give her the terrible news about the accident they'd been forced to tell her there'd been a woman with him in the car. They'd both been killed instantly when the Sierra had run into the back of a stationary wagon that had been parked on the hard shoulder, and Kate had been left to speculate what Sean had been doing to swerve so badly off the road.

At the inquest, she'd learned that they'd both been drinking, and, in the absence of any other evidence, a verdict of death while under the influence of alcohol had been returned. She'd learned later, from a well-meaning sympathiser, that Sean had been having an affair with the woman who'd died with him. It had been a long-term relationship by all accounts, which had started when she was pregnant with Joanne.

She'd realised then that she'd had her suspicions all along. Sean had been absent too many times for all his excuses of overtime to be true. She'd been burying her head for so long, it had been hard to come to terms with it and many more months had passed before she was able to face the future with any optimism.

Not that she regretted all of what had happened. Her daughter was a constant source of delight to her. But when Joanne was six Kate had known she had to get on with her life. She'd enrolled at Bristol University and finished the degree she'd started at Warwick, which enabled her to travel to college every day but come home every night to put Joanne to bed.

However, when she'd eventually tried to get a job, she'd found it wasn't that easy. There were few jobs around, and no one wanted to employ a thirty-year-old unmarried mother when there were plenty of younger, unencumbered graduates around. After months without success, her father had offered a temporary solution. He needed an assistant, he'd said, now that his secretary had retired, and Kate's legal training would come in very useful.

She'd thought he was only being kind to begin with, that, far from needing another assistant, there was barely enough work for one. But, gradually, she'd come to realise that she did have her uses, that she could do all the legwork while her father concentrated his talents in solving the cases.

They'd been a good team, too, she reflected, a lump forming in her throat. And she'd become interested in the business, and eager to learn all she could. But then her father had had his fatal heart attack and word had got around that Kate was on her own, and for a while the jobs had just stopped coming. She'd been half afraid she'd have to find something else to do.

But, slowly, she was gaining people's confidence, and because she'd had several successful results the business was coming back. Which was why she hadn't hesitated when Sawyer had asked her to see him after hours. She couldn't afford to give a negative response.

Yet...

The moonlight glinted on the strap of the tote bag she'd carried into the bedroom with her. She hadn't dared leave the envelope containing the money anywhere that her daughter might find it. Or her mother either, she conceded uneasily, not totally convinced Mrs Ross would approve. Where had the money come from? Was it legal? Why, exactly, did Henry Sawyer want her to trace his wife?

CHAPTER TWO

A BAR of sunlight squeezed between the drawn blinds, causing the man lying in its path to raise one arm to protect his closed eyes. Despite the fact that it was early November, the weakening sun could still be annoyingly brilliant, penetrating even his eyelids and arousing him from sleep.

'Damn,' he muttered, rolling onto his side to escape its rays, and then stifling an oath when his outflung arm connected with a warm body that wasn't his. He slitted his lids. Dammit, he thought in frustration, he was in Lacey's bed. God knew what time it was. He didn't remember much since last night.

'You're insatiable, do you know that?'

Lacey's drowsy voice warned him that his careless movements had been misconstrued, and he abruptly withdrew his hand from her rounded hip. It was always the same: he invariably despised himself after going on one of his binges, and it was just hard luck that Lacey had born the brunt.

Despite the fact that his head was pounding, he rolled purposefully off the bed. He staggered a little as he got to his feet, but the room soon stopped spinning. Apart from a burning desire to use the bathroom, he considered he was in comparatively good shape.

'Don't go.'

Lacey's plea fell on deaf ears, however, as he emerged from the adjoining bathroom and looked for his clothes. 'Go back to sleep,' he advised her, wondering if he'd been wearing underwear when he'd left Jamaica Hill the night before. Well, to hell with it, he thought impatiently, and stepped into the tight-fitting jeans he found lying on the floor.

'I don't want to go back to sleep,' protested Lacey

Sheridan sulkily, turning to face him, giving him the full benefit of her voluptuous breasts. 'Alex, what are you rushing off for?' She teased a nipple. 'Come back to bed. It's barely ten o'clock.'

Alex reached for his shirt, the soft folds of beige-coloured chambray falling smoothly about his olive-skinned shoulders. He caught sight of his reflection in the mirrors of the dressing table opposite and scowled at the dissipation in his face. For God's sake, what was he doing to himself? What did he hope to achieve? By behaving irresponsibly, he was just playing into Conrad Wyatt's hands.

'I'm talking to you, Alex.' Lacey's tone had sharpened, and there was resentment as well as entreaty in her gaze. 'I thought you wanted to talk about Sheridan's Fancy. You're not the only stud in King's Montford. We were going to discuss him doing some screwing, as well.'

Alex winced at the vulgarity. Despite all the money she'd inherited when her husband died, Lacey was still a Philistine at heart. She'd had elocution lessons, and Edward himself had tried to instil some refinement into her. But Lacey would never be a lady. She enjoyed shocking people too much for that.

Still, he reflected bitterly, who was he to judge? He went to bed with her, didn't he? He wasn't too proud to accept her hospitality—and her booze. It was because of the generous quantities of expensive burgundy she'd poured down his throat the night before that he was feeling so awful now. If his head was throbbing, it wasn't her fault. He was a hypocrite even to contemplate that it was.

'I've got to go,' he said doggedly, pushing the tail of his shirt into his jeans and glancing round for his boots. Dammit, he knew he'd been wearing socks when he came here. Where were they? God, he hated the pounding in his head when he bent to look.

'You're not listening to me, Alex.' Lacey switched to a plaintive tone now. 'You know I hate it when you blank me. Why can't you stay and have a shower, and then we'll—?'

'No,' said Alex flatly, finding his socks at last and hopping about to put them on. He shoved his feet into his boots. 'I've got to speak to Guthrie. Some woman is coming for an interview this morning.'

'What woman?'

Once again, Lacey's expression had altered, and as if realising she was not going to change his mind with her nude body she thrust her legs out of bed and reached for her satin wrap. Watching her, Alex had to admit she was a good-looking woman. At her age, a lot of other females had turned to fat.

'I said, what woman?' she said now, catching his arm before he could put on his jacket, giving him a wounded look. 'Alex, why are you being so mean to me? You were so eager—so passionate—last night.'

Alex stifled a groan. Last night, he'd come here with the best of intentions. Lacey's stallion, Sheridan's Fancy, was exactly what he needed to boost the quality of his own horseflesh, and he'd been prepared to do just about anything to meet her price. But this morning he was viewing the situation differently, his previous friendship with Edward Sheridan tarnished by this tawdry affair. Lacey was almost old enough to be his mother, for God's sake. And apart from that, did he really want to get involved with anyone else?

The air in the bedroom was suffocating suddenly, a combination of Lacey's heady perfume, sweat, and sex. He wanted to escape; he wanted to get on a horse—any horse—and ride until he'd outstripped his depression. But he knew it wasn't that simple; that it would take more than a simple horse ride to lift his mood. Until he got Rachel back, he didn't stand a chance of living a normal life.

Pulling free, he shrugged into his jacket. 'It's no one you know,' he told her briefly. 'Just someone who wants a job.' He checked his pockets for his wallet. 'I've got to go, Lace. I'll give you a call this afternoon.'

'You'd better.'

Lacey sounded aggressive, but Alex knew better. Despite

her sometimes coarse exterior, she could be hurt, just like anyone else. Which was probably why he hadn't severed their relationship, he conceded ruefully. Even if, just lately, he'd sensed that he was getting in too deep.

'I will. I promise,' he assured her now, eager to say anything to avoid a scene. He skimmed her lips with his, just to show there were no hard feelings, and then, raking impatient fingers through his tumbled hair, he left the room.

His Range Rover was where he'd left it, parked on the gravelled forecourt in front of the house. The air was delightful, fresh and dry, the sun burning off any lingering traces of frost from the night before. Considering it was November, the days were still surprisingly bright. If only his mood matched them, he thought grimly. Would he ever drag himself out of this hole?

The distance between Lacey's house and his own could be measured in minutes. The two estates ran side by side, with Jamaica Hill sweeping down into the valley. The River Way lay at the foot of Alex's property, widening into a lake among a copse of trees. The trees were bare now, but the sun shining on the water was brilliant, shadowing the willows that dipped down onto its banks.

There was a strange car parked near the entrance to the stables and Alex guessed it was the woman Guthrie had invited for an interview. Since all the stables' accounts had been computerised, his manager had employed a series of young women to do the job he'd previously done himself. The old man maintained he was too set in his ways to learn how to use a keyboard, but because his manner was brusque none of them had stayed very long.

Alex wasn't really in the mood to sit in on another interview, but he'd promised Guthrie to show his face and he was already fifteen minutes late. He scraped a hand across the night's stubble on his jaw and grimaced impatiently. He should have taken Lacey up on her offer of a shower. If he hadn't been so hung-over...

He pushed open the door of the Range Rover, ready to get

out, and then paused when the door to Guthrie's office opened and two people came out. One of them was his manager, unmistakable in his deerstalker and tweeds. But the other person was female. Was the interview over, or what?

He hesitated, torn by the desire not to get involved and an unwilling curiosity about the interviewee. It had certainly been brief, he reflected. Either that or she'd turned him down.

From what he could see, she was younger than the previous incumbent, with an unruly mass of permed blonde hair. Though not a teenager, he decided shrewdly. In black leggings and a tweed jacket, she looked nearer thirty than twenty.

But she was attractive, he conceded grudgingly. He couldn't see what colour eyes she had, but they were wide-set and fringed with lashes darker than her hair. Her mouth was generous, too, and when she spoke Alex was surprised to see Guthrie's face crease with laughter. So what? he wondered, eyes narrowing. Was she a contender, after all?

Deciding he couldn't sit there like some sleazy voyeur any longer, Alex pocketed his keys and thrust his legs out of the car. He might as well show his face, he thought, and get it over with. It wasn't as if he cared what she thought of him.

The slamming of the Range Rover's door attracted their attention, as he'd known it would. But if he'd expected Guthrie to look relieved at his appearance he was disappointed. The woman looked towards the sound, too, and he wondered later if he'd only imagined the sudden apprehension in her expression. But it was quickly hidden, and when Guthrie brought her over to be introduced she smiled with just the right amount of deference.

'This is Kate Hughes,' the older man said gruffly, and Alex wondered if he was anxious that his employer shouldn't interfere. 'This is the boss, Kate. Mr Kellerman.' Then, to Alex again, he said, 'I was just going to show her round the yard.'

Alex nodded, his headache briefly forgotten as he parted the sides of his jacket to hook his thumbs into the front pockets of his jeans. 'I gather the interview was successful.' He couldn't remember Guthrie behaving so enthusiastically before. 'Are you interested in horses, Miss Hughes?'

'Not particularly.' At least she was honest. 'I haven't had the opportunity to deal with them before.' She smiled at Guthrie. 'But I'm interested in the job. And I'm computer-literate. I'm looking forward to working here; to learning all there is to know.'

'A daunting prospect,' remarked Alex dryly, wondering why her words seemed to strike such a disturbing chord inside him. It wasn't just that he was attracted by her appearance, although there was no denying that she was infinitely more attractive close to. He could now see that she had grey eyes, an unusual combination with her streaked blonde hair. Though that might not be natural, he reflected. Some women coloured their hair as frequently as they changed their lipstick these days. 'Where are you working at present?'

'I'm not—' she began, only to be baulked in whatever she was going to say by Guthrie's impatient exclamation.

'I have asked Kate all these questions!' he exclaimed shortly. He gave his employer a speaking look. 'I believe there are some messages for you up at the house.'

Alex conceded defeat. Whatever his opinion of Miss Hughes might be—and he wasn't entirely sure why he should have any misgivings in the first place—Guthrie was clearly delighted by his find. And he was the one who was going to have to work with her, and if she didn't do her job to his satisfaction he was the one who'd have to fire her, too. Alex, himself, couldn't object if she satisfied his manager. When he'd hired an assistant for him, he'd let his sympathies rule his head.

'Right,' he said now, using one hand to rake his aching scalp. 'I'll leave it up to you, Sam. I'm sure you know what you're doing.'

Guthrie took the implied reproof without comment, and Alex turned back to the Range Rover to drive up to the house. 'It was nice meeting you, Miss Hughes,' he said, over his shoulder. 'I'll see you later, Sam. Good luck.'

But, as he drove away, Alex wondered why he'd made such an issue of Sam Guthrie's decision. What was there about the Hughes woman that caused him such a feeling of unease? Was it her slight resemblance to Alicia Sawyer that had thrown him? Why did he have the feeling that employing Kate Hughes might create problems he hadn't even thought of yet?

Was it because of the way she'd looked at him? He didn't kid himself that she'd been attracted to him, but there was no denying there'd been a guarded interest in her gaze. He rubbed his jaw again, feeling the harsh bristles with some disparagement. He was flattering himself if he thought there'd been anything more than curiosity in her face.

Perhaps she knew his history. He scowled. Dammit, of course she knew his history. It wasn't as if you could live in King's Montford without hearing the rumours about Pamela's death. And his own behaviour afterwards had only reinforced the speculation. Why in God's name had he let the Wyatts take Rachel away?

But he couldn't think about them. Not in his present mood. The attractions of the bottle were still far too easy to justify, and turning to drink hadn't helped him before. On the contrary, it was because he'd been so devastated by what had happened to Pamela that he'd buried his grief in a bottle in the first place, allowing Conrad Wyatt to destroy what was left of his reputation.

It was a week before he saw Kate Hughes again.

He knew Guthrie had taken her on. The old Scotsman, who had worked for the Kellermans for the past thirty years, had made a point of telling him he had. 'She's an intelligent lassie,' he'd persisted, recognising Alex's scepticism. 'It'll be nice to have a female about the place again.'

Alex wasn't so sure. Apart from his long-standing association with Lacey Sheridan, he had had little time for women in recent years. Since Pamela's death, it had been a struggle to even hang onto the stables, and there was no doubt that opinion was still mixed about whether he'd had a hand in her death or not.

Which was why it was proving so hard to get his daughter back.

When Pamela was killed, he hadn't been able to think straight. He hadn't even known she was pregnant, for God's sake, and that news had left him reeling for weeks. He knew they'd been having problems, and the eventuality of them getting a divorce had crossed his mind. But Rachel had still been a baby. He'd been prepared to put up with a lot for her sake, but he hadn't realised that Pamela was having an affair.

When she died, all he'd really known for certain was that the baby she'd been carrying wasn't his. It had been months since he and Pamela had slept together; months since they had shared a bed. Not that that fact had helped his case; it had only reinforced the opinion that he'd had something to gain by her death. And the fact that her father had invested in the business, and would obviously pull his support if Pamela left him, had seemed to prove the point.

Still, that was behind him now, and despite his own reservations Alex had assured Guthrie that he had no objections to his decision to employ Kate Hughes. 'What was she doing before she applied for this position?' he'd asked idly, not sure why he really wanted to know.

'She worked for her father; but he died several months ago, and since then she's been looking for a job.'

'Ah.'

Alex had absorbed that information, aware of Guthrie's disapproval, and had decided not to ask the old man what her father's business was. He could always find out later—providing she stayed the course, he'd reminded himself dryly; but he doubted his manager would appreciate the pun.

Nevertheless, he felt an unwelcome charge of emotion a few days later, when he turned the corner into the stable yard and found their new employee forking hay into an empty stall. This was not what she was being paid for, and he objected to the familiarity. He had some valuable horseflesh

boarded at the stables and he wondered if he'd been right to
be suspicious about her. Had she taken the job to enable her
to snoop around?

He frowned. Not that she was alone. The stable-yard was
busy, with one of the young apprentices walking two of the
mares to cool them down after the morning's gallop. He
could see Guthrie himself at the far end of the yard where
the stable block angled into the barns and storerooms. He
was talking to one of the owners, who had an appointment
to see Alex at eleven o'clock.

She must have heard his boot-heels striking the concrete
apron that ran along the side of the building nearest to her,
because she straightened as he appeared, stretching her back.
He didn't know if she was aware of it—though his instincts
told him she probably was—but as she flexed her spine her
breasts were clearly outlined beneath the fine angora of her
sweater.

Her long legs were once again encased in black leggings,
which hugged their shape with provocative intent. He could
even see the slight cleft that shaped her bottom, and he was
annoyed to feel an unfamiliar pressure in his trousers.

His frown deepened. It had been a pretty lousy week for
him, one way and another. He'd heard from his solicitor that
the latest hearing into his bid to regain custody of his four-
year-old daughter had been put back yet again, due to the
Wyatts' delaying tactics, and he dreaded to think what they
were telling her. But the longer they could maintain guardi-
anship of the child, the better chance they had of sustaining
their position. They'd already started arguing that Rachel
hardly knew him and that, in any case, his household was no
fit place for a little girl.

To add to his frustration, Lacey appeared to have taken
umbrage because he'd had to refuse her latest invitation. In
other circumstances, a couple of days at the races would have
appealed to him, but he'd been afraid it might give her the
wrong idea. He liked Lacey; he was fond of her; she was fun
to be with. But their primary connection—so far as he was

concerned, at any rate—was horses. He despised himself for allowing sex to get in the way of what had been a good friendship up till now.

In consequence, he was in no mood to be tactful with Kate Hughes. 'Exactly what do you think you're doing?' he demanded. 'I don't pay you to swill out the stalls. Or is this some kind of unpaid overtime?' He glanced at his watch. 'What is this? Your coffee break, or what?'

'I finished what I was doing, Mr Guthrie was with a client, and I could see Billy needed some help,' she retorted, with none of the deference he'd expected. Her voice was husky from her efforts and as she spoke the warm draught of her breath caressed his cheek. She seemed indifferent to his disapproval as she swept damp strands of hair behind her ears. 'Do you have a problem with that?'

Alex's mouth tightened. 'Obviously I do,' he told her shortly. 'And I'm not your father, Miss Hughes. If this is the way you used to speak to him, then perhaps you should remember where you are now.'

She coloured then, the skin of her neck and cheeks deepening to a fiery shade of pink. The change was appealing, giving her a vulnerability he hadn't expected, and his earlier reaction to her ignited in his gut.

'I'm sorry,' she said stiffly, and conversely he wanted to apologise for embarrassing her. It was disconcerting how easily she could arouse unwelcome feelings, and he found himself shaking his head.

'No, I'm sorry,' he muttered ruefully, thrusting his hands into his jacket pockets, almost as if he didn't trust himself not to reinforce his words with deeds. He grimaced. 'You'll have to forgive me. I don't usually take my grief out on the staff.'

'Your grief?' she echoed at once, and he realised how his statement could be misconstrued.

'Not literally,' he said dryly, his lips twitching at the prospect. 'No, I guess what I really mean is that I'm not in the best of moods.'

She moistened her lips with the tip of a pink tongue, her expression one of mild interest, and he guessed she expected him to explain. 'A personal matter,' he added briskly, surprised at the urge he had to confide in her. For God's sake, wasn't he in enough emotional turmoil as it was?

'They're the worst,' she said now, propping her chin on the handle of the pitchfork and looking up at him with sympathetic eyes. 'So you're not going to fire me today?'

'I'll give it more thought,' Alex promised lightly, finding himself fascinated by the impish smile that curled her lips. 'Does that mean you want to stay?'

'Why not?' Was she openly flirting with him now? He wondered if that was how she had disarmed Guthrie, who was usually known for his irascibility, not his charm. 'I just hope you'll have solved your problems by the time we meet again.'

'Unlikely,' remarked Alex wryly. Then, because he was becoming far too familiar with an employee, he brought their exchange to an abrupt halt. 'Excuse me,' he added, raising a hand in a gesture of farewell, and without waiting for her response he strode away across the yard.

But he was almost certain that she watched him go, the awareness of her eyes on his back causing an almost physical impact inside him. Irritation gripped him. He was behaving like an idiot even thinking about her, and the knowledge that he was becoming curious about her personal life really bugged him. Didn't he have enough to deal with as it was?

Nevertheless, her image remained in his thoughts for the remainder of the day and it was only sheer will-power that stopped him from asking Sam Guthrie what her background was. He could have checked the files. Whatever he lacked in a technical capacity, Guthrie was nothing if not thorough, and all her details would be neatly logged away in her personal folder.

But he didn't. Whether she'd been married, whether she was attached—she didn't wear a ring, but that meant nothing these days—whether she was in the habit of forming casual relationships was nothing to do with him. He had no intention of getting involved with anyone, least of all a woman he employed.

CHAPTER THREE

KATE watched Alex Kellerman walk away with a shiver of
anticipation running down her spine. Despite the sudden way
he had ended their conversation, she was sure she had made
some progress in her quest to gain his confidence. He hadn't
actually said anything; it was what he hadn't said that spoke
volumes about his mood. She shivered again at the realisation
that he had accepted her at face value. He had no idea that
she was anything more than another employee.

Once again, using her own name had come in handy. Her
National Insurance details were all in her married name. Of
course, she hadn't corrected his assumption that she had
never been married, but that was hardly an indictable offence.

She swallowed, turning back to forking hay with hands
that weren't entirely steady. Talking to him had been more
exhausting than she'd thought. Exhausting—and exhilarating,
she admitted unwillingly. Whatever else he was, Alex
Kellerman was definitely a most disturbing man.

Was that what Alicia Sawyer had thought?

Kate dug the fork into the bale of hay with more aggres-
sion than effect. She should know better than to start fantasis-
ing about Alex Kellerman, she told herself severely. If what
she had heard was true, he was definitely not a man to be
trusted.

Yet, in all honesty, she still knew precious little about him.
Which was the main reason she had decided to apply for this
job. Since his wife's death, there had been plenty of gossip,
but nothing of substance. He seemed to have surrounded himself with people who weren't willing to talk.

Not to a stranger anyway, she amended, rubbing the back
of her hand over her damp forehead. Despite his apparently

doubtful reputation, he evidently inspired a sense of loyalty in his staff. She hadn't heard anyone say a hard word against him, even though it was obvious that the stables were having a struggle to survive.

The only thing she had learned was that he was trying to regain custody of his daughter. Apparently, her grandparents—her mother's parents, that was—had taken her away from Jamaica Hill just after their daughter had been killed. Which was reasonable enough, considering what Kate had read about Rachel's narrowly avoiding witnessing her mother's accident, but now they were refusing to give her up.

And, naturally, Alex wanted her back. She was his daughter, after all, and whatever kind of relationship he'd had with his wife Rachel was all he had left. Kate couldn't understand why he hadn't been granted custody before now, unless the Wyatts knew something about their son-in-law that they were using to keep the child themselves.

She frowned, picking up the fork again with renewed vigour. She wasn't here to speculate on Kellerman's relationship with his in-laws. She was here to find out what had happened to Alicia Sawyer, and so far she wasn't making a very satisfactory job of it.

Henry Sawyer wouldn't be pleased to think she was entertaining any sympathy for Alex Kellerman, she mused. When he'd turned up at her office a few days after giving her the assignment and learned what little progress she'd made in those few days, he'd been well peeved. She didn't know exactly what he'd expected, but as far as she was concerned she'd done everything she could.

Of course, he wasn't interested in hearing that she'd confirmed what he'd told her: that her contact in the local social security office had endorsed the fact that Alicia had worked for Alex Kellerman, and that as far as the authorities were aware she hadn't taken up any other employment since she left. Sawyer had already told her that the small account Alicia had had with the West Avon bank hadn't been drawn on for the past two months, and there were no credit card statements available either.

Kate had gone further, of course. She'd managed to find out that Alicia had no relatives in King's Montford, and that she hadn't been admitted to any hospital in the area under her own name. She'd shown her photograph in job centres and travel agents, she'd even shown it at the bus and train stations, but without any satisfactory result. It seemed that Alicia Sawyer had disappeared, just as her husband had said.

'So what do you intend to do next?' he'd demanded. And when Kate had looked a little doubtful he'd produced the advertisement which she was sure was why he'd come in. 'That's Alicia's job,' he'd declared, tossing the scrap of newsprint onto the desk in front of her. 'Why don't you apply for that?'

Her initial response had been one of incredulity. At no time in her father's long career had he ever gone undercover to get information, and the idea of passing herself off as a secretary had seemed completely over the top.

'Then I want my money back,' Sawyer had snapped angrily, and she could see he meant it. Which would mean telling Joanne that the skiing trip was off.

She'd despised herself afterwards, of course. Giving in to a man like Sawyer was not what being a private detective was all about. But there was no doubt that applying for the job was the best way of finding out what had happened to Alicia. So far, she'd had no luck in talking to anyone from the stables, and she'd consoled herself with the thought that her father might have had to amend his methods of detection in this case.

Which was how she came to be standing in the yard at Jamaica Hill helping Billy Roach with his chores. It was true she had finished the work that Mr Guthrie had given her, and she supposed she could have spent her free time reorganising the files. But Billy seemed her best bet as far as getting any information about Alicia Sawyer was concerned, and winning his gratitude, and his confidence, would go a long way towards proving she could be trusted.

All the same, it was hard work, and her back was aching. If Kellerman hadn't still been standing in the yard, talking to Guthrie and his companion, she'd have packed it in and gone back to the office. It was cold, and although she was sweating as she worked any break in her activities caused her to shiver. Or was it the awareness of danger? Was Kellerman really as innocent as he'd have everyone believe?

He was coming towards her again now, accompanied by the man who had been talking to Mr Guthrie, and she had to force herself to meet his narrow-eyed gaze. He was talking to his companion, but he was looking at her, and she made herself offer a small smile in response.

But after he was gone reaction set in and she shuddered. God, was she really trying to make him believe she was the kind of woman who took pleasure in flirting with men? Until she'd come to the interview here, she hadn't even owned a pair of leggings, let alone worn them. When she'd first put them on, her initial thought had been to hide her backside.

She shook her head. She had to stop thinking so negatively. Whether it was an act or not, she had succeeded in drawing Kellerman's attention to herself. If he thought she was ripe for an affair, however, she would have to disabuse him. Gaining his confidence was one thing; prostituting herself to satisfy Sawyer was something else.

Nevertheless, as she drove home that evening, she was unwillingly aware that she wasn't entirely indifferent to Alex Kellerman's attraction, and talking to him hadn't been as difficult as she'd expected either. On the contrary, for the first time since Sean's death, she'd met a man she felt at ease with. What a pity he was going to hate her when he found out why she was there.

The following morning she got the chance she'd been waiting for. Guthrie was away for the morning, and he'd left her in nominal charge of the office, so that when Billy Roach came to tell the manager he'd finished cleaning the tack Kate suggested he should take a break and join her for coffee.

'I've had my break, Miss Hughes,' replied Billy, with a rueful grimace. At sixteen, and a little over five feet in height, he was the youngest apprentice in the yard. He was also the least intelligent, according to the manager. 'If Mr Guthrie's not here, I should be getting back.'

'Oh, must you?' Kate adopted her most winsome expression. 'So I've got to have my coffee on my own.' She allowed her tongue to circle her lips in what she hoped was a provocative gesture. 'I thought you might like to sit and chat with me for a while.'

'Well, I would.' Billy shifted a little uncomfortably. 'But I do have work to do. And if Mr Guthrie came back and found me here—'

'He won't.' Kate stepped past him to close the door, and then turned to smile at him encouragingly. 'He's gone to Bristol, as you know. I don't suppose he'll be back until later this afternoon.'

Billy still looked doubtful. 'I don't think the other men would like it,' he murmured uneasily.

'Well, while you're thinking about it, I'll pour us both a cup of coffee,' declared Kate, moving towards the filter. She cast him a smile over her shoulder. 'Relax. If anyone comes, I'll tell them it was my idea.'

'As if they'd believe that.'

Billy was still uncertain, and Kate realised she'd have to work very hard to allay his fears. 'If it's any consolation, I don't think Mr Kellerman would object if he found out. He seemed very impressed with your work when I spoke to him yesterday.'

'He did?'

Billy was staring at her with eager eyes now and Kate felt terribly guilty for leading him on. 'Oh, yes,' she said, concentrating on adding milk to the coffee to avoid looking at him. 'When I said I was helping you, he implied you were one of the best apprentices he'd ever had.'

'Really?' Billy took the mug she handed him now and perched on a corner of her desk. 'How about that?' He chuckled, his earlier doubts forgotten for the moment 'And I thought both he and Mr Guthrie thought I was thick!'

Kate shook her head, half wishing she hadn't been so effusive, but Billy didn't want to let it go. 'Perhaps I should ask for a rise,' he mused, arching an inquisitive brow. 'This job doesn't pay much, you know. If I wasn't still living at home, I wouldn't be able to pay the rent.'

'Oh…' Kate drew a hasty breath. 'Well, I'm not sure this is the best time to ask Mr Kellerman for a rise,' she declared, horrified that he might quote her on this. She glimpsed the truculence in his eyes, and hurried on, 'You know things are pretty tight at the moment. If I were you I'd wait until next year.'

'Things are always tight,' muttered Billy glumly, burying his nose in the beaker of coffee, but Kate was relieved to hear the resignation in his voice. That was one thing about Billy: he was easily persuaded, but she determined not to get herself into that kind of corner again.

'I—I suppose it's been hard for Mr Kellerman,' she ventured instead, deciding she couldn't afford to waste this chance, however reckless it might be. 'Since his wife was killed, I mean,' she added tentatively. 'It can't have been easy, picking up the pieces of his life.'

Billy regarded her across the rim of his cup. 'You like Mr Kellerman, don't you?' he said, getting exactly the wrong message. He lowered his cup and grinned at her. 'All the ladies like Mr Kellerman, you know? Or they used to.'

Kate sighed. 'I do not—that is, I was being objective. I meant—well, according to Mr Guthrie, there have been—problems at the yard.'

In fact, Sam Guthrie had told her nothing of his employer's problems, and she could only hope that Billy didn't know that, or betray her confidence to the manager. She grimaced. She didn't think it was likely. The old Scotsman treated Billy as a pair of hands and nothing more.

'Problems?' Billy looked blank for a moment, and Kate wondered if she was wasting her time talking to him. But then, drawing his brows together, Billy gave her a thoughtful look. 'I suppose you mean when Allie walked out?'

Kate's jaw dropped. She felt like a player on a slot machine who had suddenly hit the jackpot. 'Allie' had to be Alicia Sawyer. God, and she'd doubted she had the time to get to the other woman's disappearance today.

But then, she'd imagined she'd have to wait while Billy told her about Pamela Kellerman's accident, and although that intrigued her it wasn't why she was here. But she'd been prepared to put up with that, so long as Billy eventually reached the point of Alicia's employment, although she had to admit she'd had doubts about how long it was going to take.

Yet now, quite incredibly, Billy had brought up the very thing she wanted, and she realised, belatedly, that he'd not been working at the stables when Pamela was killed. Kate could hardly contain her excitement at this development, and she struggled to find something to say that wouldn't arouse his suspicions.

'Allie?' she echoed at last, and then had to wait impatiently while he took another mouthful of his coffee before going on.

'Mrs Sawyer,' he agreed, wiping his mouth with the back of his hand. 'The woman who worked here before you. She liked me to call her Allie. She said it reminded her of when she was a little girl.'

Kate strove for a casual tone. 'But you say she—she walked out?' She waited a beat. 'D'you mean she was fired?'

'No.' Billy was indignant now. 'Mr Guthrie wouldn't have done that. He liked her.'

'Did he?' Kate wasn't sure how to go on. 'What do you mean, then?' She remembered just in time that she wasn't supposed to know anything about her. 'Um—didn't she turn up for work one morning, or what?'

'She just left,' said Billy glumly. 'She didn't even say goodbye. Mr Kellerman said—'

He broke off abruptly. A look of undisguised horror had darkened his face, and all the hairs on the back of Kate's neck rose up in sympathy. She was sure he'd remembered something significant, something that still had the power to fill him with terror. She leaned towards him, silently urging him to finish what he was saying, and then heard the sound that had panicked him into silence in the first place.

Footsteps were approaching, and Billy slammed his mug down onto the desk, spilling half its contents in the process. 'It's Mr Kellerman,' he muttered, catching sight of his employer through the window into the yard. 'Crikey, what am I going to do now?'

Kate, who had her own reasons for not wanting to encounter Alex Kellerman at that moment, gave an impatient shake of her head. 'You're only drinking a cup of coffee!' she exclaimed, hiding her impatience. 'If anyone's in trouble, it's me.'

Billy was not convinced and, wrenching open the door, he confronted his employer with a nervous grin. 'I—I was just leaving, Mr Kellerman,' he muttered. 'I cleaned out the tack room like Mr Guthrie said.'

Alex Kellerman frowned, but before he could make any comment Billy had scooted away across the yard. The older man looked after him, an expression of momentary speculation crossing his face. Then he turned to look at Kate as he entered the office, and she had to steel herself not to look as guilty as she felt.

'Is something wrong?' he asked, coming into the small office and closing the door. Like the stables themselves, and the other buildings that made up three sides of the rectangle, the office opened straight out into the yard. He leaned against the door, but that didn't stop the feeling Kate had that the room was suddenly smaller. His eyes alighted on the pool of coffee. 'Did I interrupt something?'

'Of course not.' Kate spoke a little sharply, but she

couldn't help feeling frustrated and it showed. 'I—Billy—
well, I asked him to join me for coffee. He—he was looking
for Mr Guthrie, that's all.'

'Really?'

'Yes, really.' Kate remembered she was supposed to be
trying to gain his confidence as well and forced a smile. 'I
suppose I shouldn't have done it, but it gets pretty lonely in
here when Mr Guthrie's away.'

'Does it?'

His responses were hardly encouraging, and because she
was far too aware of their isolation she took refuge behind
her desk. She would have to soak up the coffee Billy had
spilled, she reflected, but she'd do it later. She had no desire
to get any closer to Alex Kellerman than was absolutely necessary right now.

'I suppose it was too much to hope that you hadn't heard
the rumours,' he remarked after a moment, and this time Kate
had no chance to control the sudden heat that burned her
cheeks.

'I beg your pardon?' she said, her mind racing to find a
convincing explanation. Her knees felt weak. Had he heard
what she'd been asking Billy? Had he been outside the door
long before they'd heard the betraying clatter of his feet?

Kellerman straightened away from the door, and once
again Kate had to steel herself not to react. If she was going
to have any kind of success as a private investigator she had
to stop behaving like a scared rabbit. If he was angry with
her, so what? She hadn't done anything wrong.

Except…

Except take a job under false pretences. Except lie about
her reasons for being here. Not to mention the fact that she'd
accepted payment for investigating a woman's disappearance.
Oh, yes, she was sure he'd believe there was nothing wrong
about that.

He approached the desk and she stiffened. He was dressed
all in black and she wondered if that was why he seemed so
menacing today. Didn't he feel the cold? she wondered, her

eyes flickering over the opened collar of his black silk shirt. There was no trace of the goosebumps she was suffering in the strong-muscled column of his throat.

But it was his eyes that really disturbed her. They looked almost black in his hard, accusing face. She was forced to look at them, forced to look at *him*, forced to acknowledge his physical superiority. If he intended to fire her, there wasn't much she could do about it. He was not the sort of man to suffer any kind of interference in his private life.

'My wife's death,' he said now, the tips of his fingers just resting on the rim of her desk. A look of contempt crossed his face. 'That was what you were grilling Billy about, wasn't it? You wanted to know all the gory details about how she died.'

The breath expelled from Kate's lungs almost explosively. He didn't know, she realised weakly, hanging onto the edge of the desk herself for support. 'Um—no,' she stammered hastily. 'Your—your wife's accident is nothing to do with me. Besides, Billy wasn't here when it happened, was he? He's too young. I seem to remember it was about—well, several years ago.'

Kellerman's brows drew together. 'It was,' he agreed stiffly. 'Over two years ago, as you say.' His thin lips compressed. 'Not that that matters. Billy's been working here for almost a year. He's bound to have discussed it with the other men.'

'Well, he didn't discuss it with me.' Kate was relieved to hear that she sounded almost confident. 'That's not what we were talking about.' And then, before he could ask the obvious question, she added, 'Aren't you getting a little paranoid, Mr Kellerman? People do have other interests in their lives.'

'Do they?' But she could see the doubt in his expression. 'Sometimes, I feel as if they talk about nothing else.' He took a step back from the desk, and pushed his hands into the back pockets of his tight jeans, the spread sides of his leather jerkin exposing a taut midriff above his belt. 'You have every right to think I'm over-reacting, Miss Hughes. But I'm afraid I have become very sensitive in recent months.'

She could believe it, and, ridiculously, Kate knew a sudden desire to reassure him. This man, who only moments before had seemed to present a real threat to her existence, was actually inspiring her sympathy. It couldn't have been easy living with all the gossip, she conceded. And if he was innocent of any charge, as he professed, it must have been doubly hard.

If...

'It's—understandable,' she assured him, glancing behind her at the pot of coffee sitting warming on its stand. She hesitated for only a moment before coming to a decision. 'Er—can I offer you a drink, Mr Kellerman?'

He seemed certain to refuse, and she prepared herself for his rejection. But then, he seemed to change his mind. 'Why not?' he said, nodding towards the spillage Billy had created. A small smile touched his lips. 'I'll try not to make any more mess.'

Kate found herself returning his smile, and then hurriedly turned away to take a clean mug from the shelf. Was he teasing her? she wondered. Was he trying to make amends for his earlier harshness? She didn't know, but when he let down his guard he was really nice.

Nice!

She picked up the pot with rather less complacence. Dammit, *nice* was not an adjective she could use to describe him. Aggressive, perhaps; sarcastic, definitely; maybe even dangerous. And how did she know his affair with Mrs Sawyer hadn't started exactly like this?

Her breath caught in her throat, and her hand shook as she poured his coffee. Just for a moment, she'd wondered what it would be like to have an affair with him. With Alex Kellerman? She was appalled. That was scary. She felt exposed suddenly, as if a sensitive layer of skin had been removed.

She used both hands to offer the mug of coffee to him,

just in case her shaking hands warned him of how disturbed she was. 'D'you have any sugar?' he asked, as she was congratulating herself at succeeding, and she saw she hadn't offered him any milk either.

'Sorry,' she murmured, handing him the packet of sugar. There were no social niceties in the office 'Um—do you take milk too? I'm afraid I forgot to ask.'

'Black and sweet,' he assured her wryly, another of those small smiles playing about his mouth. 'Mmm, that's good,' he added, after tasting it. 'Slightly stewed, but full of flavour.'

Kate groaned. 'You don't like it!' she exclaimed. She gestured towards the filter. 'Would you like me to make a fresh pot?'

'No. This is fine.' He glanced behind him for a chair. 'May I sit down?'

'Of course.' Kate lifted her shoulders. 'It's your office.'

'So it is.' He grimaced and dropped down into an old leather chair that was situated beside the electric heater. 'Mmm.' He stretched out his long legs. 'That's better.' He crossed his booted ankles. 'Now, d'you want to tell me what Roach was doing here?'

She should have known he wouldn't forget, thought Kate, subsiding into her own chair with some reluctance. 'Roach?' she said thoughtfully, giving herself a few moments to compose an answer. 'Oh, you mean Billy,' she added needlessly. 'I can't remember now.'

'I believe he implied he'd been looking for Guthrie,' Alex prompted, his eyes sharp as they appraised her across the rim of his mug.

'Oh, yes, that's right. He was,' Kate said gratefully. 'That's why he came to the office.' She put her mug aside. 'Were you looking for Mr Guthrie, too?'

'As a matter of fact, I wanted to speak to you,' Alex remarked now, instantly banishing her smugness.

'To me?' she got out faintly. 'Why? Is something wrong?'

'What could be wrong?' he countered now, and she

thought again how reckless she'd been in coming here. When Alex set down his mug on the floor beside his chair and steepled his hands across his flat stomach, she swallowed convulsively. But all he said was, 'I thought it was time I got to know something about the newest member of my staff.'

Kate's mouth felt unpleasantly dry. 'But didn't Mr Guthrie—?'

'Oh, sure. Sam has no complaints about you. I'm sure you know you charmed him right from the start.'

'But not you.' The words were out before she could prevent them. 'I mean—well, I don't mean that exactly.' She inwardly cringed. 'Um—do you have a problem? About my work, I mean.'

'Why should I?' Alex leaned forward in his seat, resting his arms along his spread thighs. 'But your working here is bound to cause repercussions. I just wondered what your family thought about that.'

Kate expelled an uneven breath. 'My—family is quite happy about me working here,' she told him, refusing to think about what her mother had said when Kate had told her what she intended to do.

'So they don't think I'm as wicked as the press has painted me?' His eyes were intent. 'They don't believe I killed my wife for her money?'

Kate stared at him. 'For her money?' she echoed blankly, and he stifled a bitter oath.

'Oh, haven't you heard that part of the story?' he queried scornfully. 'Well, don't worry. If you stick around here long enough, you will.'

Kate drew a breath. 'It must have been very—painful for you.'

'The standard response.' His lips twisted. 'They all say that.' He paused. 'Well, those who believe me—or say they do, at any rate—assure me of their sympathy. I think I'm supposed to be grateful, or something like that.'

'And you're not?'

Once again, Kate spoke without considering what she was saying, and Alex's face mirrored a faint respect. 'Do you think I'd tell you?' he asked, and she caught her breath. His lips twisted. 'I don't have a satisfactory answer for what happened to Pamela. I'm sorry she's dead, but the pain came long before she fell off the horse.'

Kate didn't know what to say. This was not a conversation she had ever expected to be having with him. She'd never dreamt that Alex Kellerman might talk about his wife's death to her. And if there had been money involved, people did crazy things.

'But I didn't come here to talk about me,' he said, getting abruptly to his feet, and Kate realised that she was under his mental microscope once again. He came towards the desk, idly straightening the pile of letters and bills she had yet to deal with. 'You never did tell me what you did before you took this job.'

'I worked for my father,' said Kate at once, glad she could answer truthfully. But then, when that obviously wasn't enough, she added, 'He—he had a small—insurance agency in—in Bath.'

'Not in King's Montford?'

'No.'

'And you didn't think of continuing with the agency?'

Kate shook her head. 'No. It—it wasn't the same after my father died.'

He conceded the point, but he still seemed curious. Was it only her imagination, or was he as suspicious of her answers as she was of his? 'I still don't see why you'd want to do this job,' he said at last. His eyes narrowed. 'It isn't as if there's any responsibility involved.'

'I don't need responsibility.' Kate could have added that she'd had more responsibility than he could imagine in her comparatively short life. 'I obviously wanted a job, and there aren't that many to choose from. Not—not everyone wants to employ someone as—as old as me.'

He gave her an old-fashioned look. 'Am I suppose to answer that?' he asked levelly, and her skin burned at the irony in his face. The office wasn't large, and she was far too aware of his maleness. He could have no idea how inexperienced she was at fencing with any man.

'I—I just meant a lot of employers are looking for younger women,' she explained awkwardly. 'I'm sorry if you thought I was fishing for compliments. I—I'm not like that.'

'What are you like, I wonder?' he mused, and her throat tightened almost convulsively. 'Are you one of those females who imagine it would be a thrill to sleep with a killer?'

Kate gulped. 'You're not a killer!' She refused to consider the rest of what he'd said.

'How do you know?'

She didn't, of course, and a few moments ago she'd have believed almost anything of him. 'I just know,' she declared, somewhat naively. 'Do you think I'd have taken this job if I'd thought you'd—you'd—?'

'Murdered my wife?' Alex was laconic, and she reluctantly nodded.

'When my father was alive, he always used to say I was a good judge of character,' she agreed, getting to her feet.

'Your father?' He paused. 'The insurance agent.'

'That's right.' She was grateful he had reminded her. 'I'm sure if you'd met him you'd have liked him, too.'

'Was he as gullible as you?' he asked sardonically, and Kate took a steadying breath.

'I don't think I'm gullible, Mr Kellerman. Just because I'm prepared to give somebody the—the benefit of the doubt.'

'And you think your father would approve of you working for me? Someone of your—age and intelligence typing statistics into a computer? Come on, Miss Hughes, do you really expect me to believe that?'

Kate shrugged. 'Perhaps I'm not as intelligent as you think…?' she began, and then flinched when he leant towards her.

'And perhaps you're too damn clever for your own good.'

His lips thinned. 'I'm not stupid, Miss Hughes. I can recognise a phony when I see one, whatever your editor thinks!'

'My editor!' Kate could have collapsed with relief, but instead she forced herself to meet his shrewd gaze. 'I don't have an editor,' she denied swiftly. 'Whatever you think you know. I'm not a journalist, Mr Kellerman. I've never worked for a newspaper in my life.'

'Can you prove it?'

'Can I—?' Kate tried to think. 'I—journalists usually have press cards, don't they?' She fumbled to get her handbag out of the drawer beside her. 'You can look through my personal belongings, if you like.'

Too late, she remembered her investigator's licence tucked inside her wallet, but she needn't have worried. 'I don't imagine you'd carry such an incriminating thing around with you,' Kellerman said, dismissing her offer. His expression softened somewhat, nevertheless. 'Do you swear you're not working for any publication, tabloid or otherwise?'

'Yes.' There was conviction in her voice.

'No freelance assignments? No docu-dramas for television?'

'No.' But despite the relief her knees were trembling. 'Do you believe me? I've never worked for the media.'

He studied her flushed face for what seemed like for ever, and then gave what she hoped was a gesture of assent. 'Okay,' he said at last. 'Okay, I believe you. But if I find out you've been lying...'

He didn't bother to finish the threat, but Kate knew what he meant. There'd be no second chances if he found her out. 'I think you've made your feelings very plain, Mr Kellerman,' she declared stiffly, her nails digging into her palms.

She was grateful that he seemed to accept that as a dismissal, and when he moved towards the door she sank down into her chair again and expelled an exhausted breath. But that didn't stop her from wishing she could just hand in her notice and leave while she still had all her faculties. She was very much afraid that Alex Kellerman was far more dangerous than she'd ever imagined.

CHAPTER FOUR

ALEX shoved the weights to their fullest extent for the final time and then lay panting, trying to get his breath back. Hell, he was out of condition, he thought disgustedly. Okay, he'd been pushing himself hard for the last couple of hours, but lifting the bar that last time had almost finished him off. He'd been spending too many nights with a bottle instead of with a woman, he reflected wryly. If there was one thing to say for sex it was that it didn't make you fat.

He heaved a sigh and got up from the bench-press, flexing his shoulders as he did so. What he needed was a shower, that was all, he assured himself. He'd feel a damn sight better when he got out of this sweaty gear. Then, when he was sure he'd eliminated all his frustration, he'd go and pick up Rachel. These additional visits were one concession his recent visit to court had granted him, and he had no intention of doing anything to blow the privilege now.

Even if the thought of going to the Wyatts' house to collect her still bugged him. He'd have much preferred it if his solicitor could have arranged for him to meet his daughter at a neutral point. But it was probably better for Rachel not to have to deal with too many strangers, he conceded. The muscles in his stomach tightened at the thought of losing her for good.

As he left the gym, which was in the basement of the house, and mounted the stairs to the first floor, he found himself thinking of Kate Hughes. He was slightly ashamed of the way he had treated her the previous day. He was well aware that he had intimidated the woman for no good reason. He had had no grounds for accusing her of being anything more—or less—than she claimed. Would she understand the pressure he was under if he told her about Rachel? She'd said she didn't believe he was a murderer, but that was before he'd practically accused her of working for the gutter press.

He reached his bedroom and crossed the floor to his bathroom, shedding his vest and shorts on the way. Then, kicking off his trainers, he stepped into the shower cubicle, running the water hot at first to sluice all the stickiness from his skin.

As he soaped his shoulders, he considered why he'd suddenly thought of Kate Hughes. Was it because of the way he'd behaved with her that had persuaded him to work out before going to Wyvern Hall? Perhaps he was afraid he'd let Conrad Wyatt arouse his anger. If he went there filled with resentment he'd be playing right into his father-in-law's hands.

Perhaps he should be grateful to the Hughes woman, he thought, returning to the bedroom. As he towelled his hair dry, he wondered what she thought of him now. He supposed he owed her an apology for coming on so strong, and he hoped he hadn't upset her. Guthrie wouldn't be very pleased if his protégée decided to take a hike.

He blew out a weary breath, looking round the room without pleasure. This was one of the smaller bedrooms. He'd moved out of the master suite when Pamela died. It needed some redecoration, but these days he had no enthusiasm for anything. If—*when*—he got Rachel back again, things would be different, he assured himself. He'd begin to feel that this was a real home again.

The Wyatts' estate was situated on the other side of King's Montford. Conrad Wyatt's family had farmed the land for over a hundred years, and although the old man himself no longer took an active part in running the estate he had a very efficient manager to do the job for him.

Alex had always known that Conrad regretted the fact that his wife had been unable to have any more children after Pamela was born, and when Pamela herself was expecting Rachel her father had hoped she would have a boy. At that time, though, it hadn't seemed important. Alex had assumed

he and Pamela would eventually have a son. He hadn't
known then that Pamela was going to be unfaithful, or that
the second child she carried wouldn't be his.

It was impossible not to feel some emotion, Alex thought
as he drove through the gates of Wyvern Hall. He might not
have loved his wife when she died, but that didn't alter the
fact that this was where she'd been born. Where he'd come
to visit, when he and Pamela had first got to know one another; and where her father had voiced the suggestion that
when he died they should move into the house.

He'd even asked Alex to consider changing his name to
Wyatt. Alex's own father was dead, so he hadn't seen anything wrong in that. But Alex had. The Kellermans might not
have such illustrious forebears, but under his direction the
Kellerman stables were beginning to make an enviable name
for themselves. There was no way Alex was going to deprive
his heir of his real heritage, and his relationship with Conrad
Wyatt had deteriorated from then on.

Even so, Alex had always tried to be civil to the man.
He'd had no quarrel with Pamela's father, and he'd always
hoped that some day they could really be friends. But then
Pamela was killed, and Conrad had accused his son-in-law
of contriving the 'accident.' Even Pamela's mother, who had
remained neutral throughout most of their marriage, had been
forced to take her husband's side.

There was little wonder, Alex reflected now, that he'd been
shattered. His whole world had been falling apart, and the
only solace he'd found was when he was too drunk to know
what was going on. Rachel had been too young, too vulnerable, to offer him any comfort. Little wonder that her grandfather had found it so easy to convince the authorities that
he and his wife should look after her until her father was
capable of doing so.

Alex's hands tightened on the wheel at the unwelcome
memory. But he knew it wouldn't do to go and meet Conrad
Wyatt in a hostile frame of mind. He had to convince the

Wyatts he meant to regain custody of his daughter; that he was the fit and proper person to bring her up.

And he was, he told himself fiercely. Any bitterness he had left was all directed towards himself. He'd been a fool, but he'd learned his lesson the hard way. If he got Rachel back, he'd never act so stupidly again.

Julia Wyatt opened the door to him herself. Alex, who had been expecting to encounter the dour housekeeper, Mrs Gellis, felt an immediate sense of apprehension. Although Pamela's mother had always been less antagonistic than her husband, she was not in the habit of answering doors; not when she had a perfectly good member of staff to do it for her.

'Oh—Alex,' she said, almost as if she hadn't expected it to be him. She must have heard the car, he thought. Her sitting room was at the front of the house. 'I'm afraid I've got some bad news for you. Um—Rachel isn't very well.'

Alex pushed his hands into the pockets of his overcoat. It was a cold day and he had worn the long cashmere garment because he'd intended to take Rachel to the park. He'd planned that they would feed the ducks, and then go back to Jamaica Hill for lunch. In the afternoon, he'd been going to take her down to the stables. One of the mares had foaled and he was sure she'd love to see the spindly-legged colt.

But now...

'She's ill?' he asked, aware that his tone was brusque, but he couldn't help it. Of all the stunts he'd expected Conrad Wyatt to pull, he'd never anticipated anything like this.

'She's not ill exactly,' demurred Julia, glancing somewhat nervously over her shoulder. 'She's got a nasty little cold, and I don't think she should go out on a day like this.'

'*You* don't think?' asked Alex harshly. He was fairly sure this was all her husband's idea. But it was a damp, cold morning, and he took a breath to calm himself. Then, putting a booted foot on the step, he asked, 'May I see her?'

'Oh, I'm not sure—' began Julia, and then broke off abruptly when her husband's voice sounded behind her.

'Who is it, Julia?' he was demanding. 'It's far too cold to be standing at the door.' Then he saw Alex, and his expression hardened contemptuously. 'Oh, it's you.' He turned to his wife. 'Haven't you told him that Rachel can't go out today?'

'Well, yes—'

'She's told me, Conrad,' broke in Alex levelly, aware that his behaviour now was crucial. 'I was saying that I'd like to see her anyway.'

'You can't.' Conrad Wyatt didn't mince his words. 'She's—ah—she's sleeping. Isn't that right, Julia?' He exchanged a look with his wife, and Alex wondered what else was said in that silent stare. He turned back to his son-in-law, his eyes mirroring his triumph. 'I'm sorry to disappoint you, Kellerman, but there it is.'

Alex's hands curled into fists in his pockets. He would have liked nothing better than to stuff one of them down Conrad Wyatt's throat. The man was actually enjoying this, and no wonder. It would be another week before Alex could arrange to see Rachel again.

But Alex knew better than to argue with him. Conrad would like nothing better than to be able to tell a judge that he'd been threatened by his son-in-law. It would also add weight to what Conrad had always maintained about the accident: that Alex was violent and untrustworthy, and no fit guardian for the child.

'So am I,' Alex said now. 'Sorry, I mean.' He addressed himself to Julia. 'Will you let me know how she is tomorrow?'

'Oh—yes.' Julia glanced at her husband for his approval, before going on. 'But I'm afraid—'

'I know.' Alex was sardonic. 'I won't be able to visit her tomorrow. Just give her my love, will you? I'm sure I can trust you to do that.'

'Are you implying—?' began Conrad angrily, but Alex was already walking back to the Range Rover. Pretending he didn't hear, he opened the door and coiled his considerable length behind the wheel. Raising one hand in farewell, he started the powerful engine, deliberately churning up the gravel as he gunned the motor down the drive.

But once he was out on the King's Montford road again his spurt of defiance vanished. In spite of all his efforts, he was no further forward than before. And the knowledge that he wasn't going to spend the day with his daughter was like a burning pain inside him. At times like these, he wanted to cry like a baby for the way he'd screwed up his life.

But there was no point in letting Conrad Wyatt's attitude get to him, and he decided to drive to the Wayside and make his peace with Lacey instead. He had spoken to her in the last couple of days and she'd seemed more amenable. But that was on the phone. Who knew how she'd react if he turned up in person?

He decided to swing by Jamaica Hill first. He'd told his housekeeper he'd be in for lunch and she was making her special chocolate pudding just for Rachel. He knew Agnes Muir would be disappointed that the little girl wasn't joining them, just as he was. The elderly Scotswoman had supported him throughout all his dealings with the Wyatts.

He turned in at the gates and then had to brake hard to avoid a loitering teenager. The girl was hanging about inside the gates, apparently undecided as to whether to walk up to the house or turn off towards the stable block. She was fairly tall and slim, dressed in a short pleated skirt and a parka. He was sure he didn't know her, yet there was something strangely familiar about her startled face.

He rolled down his window. 'Can I help you?' he asked shortly. He wasn't really in the mood to talk to some strange schoolgirl, who was probably here to ask about a job. He and Guthrie got them all the time: girls who were horse-mad and wanted nothing more than to brush the animals' coats or muck out the stalls in their spare time. Most of them couldn't afford the cost of riding lessons, and working with the horses meant they sometimes got lucky and had the chance to hack around the paddock.

The girl looped her haversack over her shoulder and looked at him doubtfully. 'I—er—I was looking for my mum,' she said awkwardly. 'She—er—she works here. Her name's Kate. Kate—'

'Kate Hughes?' asked Alex, and the girl coloured guiltily.

'Yes. Kate Hughes,' she agreed hurriedly, and he guessed her mother had told her not to come here.

'You're her daughter?' Alex was surprised. Not because Kate wasn't a good-looking woman, but because he hadn't known she was married. If indeed she was. And it also explained that unfamiliar resemblance. He shook his head. 'If you get in the car, I'll take you down to the yard.'

'Oh, I don't—'

'I'm Alex Kellerman,' he informed her flatly. 'I'm sure your mother's warned you not to get into cars with strange men, but I happen to own this place.'

'I know.' Her eyes widened then, as if she was afraid she shouldn't have made such an admission. 'Well—' She hesitated. 'If you don't mind, that would be cool.'

Cool!

Alex grimaced and thrust open the door nearest to her. 'Get in,' he advised her tersely, and she swiftly swung her long legs over the seat. 'Shouldn't you be in school?' he asked as she slammed the door, and she gave him a rueful grimace.

'That's what Mum's going to say, I know, but I'm not going back.' She pursed her lips. 'Not today anyway.'

Alex frowned, not altogether unhappy at the diversion. 'Is something wrong?' he asked. 'Couldn't whatever it is have waited until tonight?'

'Mum's going to say that, too.' She gave him another doubtful look. 'She's really hot on getting a good education and all that.' She hunched her shoulders. 'But sometimes it's not as easy as she thinks.'

Alex put the car into gear. 'You're having problems,' he remarked dryly. 'Convincing people you're telling the truth can be pretty tough. I know.'

'I s'pose you do.' She glanced sideways at him. Then her

colour deepened again. 'I'm sorry. I shouldn't have said that. I don't really know anything about you.'

'That hasn't stopped plenty of other people from passing their opinion,' responded Alex, with some irony. And then he smiled. It was refreshing to meet someone who admitted to having preconceived ideas. 'So, as I'm such an authority, why don't you tell me what's troubling you?' He examined her face critically. 'I guess you go to the comprehensive in town.'

'Lady Montford,' she agreed, with a nod. 'I've been going there for over a year.'

'And you're finding the work too hard, is that it?' asked Alex gently, only to have her fix him with an indignant look.

'No!' she exclaimed. 'I don't find the work hard. Well, not especially. I'm not brilliant at maths, but I'm pretty good at everything else.' She sniffed. 'That's part of the trouble,' she muttered in an undertone, stiffening as she saw the roof of the stables through the trees.

Alex wished the journey had been longer. He had enjoyed talking to her, and he was loath to let her go without finding out what was wrong. 'So what's the problem—er—you didn't tell me your name?'

'Joanne.'

'—Okay, Joanne.' A thought occurred to him. 'You're not being bullied because they think you're a swot?'

'A what?'

She turned to gaze at him, and he realised they probably had other names for it these days. 'Because you're prepared to learn and they're not,' he explained, feeling very old suddenly.

'Oh, you mean a nerd.' She grimaced. 'No.'

Alex pulled a wry face, but they'd already reached the stable yard and he switched off the engine. 'Whatever it is, I'm sure if you discuss it with your mother she'll understand.'

'You think?' Joanne pulled a face. 'You don't know Mum like I do. She doesn't seem to understand how hard it is to stay friends with girls who think you're just a wimp.' She sighed. 'Have you ever done something you know was wrong and regretted it later, Mr Kellerman? Like, you want to put it behind you, but some people won't let you forget?'

Alex's brows drew together. What was this? he wondered. Some new way Conrad Wyatt had devised to disarm him and induce him to confess? He shook his head. No, that was crazy. This was Kate Hughes's daughter. He thought even Conrad would draw the line at using a child to do his dirty work.

'Look,' he said evenly, 'everyone does something they regret sometimes.' He grimaced. 'In my case, it was getting married to the wrong woman, but we won't go into that.' He paused. 'What can you have done that's so outrageous? You're—what? Thirteen? Fourteen?'

'I'm twelve.'

'There you are then. You're twelve—' he grinned at her haughty expression '—going on twenty. What can you have done to warrant that long face?'

'You don't have to be old to break the law,' Joanne retorted, gazing at him defensively. 'Oh, God, Mum's going to kill me when she finds out.'

Alex blinked. She was so serious. Whatever she'd done, she obviously believed it would cause her mother some grief. So, what? Missing lessons? Mouthing off at her teacher? *Taking drugs?* As she gathered her haversack to her chest, preparing to get out, he felt an unexpected twinge of alarm.

'You're not—' he began as she reached for the door handle, and then stopped himself before he could go on. This was crazy, he thought. He'd just met her. This girl meant absolutely nothing to him.

'I'm not what?' she asked, a small ladder in her tights delineating the bony curve of her knee. There was something fragile about that ladder; it made her look vulnerable. And, although he'd determined not to say any more, he couldn't help it.

'You're not—sniffing glue, or anything like that?' he

asked unwillingly, choosing the least likely option he could think of, and she gasped.

'No, I'm not,' she told him shortly. 'I'm not stupid, Mr Kellerman. And I don't do drugs either, even though I have been offered them.'

Alex was horrified. To hear that this child had already been offered drugs at her young age filled him with anger. Dear God, he thought, where was it all going to end? When were children allowed to be children, for pity's sake?

'I'm glad to hear it,' he said now, making an effort to hide his real feelings. 'And if it's not drugs I don't think you have anything to worry about.'

'That's all you know,' she muttered rudely, getting out of the Range Rover and hauling her bag out after her. 'You try telling Mum that I didn't want to go shoplifting last term.'

He suspected she hadn't meant to tell him, and judging from her expression she regretted it as soon as the words were out. But she didn't say anything in her own defence. She probably thought she'd be wasting her time, he reflected, watching her a little ruefully as she clumped off across the yard.

He was going to have to leave her to it. He prepared to do a three-point turn to go up to the house. But before he could accomplish this it became obvious that she didn't know which way to go, and, stifling the voice that was warning him not to get involved, he turned off the engine and swung out of the car.

'Hey!' His initial yell didn't attract her attention, and, slamming the car door, he tried again. 'Joanne!' He used her name this time. 'Where are you going? The office isn't along there. It's over here.'

She halted, turned, and came back to him with obvious reluctance, the sturdy Doc Martens she was wearing giving her long legs a stalk-like appearance. In that respect she resembled her mother, too, he conceded. One of the first things he'd noticed about Kate was her long legs.

But before she could reach him the door that led to her

mother's office flew open, and Kate herself emerged looking
dismayed. 'Joanne!' she exclaimed, ignoring Alex for the
moment in favour of her daughter. Then, acknowledging his
presence with a nervous glance, she went on, 'What on earth
are you doing here?'

'Mum—'

'Shouldn't you be in class?' Kate didn't wait for her to
finish before examining her watch. 'It's only eleven o'clock.'
Another quick glance in Alex's direction, and then she said,
'Nothing's wrong, is it? Your grandmother hasn't—'

'Nan's fine,' Joanne said flatly, trudging nearer.

'Then why is Mr Kellerman—?'

'I met her at the gate.' Against his better judgement, Alex
sauntered up to them, noticing Kate was shivering in spite of
her ankle-length skirt and woollen cardigan. 'Hadn't you better go inside, before you catch a chill?'

'What?' She looked up at him almost blankly for a moment and he realised she was more upset than he'd thought.
'Oh, yes.' Dark lashes shadowed her grey eyes as she directed her daughter towards the lights of the office behind
her. 'I've just made some tea, Joanne. Go and pour us both
a cup.'

Alex's lips twitched. 'That's very civil of you after yesterday.'

'Oh—' Once again, he saw a trace of anxiety in her face.
'I didn't mean—' He knew exactly what she'd meant, but he
didn't make it easy for her. 'That is, if you'd like to join us,
Mr Kellerman, then naturally—naturally you'd be very welcome.'

'Would I?'

He regarded her quizzically. It was so easy to disconcert
her, he thought, and he knew an unexpected feeling of regret
that she was married and therefore out of his reach. With the
experiences he'd had, there was no way he'd put any other
man through what he'd had to go through, but nevertheless
he had to admit he was intrigued by his newest employee.

'Of course,' she said now, squaring her shoulders, and he realised she expected him to accept.

'Some other time,' he said, nodding towards the open doorway Joanne had just passed through. 'And go easy on your daughter, hmm? I think she's having a tough time at the moment.'

'You think what?' Kate stared at him coldly now and he guessed she resented his remark. 'I don't think the way I treat my daughter is anything to do with you, Mr Kellerman.' She straightened her spine, and then added with some vehemence, 'I don't think you're in any position to judge, do you?'

That stung, particularly this morning with the memory of Conrad Wyatt's latest tactics still sticking in his throat. 'Perhaps not,' he conceded coolly, choosing not to argue with her. 'I was merely offering an opinion. If I were her father—'

'But you're not,' she broke in heatedly. 'Joanne's father is dead, Mr Kellerman. He was killed in a car crash when she was barely two years old.'

'I'm sorry—'

Alex felt chastened, but this time Kate made a gesture of defeat. 'I'm not,' she told him flatly. 'And if that sounds hard to you, well—that's how I feel.' She took a breath. 'You see, he wasn't alone in the car when he died.'

'Ah…'

Alex nodded, and his understanding seemed to bring a change of heart. 'If I was rude just now,' she murmured, 'I'm sorry.' She glanced over his shoulder. 'Is your daughter waiting in the car?'

'My daughter's not coming,' he informed her firmly, not at all surprised that she should know where he'd been. The grapevine at the stables was quite efficient, and he hadn't hidden his delight at the prospect of seeing Rachel again from Mrs Muir, or Sam Guthrie, for that matter.

'Oh.' She actually looked sympathetic. 'There's nothing wrong, is there? Is she coming another day?'

'Not if my father-in-law has anything to do with it,' remarked Alex pleasantly. Then, because the temptation to confide in her was too inviting, he rocked back on his heels and turned towards the car. 'I like your daughter,' he added, as a parting observation. His lips twisted. 'You must have been a teenager yourself when she was born.'

CHAPTER FIVE

'I'M NOT sure your father would approve of what you're doing, Kate.'

Ellen Ross confronted her daughter across the supper table that evening, primed, no doubt, by Joanne that her investigation at the stables wasn't as straightforward as she'd have had them believe.

'I don't know what you mean, Mum,' Kate protested now, giving Joanne an irritated look. 'And if someone hadn't been playing hookey we wouldn't be having this conversation.'

'No, that's probably true.' Ellen Ross turned her attention to her granddaughter now, as Kate had hoped she would. 'I can't believe you behaved so recklessly, Joanne. What were you thinking of?'

Joanne hunched her shoulders. 'I just got caught up in it,' she said defensively. 'I didn't know what they were planning to do until I got there.'

'"There" being Daltons department store,' put in Kate dryly. 'You realise you're going to have to tell Mr Coulthard what's been going on?'

'Oh, Mum!'

'Well, there's no other way to handle it,' declared Kate reasonably. 'If you own up, I doubt if Daltons will bring a charge.'

'Bring a charge!' Joanne was horrified. 'Mum, I only took a lipstick, nothing else.'

'It's still shoplifting, Joanne,' replied her mother firmly. 'You knew it was wrong. That's why you stayed away from school.'

'I stayed away from school because—because they expected me to go with them again.' Joanne grimaced. 'He won't expect me to grass on the others, will he?'

'*Grass!*' Her grandmother was appalled. 'Joanne, where do you get your expressions from?'

'Television,' said Kate flatly. 'And Mr Coulthard will ask you who was with you.' She bit her lip. 'I suppose whether you tell him or not is up to you.'

Joanne slumped over the table. 'Oh, God,' she groaned, 'I can't go back to that school again.'

'You don't have any choice,' said Kate, getting up to clear the dishes. 'Joanne, you're going to have to face those girls and tell them you're not a thief. You made a mistake, that's all. If they don't like it—well, it's not the end of the world. You'll make new friends who don't think you're a wimp because you don't get your kicks at other people's expense.'

'That's easy for you to say.'

'Actually, it's not easy for me to say,' replied her mother, running hot water into the sink. She cast Joanne a rueful look. 'As a matter of fact, it's very hard. I don't like the idea that you've got to deal with something like this in your second year at Lady Montford. But I'm sure you wouldn't like me to fight all your battles for you.'

'I suppose not.' Joanne straightened up reluctantly. 'But you will come with me to see Mr Coulthard tomorrow, won't you?'

'If I can get the time off,' agreed Kate, realising she'd have to ask Mr Guthrie. He might not be very pleased. As with Alex Kellerman, she'd never mentioned having a daughter to him.

'Will you have to ask Mr Kellerman?' asked her daughter at once, and Kate was reminded of her employer's remarks about Joanne. But before she could comment the girl turned to her grandmother. 'He's drop-dead gorgeous, Nan. Have you seen him?'

Ellen Ross's lips turned down. 'I've seen his picture in the newspaper,' she said dismissively. 'And ''gorgeous'' isn't an expression I'd have used.'

'Well—sort of brooding, then,' amended Joanne. 'And sexy. I bet Mum's noticed that, if nothing else.'

'Joanne!'

'That will do, Joanne!'

The two women spoke in unison, and Kate felt an added twinge of anxiety at her daughter's words. 'You never did tell me what he said to you,' she added tautly. 'Or how you came to speak to a man you didn't know.'

Joanne pulled a face. 'Honestly, talk about the inquisition! I met him, right? I was hanging about at the gates when he drove in. He asked me what I was doing, and I told him I was looking for you. He gave me a ride down to the stables, and that's it.'

'You got into his car?' exclaimed her grandmother in an appalled tone, and Joanne looked to her mother for support.

'You knew that,' she said. 'And you didn't say anything about it.'

'Because I thought at first that his little girl was with him,' put in Kate shortly. 'And you don't need me to tell you my views about accepting lifts from strange men.'

'He isn't a strange man. He's your boss,' protested Joanne indignantly. She flung herself off her chair. 'In any case, I think he's really nice.' Her jaw jutted. 'He talked to me. He really talked to me, you know? Like I was an adult, not some dumb kid!'

'I don't talk to you like you're a dumb kid,' objected her mother at once, wondering what Alex Kellerman could have said to evoke this kind of response from her daughter. 'And—' she cast her mother a hopeful look '—perhaps we are overreacting a little bit. You were on Mr Kellerman's land, after all.'

'Even so…' began Ellen Ross, but Joanne wasn't listening to her.

'You do like him, don't you?' the young girl asked, giving her mother a sly look. 'I could tell.'

'You're talking nonsense!' exclaimed Kate hotly, plunging her hands into the soapy water in an effort to avoid any further discussion of Alex Kellerman. 'Come on. You can dry. Your grandmother can go and sit down for once.'

But later that evening, after Joanne had gone to bed, Ellen Ross returned to the subject of Kate's temporary employer. 'I still think taking a job at Jamaica Hill was going too far,' she declared. 'You don't really know anything about that man, and I don't like the idea that he's influencing Joanne now. How do you know he wasn't responsible for his wife's death? Somebody had to have put those horses into the wrong stalls, so why not him?'

Kate sighed. 'I think if Alex Kellerman had wanted to kill his wife he'd have chosen a more certain way of doing it,' she replied quietly.

'What do you mean?'

'Oh, Mum.' Kate shook her head. 'You know as well as I do that the chances of someone being killed by a fall from a horse are fairly slim. People fall from horses all the time without any serious injury. Or she could have been paralysed, brain-damaged, even. Neither of which would have achieved what he's supposed to have wanted to achieve.'

'Since when have you become such an expert?' asked her mother huffily. 'It seems to me that both you and Joanne have been taken in by Alex Kellerman's ''sexy'' manner.' She used her fingers to denote the quotation marks, and then grimaced. 'Well, just be careful, Kate. You're not infallible and Alex Kellerman is a very clever man.'

Didn't she know it?

But Kate made no comment. She preferred not to have to explain her own reasons for thinking so to her mother and the knowledge that what the older woman had said was probably true didn't help. Not least that despite what she'd heard—and the warnings she'd given herself—she still found her employer an intriguing enigma. Not sexually attractive, she assured herself, but fascinating nonetheless.

Kate went into her office early the next morning.

She made a point of calling in at the agency every two or three days to read her messages and check the post. Susie wasn't in that early, of course, and she and Kate usually kept in touch by phone. For the time being, Susie was in nominal charge of the office, and she had orders to try and postpone any enquiries and sign cheques for any service bills that came due in her employer's absence.

Today, Susie had left a couple of letters for her attention. One of them was from the insurance company who generally used her services in their inquiries, asking if she was free to accompany their assessor on a visit to see a claimant in Bath. The other was from the garage that serviced the Vauxhall, reminding her that it was due for its next road test at the end of the month.

More expense, thought Kate gloomily, appalled at how much of the two thousand pounds Henry Sawyer had given her she'd already spent. She'd earned some of it, of course, but she doubted he would think she was any further forward, and playing fencing games with Alex Kellerman wasn't getting her anywhere.

She studied the letter from Lingard's Life Assurance one more time before scribbling a note refusing the offer for Susie to type up when she came in. She thought ruefully that she would have liked nothing better than to be able to accept such an undemanding job. But insurance investigations didn't usually pay very large dividends, and in any case she was committed to her present client for the next two weeks at least.

She decided the letter from the garage could wait until later. Despite its age, the car was running reasonably efficiently at the moment, even if it did spend all its days and nights in the open air. When her father was alive, and they'd all shared the house in Edgecombe Crescent, it had enjoyed the luxury of a garage. But the apartments where they now lived provided only parking spaces, and Kate had had to invest in an alarm to protect the car.

She checked to see that there were no further messages on the answering machine, and then, after straightening the papers on her desk, she walked reluctantly towards the door.

But she paused and took a last wistful look around the office. She missed the familiarity of these surroundings, she thought. She missed the anticipation of what each new day would bring. But most of all she missed being herself. She simply wasn't cut out to live a lie.

Which was defeatist talk, she chided herself severely as she rattled down the stairs again and crossed the street to where she'd left the car. She was letting the slow progress she was making influence her thinking, when it took time to gain the confidence of her fellow employees. She had to find a way to talk to Billy Roach again. She was fairly sure he knew more about Alicia Sawyer's disappearance then he'd said. But, first of all, she had to see Mr Guthrie and ask him for some time off this morning. She doubted he'd be very pleased to hear that she was a single mother, let alone that she was going to have to try and find some way to explain her daughter's misdemeanours to her head teacher.

Her confidence received something of a blow when she arrived at Jamaica Hill to find Alex Kellerman's mud-spattered Range Rover parked at the stables. She looked about her rather apprehensively as she pulled into the space beside the other vehicle. But to her relief there was no sign of her employer. Only Billy, and one of the other apprentices, hosing down the yard.

She acknowledged their greetings, but now was not the time to look for answers. She guessed Kellerman was with Sam Guthrie, and until he left her request would have to wait. It was just her hard luck that he'd chosen to visit the stables this morning. Still, she had plenty of time. Her appointment with Mr Coulthard was not until ten o'clock.

When she opened her office door, a pleasing wave of warmth enveloped her. It was a bright morning, but it was cold, and she was glad Mr Guthrie had remembered to turn on her fire. He didn't always do so and sometimes the room felt as cold as charity. She hoped it was an omen. He must be in a good mood.

She had loosened her tweed jacket and was unwinding the

green chenille scarf from her neck when Mr Guthrie's office door opened. Half expecting it to be Alex Kellerman, Kate managed not to look too dismayed when he appeared. At least he was leaving, which was good news. But although she waited for Mr Guthrie to follow him out Alex appeared to be alone.

'Good morning,' he said, his lean dark face far too knowledgeable for her liking. 'I thought you'd like to know that Sam won't be coming in today. His wife rang to say he's not feeling so good.' He shrugged his shoulders. 'She thinks he might be getting the flu.'

Oh, great!

Kate knew an immediate—and selfish—feeling of frustration. But she couldn't help wishing that the old man hadn't chosen today of all days to be ill. She sighed impatiently. What was wrong with her? No one *chose* to be ill. It just happened.

'Something wrong?'

Alex was watching her closely, and Kate made a pretence of folding her scarf and putting it on her desk. But her mind was buzzing with the realisation that she would have to ask him if she wanted to take part of the morning off.

'Not really,' she said now, stopping short of taking off her jacket. 'Um—I hope he'll be feeling better soon.'

'Don't we all?' But Alex's green eyes had narrowed. 'Until then, you'll have to put up with me, I'm afraid.'

Kate forced a polite smile, and turned away to put her bag in the desk drawer. It was only when she straightened that she was reminded that she was wearing a short skirt this morning. She'd dressed more formally than usual to go and see Joanne's headmaster and her careless action had exposed a provocative length of thigh.

The urge to try and pull down the hem of her skirt was almost irresistible, even though her long legs were encased in warm black tights. Then she met his sensual gaze, and she was fairly sure that he knew what she was thinking. Her skin prickled with an awareness she didn't want to admit.

'Did you talk to Joanne?'

His question was so at odds with the way he'd been looking at her that for a moment Kate couldn't think what he meant. But then the audacity of his enquiry hit her, arousing a sense of outrage she was able to channel into keeping her unwelcome attraction to him at bay.

'I—whether or not I spoke to my daughter is hardly relevant, Mr Kellerman,' she declared stiffly. 'And if she turns up here again I'd be grateful if you'd remind her that this is my place of work.'

Alex's dark brows arched. 'In other words, mind my own business,' he remarked tightly. 'Okay. If that's what you want. I wouldn't like to be accused of attempting to corrupt a minor as well as everything else.'

Kate sighed. 'I'm not accusing you of attempting to corrupt her.'

'No?' He raked one hand through his overlong hair. 'It sounded like it to me.'

'Well, I wasn't.' She took a breath. 'It's just—complicated, that's all.' Then, deciding that it might as well be now as later, she said, 'As a matter of fact, I was going to ask Mr Guthrie if I could have a couple of hours off this morning. I—I have to go to Lady Montford, you see.'

'I assume you mean Joanne's school?'

Kate gripped the edge of her desk. 'That's right. I have to see her head teacher.'

Alex grimaced. 'Well, I must say you have a hell of a way of asking for a favour,' he remarked dryly. 'And at the risk of being accused of interfering again, is there anything I can do?'

Kate's shoulders sagged. 'I don't think so, thank you.' But it was kind of him to ask. She swallowed. 'My appointment's at ten o'clock. Would it be all right if I left about half-past nine?'

Alex frowned. 'If you think that will give you sufficient time.' He paused. 'I suppose Joanne is going with you?'

Kate looked up. 'What makes you think she's not in school?'

Alex lifted his shoulders. 'Call it intuition,' he responded flatly. He massaged the back of his neck with a weary hand. 'You can go whenever you want.'

'Thanks.' But Kate still regarded him warily. 'Um—what exactly did Joanne say to you?'

'Do you expect me to betray a lady's confidence?' he mocked her gently, his hand falling to his side. 'Besides, it isn't—relevant—is it?'

Kate slumped. 'She told you, didn't she?'

'What?' He gave her an innocent look and she wanted to scream.

'Why—why she wanted to see me!' she exclaimed at last, gazing at him frustratedly. 'Why I have to see her head teacher this morning.' She groaned. 'That's why you told me to go easy on her. God, you must think I'm such a fool!'

'I don't think you're a fool, Kate.' He abandoned his stance beside the door into the manager's office and came further into the room. 'As a matter of fact I have nothing but admiration for you. You're doing a great job. It can't have been easy bringing up a child on your own.'

'No.' Kate blew out breath. 'No, it hasn't been,' she conceded ruefully, trying not to feel threatened because he was now standing just an arm's length away. But in black jeans and a dark green corded jacket he was disturbingly familiar. It was odd how in such a short time she had come to know his appearance so well.

'That's what I thought.'

There were waistline pockets in his jeans and now he hooked his thumbs inside them, drawing her attention to the powerful thighs they enhanced. Reminded her, too, of his sexuality, and the not unimpressive bulge against his zip.

God!

She was horrified at where her thoughts were leading her. She had to remember that he was the man she had come here to investigate. She must be crazy to be entertaining any ideas about his masculinity when his relationship to the missing woman was still in doubt.

'Would you like to talk about it?'

She realised suddenly that he'd misinterpreted her silence. He'd assumed she was still worrying about Joanne when her daughter's problems had been far from her thoughts. She wondered what he'd say if she told him she'd been speculating about his sexual preferences. He was a sensual man; there had to be some woman in his life.

'Talk about what?' she asked now, buying a little time, and a look of resignation crossed his face.

'What indeed?' he countered quietly, turning back towards Mr Guthrie's office. 'Let me know when you're leaving. I'll have all calls switched through to me.'

'No—wait—' Kate went after him, stopping herself just short of grabbing his arm. 'That is, I'll tell you what happens when I get back.' She bit her lip. 'If you're interested.'

'I am,' he agreed gently. 'Good luck.'

When the door closed behind him, she filled her lungs completely for the first time since he'd come into her office. What was there about him, she wondered, that put every nerve in her body on red alert? When she was near him, she was conscious of herself in a way she'd never experienced before. No wonder Alicia had been infatuated with him—if she had, she amended swiftly. It was far too easy to jump to the wrong conclusions where he was concerned.

Deciding there wasn't much point in starting anything until she got back, Kate decided to take him up on his offer and make an early start. With a bit of luck, she should be back by eleven o'clock, and she'd make sure she caught up on all her correspondence before she went home.

But, as she wrapped her scarf around her neck again, she knew she was being rather optimistic. She had no idea how long the interview with Mr Coulthard might take, and the thought that Joanne could end up with a suspension from school, or worse, filled her with apprehension.

Lifting her bag out of the drawer again, she crossed to the

door leading into Mr Guthrie's office. Tapping lightly on the panels, she waited until Alex answered before putting her head around the door. 'I'm leaving now,' she said, when he looked up from the stock book. 'I've switched the phones through to you. Is that okay?'

'Okay.'

Alex nodded, and Kate closed the door again and started for the door. So far, so good, she thought, trying to be optimistic. All she had to do now was pick up Joanne, which would give her plenty of time to cope with the morning traffic.

The old Vauxhall looked more shabby than usual beside the Range Rover. Alex's vehicle might need a wash, but even dirty it possessed a powerful appeal. Much like its owner, reflected Kate as she slid behind the wheel of her own car. Her lips twitched. Not that she was in any position to judge.

Nevertheless, as she turned the key in the ignition, she had to admit that the night's growth of beard on his jaw this morning had suited him. He'd obviously left the house in a hurry after learning that Mr Guthrie wasn't going to be in that day. The car hiccupped, but didn't start, and she stifled an expletive. She had to stop thinking about Alex Kellerman so personally and concentrate on why she was here.

She tried to start the car again, but once again it refused to respond to her efforts. And, no matter how she tried to coax it into action, the engine simply wouldn't fire. 'Oh, great,' she muttered irritably. This was all she needed. She would have to go and call a taxi now and hope that one could get here in time.

She'd attracted the attention of a couple of the hands who worked at the stables, but before one of them could come and offer his help the office door opened and Alex himself came out. At once, the other men reverted to what they'd been doing, and Kate thrust open her door and got out of the car as her employer strolled across the yard.

'I won't ask if you're having problems, because I can see

you are,' he remarked without sarcasm. 'What's wrong? Have you flooded the carburettor, or what?'

'You tell me,' muttered Kate frustratedly. 'I just know it won't start.'

'Let me try.' Alex got into the car and flicked the ignition. But although the engine turned over a couple of times it remained obstinately uncooperative. 'I think it may be flooded,' he said at last, getting out again. 'Would you like me to get my mechanic to take a look at it? In the meantime, I could give you a lift into town.'

Kate thought ruefully of the letter she'd read that morning. If she'd kept up to date with the car's maintenance, this might never have happened. 'Um—well, if you could give me a lift to the taxi rank at the bus station, I'd be grateful,' she acknowledged weakly. 'But I'll get the garage where it's serviced to come and collect the car.'

Alex shrugged. 'If you like.' He paused. 'But it's possible they'd have a wasted journey. If it is flooded, it will start again once the petrol's had time to evaporate, you know.'

Kate hesitated. There was no doubt that she could do without another bill if it wasn't necessary. 'Well—if your mechanic doesn't mind,' she murmured awkwardly, wondering what her father would have done in a case like this.

But, of course, her father would never have got himself into a situation like this, she conceded, after Alex had closed the office door and unlocked the Range Rover so that she could get in. He'd never have become involved with someone he was investigating, let alone got himself into a position where he was indebted to the man himself.

'Right.' Alex climbed into the vehicle beside her, and she was instantly aware of how much she wanted to believe he was innocent of the charge she was investigating. In the confined space of the car, she couldn't help inhaling the clean male scent of his body, the piney scent of his aftershave lingering so pleasantly on his skin that she almost started when he spoke again. 'Do you want to remind me of your address?'

'My address?'

'I assume you want to collect your daughter before going to the school?'

'Well, yes.' Kate swallowed. 'But there's no need for you to take us. If you'll drop me at the taxi rank, I can take it from there.'

Alex gave her a sidelong glance as he reversed the powerful motor, and she wondered what he was thinking. But she could hardly explain that her apparent lack of gratitude was due to the fact that she didn't want him to see exactly where she lived. She'd had to give her address, of course, when she'd applied for the job at the stables, but she'd hoped he'd never have occasion to notice it himself.

'I'll take you to the school,' he said now, and she decided not to argue with him. After all, at least twenty other families lived in the block of flats where she and her family lived. Unless he checked, he'd never know there wasn't a Hughes among them. That there was a Ross could surely mean nothing to him.

'Well—if you don't mind,' she murmured as they accelerated towards the gates.

'If I had, I wouldn't have offered,' he remarked sardonically. 'What's the matter? Are you afraid your boyfriend will find out I've been chauffeuring you around?'

'I don't have a boyfriend,' retorted Kate, without thinking, and she scolded herself for the lack of professionalism she'd displayed. If she wasn't careful, he'd trick her into revealing what she was really doing at the stables, and her nails dug into her palms at the prospect of what that would mean.

'Why not?' he asked, and she looked at him blankly. 'Why don't you have a boyfriend?' he amplified mildly, and she hurriedly looked away.

'I don't have time for men,' she said at last, staring out of the window. 'And I live in Milner Court. That's off Marlborough Road.'

'Okay.' Alex absorbed the information. Then, as if this was some game he liked to play, he said, 'Joanne's father must have hurt you very badly. Didn't you say she was little more than a baby when he died?'

Kate heaved a sigh, wishing she'd never confided in him. 'It was a long time ago,' she said dismissively. She clenched her fists. 'I suppose I could say the same about you,' she added, deciding he could hardly object if she answered in kind.

He was silent for a few moments, and she half thought he wasn't going to respond to her challenge. His expression had darkened, and his long fingers had tightened on the wheel. But then, with a shrug of his shoulders, he seemed to come to a decision. 'I hardly think my situation qualifies, do you?'

Kate took the opportunity he was offering. 'Why not?' she asked innocently, and he glanced her way, his thick lashes shadowing the expression in his eyes.

'What woman would trust herself with me after what I've been accused of?' he enquired dryly. 'Oh, no, Mrs Hughes, I'm in no doubt as to what most of your sex would think of me.'

'Well, I think you're exaggerating,' declared Kate swiftly, and a look of wry amusement crossed his face.

'And I think you're being charitable,' he countered. 'Let's talk about your daughter. That's a safer topic, don't you think?'

Kate shifted a little restlessly in her seat. She might never have another chance to talk to him like this. 'I'm sure there are plenty of women who'd like to get to know you,' she persisted. 'Who'd jump at the chance to visit Jamaica Hill.'

Alex expelled a resigned breath. 'Really?'

'Yes, really.'

'Why? So that they could say they'd seen the spot where the dastardly deed took place?'

'No.' Kate sensed that despite his mockery it still hurt him to talk about it, but she told herself she mustn't feel sorry for him. 'Are you telling me you haven't brought any other women to—to the house since your wife died?'

Alex's eyes narrowed. 'I don't think that's anything to do

with you, Mrs Hughes,' he responded harshly. 'Are you sure you're not working for someone else as well as me?'

Kate went cold. 'I don't know what you mean.'

'I mean my father-in-law, Mrs Hughes. Perhaps he can't get the answers he wants from my staff, so he's sent you.'

Kate gasped. 'I don't even know your father-in-law, Mr Kellerman,' she protested, glad she could be honest. 'And I can assure you, I'm not working for him.'

'Well, good.' His lips twisted. 'I believe you. I guess I'm just not good at answering questions any more.'

Kate managed to hide the relief she was feeling. For a moment there, she'd thought he'd guessed why she'd taken the job. But in his position she supposed he had to be careful what he said, and to whom. The case of how his wife had died was considered closed, but if any further evidence was forthcoming she supposed it could be opened again…

CHAPTER SIX

IT WAS after twelve o'clock by the time they got back to Jamaica Hill.

Although Kate had insisted that there was no need for him to wait, Alex had hung about the school gates for over an hour while she and Joanne had their interview with Mr Coulthard, Joanne's head teacher.

And it was just as well he had, Alex reflected now, glancing once again at Kate's white face. The head teacher had proved to be tough and intractable, and she had taken his decision badly. He also knew she blamed herself for Joanne's behaviour and no amount of persuasion on either his or Joanne's part would change her mind.

Joanne, herself, had proved surprisingly resilient, though Alex suspected she might behave somewhat differently in the privacy of her own room at home. But she seemed to realise how upset her mother was and in consequence she'd kept her own feelings to herself.

Alex admired her sensitivity, and after they'd dropped the girl at the flat he'd done his utmost to convince Kate that, far from letting her daughter down, she'd given her values anyone would admire. But he couldn't do anything about Joanne's suspension, or make Kate see that Mr Coulthard had really had no choice.

Now, he realised, he didn't want to return her to the office. Despite her assertion that she'd be better off at work, he was of the opinion that she needed a break. Her mother, whom he'd met briefly that morning, had suggested that he might be agreeable to giving her the rest of the day off, but although he had willingly concurred Kate had insisted on returning to the stables.

'Have lunch with me,' he offered abruptly as he swung the Range Rover between the stone gateposts, and Kate turned to give him a startled look.

'Lunch?' she echoed, and he nodded. 'Oh, really, that's not necessary. Um—I've got some biscuits in my office. That's all I need.'

Alex slowed the car. 'Is that what you usually have for lunch? Biscuits?'

'Well—no.' Kate moistened her lips. 'As—as a matter of fact, I usually get a sandwich from the van.' A firm from King's Montford delivered fresh sandwiches every morning, but of course today she hadn't been there when they came round.

'Then why not join me today?' Alex persisted, allowing the engine to idle. 'Mrs Muir will be glad to have someone to cater for, for a change.'

Kate drew a breath. She was hesitating, and Alex pressed his advantage. 'You can tell me what Coulthard's going to do about the other girls who were involved.'

Kate sighed. 'Are you really interested?'

'I am, as a matter of fact. I like Joanne.'

'And she likes you,' murmured Kate almost inaudibly, and then blushed when she realised he'd heard her. 'Well—if you're sure your housekeeper won't object.'

'It is my house,' Alex reminded her mildly, turning up towards the main building. He parked on the paved forecourt. 'Come on. You look as if you could use a drink.'

Mrs Muir appeared as they entered the large reception hall, where a Waterford crystal chandelier was suspended from the ceiling of the second floor. As the little woman came to meet them, he was aware of Kate looking about her with interest and for the first time in years he wondered what someone else thought of his home.

Agnes Muir was thin and angular, not at all the rosy-cheeked retainer so lovingly described in popular fiction. Yet, for all that, she was loyal, and she had a kind and generous nature, and it had hurt her very badly when Rachel was taken away.

'Och, there you are, Mr Kellerman!' she exclaimed, her eyes darting swiftly between them, and he guessed she was curious about why he'd brought Kate here. 'Mrs Sheridan's been on the phone half a dozen times this morning already. Didn't you promise her you'd go and look at her new colt?'

'Damn.' He'd forgotten all about Lacey's invitation, and he saw Kate turn to give him a doubtful glance. He should have rung Lacey before he left, but he'd been thinking of other things at the time. 'Not to worry,' he added reassuringly, more for Kate's benefit than his housekeeper's. 'If she rings again, I'll explain that I had to go out.'

'Very well.' Mrs Muir folded her hands at her waist, and he knew she was waiting for him to tell her where he'd been. Either that or introduce her to his companion, he conceded without rancour. Agnes had begun to consider herself the mistress of the house.

'If you'd rather—' began Kate awkwardly, and he realised she'd misunderstood his hesitation, probably imagining he would rather have kept his appointment with Lacey.

'I wouldn't,' he assured her, taking her arm to bring her forward, and then frowning when she jerked away.

But he had no time to consider that rejection, or what it might mean, and, keeping his temper in check, he introduced her to the housekeeper without delay. 'Mrs Hughes works with Sam, as you know,' he added, aware that his tone was clipped and formal. 'I've invited her for lunch. Is that a problem?'

'As if it would be!' exclaimed Agnes, evidently liking what she'd seen of Kate. 'If you'll give me thirty minutes, I'll have the meal ready for you.'

'Thanks.'

Alex knew his voice was curt, but he couldn't help it. He hadn't realised until then how much Kate's confidence in him had meant. But the way she'd pulled away, as if she was revolted by his touch, had dealt him quite a blow, and he wondered if she'd been fooling him all along.

The thought was repellent, and rather than allow it to fester he pushed it aside and led the way into the library, which was situated at the front of the house. The leather-bound volumes on the shelves were seldom moved, but the room was one of his favourites, the open fire in the huge hearth giving it a warmth and familiarity he normally enjoyed.

'What would you like to drink?' he asked, moving to a cabinet in the corner, where a selection of bottles and decanters occupied a silver tray. There was a built-in fridge below which Mrs Muir kept stocked with beer and mixers, despite her contention that Alex drank too much.

'Oh—just an orange juice, please.'

Kate was hovering in the entrance, and he wondered if she was afraid he might jump her if she closed the door. He might, too, he thought aggressively, if only to punish her for treating him like one of the untouchables, but then he saw her anxious face and his anger cooled.

'Orange juice,' he said, bending to swing open the door of the cool-box. He found what he wanted, flicked the tab, and poured the contents into a stemmed glass. 'Is that okay?'

'Thanks.'

She took the glass from him, but this time he made sure their fingers didn't touch. If she thought he'd invited her here for any ulterior motive, she could think again. He'd felt sorry for her, that was all. He'd have done the same for anyone.

Like Alicia…

He scowled. He didn't want to think about her now. He didn't want to remember how she'd deceived him, too. All that talk about her husband beating her; how she was too afraid to go on living at home. He should have put her in touch with social services or one of those hostels that catered for battered wives, instead of giving her temporary accommodation in his home.

The memory of how she'd duped him caused him to regard Kate with even less sympathy. What if she was only here to see how much she could get out of him? He still wasn't entirely satisfied she'd told him the truth about taking this job.

'You've got a lovely home,' she murmured as he was opening a bottle of beer for himself. 'Is—is the house very old?'

'Parts of it date back to the seventeenth century,' he told her coolly. He took a swig of beer from the bottle and wiped the back of his hand across his mouth. 'Thankfully, my grandfather decided to modernise the old place. Much as I appreciate its history, it's bloody hard to keep it warm.'

Kate smiled. 'I love open fires, don't you?' she said, gesturing towards the logs burning in the grate. 'We just have electric heating at the flat.'

Alex watched her. 'And you live there with your mother and your daughter?'

'That's right. I couldn't have got—got a job without her help.'

Now why did he think she had been going to say something other than that she'd been able to get a job? he wondered. There was no doubt that when Joanne was younger she'd have needed a babysitter for the child. He lifted the bottle to his lips and took another swallow. He was letting his irritation at her edginess affect his mood.

'Why don't you sit down?' he suggested, gesturing towards an armchair nearer the fire, and although he was sure she would have preferred to stand she moved to take the seat.

'I envy you all these books,' she remarked rather nervously, when he came to stand in front of the fire. 'I've always loved books and reading.' She grimaced. 'I just wish Joanne felt the same.'

Alex hesitated, and then, because he wasn't naturally aggressive, he subsided into the chair across the hearth. 'I shouldn't worry,' he said, with rather more warmth. 'Maybe being suspended will prove a godsend in the long run.'

'How can you say that?'

She wasn't prepared to be polite where her daughter was

concerned and Alex noticed how her eyes sparkled when she was provoked. He found himself wondering how she would look if he was making love to her. Would her mouth taste as hot and sensual as it looked right now?

'I mean,' he said mildly, 'it will give her time to consider her options, and if Coulthard's going to put her into a different class next term it will be like a new start.'

Kate hunched her shoulders. 'I suppose.'

'Well, he had to do something, Kate!' Alex exclaimed reasonably, and then cursed himself when her arching brows told him she'd noted the familiarity. 'Shoplifting is a serious offence,' he added, trying to cover himself. 'If he'd let her off, he'd have had to let the other girls off as well.'

'He doesn't know who the other girls are!' exclaimed Kate at once. 'Joanne refused to tell him.'

'Still, I'd say he has a fairly good idea,' retorted Alex shrewdly. 'He'll be watching them like a hawk. They won't get away with it for long.'

'I wish I could believe that,' muttered Kate, sipping her orange juice almost without thinking. 'But you're right. Joanne did deserve some punishment. I just wish I didn't feel so helpless.'

Alex rolled the bottle he was holding between his palms. 'At least you don't lie awake nights wondering what lies other people are telling her about you,' he said heavily. 'Believe me, that's the hardest thing to take.'

She frowned then. 'You're talking about your own daughter, aren't you?'

'Rachel. Yes.' Alex wondered again why he found it so easy to confide in her. 'You probably know that she lives with my in-laws. What you may not know is that they don't intend to give her up.'

Kate stared at him. 'Intend?' she said curiously. 'That's an odd word to use. Don't you mean they don't *want* to give her up?'

'I mean intend,' he told her grimly. 'Conrad Wyatt will do anything to stop me getting my daughter back.' He grimaced.

'I guess you could say I've been making it easy for him. For a while after Pamela died I hit the bottle pretty badly.'

Kate shook her head. 'That's understandable.'

'Is it?' Alex wished she'd been around then. He might have had more sense than to destroy what was left of his reputation. He scowled as the memories came flooding back. 'You can't imagine what it was like, being accused of killing my own wife.'

'No.'

Kate conceded the point, but there was no trace of censure in the word. On the contrary, she seemed almost willing to believe him. Or was he being absurdly naïve to think that?

'You said your husband was killed in a car crash,' he observed now, deciding he'd said enough about himself. 'That must have been tough on you.'

She stiffened at his words. He sensed it immediately, without the sudden straightening of her spine. He had evidently stepped into territory that was still painful to her, and he cursed himself for destroying their unexpected rapport.

'It was,' she told him tensely. 'I suppose you think it's because Joanne doesn't remember what it was like to have a father that she's so rebellious now.'

'I didn't say that,' he replied evenly. 'I was merely comparing your situation with mine.' He grimaced. 'At least no one has accused you of being responsible for the accident.'

Kate put down her glass. He sensed she would have liked to get to her feet and pace about the room, but perhaps the fear of what he might do deterred her. 'Perhaps I was,' she said at last. 'Responsible, I mean.' She pressed her knees together. 'If Sean had been happy with me, he wouldn't have gone off with someone else.'

Alex's expression was sympathetic. 'I doubt if it's as simple as that,' he remarked gently, and she gave him a rueful look.

'You'll have gathered that I don't like to talk about Sean,' she murmured. 'It just reminds me of what a fool I was.' She paused. 'I should have listened to my parents. If it hadn't

been for them I'd never have been able to finish my degree—'

'You've got a degree!' Alex was stunned, and, looking at
her suddenly flushed face, he realised she hadn't intended to
tell him that. But the words had just slipped out, and now
she was stuck with them. 'A degree in what?' he demanded,
trying not to feel suspicious. He filled his lungs. 'Not journalism, I hope.'

'Law,' she got out jerkily. 'I got a degree in law.' And
then, seeing his scepticism, she added, 'It's true. But I
couldn't find a firm of solicitors willing to take me on so, as
I told you, I went to work for my father.'

Alex breathed deeply through his nostrils. Then he got
abruptly to his feet. A degree in law, and she had taken a
job at his stables. Was he being unnecessarily paranoid to
wonder why?

He was staring out of the long windows when he realised
she had come to stand beside him. Beyond the windswept
gardens that surrounded the house, the land sloped away towards the river, and he noticed the lower meadow was partly
flooded. They'd had so much rain in the last few weeks, it
was to be expected, he supposed, trying to ignore her and
not succeeding.

'I'm sorry if you think I should have told you,' she ventured, to attract his attention. 'I know I didn't put it on my
CV, but that was because so many employers are put off by
qualifications like that.'

Alex half turned towards her. 'And you thought I would
have been one of them?' His lips twisted. 'You didn't want
to embarrass an ignorant horse-trader like me?'

'You're not an ignorant horse-trader.'

His eyes narrowed. 'How do you know?'

She shifted a little uncomfortably. 'I should have thought
it was obvious.' She took a breath. 'Ignorant people aren't
usually sensitive, and—and you've just proved you are.'

'Am I?'

Alex knew it wasn't the most sensible thing to tease her,

but he was enjoying having her trying to placate him for a change. Besides which, he conceded tersely, she was a beautiful woman. Despite his self-derision, he was not entirely immune to the appeal in her grey eyes.

'You—you were kind to Joanne,' she told him firmly, turning her head slightly to avoid his gaze. A strand of crinkled hair fell forward and she looped it back behind her ears. 'I—I was glad you came with us today.'

'Yeah, so was I.'

Alex felt an instantaneous response to her admission, a recognition that his own motives hadn't been exactly impartial either. As she stood there beside him, the smell of her warm skin drifted irresistibly to his nostrils, a delicate fragrance that was overlaid by the sudden sharpness of his own desire.

God, he acknowledged darkly, he wanted to touch her. He didn't care at that moment who she was or what she'd done, he only wanted to ease her jacket off her shoulders and slide his sweating palms into the demure neckline of her shirt. What would she do? he wondered. How would she react if he took her small, high breasts into his hands? He wanted to see her eyes widen as he caressed them and squeezed them. Would her nipples be taut? Would they swell like hard buds against his palms?

'So—so I'm forgiven?'

When she spoke, he had to pull himself together before he could answer her. His head was swimming, and he hoped to hell she didn't look below his waist. 'Forgiven?' he echoed thickly, and she must have thought it was safe to turn her head and look at him, but when she met his burning gaze the hectic colour rose hotly into her cheeks.

'For—for not telling you about my degree,' she got out jerkily, clearly disturbed by his appraisal, and he remembered why he'd felt he needed some time to think about what she'd said. 'Um—why—why don't you tell me about your daughter?' she added hurriedly. 'I—I expect you miss her a lot.'

Alex blew out a breath. He wondered if it was only his

imagination that made him think she looked guilty, or was it fear that had brought such a look of agitation into her face? But one thing he did know: he didn't want to talk about Rachel right now. There would be something almost profane in using his daughter to dispel the way he felt.

'Are you afraid of me?' he asked abruptly, and this time he was not mistaken when she drew away.

But, 'No,' she said tensely, though her voice was slightly higher than before. 'Why should I be afraid of you, Mr Kellerman? I—I hardly know you.'

Alex couldn't let it go. 'Oh, I think you do,' he insisted softly, aware that his efforts to get rid of his own unwilling attraction weren't working. 'Know of me, at least,' he appended, moving closer. 'Perhaps you're beginning to wonder if there was any truth in the rumours. Do you think you're woman enough to find out?'

He heard the catch in her breath as she backed away from him. 'I think you're just amusing yourself at my expense, Mr Kellerman,' she said, forcing a valiant smile. But the smile didn't reach her eyes, and he realised she was still apprehensive. 'Shall we go and sit down again? I haven't finished my drink.'

Her efforts to reason with him didn't please him, however, they annoyed him. For God's sake, she was behaving as if he'd stepped out of line and it was up to her to rap his knuckles and send him back. Did she really think he was deceived by her pathetic attempts to appear sophisticated? If she'd had any sense, she'd never have left her seat.

'You know what I think?' he drawled now as she came up against the bookshelves. She'd been so intent on putting some distance between them that she hadn't realised she'd backed into a corner. 'I think you are afraid of me, Miss Hughes.' He lifted his hand and stroked her cheek with a carefully controlled finger. 'Don't be. I'm not half as dangerous as I look.'

She tilted her head away from his hand. 'I don't think you are dangerous,' she retorted recklessly. 'I think you're rather sad, if you want the truth. You've lost your wife; you've lost your child; you've lost your reputation. Why should I be afraid of someone who's just given up?'

'Damn you, I haven't given up!' Her words caught him on the raw, and he was furious with her for saying them. Without really thinking about what he was doing, he grabbed her shoulders in a savage grasp. 'You know nothing about me,' he snarled, forgetting that just minutes before he'd maintained the opposite. 'I should break your bloody neck for that remark!'

It wasn't until the words were out that he realised what he was saying, that she was bound to associate the threat with his wife's death. She probably thought he was capable of anything if he could lose his temper so easily, and Pamela had done a hell of a lot more than provoke him about his life.

But, by then, it was too late. Too late to withdraw his careless words; too late to wish he'd never started this; too late to ignore the woman beneath his hands. She was so warm, so feminine, so everything he'd been trying to shut out of his mind since she'd walked into his house, and, ignoring her stunned expression, he pulled her into his arms.

It was a mistake; a big mistake. He knew that as soon as he felt her yielding body against his own. Looking down into her wide, dilated eyes, he knew she was incapable of fighting him and although her fists were balled against his midriff it was a token gesture at best.

'I have not given up,' he repeated harshly, making one last attempt to bring some sanity into the situation, but she only shook her head. Whether she believed him or not, she expected him to exercise some restraint, but Alex found he couldn't let her go.

Instead, he bent his head to brush the pale curls of hair that nestled at her temples with his lips. She had secured her hair in a braid today, probably to try and impress the head teacher at Joanne's school with her severity, but several unruly strands had broken free and now clustered about her face. Her hair was soft and tasted of her skin and his senses spun in dizzying circles. He knew it was becoming impossible to let her go without tasting the dewy softness of her mouth.

He thought she sensed what he was going to do before he did it. Which was why her lips were pressed so tightly together when he sought her mouth with his. She was determined not to give in to him, even though he could feel her trembling, and he despised himself for frightening her this way.

But he didn't stop. He couldn't stop. Some inner hunger was driving him on, and with one arm lodged securely about her waist he brought his free hand to her face.

His thumb brushed her clamped lips, feeling their instinctive stiffening at the intimate caress. The tips of his fingers probed her ear, finding the sensitive hollow beneath the soft lobe, registering her rapidly beating pulse. She was all woman, all warmth, all sanity, and he wouldn't have been human if he hadn't been aware of it, and of the desire he had to make her respond to him in return.

When his thumb found the curve of her chin and tilted her face up to his, he could see the raw uncertainty in her expression, and it drove him on. Although she said nothing to encourage him, he sensed that she was weakening, and he wanted her to tell him how she felt.

'You don't hate me, do you, Kate?' he asked roughly, bringing his other hand to cup her face between his palms. 'Believe me, I won't hurt you.'

'Won't you?'

There was still a trace of doubt in her voice, but her parted lips were too much of an invitation for him to resist. She was in his arms, he wanted her, and he lowered his head and fastened his mouth to hers.

Alex's head swam. It was heaven and it was hell. Heaven in the sensuous sweetness of her lips and hell in the knowledge that he could never have her. Why didn't she stop him? he wondered frustratedly. Why didn't she fight him with every scrap of strength she had? He was giving her the opportunity. Hell, he was as vulnerable as a schoolboy in his present position.

But, when he permitted his tongue to slip between her teeth, it met no obvious opposition. The moist hollow of her mouth lay open to his eager assault, and his hands were not entirely steady as they slid the jacket from her shoulders and moved down her spine to clutch the slender contours of her hips.

Another mistake. When he thrust his leg between hers to bring her closer to him, he felt his hardness digging into her soft stomach. The feeling was indescribable, and he wanted desperately to ease his male arousal in her woman's body.

Her shirt had come free of the waistband of her skirt and his fingers sought the silky heat of her bare skin almost without his volition. His palms spread against the smooth flesh of her back before seeking a more intimate exploration. The clip of her bra was no obstacle and then, taking a shuddering breath, he allowed his thumbs to caress the undersides of her breasts.

Suddenly, he couldn't breathe, and, releasing her mouth, he buried his hot face in the scented hollow of her neck. God, he must be crazy, he thought unsteadily. Not for the first time, he was in danger of making a complete hash of things. Did she have any idea what she was doing to him? Did she realise how close to losing it he was? Perhaps she did, he mocked himself derisively. Perhaps that was what he could see in the sensual mystery of her gaze.

The sound of the door opening behind him brought him partially to his senses. Agnes Muir, he thought bitterly. She never had learned to knock before barging in.

Straightening, he barely glanced at Kate's flushed face before swinging round to confront his housekeeper. Only it wasn't his housekeeper, he saw at once. It was Lacey Sheridan, and she was staring at him with a look of harsh contempt on her face.

'Well, well,' she said, whatever pain she might have felt

quickly concealed beneath a mask of sarcasm. 'And I thought you'd have learned your lesson by now.'

'Lacey,' he groaned frustratedly, shaking his head, but before he could offer any words, whether of protest or explanation, he had to save himself as Kate brushed past him, almost knocking him over in the process.

'Excuse me,' she muttered, though he doubted she meant it, and, draping the jacket she had snatched off the floor about her shoulders, she barrelled out into the hall.

'Kate! Wait!' he yelled, starting after her, but before he could catch up with her she had let herself out of the front door.

'I don't think the lady's interested,' remarked Lacey mockingly from behind him, curving a detaining hand over his shoulder. 'I'd advise you to let her go, darling.' And when he jerked away from her possessive touch her eyes narrowed maliciously as she added, 'You will if you want my continued support...'

CHAPTER SEVEN

'IT'S Mrs Hughes, isn't it?'

Kate had been trying to decide whether to put sausage or mince into her shopping basket when an unfamiliar voice accosted her. Or someone else, she acknowledged, glancing somewhat apprehensively around the supermarket. She turned to find Alex Kellerman's housekeeper regarding her with a mixture of wariness and doubt, and breathed a little easier when she saw there was no one else about.

'Mrs Muir.'

Kate's response assured the little woman she hadn't made a mistake, and her angular features creased into a smile. 'I thought it was you, Mrs Hughes,' she said warmly. 'I hope you're feeling better. Mr Kellerman explained how you had to rush away the other day.'

'Oh.' Kate's brain struggled to function. 'Oh, yes. I—I'm sorry about that.'

'No worries.' Mrs Muir patted her arm. 'Mrs Sheridan stayed for lunch instead. Still, it was a pity you and Mr Kellerman didn't have time to talk.'

'Oh—we talked,' murmured Kate wryly, a shiver at the memory of that conversation causing goosebumps down her spine. She wondered what Mrs Muir would have thought of her employer if it had been she who had interrupted them and not this Sheridan woman. 'Um—it's been nice seeing you again,' she added, hoping the diminutive Scotswoman would take the hint.

She didn't.

'You're managing all right on your own, are you? Down at the office, I mean,' she continued pleasantly. 'It was such a shame that Mr Kellerman had to go away this week. What with Sam Guthrie being off, and all. Though I've heard he's feeling much better than he was.'

'That's good news.' Kate expelled a cautious breath. 'And—and with Ted's help I'm managing fairly well.' Ted Lowes was the head groom, and Kate suspected he knew as much about the stables as anyone, although, like Mr Guthrie, he always referred to Alex as the boss.

'Do you have time to join me for a cup of tea?' Mrs Muir suggested now, indicating the small café that was owned by the supermarket. And then, as if thinking better of it, she shook her head. 'Och, it's after five. You've probably got things to do.'

Kate had. Lots of things, she thought ruefully, remembering the agency's accounts, which Susie had left for her that morning. Not to mention a rebellious teenager, who had too much time and too little to do, and her mother who had taken her granddaughter's suspension very badly.

But… She hesitated. She doubted there was anyone at Jamaica Hill who knew what went on better than Mrs Muir. 'Um—I'm not in a hurry,' she protested firmly. 'Thank you for inviting me.'

With her groceries packed into two carriers and stowed in the boot of her car, Kate joined Mrs Muir in the café. The older woman had already been served, Kate found, and now two individual pots of tea and two scones with butter and jam resided on the table she'd taken in the window.

'Isn't this cosy?' asked Mrs Muir happily, passing Kate a cup and saucer. 'I like to come in here, but I don't often have company. Since Mr Muir died, I don't find it so easy to make friends.'

'Oh, I'm sorry.' Kate was sympathetic. 'I know how hard it can be when—when a loved one dies.'

'Well, it has been almost two years,' said her companion, making a valiant effort to dismiss it. She started to butter one of the scones. 'Tell me about yourself. How long have you been married?'

'My husband's dead.' Kate had no wish to talk about herself, but she knew she couldn't get away with saying nothing. And, as Alex knew about Joanne… 'I do have a daughter, however. She'll be thirteen in a couple of months.'

'Thirteen!' Mrs Muir was obviously surprised. 'Why, you don't look old enough to have a daughter that age.'

'Well, it's very nice of you to say so, but I was nineteen when she was born,' said Kate dryly.

'Really?' Mrs Muir was impressed. 'Well, they say having a family keeps you young.'

'Don't you believe it,' murmured Kate, adding milk to her cup, and Mrs Muir put a hand up to her mouth.

'Oh, my!' she exclaimed. 'Here I am, asking you to have tea, and your daughter's probably waiting for you at home.' She shook her head apologetically. 'I'm afraid I didn't think. I hope she's more patient than my Jim used to be.'

'We live with my mother,' admitted Kate reluctantly, realising she was saying more than she'd intended. And then, because Mrs Muir still looked as if she was waiting, she said, 'My husband died in a car accident over ten years ago.'

'Oh, that's a shame.' Mrs Muir tutted. 'You must have been devastated, my dear. I hate to hear about young people getting killed. It's every parent's nightmare: burying a son or daughter.' She hesitated. 'My Jim was never the same, I know that.'

Kate's brows drew together. 'You've lost a child yourself?'

'Yes. Our son, Philip.' There were tears in Mrs Muir's eyes now, which made Kate feel even worse. She wondered if she was cut out for asking awkward questions, but the opportunity was too good to miss.

'I suppose the Wyatts must have felt that way when— when their daughter died,' she murmured carefully, and Mrs Muir pulled a tissue from her pocket.

'I can't speak for them,' she said shortly. 'I only know that they've made Mr Kellerman's life a misery. It wasn't his fault that Pamela broke her neck.'

'No.'

Kate didn't dare question her belief, but the housekeeper must have suspected that she wasn't convinced, because she went on, 'He's a good man, Mrs Hughes. He's been like a son to me. If it wasn't for him, I don't know where I'd have found the strength to go on.'

'When your husband died,' nodded Kate, but Mrs Muir wasn't finished.

'We keep each other company, Mr Kellerman and I,' she said, pushing the other scone towards Kate. 'He'll get the lassie back; I know he will. These things take time, that's all.'

Kate could have remarked that Alex Kellerman had had time, lots of it, but he'd apparently chosen to drown his sorrows in a bottle; but she didn't. Nevertheless, thinking of him and what he had done to her caused another prickle of apprehension to ripple through her veins. What might he have done if Mrs Sheridan hadn't interrupted them? What might *she* have done if that sensual assault had lasted any longer? She hated to admit it, but she had been weakening, the hungry urgency of his hands on her body driving all sane thoughts out of her head...

'Eat your scone,' urged Mrs Muir now, and Kate was obliged to break off a corner and spread the crumbling cake with butter. But she wasn't very hungry, her thoughts of Alex Kellerman leaving a bitter taste in her mouth.

Not that she'd seen him since that scene in the library at Jamaica Hill. As Mrs Muir had said, he'd been away for the past couple of days, and she was grateful. She didn't know what she'd have done if she'd had to face him the following morning. She'd been tempted to send a message pleading illness, but that had seemed such a cowardly thing to do.

All the same, she was being forced to view Henry Sawyer's accusations about Alex and his wife rather less sceptically. A man who would take advantage of someone he barely knew would not quibble over starting an affair with a woman who was actually living in his house. At least, that was the way she was beginning to see it—even if some small part of her shrank from pre-judging him this way.

'Anyway, how are you settling down at the stables?' Mrs Muir asked warmly. 'I know Sam Guthrie has no complaint about your work.' And then she abruptly turned to the subject Kate was struggling hard to find a way to broach. 'It's to be hoped you stay longer than the rest.'

'The rest?' Kate was hardly aware she was crumbling the rest of the scone until Mrs Muir pointed it out to her.

'The other girls who worked for Mr Guthrie,' she continued after Kate had dropped her hands into her lap. 'Of course, they weren't like you. They were fly-by-nights, most of them. The wages were never good enough, and as soon as something more lucrative came along off they'd go.'

Kate tried not to sound too interested. 'That's a shame,' she murmured casually. 'I expect Mr Guthrie got sick of having to train new staff.'

'Ay, well, I'm not saying he's an easy man to work with,' went on the housekeeper sagely. 'And his judgement isn't always what it should be.' She grimaced. 'But even Mr Kellerman was taken in by the last woman to do your job.'

Kate hesitated. 'Wasn't she any good?'

'She was a liar,' declared Mrs Muir staunchly. 'She told Mr Kellerman her husband used to beat her, and that wasn't true. It's obvious she only said it to gain his sympathy. She wanted to get into the house, that was all. She must have been planning it all along.'

'Planning what?'

Kate couldn't help the question, but Mrs Muir took a deep breath before she said, 'I really shouldn't be discussing it. It's Mr Kellerman's business, not mine.' She paused, and smiled at her companion. 'All I will say is that I'm glad Mr Guthrie's found a decent assistant at last.'

Kate almost groaned aloud. For a few moments, she'd actually believed she was making some progress, that Mrs Muir might hold the key to everything she wanted to know. But now all she felt was frustration, and the guilty knowledge of her own deception that wouldn't go away.

'Kate! Hi! How are you? Long time, no see.'

Kate had been so sunk in depression that she hadn't noticed the woman who had come up to their table and she was immediately reminded that there were worse things than losing out on a hot lead. Marian Garvey was someone she'd known while she was at university, someone who'd known she was working with her father, and who might conceivably blow her cover.

But, to her relief, Mrs Muir seemed grateful for the interruption. Perhaps she'd decided she'd said more than she should, Kate reflected ruefully. In any event, when Kate returned the other woman's greeting, Mrs Muir gathered together her bags and got to her feet.

'I'd better be going,' she said. 'Mr Kellerman will be wondering where I've got to. Goodnight, Mrs Hughes. I've enjoyed our little chat. Perhaps we'll see one another again next week.'

Kate managed a polite rejoinder, but when Marian dropped into the seat Mrs Muir had vacated, and said, 'A client?' she wished she'd made an excuse to leave, too.

'Just someone I know,' she murmured, using her teacup to hide any embarrassment Marian might see in her face. 'Her husband died quite recently. I was just keeping her company, that's all.'

'How charitable,' remarked Marian sardonically, regarding Kate with a faintly jaundiced eye. 'But did I hear her say *Mr Kellerman*? She's no relation of the notorious Alex, is she?'

'No.' Kate was defensive, but then, realising it wouldn't be wise to get into a discussion about her employer, she changed the subject. 'How are you, Marian? You're looking well.'

'Thanks.'

Marian took the compliment complacently, and in actual fact Kate had to admit that she hadn't changed a lot since their college days. She'd put on some weight, but she was fairly tall so she could carry it. However, Kate had always found her rather supercilious and far too inquisitive about other people's affairs.

'Well, I'd better be going, too,' Kate said awkwardly, hoping to avoid any further questions about herself. But when Marian stood up as well her heart sank.

'I'll come with you,' Marian declared, accompanying her to the exit. 'The store's so busy on Fridays. You can never get what you want.'

'Oh—but you haven't had your tea,' protested Kate, gesturing towards the self-service counter.

'I don't want any,' replied Marian, looping the strap of her bag over her shoulder. 'I only came into the café because I saw you. It's such an age since we've had a gossip.'

'Oh.'

Kate managed to hide her dismay, but there was no way of escaping her until they reached the car park. 'How's your daughter?' she asked, tucking her arm through Kate's as if they were bosom friends. 'Joanne. She must be—what? Twelve or thirteen now.'

Kate frowned. 'She's nearly thirteen,' she conceded, not sure where this was leading. 'She's very well, thank you. I expect your little boy is growing up, too.'

'Bobby, yes.' Marian dismissed her son almost carelessly. 'But imagine, Joanne's almost a teenager. I bet she's quite a handful, isn't she?'

Kate sucked in her breath. She was beginning to see where this was heading. 'Joanne's okay,' she said as they reached the revolving doors. 'It was good of you to ask.'

'Well, I know what teenagers are like,' said Marian, accompanying her outside. 'My Bobby may be too young yet, but my younger sister's at Lady Montford, you know.'

Like Joanne.

She didn't say the words, but she might as well have done. It was obvious Marian knew about Joanne's suspension and had decided to gloat. Kate supposed she should be grateful for the distraction, but she resented the sly way Marian had brought it up.

'How's Marcus?' she asked casually. 'I saw his picture in the newspaper just last week. You must be very proud of him.'

She omitted to mention the fact that she already knew that Marian and Marcus were divorcing. It was cruel, perhaps, reminding the other woman of her ex-husband's success as an entrepreneur, but she deserved the dig. Kate might be disappointed in Joanne herself, but that was her business. She'd do anything to protect her daughter from Marian's gossiping tongue.

'Marc and I split up some time ago,' Marian eventually told her tightly. 'But we're fine. Bobby's nearly six.' She seemed to recover her composure as they walked out into the car park. 'I can hardly believe it. But I imagine having a child of Joanne's age makes you feel quite old, aside from anything else.'

'Positively ancient,' agreed Kate, refusing to accept the challenge. She paused a moment, waiting to see which way Marian was heading before turning in the opposite direction. Then, after turning up the collar of her coat, she raised a hand in farewell. 'Take care,' she added pleasantly, and walked away.

In fact, Marian's car was parked practically next to the old Vauxhall, and Kate had to wait several minutes for the woman to drive away. She was shivering by the time she'd unlocked the car and got behind the wheel, and she reflected that it would serve her right if the car refused to start.

Thankfully, it didn't. Since Alex's mechanic had checked it out, she'd had no more trouble with it. According to the note he'd left sellotaped to the steering wheel, he couldn't find anything wrong with it. She'd evidently flooded the carburettor as Alex himself had said.

Nevertheless, she was in no mood to humour her daughter when she got home and found Joanne moping about the house. She had only herself to blame if she was bored, she told her shortly, ignoring her mother's look of warning, and Joanne muttered something under her breath before flouncing into her room.

'That wasn't very kind, Kate,' murmured Ellen Ross, helping her daughter unpack the groceries from the carrier bags. 'It isn't easy for her, spending all day cooped up in the flat.'

'And whose fault is that?'

Kate refused to let her mother make her feel guilty, and Ellen Ross's nostrils flared with sudden irritation. 'And you're not letting her forget it, are you? Not for a minute. Despite the fact that if it hadn't been for Joanne you'd have known nothing about it. Nor Mr Coulthard, either, though I suppose he was only doing his job. She could have gone on doing what the other girls were doing, but she didn't. You should be thankful she's not into drug-taking or something like that.'

Kate heaved a sigh. 'I should have known you'd take her side.'

'I'm not taking her side.' Ellen was indignant. 'I'm just trying to make you see that Joanne's not a bad girl, whatever you think.'

'I know.' Kate shook her head. 'Oh, I suppose I'll have to apologise. But, honestly, it's not been an easy day for me either.'

'Why?' Her mother regarded her with interest. 'Has something happened? I thought Mr Kellerman was away.'

'He is.' Kate hoped her mother would put the slight deepening of colour in her cheeks down to exertion. 'But I saw Marian Garvey in the supermarket. She couldn't wait to let me know she knew about Joanne.'

'I see.' Ellen looked thoughtful. 'Of course. The Westons' younger daughter goes to Lady Montford, too.'

'Yes.' Kate grimaced. 'I wouldn't be surprised if the whole town knows our business by now.'

'Stop exaggerating.' Kate's mother was philosophical. 'I doubt if anyone's interested in Joanne's suspension but us.

She's not unique, Kate. I'm sad to say that being suspended these days is quite a common punishment.'

Kate finished putting the frozen items into the freezer and then propped her hips against the cupboard. 'I suppose you're right.'

'I am.' Ellen held her daughter's gaze for a moment and then looked away. 'So why do I get the feeling you're still on edge?'

Kate blew out a breath. 'I'm not on edge.'

'Of course you are.' Ellen was impatient. 'We've lived together too long, Kate. I always know when you've got something on your mind. What is it? You've been like this since you came home on Wednesday afternoon.'

Kate turned back to the counter. 'You're imagining things.'

'No, I'm not. What did Mr Kellerman say after you'd dropped Joanne off at the flat?' She paused, and when Kate still didn't speak she made a terse sound of frustration. 'I thought when he let you off early that he'd understood how you felt.'

Kate sighed. 'He did.'

'And you say he's been away for the past couple of days, so it can't be anything he's done.' She sighed. 'Oh, well, if you don't want to tell me, I'll have to assume it's me.'

Kate groaned. 'Give it a rest, Mum, please. Nothing's happened, all right? I'm—just not sure where this case is leading, that's all.'

'You mean you think it's a waste of time?'

'Not exactly.'

'Then you do suspect that Alex Kellerman may be responsible for this woman's disappearance?' Her mother frowned. 'Oh, Kate, you will be careful, won't you?'

Kate shook her head. 'I don't know what I believe any more,' she said bleakly. She wrapped her arms about her midriff, as if to try and calm the churning nerves in her stomach. 'I—I think he may have had an affair with her. And if he did…'

'That doesn't make him a murderer,' argued Ellen practically. 'But I think you ought to tell Mr Sawyer what you've told me. It's not as if you're making any progress. Perhaps it is time you admitted defeat.'

It was a temptation to do as her mother suggested, but Kate ignored it. Despite what had happened, she was reluctant to give up her job at Jamaica Hill. She told herself it was because she'd made a start at gaining Mrs Muir's confidence, but the fact was that was very far from the truth.

'I'll give it another couple of weeks,' she said now, reaching for a bag of pasta. She split the Cellophane and dropped the contents into a pan. 'I thought we'd have spaghetti tonight,' she added, hoping her mother would take the hint. She didn't want to get into a long discussion about Alex Kellerman. She was far too unsure of the way she felt about him.

'Well, I think you're just filling in time until the money stops coming,' remarked Ellen reprovingly, but Joanne's reappearance from her bedroom prevented her from saying anything more. And Kate took the opportunity to make her peace with her daughter, thus evading any further discussion of the case.

The weekend passed much too quickly. Kate, who had spent Saturday and Sunday trying to avoid thinking about Alex Kellerman, had to summon all her courage just to get into the car and drive out to Jamaica Hill on Monday morning. Perhaps Mr Guthrie would be back, she cheered herself hopefully, and then was grateful when the traffic lights at the end of the high street turned to red at her approach.

Anything to delay her arrival at the stables, she thought ruefully, wondering how her employer would react when he saw her again. Perhaps he'd already thought of a reason to dismiss her, she reflected, and then chided herself for the hollow feeling that evoked inside her.

The trouble was, she'd started to like him, she conceded. It had been so kind of him to take her and Joanne to the school and then hang about until they came out. They'd both been grateful for his understanding, and when he'd invited her to have lunch with him she'd been happy to accept.

But that was when it had all started to unravel, she remembered. She'd been so edgy when he'd taken her arm to introduce her to the housekeeper that he'd got the idea that she was repulsed by his touch. If only he knew, she brooded tensely. It was because he disturbed her so much that she'd been forced to pull away.

It had proved impossible to rescue the situation after that. He'd been so tense when they first went into the library that it had been a struggle to keep any kind of conversation going. She'd wanted to talk about his daughter, but it had been difficult to find an opening, and then, when she had, she'd ruined it all by accusing him of giving up.

She cringed now when she recalled his anger, and the sarcasm he'd used to such good effect. By the time he'd yanked her into his arms, she'd been so bemused, she was shaking, and she'd have believed anything of him before he touched her mouth.

Kate was brushing her lips with a wondering finger when the sound of a horn behind her alerted her to the fact that the lights had changed. She put the car into gear and let the clutch out too fast so that the engine stalled. She was anxiously revving the Vauxhall's engine when the pock-faced youth in the car behind accelerated past.

Kate wished for a moment she had a powerful car that she could compete with, and then, kangaroo-ing across the junction, she chided herself again. She wasn't a youth, she reproved herself, she was a woman fast approaching middle age, with a pre-pubescent daughter to boot.

And allowing other road users to get up her back—literally—wasn't going to help her. She'd need a cool head if she was going to come out of the present situation with even an atom of self-respect. Because nothing could alter the fact that despite all her efforts to fight him off Alex had overcome her resistance. When Mrs Sheridan had walked in the door, Kate had been on the verge of kissing him back.

And he'd known it, damn him. That was why he'd come chasing after her when she'd grabbed her jacket and high-tailed it out of the door. Her only compensation was that she'd been too quick for him. She'd cut across the paddock to the stables, collected her car, and driven home.

Well—not immediately home, she amended as the stone gateposts that marked the entrance to Jamaica Hill hove into view. She'd had no desire to face her mother and daughter until she'd had time to recover from that sensual embrace, so she'd gone to the agency, sneaking into her office while Susie was out for lunch.

Of course she'd dreaded going to work the following morning, and she'd been so relieved to find Ted Lowes occupying Mr Guthrie's desk. That was when he'd explained that the boss had accompanied Mrs Sheridan to Doncaster races, and that he wouldn't be back in the office until the following week.

Today?

Kate turned in at the gates with an involuntary shiver. She'd know soon enough if the Range Rover was parked down at the stables. It was, and her stomach clenched in protest. Oh, God, she thought, why hadn't she turned down his invitation to lunch?

Well, she hadn't, and she had to live with it. At least, until she'd satisfied herself that she'd done all she could to locate Alicia Sawyer. Someone must know something. The woman couldn't just disappear off the face of the earth. Perhaps to-day would be the day she'd get another chance to tackle Billy Roach. Despite her hopes about Mrs Muir, she sensed the young apprentice was more likely to be indiscreet than the housekeeper.

She parked her car and got out, brushing down the seams of her black woollen trousers and checking that her hair was neat before locking the door. She'd secured it in a French pleat today and she thought it looked satisfyingly business-like. She smoothed a couple of wisps behind her ears before setting off across the yard.

What could be so bad? she asked herself as two of the stable boys called a greeting. It was Kellerman who ought to be feeling ashamed of himself, not her. If he fired her, so what? She was hardly likely to take the case to an employees' tribunal. And Henry Sawyer could hardly complain if Alex threw her out.

This morning her office felt decidedly chilly. Unlike that other occasion, he hadn't bothered to turn on the fire in her room. With a tightening of her lips, she went across to attend to it, and then almost jumped out of her skin when Alex spoke behind her.

'Will you come into my office?' he asked, before she had time to bend down and flick the switch on the electric fire, and Kate schooled her nervous features before turning to face him. But she needn't have bothered. He'd already gone back into the other room, so her efforts to appear calm and composed were wasted. Still, she decided not to take off her fur-trimmed parka. It didn't look as if she was going to be there long enough for that.

He was standing behind Mr Guthrie's desk when she entered the office, his back to her, staring out through the somewhat grimy windows into the yard. His hands were tucked beneath his arms and Kate's gaze moved almost greedily over his broad shoulders. He was standing with his feet slightly apart, the powerful muscles of his thighs clearly outlined beneath the tight-fitting fabric of his trousers. Dear God, she thought, why did he arouse such a feeling of unwanted excitement in her? He wasn't the first man who'd come on to her since Sean died, and it was pathetic that this man, of all the men she'd known, had the ability to turn her bones to water.

'Sit down,' he said now, without turning. 'I expect you're wondering what this is all about.'

'Well, yes.' *No!* She thought she knew exactly what he was going to say. She just wished he'd get on with it instead of dragging it out.

He expelled a breath. 'Well, first of all, I suppose I should apologise for the way I behaved last week.' He paused. 'I've got no excuse. What I did was unforgivable. I invited you into my house and then abused your confidence in the most despicable way.'

Kate hadn't intended to sit down, but now she sank weakly into the chair at her side of the desk. She'd never imagined that he might be going to apologise, and the realisation of how quick she'd been to misjudge him filled her with remorse.

'Really, I—' she began awkwardly, but he wasn't finished.

'You probably think that's why I didn't come into the office for the rest of the week,' he continued, turning to face her, and although she was loath to meet his eyes her glancing look took in the stark contours of his face. 'Perhaps it was,' he added, his arms falling to his sides, his fingers finding diversion in the papers on the desk. 'Perhaps I was reluctant to admit the baseness of my actions even to myself. And it was easier to go away and put off this confrontation.'

'Mr Kellerman, please—'

'In my own defence, I have to say that I had good reasons for going to Doncaster. It's the last flat-racing classic of the year.' His lips twisted. 'I could also make the excuse that you—provoked me. It isn't very flattering to hear that your staff think you've got no guts.'

'I never said that—'

'Whatever.' Once again, he interrupted her. 'I've got only myself to blame for the opinion you must have of me now. I was half prepared to hear you'd given in your notice. You've probably got a case for sexual harassment, if you chose to take it that far.'

'I don't think so.' Kate shook her head rather bemusedly. She hesitated for a moment, and then went on, 'I'd rather forget it, if you don't mind.'

'So it didn't persuade you that I must be guilty of all the crimes I've been accused of?'

'No.'

'That's a relief.' His small smile was ironic. 'You must be the only woman in King's Montford who'd react that way.'

Kate lifted her shoulders. 'If—if you want me to leave—'

'I don't.'

His response was vehement, and she felt confident enough to stand again. 'Then I'll go and get on,' she said, moving round the chair and heading towards the door.

'Wait.' His hastily uttered summons arrested her, and she turned somewhat reluctantly to face him.

'Yes?'

'I've got a favour to ask,' he muttered, raking an impatient hand through his hair. 'I contacted my solicitor over the weekend, and he's arranged for me to have Rachel for the day.' He sucked in his breath. 'As I've only seen her a couple of times in the last two years, I want you to come with me to get her. Then, if her grandfather tries to pull any more stunts to stop me, it won't just be my word against his if he denies it later on.'

CHAPTER EIGHT

WYVERN HALL was an impressive sight. Its crenellated façade was more Victorian than Georgian, despite the fact that Alex had told her that parts of it dated back to the early nineteenth century. Nevertheless, Kate thought it was ugly, though that might have been because she was so apprehensive at being there.

She hadn't wanted to come. When he'd first made his request, she'd sought desperately for some means to avoid accompanying him to his father-in-law's house. Even though she knew that a good investigator would welcome any chance to learn more about her subject, she was reluctant. She was always afraid that someone might recognise her, for one thing, and for another, did she really want to get to know his daughter?

But her prime reason for wanting to refuse was a more personal one. She was already far too involved with Alex Kellerman, and getting caught up in his private affairs was the very last thing she should be doing. She was supposed to be *im*partial, *un*biased, not taking sides with him against a possibly innocent man. Conrad Wyatt only wanted to do what was right by his dead daughter. In his position, would she have behaved any differently?

'Pam's father wanted me to change my name to Wyatt,' Alex commented now as they reached the gravelled forecourt, and Kate acknowledged that all the misgivings in the world weren't going to do her any good. She was here; she'd agreed to do this favour; she was committed. She had to make the best of it for Rachel's sake, if nothing else.

'And you didn't want to do it,' she murmured now, and he gave her a sidelong look.

'No,' he said flatly. 'I prefer to bear my own name. But it wouldn't surprise me to learn that Conrad's trying to change Rachel's name to Wyatt, too.'

He was very bitter, thought Kate as he brought the Range Rover to a halt before the impressive entrance. But perhaps he had good reason. How would she have felt if Sean's parents had tried to take Joanne away from her? It hadn't happened, of course. Sean had never known his father, and his mother had died when he was just a teenager. Which perhaps explained why Kate's husband had had so little respect for his own marriage.

Kate wondered if Alex would expect her to stay in the car while he went and collected his daughter, but after pushing open his own door and getting out he came round the bonnet to open hers. He'd put on a long dark overcoat over his jacket, and she couldn't help noticing how well it suited him. But he'd left it unfastened so that when she passed him she smelt the clean male scent of his skin.

'Ready?' he asked, and she bit her lips to stop them from trembling.

'As I'll ever be,' she conceded, with more confidence in her words than in her voice.

'Good,' he said, and to her dismay he put a possessive hand beneath her elbow. 'Come on. You can take your cue from me.'

Which meant what? Kate looked up at him, aghast, but his attention was already concentrated on the house. His lean, dark features were harsh, and unforgiving, and she was very much afraid that Rachel would think so, too.

'Can I say something?' she asked in a low voice as he rang the doorbell, and she could tell by the way he turned to her that he half resented the distraction. But he nodded, albeit with some impatience, and she took a chance that he wouldn't bawl her out here. 'Lighten up,' she said. 'You don't want to frighten your daughter, do you?'

Alex blew out a breath. 'You don't know what—' he was

beginning harshly, when the door opened to reveal a young woman in a maid's uniform, and he bit off the words.

The maid regarded the visitors unsmilingly. 'Yes?' she said insolently, and Kate waited apprehensively for Alex to put the girl in her place.

But to her astonishment he didn't, and she watched the change come over his face. 'Will you tell Rachel's nanny that her father's come to collect her?' he asked, with a polite smile. 'She is expecting me.'

Kate breathed out slowly, hardly aware she had been holding the air in her lungs until the maid flounced away. 'Didn't I do well?' Alex asked softly, and she was amazed to see that he was still smiling. 'Oh, and thanks for the advice. I do tend to let the Wyatts rattle my cage.'

Kate smiled back, aware that her attraction to this man was as strong as ever. What was wrong with her? she wondered. She ought to have cut her losses last week and run. Now that Joanne had been suspended from school, she was unlikely to be allowed to go on the skiing trip, which had previously provided a justification for being here.

The maid was coming back accompanied by a middle-aged woman dressed in a beige sweater and a brown pleated skirt. 'The nanny,' said Alex in an undertone, but there was no sign of the little girl. Kate practically felt him stiffening beside her, and she prayed he wouldn't blow it now.

'I'm afraid Rachel and her grandfather are still down at the paddock,' said the nanny politely, and to Kate's relief there was no trace of animosity in her tone. 'I don't think Mr Wyatt expected you so early. If you'll come in, I'll have someone go and tell him you're here.'

'We'll go and meet them,' declared Alex at once, his relief evident. And, before the nanny could voice any objections, he anchored Kate with a hand at her wrist, and strode away.

They went around to the back of the house, where the Wyatts' stables adjoined a walled garden. It was not a professional operation like Alex's, but one or two horses nodded over the gates of the stalls. Apparently unaware that he was still gripping her wrist, Alex led the way down a path between the garden and a barn. As they reached the end of the path, Kate could see the paddock the nanny had mentioned, and a little girl, riding a sorrel pony, being led around the grassy enclosure by an elderly man with a deerstalker pulled down over his ears.

Alex's hand tightened around her wrist for a moment and then, as if realising he might be hurting her, he let her go. And, in the same instant, the little girl noticed them, and her excited cries of, 'Daddy, Daddy,' caused the elderly man to turn his head in their direction.

The look Conrad Wyatt bestowed on his son-in-law was full of malevolence, and Kate, who had tended to regard the explanation Alex had given her as an exaggeration until now, shivered. There was so much resentment in the old man's gaze and a hatred that bordered on violence. She could believe anything of him, she realised incredulously, and she looked at Alex to see how he would react.

But, to her relief, the younger man wasn't even looking at his father-in-law. His attention was focussed on his daughter, and, ignoring her grandfather's warning, Rachel swung her leg across the saddle and, releasing her foot from the stirrup, slid excitedly to the ground. Then, tossing her helmet on the grass, she ran towards the white railings, and Alex leant across the barrier and plucked her into his arms.

'Hello, sweetheart.'

His voice was gentler than Kate had ever heard it, and the little girl wrapped her arms about his neck. 'I thought you were never coming!' she exclaimed, pressing her pink cheek against his neck. 'Grandpa said you'd prob'ly forgotten. Like you did last week.'

Kate saw Alex's expression darken. 'Last week?' he echoed ominously as the old man handed the reins of the pony to a waiting groom and came towards them, and Kate wanted to grasp his arm and warn him not to say anything aggressive.

'Yes. Last week,' Conrad Wyatt repeated maliciously.

'Last Tuesday, as a matter of fact. Weren't you supposed to be coming to take Rachel out for the day?'

'He couldn't come,' broke in Kate, before Alex could answer him. Rachel had lifted her head from her father's shoulder and was looking at her now, and Kate gave her a big smile. 'Didn't your grandpa tell you?' she continued, much to the amazement of both men. 'Daddy phoned to say he was really sorry but he couldn't make it. It was my fault. I'm afraid I'd made an absolute mess of some work I was doing, and your daddy had to help me out.'

'Who are you?' asked Rachel, staring at her suspiciously, and her grandfather made a sound something like a hiss.

'Yes, who are you?' he snapped. 'And what do you know about it?' He sneered. 'Oh, yes. I suppose you're another of Kellerman's women.'

'She's my personal assistant,' put in Alex coolly, and Kate could tell from his expression that he understood exactly what she was trying to do. He looked at the little girl. 'I want you to meet Kate,' he said, gesturing her towards him. 'Kate, this is Rachel.' He cast a disparaging glance in his father-in-law's direction. 'My daughter.'

'Hello, Rachel.' Kate bestowed another warm smile on the little girl. She was a pretty little thing, though slightly underweight for her age, Kate decided, her seal-dark hair the image of her father's.

'Do you live at my daddy's house?' the child asked curiously, and before Kate could reply her grandfather gave another contemptuous snort.

'Of course she does, baby, just like all the others. Your father always had more time for his—'

'Are you coming to see your daddy's horses?' broke in Kate, before Conrad Wyatt could provoke Alex into violence. 'You're ever so lucky that your daddy has a farm. I wish mine did.'

'Rachel lives here, Miss Whoever-you-are,' ground out the old man angrily. 'And I'll thank you not to interrupt when I'm talking to my son-in-law.'

'I thought you were talking to Rachel,' remarked Alex calmly, and Kate realised he had no intention of playing the old man's game. He swung his daughter up onto his shoulders and she screamed excitedly. 'Now, if you don't mind, we're wasting far too much time. Say goodbye to your grandfather, sweetheart,' he added, and with Kate at his side he started back along the path.

'Bye, Grandpa,' Rachel shouted back over her shoulder. Then, clinging to her father's neck, she settled down to enjoy the ride.

'Don't forget to have her back for five o'clock,' Conrad Wyatt called after them. 'Any later than that and I'll be in touch with the police, Kellerman.'

'You do that,' muttered Alex, his long strides quickly opening up a space between them. Kate guessed there were other words he'd have liked to use to describe his feelings, but to her relief he kept them to himself.

'Where are we going?' demanded Rachel, after her father had settled her into the back of the Range Rover and secured her seat belt. She hesitated for just a moment. 'Jamaica Hill?'

'Eventually,' agreed Alex, folding his length behind the wheel. 'As it's a fine morning, I thought you might like to go and feed the ducks first. Then Kate and I can have a coffee at the snack bar, and you can have a chocolate milk shake.'

'Oooh, can I?'

This was evidently a treat and Kate found herself smiling as she looked out of the car window. But she would not be sorry to leave Wyvern Hall behind. Its grim façade seemed to reflect the personality of the people who lived there, and as she looked up at the windows she saw a pale face sheltering behind the glass.

Rachel's grandmother?

Kate frowned. The face was too quickly withdrawn to be seen clearly. All she got was an impression of vague hostility, and as there was no one else likely to look at her in that way she decided it must be Alex's mother-in-law. Naturally, she wouldn't approve of him bringing a woman with him, however innocent their relationship might be, and she was glad when Alex spoke again and distracted her attention. She didn't like the feeling that shadowy face had left her with.

'You don't mind, do you?'

Kate forced herself to remember what Alex had suggested, but his words were barely audible over the roar as he gunned the engine of the car. Still they reminded her that she'd only agreed to come with him to pick up his daughter. Glancing at Rachel again, she thought how long it seemed since she and her daughter had done anything together. Was that why Joanne had turned to shoplifting? To gain her mother's attention?

'Do you mind?'

Alex was speaking to her again, and she blinked away her emotion. 'You're the boss,' she murmured, and his lips took on an ironic curl.

'I wish I could believe that,' he remarked, and she wondered rather curiously what he meant.

Still, despite its rather shaky beginning, it was a good morning. For a while, Kate managed to put her own problems aside and concentrate on putting the little girl at her ease. It didn't take her long to realise that although she reacted like an ordinary four-year-old Rachel was by no means as confident as she appeared. Was that Alex's fault, Kate wondered, or Conrad Wyatt's? She suspected it was a combination of the two.

But Alex was trying his best to be a good father now, she acknowledged. And there was no doubt that Rachel idolised her father and hung on his every word. Without Conrad Wyatt's interference these two could have worked things out, she was sure of it. And, while it was true to say that the child's grandfather had been there when she needed him, he should have agreed to back off long ago.

Unfortunately, Conrad Wyatt wasn't the 'backing off' type. Kate had realised that within a couple of minutes of meeting the old man. If she hadn't been there, she wondered if Alex would have let him get away with telling lies about

his absence. She doubted it. Which was probably how the
Wyatts had retained control of Rachel for so long.

Alex was his own worst enemy, she realised. But, for all
that, she could understand why he'd behaved as he had when
Pamela was killed, so why couldn't his in-laws? The truth
was, they probably could have, if they'd chosen to do so.
But their daughter was dead, and Alex had played right into
their hands.

Sitting in the snack bar later, watching Rachel making a
valiant attempt to look as if she was enjoying the milk shake,
Kate tried to understand Alex's feelings. She guessed he was
worried about the child, and she could see why. Rachel was
so delicate; so fragile; she looked as if the least thing would
cause her to shatter. Her eyes, green, like her father's, were
huge in the small oval of her face.

'Does he often tell Rachel lies about you?' Kate asked
softly, cradling her coffee mug between her hands.

'How should I know?' Alex's tone was grim. 'I'm only
her father.' He forced a smile to reassure the little girl, and
then shrugged his shoulders wearily. 'It's all my fault. I
should never have gone to pieces as I did.'

'Oh, I think that was justifiable,' murmured Kate, encouraging Rachel to taste one of the warm muffins her father had
brought to tempt her. 'Mmm,' she said dramatically, breaking
off a piece and eating it herself. 'That's scrummy. Can I have
some more?'

'You can have it all,' said Rachel indifferently, pushing
the plate away when Kate tried to persuade her. 'I don't have
to eat anything I don't want to. My grandpa said.'

Alex expelled a controlled breath. 'He's got a lot to answer
for,' he muttered. And then, forcing himself to taste the muffin, he endorsed Kate's opinion to the little girl. 'Sometimes
we have to do things we don't want to do,' he told her gently.
'If you don't eat anything, you're never going to get as fat
as me.'

'You're not fat!' exclaimed Rachel at once, her face dimpling, and while she was giggling her father popped a small piece of muffin into her mouth.

'I tell you what,' he said as she chewed experimentally. 'Let's see who can eat the most, shall we? And if you don't want Daddy to blow up like a balloon you'll have to make a proper effort.'

'All right.' Rachel sounded as if she might accept the challenge, but after swallowing only a couple of mouthfuls she pushed the plate away again. 'I'm not hungry,' she said. 'I want to go to your house. You said you were going to show me the new baby horse.'

'It's not a baby horse, it's a foal,' Alex corrected her, but he accepted defeat gracefully and got to his feet. 'Okay,' he said. 'Let's get this show on the road. And Jamaica Hill's not just my house, it's yours, too.'

'I don't want to live at Jamaica Hill,' said Rachel as they drove out of the park onto the Bath Road, and Alex exchanged a look with Kate that was full of pain.

'Why not?' he asked. 'It's your home. You've only been staying with Grandpa and Grandma because Daddy's been sick.'

'Have I?' Rachel sounded surprised at this explanation. 'Grandpa said you didn't want me to live with you any more.'

Alex clenched his teeth. 'That's not true,' he said harshly, and then, softening his tone, he added, 'I've missed you a lot. Jamaica Hill's not the same without my little girl.'

Kate glanced around and saw that Rachel was looking puzzled. 'It's true,' she said. 'Your daddy's really lonely in that big old house on his own.'

Rachel pursed her lips. 'But Grandpa said that now that Mummy's gone I'd be just an-noosuns. He said you'd prob'ly give my room to another little girl.'

'God!'

Alex swore violently, and Kate hurried to distract his daughter from her father's grief. 'You couldn't be more wrong,' she said. 'There are no other little girls at Jamaica

Hill.' She glanced at Alex. 'I'm sure Daddy told me your teddy was asking when you were going to come and see him again.'

Rachel's lips parted. 'Which teddy?'

'All of them,' put in her father, with a grateful look at Kate. 'So—does that mean you'd really like to come back and live with Daddy? Kate's right. I have been lonely since you went away.'

Rachel smiled. 'I want to live at Jamaica Hill,' she declared, nodding, and Kate saw Alex's hands tighten on the wheel.

'You will,' he said. 'Just as soon as I can arrange it.' He blew out a breath. 'Let's pretend you really do live there today, shall we?'

They were turning in to the gates of the estate when Rachel spoke again. 'Do you wish you had a little girl, Kate?' she asked thoughtfully, and Kate wondered what she was thinking. Was it just a casual question or did it mirror something else her grandfather had said?

'I have a little girl—well, quite a big girl really,' Kate replied, glancing at Alex. 'She lives with me in King's Montford, and her name's Joanne.'

'Joanne?'

'That's right.'

Rachel considered. 'Does she go to school?'

'Well, she does.' Kate pulled a wry face. 'But she's—on holiday at the moment.'

'Can I see her?'

'May I see her?' corrected her father automatically. And then he said, 'I don't see why not.' He raised his eyebrows at Kate. 'Why don't you bring her down to the yard one day?'

'To the stables?' Kate stared at him.

'Why not?' His lips twitched. 'She's got nothing else to do, has she?'

'That's not the point—'

'What is the point, then?' Alex frowned. 'Oh, I see. She's in the doghouse right now.'

And then his features relaxed into a grin when Rachel asked, 'What's a doghouse?'

'Joanne was—naughty,' Kate explained, unhappily aware that she and Alex were becoming far too familiar. But that was what happened when you allowed a relationship to encroach on your private life, she reflected. He already knew more about her than was strictly sensible. And it wasn't just unwise, it was downright dangerous to let it go on.

'How was she naughty?' asked Rachel, and Kate was thinking so hard about how to answer her that she didn't notice that Alex had driven up to the house. She'd been expecting him to drop her at the stables, but now he was turning off the engine and Mrs Muir was at the door of the house, waiting to greet them.

She turned to him then, her eyes wide with enquiry, and he gave her a rueful look. 'Humour me,' he pleaded softly. 'I want to make up to you for what happened last week.'

'But, Rachel—'

'Rachel won't mind.' He glanced round at his daughter who was busily removing her seat belt. 'You don't mind if Kate has lunch with us, do you?'

'Will Joanne be having lunch, too?' Rachel asked at once, scrambling forward, and Alex exchanged another amused look with Kate.

'Not today,' he said at last. 'But maybe next time you come to visit. Look, there's Mrs Muir. You'll have to make do with her for today.'

Rachel looked as if she might protest, but then she saw the fluffy toy Mrs Muir was carrying and Joanne was forgotten. 'Peter!' she exclaimed. 'It's Peter Rabbit.' And as soon as the door was opened for her she jumped out, wrapping her arms around the cuddly bunny, and beaming all over her face.

Kate got out rather more sedately. She wasn't at all convinced that she was doing the right thing. In fact she was

fairly sure she was doing the wrong one, and even the
warmth of Mrs Muir's welcome didn't help to put her at her
ease.

Still, there wasn't a lot she could do about it now.
Everyone seemed to be taking it for granted that she was
staying, and it would have been churlish to refuse. Besides,
much as she feared their developing relationship, it could
prove useful, and she squashed her initial prejudice beneath
a veneer of polite forbearance.

All the same, that forbearance quickly wore thin when Mrs
Muir took Rachel off to the kitchen with her, leaving Kate
and Alex in the library. Once again, they were alone together,
and Kate had the added distraction of knowing that she was
nowhere near as indifferent to him as she'd have him believe.

'Drink?' he offered, as before, and this time Kate decided
she needed something slightly stronger than orange juice to
sustain her.

'Um—do you have a martini?' she asked, linking her cold
fingers together, and Alex bent to open the cabinet door.

'I think so,' he said, dropping ice cubes into a tall glass.
Then, looking up, he said, 'Make yourself at home.'

As if she could!

Kate managed a tight smile nevertheless, and subsided into
the armchair she'd occupied the last time she was here.
Holding her hands towards the fire, she tried to force herself
to relax, but her knees persisted in trembling and she pressed
them together to hide her nervousness.

'There you go.'

She hadn't heard Alex cross the room. The richly patterned
carpet had silenced his footsteps, but now he was beside her,
the drink she had requested extended towards her.

'Oh—oh, thanks.' Her face burned suddenly, and she
heard him mutter something under his breath.

'It's okay.' His voice when he spoke revealed his frustration. Then, going back to the cabinet, he helped himself to a
beer from the fridge before continuing, 'You can trust me,

you know. I don't usually try to seduce my guests.' His lips twisted. 'Well, not on a first date anyway.'

'It wasn't a date.'

'No.' He acknowledged her correction. 'Which makes it worse, doesn't it? I took advantage of you without even paying the bill.'

Kate pressed her lips together. 'Let's forget about it, shall we?' She sipped her martini. 'This is nice.'

'Not too strong for you?' he asked mockingly. 'I wouldn't want to be accused of trying to get you drunk.'

Kate sighed and looked up at him. 'Would you like me to go? I can, you know. You can always tell Mrs Muir that Joanne is ill or something.'

'Why would I want to do that?' Alex sighed, too, his impatience evident. 'No, I just want us to stop sniping at each other. I'd like you to stay.' He paused, and then added softly, 'I hope we can be friends.'

Friends?

Kate almost choked on her drink. Dear God, if he ever found out who she was he'd be—uncontrollable. She had been thinking 'furious', but that wasn't a strong enough adjective to describe how he'd feel. Her breath caught in her throat. He'd never forgive her; never. She'd have to spend the rest of her life looking over her shoulder, afraid of every shadow after dark.

'Look,' she began awkwardly, 'you don't have to say anything. There's nothing either of us can do to change the past, and I'd rather pretend it never happened.' She waited a beat, and then, with a complete change of subject, asked, 'Are—are you and Mrs Sheridan good friends?'

'Lacey?' His eyes narrowed. 'I guess so. Why do you ask?'

Kate shrugged. 'Um, Ted—Ted Lowes, that is—said she'd gone to Doncaster with you.'

'Ah.'

He sounded resigned, and she hoped she hadn't said anything she shouldn't. The last thing she wanted to do was make him think she'd been gossiping about him. Or that Ted had been gossiping either. Especially since the head groom had proved depressingly reticent about his boss.

'That was Mrs Sheridan who—who—'

'Interrupted us last week?' suggested Alex dryly, and she hoped he'd been diverted by her words. 'Yes, that was Lacey,' he agreed, and then grimaced. 'She and I have known one another a long time.'

'Really?'

Kate tried not to sound too interested, and, as she'd hoped, he continued in a similar vein. 'Her land adjoins Jamaica Hill on the western boundary. When my father was alive, he and her husband were good friends.'

'But he doesn't accompany her to race meetings?'

Kate couldn't hide her curiosity and Alex regarded her sardonically. 'She's a widow,' he amended. 'Her husband was much older than she was and he died a few years ago. Since then...' he paused '...since then, she and I have attempted to sustain the connection. Unfortunately, it hasn't always worked.'

'No?'

'No.' Once again Kate's comment had prompted a reaction. 'She never did forgive me for marrying Pam.' He mused. 'And when Alicia was here she didn't like that either. She couldn't wait to get her out of the house.'

'Alicia?' Kate managed to sound as if the name was not familiar to her.

'Yeah, Alicia Sawyer,' he conceded, but she sensed she'd spoken out of turn. 'She worked at the stables before you came,' he added, almost as an afterthought. He nodded towards the glass in her hand. 'Would you like another?'

'What?' Kate had been so intent on what he was saying that she hardly heard the question. 'Oh—oh, no,' she mumbled, when her brain kicked into action again. 'Um—' She hesitated. 'This is fine, thank you.' And then, after another pregnant pause, she asked, 'Did she find another job?'

'Who?'

Now it was his turn to be obtuse, and she had to force herself to continue. 'Al—Alicia,' she murmured, pretending an innocence she didn't feel.

'She left,' he responded shortly. 'Rather suddenly.' His face hardened. 'I prefer not to discuss Mrs Sawyer, if you don't mind.'

'I'm sorry.'

Of course, Kate did mind, but she could hardly tell him that. And at least he wasn't afraid to discuss her departure, which must say something about his state of mind.

'It doesn't matter,' he declared indifferently now. 'I guess I'm touchy where Mrs Sawyer is concerned.' He paused. 'But Lacey means well,' he added, reverting to his earlier topic. 'I'm not always the most tolerant of men.'

Kate saw the opening and took it. 'Does Mrs Sheridan breed horses, too?'

'She owns a couple of mares and a prize stallion, but I wouldn't call her a breeder,' replied Alex flatly. 'She doesn't have the facilities for breeding. She prefers someone else to deal with that side of things.'

'You?' asked Kate guilelessly, and then coloured at the possible connotation. 'I mean, you do breed horses, don't you? You have such a lot.'

'I actually own very few horses,' Alex told her tolerantly. 'But, yes, I have the facilities for breeding here at Jamaica Hill, as you say.'

'But—'

Kate was confused now, and he went on to enlighten her. 'My business is mainly concerned with boarding other people's horses,' he explained levelly. 'We can arrange for a mare to be covered—serviced—if that's what the owner wants, but most of our work is involved in exercising and training young animals, as I'm sure you'll have gathered by now.'

'But you go to race meetings.'

'I go to horse sales, too, both here and in the United States, but I'm usually acting on behalf of someone else.'

Kate shook her head. 'I thought—' she began, before breaking off, and he uttered a short laugh.

'What? That I owned all the horseflesh in my stables?' he asked drolly. 'I'm not a rich man, Kate, whatever impression you may have gained from the tabloids when Pam died.'

Kate was embarrassed. 'I didn't mean to imply—' She made a helpless gesture. 'Tell me about how you started. Have you always wanted to work with horses?'

'Actually, I wanted to be a psychologist,' he admitted ruefully. 'But my father wasn't having any of that. I was his only offspring, you see, and he was determined I'd take over this place when he retired.'

Kate nodded. 'But you didn't mind?'

'I minded like hell, but it didn't do me any good,' Alex replied, pulling a wry face. 'But I like to think I've put some of that instinctive training to good use.'

Kate was interested. 'How?'

'Well, they say that to train a horse you've got to use psychology. You concentrate on three things: its physical abilities, its skill, and its mental fitness. A lot depends on a horse's temperament. You can have the fittest animal in the world, but if its nature is inherently bad there's not a lot you can do with it.'

'But how do you know? I mean—' Kate tried to clarify what she meant '—how do you know when a horse is—say, bad-tempered?'

Alex was silent for so long, she thought he wasn't going to answer her. But then he said, 'Vicious horses tend to lay their ears back and bare their teeth.' He paused. 'If you're trying to find out why my wife would choose to mount a horse like that, why don't you come right out and say so? It's not as if I haven't been asked that question before.'

'I'm not.' Kate was ashamed to admit that nothing had been further from her thoughts.

He scowled. 'Well, the truth is, Jackson—that was the name of the horse she was riding when she had the accident—didn't always exhibit his psychosis. He was only uncontrollable at times, but I'd already decided to get rid of him.'

Kate hesitated. 'I suppose you wish you had now.'

'Yeah, right.' Alex was predictably bitter. 'Then I might have been dumb enough to be bringing up two children that weren't my own.'

Kate gasped. 'Rachel's yours!' she exclaimed. 'I don't know how you can doubt it. Her hair, her eyes, her mouth—' She caught herself before she incriminated herself further. 'I—I'm sure you don't need to have any worries on—on that score.'

Alex's expression had softened. 'I'm glad to hear it.' His eyes played about her mouth. 'And I suppose I should be flattered that you seem so well-informed.'

Kate buried her nose in her drink, conscious that the atmosphere between them was subtly changing again. It seemed she couldn't be alone with this man without becoming aware of him in a totally personal way.

Rachel's return a few moments later, to announce that lunch was ready, provided a welcome escape from her dilemma. Instead of watching her, Alex was obliged to watch his daughter, and she kept him busy with a host of questions of her own. They ranged from when she was going to be allowed to spend the night at Jamaica Hill with him to the new foal he intended to show her that afternoon. When they went in to lunch, Kate noticed that the little girl only picked at her meal again, but what she lacked in appetite she definitely made up for in charm.

After the meal, she insisted on showing Kate her bedroom. She was obviously reassured to find it looked exactly the same as it had done the last time she was here. Kate guessed Alex kept it that way deliberately. The toys, the paper on the walls, even the soft furnishings, were all to suit a much younger child than Rachel was now.

Once back at the stables, Kate excused herself and went into her office. Much as she would have liked to stay with Alex and his daughter, she knew she had to remember why she was here. The trouble was, the longer she knew Alex, the more she became convinced that he was innocent. Which wasn't at all the purpose behind why Henry Sawyer had persuaded her to take this job…

CHAPTER NINE

'So what have you found out?'

Henry Sawyer faced Kate across the desk in her office at the agency, a scowl of impatience darkening his already sullen features. He'd rung Susie the day before to arrange this meeting, once again after normal working hours, which Kate thought was just as well.

She could hardly have asked for any more time off, she reflected ruefully, fidgeting with her pen. What excuse could she have given Alex? That she was meeting with the man who was trying to ruin his life?

She knew Sawyer expected her to have some information for him, but the fact was, she needed more time. It wasn't possible to gain a person's confidence in the space of a few short weeks, particularly when the press had already given Alex such a raw deal. And everyone who worked at Jamaica Hill was sensitive to any questions of a personal nature.

'I know that your wife worked for Mr Kellerman until about eleven weeks ago,' she said now, and Henry Sawyer gave a derisive snort.

'I know that. I told you!' he exclaimed scornfully. 'I mean—do you know where she is? Has Kellerman dropped any clues?'

As if he would!

'He—he did say she left quite suddenly,' she admitted at last, chiding herself for the sense of guilt she felt at revealing this much to him.

'I'll bet he did,' muttered the man opposite. 'If she ever left at all. That bastard's got all the answers. You want to watch yourself, Mrs Ross. You're not unlike Alicia yourself.'

Kate caught her breath. 'That's nonsense,' she protested at

once, pretending to be checking some detail in the file to avoid meeting his accusing gaze. But she couldn't disguise her burning cheeks, and she prayed he'd think it was embarrassment and nothing else.

'No.' Sawyer leaned towards her confidingly. 'You're a good-looking woman, Mrs Ross. He likes them slim and blonde, though it's a pity you don't have more up top, if you know what I mean.'

Kate didn't know whether to be flattered or offended but she chose the latter. 'We're not here to talk about me, Mr Sawyer,' she said tersely. 'And—and as far as your wife is concerned I'm fairly sure she left of her own free will.'

'So where is she?'

He was belligerent now, and Kate expelled a weary sigh. 'I don't know,' she conceded honestly. 'I am making some progress, but it's a slow business, I'm afraid.'

'You call telling me what I already know ''some progress''?' he snapped irritably, and Kate wished she could wash her hands of the whole affair.

'It takes time to gain people's confidence,' she said. 'I don't want to draw attention to myself. If I start asking a lot of awkward questions, Mr Kellerman will become—suspicious. If he does and throws me out, I'll have wasted my time and your money.'

'My money? Oh, yeah.' Henry Sawyer chewed on his lower lip. 'It wouldn't do to waste that, would it?' His eyes narrowed. 'I might just decide I want it back.'

'Not a chance.' Kate was angry now. How dared he sit there patronising her, and behaving as if he was doing her a favour by calling in? 'My time is money, Mr Sawyer. I explained that before I agreed to take the case. And by my reckoning, your payments are now in arrears. Now, if you don't like what I'm doing, I'll give you an invoice showing what's been spent and then you can settle the balance.'

'That won't be necessary.' His voice was sulky now, and she breathed a little easier knowing she had had her say. 'But, well, Mr—that is, me—*I'm* getting really worried,' he muttered disjointedly. 'In another week or so it'll be three months since she disappeared.'

Kate wished she felt like sympathising with him, but the more she saw of Henry Sawyer, the more convinced she became that Alicia had left of her own accord. She couldn't imagine what the woman had ever seen in him, unless it was Alicia's disappearance that had caused him to lose interest in himself.

Having given her another substantial sum of money, he left soon afterwards with Kate's promise that she'd be in touch if she had any news. She had his address, though no phone number, she noticed. Evidently Mr Sawyer preferred to do business face to face.

She got home about half-past seven to find a note from her mother propped beside the kettle. It appeared that Ellen Ross had taken Joanne to the cinema in Bath and they wouldn't be back until fairly late. Kate remembered now that Joanne had mentioned the film she wanted to see and her grandmother must have decided to treat her. Kate guessed her daughter would welcome any chance to get out of the house.

Which reminded her of what Alex Kellerman had said about bringing Joanne down to the stables. But it had been mooted when she had had lunch with him and his daughter and it hadn't been mentioned since. Of course, she hadn't seen much of him since Sam Guthrie's return to work. Had he meant it, or was it just something he'd said in passing? After all, it had been Rachel who'd expressed a desire to meet her.

But there was no denying that Joanne would have loved the chance to visit the stables. She'd never had much to do with horses, but she loved all animals and it was only because of the local council's regulations that she didn't have a pet at the flat. Still, it probably wasn't the most sensible thing to do in the circumstances. She was already regretting her involvement with Alex Kellerman. It would be most unwise to involve her daughter as well.

Ellen had left Kate's evening meal in the oven. It was giving off an appetising aroma of meat and onions, but when Kate lifted the casserole onto the hob it quickly lost its appeal. At least an hour stewing in its own juices had left the meal looking dark and rubbery, and a burnt skin of gravy clung to the edges of the dish.

Deciding she'd rather make herself an omelette later, Kate hung her coat in the closet and went into her bedroom. Turning on the lamp, she dropped her bag on the bed and viewed her reflection in the dressing-table mirror. She looked as dejected as she felt, she thought dully, pulling the elastic band from her braid and threading her fingers through her loosened hair. Was she really cut out to be an investigator? she wondered. Wouldn't she be happier if she was working at the stables for real?

She suspected the answer was yes, which meant that Henry Sawyer had some justification for his impatience. Was he right? Was Alex Kellerman really a dangerous man? One thing was certain and that was that her loyalties were becoming hopelessly divided. She was a fool. Any dimwit would know better than to get personally involved with a case.

Abandoning such depressing thoughts, she went into the bathroom. A soak in the tub was what she needed, she determined, turning on the taps. And then afterwards she might open a bottle of wine, she thought, peeling off her shirt and bra. She'd forget all about Alex Kellerman and Henry Sawyer. By the time her mother and Joanne got back, she'd be feeling pleasantly mellow.

She was drying herself when she heard someone ringing the doorbell. She'd taken the portable radio into the bathroom with her so she couldn't be sure how long the ringing had been going on. It couldn't be her mother and Joanne. Her mother would have used her key. Unless she'd lost it. Kate frowned, reaching for her velvet sweatpants. Either way, she was going to have to find out.

The loose-fitting shirt that matched the purple sweatpants clung to her damp body, but she couldn't help it. It was better than wrapping a towel about herself to go to the door. The pants clung to her legs, too, but at least her body was drying. Her hair was another matter, and she scooped it up into a knot on top of her head.

She half hoped the ringing would have stopped by the time she got there, but it hadn't, and she secured the safety chain before opening the door. It was just a precaution, and she doubted it would hold a determined assailant, but her mother felt safer with the sturdy chain in place.

However, her jaw sagged when she saw who had disturbed her. Alex Kellerman was standing in the corridor outside. 'Hello,' he said stiffly. 'I hope I'm not interrupting anything.'

Kate didn't know what to say; what to think even. She couldn't imagine why he might have come to see her, unless by some awful mistake on her part he'd found out who she was.

'I—no,' she said now, putting a nervous hand up to her damp hair. 'I—I was just getting out of the bath, that's all.' She licked her dry lips. 'Have you been waiting long?'

'Not long,' he replied, with a dismissing shrug of his shoulders. He was wearing a dark blue three-piece suit this evening and the more formal clothes added to his darkly sensual appeal. 'I saw your car downstairs, as it happens. I took the chance that you might be in.'

'Oh—yes.' Kate acknowledged the fact with a shiver of awareness. It reminded her of how vulnerable she was. Thank goodness he'd known where to find her. If he'd asked someone for directions, they might have mistaken him for a client. It was frightening to think she could have been found out.

'I expect you're wondering what I'm doing here,' he said now, and she realised she'd have to remove the safety chain. Despite her misgivings, she couldn't go on talking to him through the crack.

'You'd better come in,' she said, putting the chilliness she was feeling down to the draught that blew along the corridor. She unfastened the chain and opened the door. 'It's through there.'

'Thanks.'

Although she stepped aside, he still brushed her arm as he went past her into the living room of the flat. She wondered if he was as aware of it as she was. Probably not, she reflected wryly. For the past few days, he'd seemed more than willing to forget that he'd wanted them to be friends.

Because he hadn't meant it, she chided herself irritably, closing the door and following him along the hall. The last thing he'd have wanted was for there to be any unpleasantness between them while Rachel was visiting. He'd needed someone to go with him to fetch his daughter and she'd been available. Giving her lunch had been for Rachel's sake, not hers.

He was standing in the middle of the floor when she entered the lamplit living room, and Kate was immediately conscious of how ill-at-ease he looked. He didn't belong here, she thought. Despite his notoriety, he belonged in more elegant surroundings. In his expensive suit and hand-made shoes, he made the modest room look cheap.

'Do you want to sit down?' she asked offhandedly, gesturing towards the sofa. Then, smoothing her sweating palms over her rear, she said, 'Can I offer you a drink?'

'I don't want anything right now,' Alex said, but he subsided onto the edge of the sofa. He glanced about him with what Kate was sure was feigned interest. 'I've often wondered what your home was like.'

'So now you know.' Kate's bare feet curled into the rust-coloured carpet. 'It's nothing like Jamaica Hill, as you can see. But we like it.' She gripped the backs of her thighs self-consciously. 'Is something wrong? Is that why you're here?'

His eyes seemed mesmerised by her nervous probing. He'd been watching her hands, but now he dragged his gaze up to her face. There was a certain satisfaction to be gained from the fact that he had to look up at her. It was an advantage that she'd never had before.

'No,' he replied now, his low voice fairly scraping over her nerves. 'As a matter of fact, I came to see Joanne.'

'Joanne?' Kate couldn't hide her astonishment. 'Um—well, she's not here. She's gone to the movies with my mother.'

'A pity,' he said, seeming to see that as his cue to get to his feet again. 'Then I suppose there's no point in asking what time she'll be home?'

Kate shook her head. 'They've gone into Bath,' she murmured. 'I could give her a message.'

His green eyes darkened. 'Yeah, I guess you could,' he agreed. 'But I'd prefer to speak to her myself.'

Kate stepped back. 'All right,' she said. 'If it's something private.'

'It's not.' He took a breath. 'Perhaps I just wanted an excuse to come and see you again.'

'I don't think so.' Kate gave him a thin smile. 'You can see me any time. I'm still working at the stables, you know.'

'I know.'

His gaze was disturbingly intent and Kate wondered why he'd really come here. She didn't buy his story about speaking to Joanne. Yet he knew she lived here with her mother and daughter, so he could hardly have anticipated that she would be alone.

'Tell me,' he said, taking a deliberate step towards her, and Kate had to steel herself not to panic as she'd done in the library at Jamaica Hill, 'what do you really think of me? Do I scare you? Do you still have doubts about my innocence, about the way Pam died?'

Kate pulled a breath deep into her lungs before answering him. 'You don't scare me,' she insisted firmly, but that wasn't all he'd asked and she knew it.

'But you're not sure if I was to blame for Pamela's accident,' he stated flatly. His expression hardened. 'Well, at least I know where I stand.'

'I didn't mean—'

'Tell Joanne I'll be in touch with her in the next few days,' he said, stepping around her, and before she could gather her thoughts he'd reached the living-room door.

'No. Wait—' she began, knowing she couldn't let him go thinking the worst of her, and his shoulders slumped as he swung back against the jamb.

'What?' he demanded harshly. 'Oh, right. You don't want Joanne anywhere near me.'

'It's not that—'

'Then what is it? Some new excuse for not inviting her to Jamaica Hill?'

'No.' Kate sighed, and then, reluctantly, she closed the space between them. 'I—I do think you're innocent. I don't think you—deliberately—brought about your wife's death.'

Alex tipped his head back against the frame of the door behind him and looked at her through his lashes. 'Is that supposed to be an apology?' he asked. 'You don't think I *deliberately* put Jackson in that stall?' He gave a bitter laugh. 'But you do think I put the horse in there, don't you? Whether by accident, or simple misjudgement, I'm to blame?'

Kate's hair was starting to come loose from its band, and, pulling it off, she thrust her fingers into the damp mass of curls. 'I don't know what to think,' she admitted helplessly. 'I wasn't there. I don't know all the facts. But I don't believe you're guilty. Isn't that enough?'

Alex expelled a weary breath. 'I guess it's going to have to be.'

He sounded totally defeated, and Kate suppressed an almost irresistible urge to scream. She wanted to tell him she trusted him, that there was no way he could have hurt his wife, but the reason why she wanted to believe him was what really held her back.

He was turning towards the outer door when she spoke again. 'What—what you said,' she murmured. 'About—about inviting Joanne to the stables. Is that really why you came tonight?'

'What else?'

His response was muffled. Deliberately, she suspected. He was feeling in his pocket for his car keys and the words were

lost as he reached for the latch. Which was when Kate reacted, when she knew she couldn't let him go like this, and,
shouldering past him, she pressed her back against the door.

'Don't go.'

'Why not?' Alex's expression didn't alter. 'I'm sure you'd
rather I left before your mother and daughter get home.'

Kate hesitated for a moment and then surrendered to a
force stronger than herself. 'They won't be home for hours,'
she told him huskily. 'At least stay and have a drink.'

Alex stepped away from the door. 'I don't think that would
be entirely wise in the present circumstances,' he said tightly.

'Why not?' She threw his words back at him now. Then
she asked audaciously, 'Have you got something more important to do?'

His lips twisted. 'I think so.'

She couldn't stop herself. 'What?'

'Getting out of here,' he answered, without emotion.
'Now, do you want to get out of the way so that I can open
the door?'

'And if I don't?'

His lips parted to deliver what she was sure would have
been a passionate response, but then he seemed to gather
himself and when he spoke again his voice was low and
controlled. 'Let's stop playing games, shall we? We both
know what would happen if I accepted your invitation, and
I have no desire to be accused of harassing you again.'

Kate was indignant. 'I didn't accuse you of harassing me,'
she protested, and he gave her a weary look.

'No. Okay. You didn't accuse me of it, but you damn near
sprinted out of the library the last time I laid a hand on you.'

Kate bent her head. 'That woman came in.'

'Lacey; right.' He conceded the point. 'But you weren't
exactly—co-operating before that.'

'No.' Kate had to admit that was true.

'No.' He breathed deeply. 'Point taken, I think.'

Kate frowned. 'But—didn't you care?'

His eyes narrowed. 'Yeah. I cared like hell.'

'No.' She shook her head. 'I meant about—about Mrs Sheridan interrupting us.'

'Not particularly.'

'But you must have done.'

'Why?'

'Well—you're close friends.'

His nostrils flared. 'Kate, I've known Lacey for more than ten years, and if she chooses to walk into my house unannounced she can't complain if what she sees doesn't meet with her unqualified approval.'

'Do you think she'd have walked out again?'

He grimaced. 'Knowing Lacey, I doubt it.'

'There you are, then.'

'What? Are you saying her arrival gave you the excuse to go haring out of there as if the devil himself was at your heels? For God's sake, a stranger would have thought I'd been assaulting you!' Then he gave a cynical snort. 'Well, hell, I suppose I was.'

'You weren't.' Kate spoke impulsively, and then had to stand his disbelieving appraisal. 'It—it wasn't like that,' she muttered awkwardly. 'I—I provoked you, like you said. I had no right to criticise your way of dealing with—with your life.'

Alex's dark brows arched. 'And that gave me the right to take advantage of you?' he asked mockingly, and she sighed.

'You're making this very hard.'

'Perhaps that's my purpose in life.'

'What?'

'To make things hard for people.'

'To make things hard for yourself,' burst out Kate impatiently. 'I thought you wanted us to be friends.'

'I find I no longer have any inclination in that direction,' he told her harshly. 'And as far as making things hard for myself is concerned, believe me, you have no idea.'

Kate pushed herself away from the door. 'Then tell me,' she said imploringly. 'I do want to understand.'

'Do you?' His eyes moved to some place behind her head

and she could see the battle he was having with himself to resist her argument. 'I don't think you have any conception of how I feel.'

'Then tell me!' she exclaimed urgently, and with a groan of defeat he turned back towards the living room.

'I guess I will take you up on that offer of a drink,' he said flatly, and Kate felt a mixture of apprehension and relief.

This time, Alex didn't wait for her invitation to sit down. Unbuttoning his jacket again, he flung himself onto the sofa, and Kate gathered herself sufficiently to ask him what he'd like to drink.

'You don't have a great deal of choice,' she admitted ruefully. 'Just wine, or beer, or a soft drink.' She hesitated. 'Have you eaten?'

Alex tilted his head to look up at her. 'Are you going to feed me, too?' he asked, with gentle mockery, and the warmth of his smile sent rivulets of heat into her quivering stomach.

'Well, I was going to make myself an omelette,' she admitted. 'And maybe a salad.' She paused. 'If you'd like to join me, I'm sure there's enough for two.'

Alex studied her face for what seemed like eons, but which was probably just a few seconds, and then he nodded. 'Sounds good,' he conceded. 'If you don't mind?'

In fact, Kate was wondering what had possessed her to invite him for a meal. After tasting Mrs Muir's cooking, she was unhappily aware that her efforts just didn't compare, and eggs and salad were hardly appropriate fare.

'You wouldn't rather have pizza, would you?' she asked hurriedly. 'I can send out for—'

'An omelette is fine with me,' Alex told her firmly, and, getting to his feet again, he took off his jacket and slung it over the back of a chair. 'Come on. I'll help you.'

Kate led the way into the kitchen wishing she'd stuck at offering him a beer. The kitchen at the flat was small and obviously much different from the kitchen at Jamaica Hill, and she was overwhelmingly aware of his powerful bulk in the confined space.

'Did—did you decide what you wanted to drink?' she asked, determining not to let him see how he disturbed her, thrusting the cold casserole back into the cooker out of sight.

'I'll wait till we eat,' he said, propping his hips against the breakfast bar. He shrugged. 'What do you want me to do?'

'There's not a lot to do.' Kate took the bag of lettuce from the fridge and shook it into a dish. 'You could open the wine, I suppose.'

'Fine. Where is it?'

'It's in the fridge, too,' she replied, turning back for eggs and tomatoes. She handed the bottle to him and indicated a drawer. 'The corkscrew's in there.'

She noticed that he loosened the collar of his shirt and pulled his tie away before tackling the bottle. He'd already turned the sleeves of his shirt back to his elbows, and she was unwillingly fascinated by the light covering of hair that darkened his wrists. His watch was a plain gold one, she observed, on a tan-coloured leather strap.

'Did you know your husband was seeing another woman?' he asked abruptly, and she bit back an unwary exclamation.

'I beg your pardon?'

He fixed the corkscrew in place before giving her a side-long look. 'I think you heard me,' he said quietly. 'Did you?'

Kate caught her breath. 'Why do you want to know?'

'Humour me.'

She hesitated for a few moments, and then said tightly, 'No. No, I didn't.'

'Me, neither,' he remarked, attacking the cork. 'Know that Pam was having an affair, I mean.' He gave a derisive snort. 'I must have been the only one who didn't.'

Kate turned her head to look at him. 'What do you mean?'

He paused in what he was doing and blew out a breath. 'Because the man involved worked for me.'

Kate's lips parted. 'He was a groom?'

'No.' Alex sighed. 'He worked on the estate.' He consid-

ered for a moment, and then said flatly, 'His name was Muir.
Philip Muir.'

Kate gasped. 'Mrs Muir's son?'

'You know about her son?' Alex frowned, and Kate hurried to explain.

'I know he died,' she said quickly. 'I—I met Mrs Muir in
the supermarket last week, and she invited me to have tea
with her in the café. She was asking me about Sean, and I
told her he'd been killed in a car crash. That's when she told
me that both her son and her husband were dead.'

The furrow between Alex's brows deepened. 'And did she
tell you anything else?'

Guessing he meant had the housekeeper been gossiping,
Kate shook her head. 'It was all perfectly innocent,' she assured him. 'Your name was hardly mentioned. She certainly
didn't talk about your wife, if that's what you're getting at.'

Alex's shoulders sagged. 'No.' He gave a slight nod of his
head. 'I should have known better than to ask something like
that. So you won't know that Philip took his own life about
six weeks before Pam was killed?'

Kate looked stunned. 'I had no idea. Was it—was it—
connected?'

'With Pam being pregnant, you mean?' Alex pulled out
the cork with undue force. 'You could say that, I suppose.
She'd apparently finished with him a couple of weeks before
it happened.'

'Oh, no.' Kate was appalled. Then she frowned. 'But I
thought you said you hadn't known about the affair.'

Alex's expression grew sardonic. 'Still checking up on me,
Mrs Hughes?' he mocked disarmingly. 'I didn't. The Muirs
told me—after Pam was dead.'

Kate expelled an unsteady breath. 'I wasn't checking up
on you,' she protested, but to herself she wondered if that
was entirely true. Yet she doubted she would be reporting
their conversation to Henry Sawyer. It was far too important
to her to be sullied by his coarse claims.

'Whatever.' Alex turned to watch her now as she broke

half a dozen eggs into a bowl. Then, as she picked up the whisk and began to beat them, his eyes lowered to her bosom, and in a strangled voice he said, 'Are you wearing anything under that suit?'

The whisk clattered into the bowl and Kate's face turned scarlet. 'Do you always ask such personal questions?' she asked. 'Or do you just enjoy shocking me?'

'I was interested,' murmured Alex huskily. 'I was remembering how soft your skin was that afternoon in the library, and how much I wanted to take your clothes off.' His eyes grew sensual on hers. 'Of course, I wouldn't have done it. Take your clothes off, I mean. I wouldn't have wanted to embarrass Mrs Muir.'

Kate expelled a sound that mingled disbelief with outrage. 'But you don't have any qualms about embarrassing me!'

'Am I embarrassing you?' He had been lounging against the counter beside her, but now he came abruptly to his feet. 'I'm sorry. I guess I was just thinking out loud.'

'Do you think that makes me feel any better?' Kate groped for the whisk again but her hand was shaking so much that she couldn't go on beating the eggs.

'Do you want me to go?' he asked tensely, and she knew that even now she had only to say the word and he'd walk out of the apartment. She wondered how she could ever have doubted this man's innocence. If it wasn't such a crazy—futile—notion she'd have said she was falling in love with him herself.

'What do you think?' she demanded now, half snappily, her own emotions working overtime as she fought to bring them under control. She caught her breath. 'You should know better than that. Dammit, you know that's not what I want.'

'Do I?'

He looked down at her with eyes that seemed to burn with a latent fire, and she swayed towards him, half afraid he still doubted her even now. Her hands spread against his waistcoat, her thumbs catching on the buttons, feeling the strong beat of his heart throbbing in his chest.

She breathed a little sigh of relief when he bent his head towards her, and when his lips brushed hers she parted them to his tongue. His hand gripped the back of her neck, pulling her closer to him, and he deepened the kiss with the hungry pressure of his mouth.

His hands possessed her, moving over her shoulders with spine-tingling familiarity, creating an intimacy between them that she'd never known with any other man. His fingers explored the sensitive curve of her back as his tongue sought and stroked the quivering length of hers, drawing her lower lip into his mouth and biting gently on the vulnerable inner flesh.

Kate's knees almost buckled when his hands invaded the waistband of her sweatpants, cupping her bare bottom and bringing her fully against him.

'I knew you weren't wearing anything else,' he muttered huskily against the whorl of her ear, and she clutched his neck to prevent herself from sagging to the floor. 'Open your legs,' he added urgently, and although she was too bemused to consciously follow his direction he had no difficulty in inserting his muscled thigh between hers.

The touch of his leg pressing against that most sensitive part of her anatomy was breathtaking, the rub of the soft cloth of the sweatpants causing a damp heat that she was sure he must be able to feel. She felt as if she was drowning in sensual sensation, and she was almost relieved when he swung her up into his arms and carried her into the other room.

It wasn't until she felt the cool linen of the sofa cushions at her back that she realised her sweatpants were around her knees, but by then Alex had joined her. His hand took the place of his thigh between her legs, and she clutched the unbuttoned collar of his shirt when he found the moist petals that opened to his touch.

'Wait...'

Kate fumbled frantically with the rest of the buttons on his shirt and waistcoat, but although Alex allowed her to tear his shirt open he made no attempt to help her.

'Relax,' he told her roughly, bending to stroke her ear with his tongue, caressing the fluttering pulse he found there as his thumb caressed the sensitive nub between her legs.

Kate had barely pressed his shirt from his shoulders when her body convulsed, and she let out a little cry of anguish as wave upon wave of uncontrollable feeling swept over her. Her body throbbed around his fingers, soaking him with her heat, and he bent his head and covered her lips with his.

When she was capable of coherent thought again, Kate gazed at him with indignant eyes. 'That wasn't fair.'

'What wasn't fair?'

She moved her head from side to side, reaching for her sweatpants, trying to drag them up her legs. 'You—you didn't—'

'I know.' He prevented her from covering herself with very little effort. He shrugged. 'I don't have any protection. Besides, I wasn't sure you'd want—'

'Well, I did. I do,' she told him hotly. And, realising she had to prove it, she wriggled into a sitting position and reached for his belt. 'Take your clothes off.'

Alex's eyes darkened. 'What if someone comes—?'

'I've told you! My mother and Joanne won't be back for hours!' she exclaimed fiercely. 'Go on. I mean it. Take your clothes off.'

'All of them?' he asked mockingly, and she struggled onto her knees, kicking off her own sweatpants in the process.

'Yes,' she said huskily. 'I want to see you too.'

She thought he wasn't going to obey her, but she could see the pressure of his arousal swelling against his zip, and with a temerity she hadn't known she possessed she covered it with her hand.

His reaction was violent, and, holding her gaze with his, he unbuckled his belt and opened his zip. Beneath silk boxers, his thickness thrust into her hand, but he held her away from him while he disposed of the rest of his clothes.

'Don't,' he said hoarsely, and she could see how close to losing control he was.

It was then that she realised she was still wearing the top of her suit, and, peeling it off, she subsided against the cushions again. This time, Alex stretched his length beside her, and his mouth moved down her throat to her breasts. Although she was sure he was impatient to satisfy his own needs, he took the time to suckle each hard nipple, and she could feel herself getting aroused again by the hot hunger of his lips and teeth.

She almost stopped breathing altogether when he buried his face in the curls between her legs. But, apparently, there were limits to even his control, and when he moved over her again he nudged her legs apart.

She raised her knees as he knelt between them, and then he was pushing into her moist passage and her muscles were stretching, stretching to accommodate his length.

She ached at the unaccustomed invasion. It was so long since she'd been with a man, but it was heavenly, too, feeling Alex as a part of her at last. She wanted to wind her legs and arms around him, and keep him there inside her, but already other needs were demanding satisfaction.

'You're beautiful,' he muttered unsteadily, looking down at where their bodies were joined, and she uttered a quivery sigh.

'So are you,' she told him, and when he put his hand beneath her bottom and lifted her against him she eagerly wound her legs about his waist.

It was all over much too quickly. Almost as soon as Alex began to move, thrusting himself against her, her senses spun wildly out of control. And by the time he was shuddering with his own release rippling spasms of ecstasy were taking her up and up, ever higher, penetrating the very core of her being and tilting her into space…

CHAPTER TEN

ALEX drove back to Jamaica Hill feeling better than he'd felt in years. Maybe better than he'd ever felt before, he conceded ruefully, aware that he'd never been with a woman who responded so delightfully to his every touch.

And he'd wanted to touch her, he acknowledged now, right from the very first moment he'd seen her standing talking to Sam Guthrie. He'd known even then she was provocation, in tight leggings and a tweed jacket, and he mocked himself for the instantaneous way he'd responded to her appeal.

But, in the event, it had turned out that she had wanted him too, and in the aftermath of this evening's lovemaking she had admitted it. Indeed, they'd spent so long exploring one another's attraction that they had barely had time to get dressed again before her mother and Joanne had got back from Bath. That would have been something for the tabloids, he thought dryly. A picture of him and Kate cavorting on the sofa in her living room would just about finish him off.

An exaggeration, perhaps, but there was no doubt that the stables' recovery was a fragile thing at best, and another scurrilous piece of journalism was exactly what Conrad Wyatt needed to persuade a judge that he was totally amoral, and therefore no fit guardian for his daughter.

But, thankfully, that hadn't happened. Indeed, when Kate's daughter had found that he'd spent the evening with her mother she'd been gratifyingly positive about the whole affair.

'I knew it was your Range Rover that was parked downstairs!' Joanne had exclaimed, turning triumphantly to her grandmother. 'Didn't I say so, Nan?'

'You may have done so.'

Mrs Ross had been slightly less enthusiastic about his appearance, but Alex decided that was understandable. She hardly knew him, after all, and it was too soon to expect her to welcome him with open arms.

Too soon?

Alex frowned as he swung into the gates of Jamaica Hill. What did he mean by that? He surely wasn't seriously considering a permanent relationship on the basis of a couple of hours of good sex.

And that was all it had been, he assured himself firmly. Okay, it had been incredible sex, and Kate was every bit as desirable to him now as she had been earlier in the evening. But he was too old to start looking for constancy between a woman's legs. If his experiences with Pam had taught him anything it was that nothing was ever that simple.

But he liked Kate; he enjoyed her company. And, what was equally important, Rachel liked her, too. Despite the lateness of the hour, he'd taken the opportunity to ask Joanne if she'd like to come down to the stables some time when his daughter was there, and she'd been more than willing to accept his invitation. Indeed, he'd have gone so far as to say that Joanne had suspected that something had been going on between him and her mother, and her mischievous smile had not been entirely unbiased.

Which might be a reason for him to steer clear of Kate in future, he reflected dourly, his mood changing when, after leaving the Range Rover on the forecourt, he let himself into the house. He didn't want to give either of them the wrong impression, but when he thought of the consequences of not seeing Kate again he dismissed the alternative out of hand. He wanted to see her again; he intended to see her again; and, however reckless it might seem, he was prepared to take the risk.

Nevertheless, after he'd showered and slipped naked between the cool sheets on his bed, he determined not to take any further risks so far as unprotected sex was concerned. Kate had assured him she was unlikely to get pregnant at this particular time of the month, but there was always the danger that she could.

He groaned. God, why did the prospect of her having his baby not fill him with the dismay it should? Why did the very idea of his child swelling her stomach tighten his own? It was crazy but he wanted to make love to her again, sex against sex, skin against skin…

Despite his intentions to the contrary, he didn't see Kate again for a couple of days.

An owner, someone he'd dealt with for a number of years, and who had stuck with him throughout all the publicity surrounding Pamela's death, had phoned from the north of England. The man, who'd been attending a horse sale at a stud near York, had wanted Alex's opinion on a mare he'd seen there. He'd asked if there was any chance of Alex's driving north to join him, bringing a horse-box, if possible, to transport the animal back to Jamaica Hill should the sale go through.

It meant being away overnight and in other circumstances Alex might have asked Ted Lowes to go in his place. But the owner was a good friend, and a good customer, and he wasn't in the habit of asking for favours. In consequence, Alex felt obliged to go himself.

He considered ringing Kate before he left King's Montford, to explain where he was going and when he hoped to be back. But he didn't. He decided it might do them both good to have a breathing space before they saw one another again. It was probably better if he tried to cool it. Despite the warnings he'd given himself the night before, he was still far too eager to continue the affair.

Yet, as soon as he hit the M1, he started wishing he'd ignored his conscience. Kate was bound to wonder why he'd left town the morning after he'd visited the flat. So long as she didn't think he was avoiding her, he brooded irritably. Could he ring her from his hotel? What excuse could he give if her mother answered the phone?

In the event, he decided against doing anything so reckless. Guthrie would tell her where he was, he assured himself. Sam would explain the circumstances and he'd be back the following afternoon. He had to concentrate on his job, and on the fact that his solicitor was presently negotiating for him to have Rachel to stay for a whole weekend. His relationship with Kate—if they had a relationship—must not be allowed to interfere with his daughter's future.

Which was all very well. And, while he was discussing breeding schedules and blood lines, and deciding how much the mare he'd come to see was worth, he was almost able to convince himself he meant it. But, despite his concern for Rachel, he couldn't get Kate out of his thoughts, and in consequence he slept badly and awoke the next morning feeling heavy-eyed and depressed.

It didn't help that it was a lousy day, heavy rain making all driving a hazard. It was particularly frustrating to be driving a horse-box, which meant he had to limit his speed. He was eager to get back to King's Montford, but the weather slowed him down considerably. That, and the fact that an articulated wagon had jackknifed on the motorway, leaving a tailback of traffic five miles long.

He got soaked when he stopped to give the mare a breather, but he got himself a strong cup of coffee at the same time and that helped his headache a bit. But it was well into the evening before he reached his destination, and his head was throbbing so badly he felt physically sick.

Finding the gates to Jamaica Hill closed was another source of irritation. For God's sake, he thought, he'd told Ted Lowes he was driving back today. Why on earth would he close the gates?

It meant him getting out into the rain again to open them, and after getting back into the cab he drove straight down to the stables. Finding his head groom standing in the open doorway of the office, he was tempted to demand an explanation, but the man was looking edgy and Alex guessed he'd remembered what he'd done.

Instead, after exchanging the briefest of formalities, Alex
grabbed his overcoat from the cab, and stamped across the
paddock to the house. He was tired and not in the best of
tempers. It was too late to contact Kate tonight and that was
what was really bugging his mood.

He went straight into the library, and he was helping himself to a can of Coke when his housekeeper appeared. 'Och,
thank God you're back!' she exclaimed, and he noticed how
anxious she was looking. 'Could ye not have warned me ye'd
be so late?'

It was a sign of her agitation that she'd relapsed into the
dialect of her childhood, and Alex knew a moment's sympathy before his own resentment kicked in. 'I'm sorry,' he
muttered. 'I didn't know I was under curfew. You try driving
nearly three hundred miles in the pouring rain and see how
accurate your timekeeping is.'

Mrs Muir twisted her hands together. 'You don't know,
do you?' she cried. 'Ted didn't tell you that the police have
been here?'

'The police!' Alex slammed down the can and turned to
the old woman in disbelief. Then, in a whisper, he said, 'My
God, something's happened to Rachel! Just tell me: has she
had an accident, or what?'

'There's nothing wrong with Rachel—as far as I know,'
Mrs Muir assured him hurriedly. 'The police came to interview you, Mr Kellerman.' She licked her lips rather nervously. 'They say that Mrs Sawyer has gone missing. No
one's seen her since she left Jamaica Hill.'

'Alicia?' Alex blinked. 'They wanted to ask me about
Alicia?' He relaxed a little. 'What does Alicia's disappearance have to do with me?'

'You may well ask.' The housekeeper grimaced. 'I told
them we knew nothing about it. But I think they think they've
found some evidence that connects with her disappearance.
They asked when I'd last seen her.' She sniffed. 'I can't be
sure, but I think they suspect something terrible has happened
to her.'

Alex felt as if all the air in his lungs had been expelled in a rush and he couldn't seem to take in any more. Alicia, missing? He couldn't believe it, and he sank into the nearest chair, resting his arms on his spread thighs and dropping his head into his hands.

'Are you all right, Mr Kellerman?'

Mrs Muir was obviously anxious about him, and, bustling across to the refrigerated cabinet, she opened a bottle of mineral water and poured some into a glass.

'Drink this,' she said, tugging his arm and pushing the glass into his hand. 'Don't worry. They won't be back until tomorrow morning. I told them I didn't know what time you'd be home tonight.'

'Thanks.'

Alex took the glass and drank thirstily from it, the chilled water giving some relief to his pounding head. But, for God's sake, he thought, he'd hoped he was through with police interviews. Alicia couldn't be dead. And if she was, why the hell were they pointing the finger at him?

Of course, she had worked for him, and thanks to Conrad Wyatt there were still rumours circulating about the circumstances surrounding Pamela's death. Hell, the old man would be clapping his hands in delight if this was made public. How was he ever going to get Rachel back if this became another *cause célèbre*?

'You're going to have to tell them,' said Mrs Muir suddenly, and his head swung up to face her.

'Tell them what?' he demanded harshly. 'You don't think I had anything to do with Alicia's disappearance, do you?'

'Of course not.' The old housekeeper was impatient. 'You forget: I know how that woman used to pursue you. It was because you'd have nothing to do with her that she walked out.'

'Who's going to believe that now?'

'Well, I do.' Mrs Muir put her hand on his shoulder and squeezed gently. 'I mean, you're going to have to tell them about Jim,' she declared steadily. 'You've protected us both for far too long, and I can't let you go on destroying your-self.'

'Oh, Agnes…' Alex tipped back his head and flexed his shoulders wearily. 'I don't think the police will believe any-thing I say at this point in time. Let's hope they find Alicia, or that she hears what's going on and comes forward herself. Until that happens, it looks like I'm their prime suspect.'

'But it's not fair.'

'No.' Alex conceded the point, getting to his feet and set-ting the empty glass on the corner of his desk. 'Did they say what this new evidence was, or who'd drawn their attention to it? Do you think it's possible that Pam's father's in-volved?'

'I don't know.' Mrs Muir bent her head. 'But there's some-thing else I haven't told you, Mr Kellerman.'

'What?' Alex gazed at her, narrow-eyed. 'Don't tell me they've found a body as well?'

'No.' The housekeeper pursed her lips. 'But they told me her husband—'

'Henry Sawyer?'

'Yes. He apparently reported her missing.'

'So?'

'Well—they said he'd used the services of a private in-vestigator here in town to corroborate his suspicions.'

'So?' Alex shook his head. 'I didn't even know there was a private detective agency in King's Montford.' And then, seeing the old woman's expression, he asked, 'Are you say-ing that I've spoken to this—investigator myself?'

'Oh, yes.' Mrs Muir backed up a bit, as if she feared an explosion. 'She—she's been working here for the past three weeks, Mr Kellerman. I'm afraid—I'm afraid it's Mrs Hughes.'

Alex eventually crawled into bed but he didn't sleep. In fact, he didn't know how he restrained himself from getting back into the car and driving to Milner Court to confront Kate, late as it was. Every nerve in his body was crying out for retribution, for the chance to tell her what a deceitful bitch he thought she was.

Yet it was hard to accept that what Mrs Muir had said was gospel. Had Kate really tricked him, and tantalised him, and reduced him to an emotional wreck, just to satisfy some perverted belief of Henry Sawyer's that he was responsible for his wife's disappearance? That was what hurt the most—the fact that she'd taken some other man's word as to his character. He'd put his daughter's life on hold while he made love to a woman who'd been sent to destroy him.

Which meant everything they'd shared had been a mockery. She'd probably encouraged his interest in the hope of hearing some incriminatory pillow talk from him. His fist slammed into his pillow. God, did she really suspect that he was capable of murder? And if so, hadn't she taken an enormous risk by letting him into her flat when she was alone?

He didn't know and he tried to tell himself he didn't care when he hauled himself out of bed the following morning. Dammit, he had more to worry about than the circumstances behind why he'd got laid. The police were coming back this morning to interview him, and, remembering their diligence two years ago, he doubted they'd care whether he'd had breakfast or not.

Not that he wanted anything to eat, he thought, his stomach churning nauseously. Despite the fact that he hadn't had a decent meal since dinner two nights ago, Alex couldn't face the thought of food. Caffeine was what he needed, and much against Mrs Muir's advice he drank several cups of strong black coffee, so that by the time the detective inspector and his sidekick were shown into the library he felt as hyper as an addict on crack.

The interview was fairly short. Detective Inspector Rivers, a dapper individual wearing a slightly shiny suit, seemed very much concerned with his own importance, and he looked around the library as he came in, as if assessing how much Alex might have gained from his late wife's death. He hadn't been on that case, but that didn't matter. Alex guessed he'd have read through the files before coming here.

The inspector's first question was predictable. He asked when Alex had last seen Alicia Sawyer, and then, under what circumstances had she left his employ? Speaking quietly, Alex explained that Mrs Sawyer had not found the work to her liking and that, after a short period, she'd decided to leave.

'It was Mrs Sawyer's decision to terminate her employment, was it, sir?' The inspector's question was polite enough, but Alex thought he could hear the veiled insolence in his voice.

'No, it was mine,' he said, refusing to compromise about Alicia's departure. 'We—had a difference of opinion, and she walked out.'

'And when did this row take place, sir?'

'It wasn't a row.' Alex balled his fists, and in his ear he could hear Kate telling him to lighten up. She'd implied he was his own worst enemy, and it was probably true. He showed his real feelings too well.

'But you admit you did have an argument, Mr Kellerman,' suggested the detective constable, only to fall silent again when his superior sent him a glowering look.

'We had a difference of opinion,' Alex repeated, breathing deeply. 'I've no idea where she went after she left here.'

'She left no forwarding address?'

'No.'

'She had no friends here who might know where she's gone?'

'You'd have to ask the men,' said Alex, mentally dreading the thought of another investigation into his life. 'If that's all—er—Sergeant—'

'It's not. And it's *Detective Inspector* Rivers, Mr Kellerman.' The dour little man scowled, and Alex hoped he wouldn't regret the urge to put him down. 'There's been another development; you might say, a rather serious development, Mr Kellerman. Mrs Sawyer's suitcases have been found. At the bottom of a rubbish skip in town.'

Alex could feel the colour draining out of his face. 'I see,' he said, and he knew his voice was strained. But, for God's sake, Alicia's suitcases in a rubbish tip! 'Who—who found them?' he asked, hoping he didn't sound as guilty as he felt.

'Some children,' replied Rivers, watching him closely. 'Do you have any idea how the suitcases got into the tip, Mr Kellerman?'

'Of course not.' Alex was appalled. But he was aware that they didn't believe him. Yet how was he supposed to act when he was apparently the last person to see her—what? Alive?

'I understand you've been away.'

Rivers was speaking again, and Alex struggled to answer him. 'That's right,' he said, wondering if they really suspected he'd been disposing of the body. 'Um—I've been in York,' he added. 'With one of my owners. We bought a horse: an Arabian. I brought it back to Jamaica Hill.'

'In a horse-box, Mr Kellerman?'

'Of course.' Alex could only guess what he was thinking.

'I see.' Rivers drew himself up to his full height and attempted to look Alex in the face. 'I assume this—owner—can confirm your whereabouts for the past two days?'

'If necessary.' Alex's jaw clamped at the prospect of having to ask someone else to vouch that he was telling the truth. 'Now, will that be all? I do have quite a lot of work to catch up on.'

'So long as you don't go away again, sir,' said Detective Inspector Rivers crisply. 'At the moment we're trying to find out how long the suitcases have been in the skip, so we may need to speak to you again.'

'I didn't put them there,' said Alex, forcing himself not to react to the inspector's attitude. 'But I'll be here.' He took another steadying breath. 'I'm sorry I couldn't be of any more help.'

Alex waited until Mrs Muir had shown the two men out

before flinging himself into the leather chair behind his desk. 'Bastard,' he muttered harshly, levelling his gaze on the half-full decanter of Scotch residing on the top of the cabinet at the other side of the room. Who in hell would have put Alicia's suitcases in the rubbish skip? Remembering how particular she'd been about her appearance, he couldn't believe she'd do something like that herself.

Then who?

And why?

One name sprang into his mind instantly. But would his father-in-law go as far as to hire a private detective to find a woman he knew only by reputation? It didn't make sense. When he'd met Kate at Wyvern Hall, there'd been no recognition there. Unless they were both better actors than he was giving them credit for. But Kate had defended him to Conrad. Would she have done that if the old man was paying her fee?

Kate...

The thought of what she'd done to him was a painful torment. The Scotch looked even more of a temptation with her on his mind. It would be so easy to give in, so easy to pour himself a glass of the rich dark malt and let the alcohol dull his senses. Dear God, was it only forty-eight hours ago that he'd begun to believe he might have a future, after all?

'They've gone.' Mrs Muir stood in the open doorway gazing anxiously at him. 'Well? Are you going to tell me what they had to say?'

Alex's shoulders slumped. 'They've found Alicia's belongings; her suitcases. Someone has dumped them in a rubbish skip in town.'

'What?' Mrs Muir looked totally staggered. 'So that's why they've started an investigation. Did Mr Sawyer find them? Is that why he—?'

'Some children apparently found them,' Alex interrupted her heavily. 'As far as I know, they don't know how long they may have been lying there. They probably think I dumped them after I'd got rid of her body.'

Mrs Muir gasped in horror. 'They're surely not accusing you of having anything to do with her disappearance?'

'Well, not yet,' said Alex flatly. 'Give them time.'

'But—that's ridiculous.' Mrs Muir was angry. 'What about her husband? She always said he resented you giving her a room here. Isn't it far more likely that he's involved?'

'She also said that he used to beat her,' Alex reminded her. 'And we soon found out that that wasn't true.' He grimaced. 'It's not up to me to accuse anyone else of being involved. I've had enough of that myself.'

'But it was Mr Sawyer who hired—well, the private detective, wasn't it?'

'Was it?'

Mrs Muir frowned. 'You're not thinking that Mrs Hughes herself—'

'No.' Alex scowled at the mention of Kate's name, and continued harshly, 'I mean Wyatt. Perhaps I'm getting too close to persuading the authorities that Rachel belongs with me, and this is his way of scaring them off.'

'By getting rid of Mrs Sawyer?'

Mrs Muir looked alarmed now, and Alex pulled a wry face. 'No,' he said impatiently. 'By using her disappearance to implicate me. Perhaps those weren't her suitcases at all. If Henry Sawyer identified them they could be anybody's.'

'Oh, yes, I see.' Mrs Muir nodded. 'So you think they might have put her name inside?'

'How else were they able to identify them?' asked Alex practically. He glanced at his watch. 'It's time I found out. Mrs Hughes should be arriving soon.'

'Oh, Mr Kellerman, is that wise?' Mrs Muir gazed at him dubiously. 'She may not come in, of course, but I'd stay away from that young woman if I were you.'

'But you're not me, Mrs Muir,' declared Alex, his eyes glittering malevolently. He cast one last look at the Scotch, and got to his feet. 'Get rid of that whisky, will you? I have the feeling I'm going to need all my faculties about me to survive the next few days.'

CHAPTER ELEVEN

KATE wondered why she'd allowed Joanne to accompany her to the stables that morning. She knew Alex was due back from York today, and he obviously wouldn't be expecting her to have taken him up on his offer so soon. Apart from anything else, he would probably be too busy to come down to the yard, and she'd be left with the awkward task of having to explain his invitation to Mr Guthrie.

Joanne, of course, was delighted. Apart from the fact that it was a special treat, she'd have done anything if it meant getting out of the flat. And she had worked reasonably well at the schoolwork Mr Coulthard had had her teachers send home for her. Kate supposed she deserved the break. She just wished she'd waited until she'd spoken to Alex again.

But, if she was honest, that was one of the reasons why she'd given in to Joanne's pleading. She hadn't seen Alex since the night before he went to York, and the truth was, she was half afraid he might have regretted what had happened at the flat. She had been the instigator, after all, however eager Alex might have been to play along with her. What if he'd never intended things to go that far? What if he really had just come to speak to Joanne, as he'd said?

And, in all honesty, she was appalled at her own conduct. She'd never been the kind of woman to do anything more than indulge in a light flirtation with a man. Apart from Sean, her experience with men was limited. Which made what she'd done so totally out of character for her.

And, during the last couple of days, she'd struggled to find a reason for her wanton behaviour. Just remembering how she'd thrown herself at Alex could still bring a film of sweat to her brow. But she'd never known what it was like to actually desire a man before; to need his touch so badly that she wanted to get under his skin.

Instead of which, he'd got under hers, she acknowledged ruefully, a pulse in the pit of her stomach reminding her of the restless nights she'd spent since he went away. If she allowed herself to think of him at all, she got an actual ache between her legs, and she'd taken so many cold showers, her mother was beginning to think she'd got a fever.

And she had, she admitted tensely as they approached the entrance to Jamaica Hill. But it wasn't a fever that she could cure with drugs. She'd fallen in love with Alex Kellerman. He was the fever in her blood. And, as soon as they were alone together, she was going to tell him the truth.

Which was another reason why she'd brought Joanne along this morning. She fully expected him to be furious with her when she told him she was a private investigator, but she hoped he might be more tolerant if her daughter was there. She'd asked Susie to make up the account, severing her connection with Henry Sawyer, and if Alex fired her, as she expected he would, she'd have to go back to investigating insurance claims and try to forget him.

There were some people gathered outside the gates to the estate. The gates were closed, which was unusual, but she didn't recognise the two men and one woman who were hanging about outside. She slowed, feeling a surge of apprehension when she noticed that two of them were carrying cameras, and when Joanne turned a puzzled look in her direction she said, 'You get out and open the gates, Jo. And don't answer any questions, do you hear?'

But when Joanne got out, leaving the door of the car open, it was Kate who had to suffer an onslaught of questions about who she was and what she was doing there. 'You work for Alex Kellerman, right?' demanded the woman pushily. 'What's your opinion about Mrs Sawyer's suitcases turning up?'

Kate blanched, but although she was dying to ask what the woman meant she kept her mouth shut. But, 'Mrs

Sawyer's suitcases'? she thought, shaking her head confusedly. What on earth were they talking about? And where had the cases been found?

Surely not here!

She leant across and slammed the door, before the woman could push into the car, and then drove through the gates when Joanne opened them. Joanne closed the gates again, ignoring the questions they threw at her now, and then scrambled into the car with an anxious look on her face.

'What's going on, Mum?'

'I wish I knew.' But Kate was feeling more and more uneasy. If it was true that they'd found Alicia's belongings, then obviously Alex must have been interviewed when he got back from York. Why else would the reporters—for that was what they were—be camping on his doorstep? She swallowed. Oh, God, what else might he have found out?

She half expected his car to be standing in the yard, but it wasn't. And no one gave her and Joanne any suspicious looks as she parked her car. Indeed, the work of the stables seemed to be proceeding as normal, were it not for a certain tension in the air.

Which probably only she was conscious of, she told herself impatiently as she and Joanne crossed the yard and went into her office. Even the electric fire was glowing cheerfully, and the mail was piled on her desk, as usual, waiting for her attention.

The phone rang before she had had time to check whether Mr Guthrie was in his office. To her alarm, it was Susie, and she knew something must have happened because her assistant had been warned never to contact her here.

'What is it?' she asked, keeping a wary eye on her daughter as she spoke. She knew Joanne must be curious about what was going on, but she couldn't discuss Alex's affairs with her.

'The police have been here!' exclaimed Susie, her voice high and agitated. 'They wanted to see you, and I had to tell them where I thought you were.'

'What, here?' Kate pressed a hand to her chest where her heart was beating erratically.

'That's right.' Susie was distraught. 'There was nothing else I could do. I couldn't tell lies.'

'No.' Kate conceded the point, her mind racing madly. Were the police already here? she wondered. Dear God, Alex would blow his top if he found out why they wanted to see her. She had to try and speak to him before they arrived, but that wasn't going to be easy. She had no way of knowing whether he intended to come down to the yard today.

'They've found that woman's luggage,' continued Susie, interrupting her abstraction. 'Some children found two suit-cases in a skip.'

'A skip!' Kate was horrified. 'My God, have they found a body?'

'Not yet,' said a cold, sardonic voice behind her, and she swung round to find Alex propped in the open doorway of Mr Guthrie's office. 'But I'm sure they think it's just a matter of time.'

Kate's jaw sagged. Her mouth opened and closed as she struggled with the dilemma of how to answer Alex with Susie's faintly hysterical voice still chattering in her ear.

But, in the event, Joanne saved the situation for her. 'Hello, Mr Kellerman,' she greeted him brightly. 'I hope you don't mind. Mum said it would probably be all right if I came to the stables today.' She gestured towards her mother. 'Mum—Mum's just speaking to—to a friend—'

'Is she?' Kate told Susie she would ring her back, and replaced the receiver before he spoke again. 'Well—why don't you go and have a look around while I have a few words with your mother?' He pointed through the window. 'See that young man there: that's Billy Roach, one of the apprentices. If you tell him who you are, he'll give you a guided tour.'

Joanne hesitated, looking half anxiously at her mother. 'Will you—will that be all right, Mum?' she asked, and Kate guessed she'd picked up on the atmosphere between her and Alex, which she was sure you could have cut with a knife.

'Yes,' she said, her throat tight. 'You'll like Billy. He's a nice boy. He's always been very friendly with me.'

'And what could be a higher recommendation?' asked Alex sarcastically. He turned back into Guthrie's office. 'Will you come in here, Mrs Hughes?'

'Mum—'

Joanne still looked troubled, but Kate knew she couldn't let her daughter get involved in her problems. 'Go on,' she said. 'You'll enjoy yourself.'

'But will you be all right?'

Joanne's nod towards the inner office was uneasy. 'I'll be fine,' Kate assured her firmly, wishing she felt as confident as she sounded.

With Joanne gone, Kate walked apprehensively to the open doorway, glancing in to find Alex was standing staring out of the window as before. 'Sit down,' he said, and this time she obeyed him. Maybe her stomach would stop turning cart-wheels if she took the weight off her legs.

The silence that followed was ominous, and Kate's stomach started churning all over again. Oh, God, she thought, why couldn't she think of something to say in her own defence? She'd been doing a job, earning a living, just like anyone else.

'Who hired you?'

Alex's question came as something of an anticlimax. She'd expected him to accuse her of deceiving him, of using his apparent attraction towards her for her own ends. But perhaps that hadn't been as important to him as it had been to her. His pride was hurt, but probably nothing else.

'Henry—Henry Sawyer,' she said now, realising she was breaking a confidence, and he swung round to face her with malevolent eyes.

'You expect me to believe that?' he snarled, and she quickly revised her estimates of his emotions. Alex was angry, and she felt a twinge of fear as he stalked round the desk towards her.

'It's the truth,' she got out quickly, trying not to let him see her feelings. 'He told me his wife had disappeared. I thought it would be a fairly straightforward investigation.'

'Investigation!' Alex made the word sound dirty. 'Well, forgive me for sounding sceptical, but you don't seem to have done a great deal to earn your fee. I assume this man—Sawyer—did pay you? I always wondered how you managed to live on what you earned here.'

Kate sighed. 'It's a job, Al—Mr Kellerman. And, yes, he paid me.'

'Not a lot, I trust,' said Alex harshly. 'You don't appear to have succeeded in your quest.'

'No.' Kate's lips tightened. 'I—I told Mr Sawyer I had no idea where his wife went after she left here. But I made all the usual enquiries. I earned my money, Mr Kellerman.'

'How?' Alex put one hand on either arm of her chair now and thrust his face towards her. 'By seducing your client's suspect, I assume.'

'No.' Kate's face burned, but his means of belittling her caught her on the raw. 'I earn a hundred pounds a day, plus expenses. Someone must think I do a decent job.'

Alex released the chair and stepped back, his expression staggered. 'You're saying Sawyer paid you that kind of money to look for his wife?'

'Yes.' Kate swallowed. 'It's the going rate at the moment. I explained that to him before I took the job.'

Alex's dark brows descended. 'And has he paid you?'

'That's my business—' she began, but the fury in his face caused her to break off. 'All right, yes,' she conceded. 'I always ask for an advance payment. Otherwise a client might not want to pay if—if—'

'If you foul up?' Alex was disparaging. Then he said, 'So tell me, where would Sawyer find—what? A thousand pounds?—when he's out of a job?'

Kate decided not to admit how much Henry Sawyer had

paid her. Then, as her brain kicked into gear, she asked, 'What are you saying? That you think someone else put Sawyer up to it? Someone else gave him the cash?'

Alex raked back his hair with an angry hand. 'What do you think?' he snapped. Then, his lips twisting, he added, 'But I forgot: you're in on this, too. You probably know damn well who financed this little conspiracy. But I have to give it to you—you'd never have guessed it from the way you stood up to him last week.'

Kate pushed herself up from her chair. 'You're saying you think—your father-in-law is behind it?'

'Who else?' Alex gave her a savage look. 'Well, he certainly knew how to bait his hook!'

'Me?' Kate was indignant. 'I had nothing to do with him. I was getting nowhere with the investigation and Sawyer—Sawyer brought the advertisement for this job to me and suggested I apply.'

'Why?'

'Why?' Kate licked her lips before replying. 'Well, his original claim was that you and she had had an affair.'

'An affair?'

'Yes.' Kate tried to ignore his stunned expression and continued doggedly, 'He said that he and his wife were happy until she came to work for you.'

Alex shook his head. 'And you believed him, I suppose.'

'I had no reason not to.' Kate hesitated. 'Well, not then. You were a stranger to me.'

'A stranger who everyone suspected of murdering his wife,' put in Alex bitterly. 'Oh, I bet you and Sawyer had some cosy discussions about what went on at Jamaica Hill.'

'That's not true.' Kate knew she couldn't let him go on thinking that. 'As a matter of fact, I didn't tell him anything about you at all. That—that's probably why he was threatening to ask for his money back.' She took a breath. 'You have to believe me. I was going to withdraw from the investigation today.'

Alex snorted. 'You expect me to believe that?'

'It's true.' She touched his sleeve. 'I was hoping you might forgive me. After—after what happened between us—'

'The good sex, you mean?' asked Alex crudely, moving so that her arm fell to her side. 'Please, don't perjure yourself on my account. Remember, you've only my word that I didn't have an affair with Alicia. Perhaps I did. Perhaps I killed her as well.' He caught her chin with cruel fingers, and bent to assault her mouth with a hard, punishing kiss. 'Face it, Kate, you're never going to find out the truth!'

'Oh, I think she will.' The cool, invasive voice caused Alex to release her abruptly, but she thought the oath he uttered was only audible to her. 'We meet again, Mr Kellerman,' the hateful voice continued. 'Rather sooner than I had anticipated. But, don't worry, on this occasion I've come to interview Mrs Hughes.'

'I'm sure nothing you did could worry me, Inspector,' said Alex insolently, and Kate groaned inwardly at the dangerous light in his eyes. 'And, if you'll excuse me, I, too, have matters to attend to.' He looked at Kate. 'Places to go, people to see.'

A shadow appeared in the office doorway as Kate was clearing her desk. For a moment she thought—*hoped*—that it might be Alex, that he might have thought better of his accusations and decided to listen to what she had to say. She couldn't believe—wouldn't believe—that he could dismiss what had happened between them so derisively. He was angry, with good reason, but he had to know that she believed in him.

She was so afraid he was going to do something stupid, like going to see Conrad Wyatt, and confronting him with his suspicions about Alicia's disappearance. God knew, Wyatt had done his best to provoke his anger when he'd gone to pick up his daughter last week. In the present situation, Alex couldn't afford to give the police a reason to believe he was a violent man.

But it wasn't Alex, she saw at once, her heart sinking. It

was Mrs Sheridan, the woman who owned the estate that adjoined Jamaica Hill. The woman who Alex had said was a good friend—though she didn't look particularly friendly at the moment. Had she heard why Kate had been working at the stables? Had she come to add her accusations to the rest?

'If you're looking for Mr Kellerman, he's not here, Mrs Sheridan,' said Kate bluntly, deciding there was no point in pretending she didn't know who she was.

'I know.' Lacey came into the office and closed the door, leaning back against it. 'It was you I wanted to speak to, Mrs—Hughes, isn't it? Alex is out at present. I don't think Mrs Muir knows when he'll be back.'

Alex was out!

Kate wanted to groan with frustration. Had he gone to Wyvern Hall? Oh, God, she fretted, if he had she should have gone with him. But she knew he'd never have allowed her to do it, even if she'd begged him to take her along.

Meanwhile, Lacey was looking round the office. She was an attractive woman, Kate thought reluctantly, though obviously much older than she'd like everyone to believe. Her shoulder-length bob was expertly tinted, and the vee of her suit jacket was cut low enough to give a tantalising glimpse of her impressive cleavage.

'Do I take it you're leaving?' Lacey asked, nodding towards the box of personal belongings the other woman had set on the desk, and Kate sighed impatiently.

'That's right,' she said, bending over the box again, determined not to discuss the terms of her employment with Lacey. 'If you'd like to tell me what you want? As you can see, I am rather busy right now.'

'I gather Alex has fired you?'

'Not exactly.' But Kate could feel the hot colour entering her cheeks at Lacey's sardonic words.

'But you are leaving,' Lacey pointed out. 'Are you saying that it's your decision? I find it hard to believe after what he told me last night.'

Kate lifted her head. She knew Lacey wanted her to ask what Alex had said about her, but she wouldn't give her the satisfaction of knowing she cared. 'Does it matter?' she asked instead, knowing it was a cop-out. 'Is that why you came, Mrs Sheridan? To make sure I left the premises?'

Lacey shook her head and straightened away from the door. 'No,' she said smoothly. 'I just wanted to give you a warning. If you care anything for Alex, you'll take my advice and stay out of his life.'

Kate did look at her now. 'Are you threatening me, Mrs Sheridan?' Her heart was thumping and there was a sense of unreality about this whole scene. For heaven's sake, Lacey Sheridan had to be nearer fifty than forty. Was she implying she had some emotional influence in Alex's life?

'No. Just warning you,' responded Lacey carelessly. 'Alex and I go back a long way, and I've no intention of allowing some trashy little secretary to come between us now. What I'm saying, Mrs Hughes, is that Alex and I are lovers.' She was so close to Kate now that Kate could smell the other woman's heavy perfume mingling with the heat of her body. 'I wouldn't want you to get the wrong idea.'

To Kate's relief, Joanne chose that moment to come bursting into the office. 'Hey, Mum!' she was exclaiming, her excitement evident in her voice. 'You'll never guess what Billy said—'

She broke off in some confusion when she saw her mother wasn't alone, and Lacey turned towards her with an irritated expression. 'Didn't anybody ever teach you to knock on doors before opening them?' she snapped.

Joanne seemed hesitant for a moment, but then she looked at her mother and saw Kate's strained face. She immediately adopted her most insolent attitude, and, placing her hands on her hips, she responded, 'No, they didn't. And this is Mr Kellerman's office, not yours. You've got no right to tell me what to do.'

It was almost lunchtime before Kate got to her office. Susie had already left to meet her current boyfriend, and Kate sank gratefully into the chair behind her desk. What a day! she thought. What a nightmare! The only bright spot was Joanne's rout of Lacey Sheridan.

Not that Kate hadn't reproved her daughter for it. But it had been so nice to have someone taking her side for a change. After the things Alex had said, the scathing way he had dismissed their relationship, she had felt raw and used, and hearing that woman, that flashy woman, telling her that she and Alex were lovers had been the final straw.

And she had had the nerve to call Kate a 'trashy secretary'. As if she looked as if she'd ever done an honest day's work in her life! Even the clothes she'd worn had been more suitable for a woman half her age. She was a sad and jealous woman and Kate was secretly glad that Joanne had pricked her bubble of conceit.

What had hurt most, though, was hearing Lacey declare that she and Alex had a relationship. It meant that what he'd scornfully described as 'good sex' had not been said in the heat of the moment. He'd meant every word.

Of course, Lacey had taken umbrage at Joanne's words, and walked out threatening to tell Alex what had been going on, but that could hardly matter in the circumstances. Kate wondered if she'd threatened Alicia Sawyer too, it might explain why the other woman had left Jamaica Hill so precipitately. Left without leaving a forwarding address.

And then there'd been that interview with Detective Inspector Rivers. She hadn't liked the man, or his questions, though she supposed he was just doing his job. Not that she could help him with his investigations. She could only reiterate what she'd told Alex himself. She'd been doing a job—and not very successfully. She hoped the inspector hadn't suspected she'd let her personal feelings get in the way of objectivity where Alicia's disappearance was concerned.

Alicia…

Kate sniffed. She wished she'd never heard of Alicia. If she hadn't, she'd never have met Alex Kellerman or got involved in his personal affairs. She found no comfort in the old saying that it was better to have loved and lost than never to have loved at all.

She frowned and, unlocking the drawer at the side of the desk, she drew out the folder that contained all the details of the case. Her notes were there, along with the accounts she'd kept of her interviews with Billy Roach and Mrs Muir, and the snapshot Henry Sawyer had given her of his wife.

She scowled at the smudgy picture, then, reaching into the drawer again, she pulled out her eye-glass. She thought its magnifying lens might give her a clearer image of the missing woman, and when she turned on the lamp over the desk Alicia's face came slowly into focus.

But the photograph was still blurry, giving more of an impression of her appearance than anything else. Her face was there, a very attractive face as she'd recognised originally, her cloud of blonde hair serving to soften her rather sharp features.

They were almost hostile features, thought Kate, wondering why she suddenly felt that that was important. She had the strangest feeling that she'd seen that face before. Well, she had. She grimaced impatiently. In the beginning, she'd studied it to distraction. Her mind was simply creating a memory of that.

Or was it?

She chewed on her lower lip. She was sure she'd seen that face, and recently. But where? And in what connection? It didn't make sense. She tried to think. Apart from the supermarket and the snack bar, when she'd been with Alex and his daughter, she'd hardly got a social life.

She blew out a breath. It was so frustrating. Not as frustrating as Alex's dealings with his in-laws, perhaps, but close. *His in-laws!* Kate's breath caught somewhere in her throat and she strove for air. God Almighty, she breathed, when she'd recovered, that was where she'd seen Alicia. It hadn't been Mrs Wyatt she'd glimpsed peering through the window at Wyvern Hall. As crazy as it seemed she was almost sure it had been *her*!

CHAPTER TWELVE

'THERE'S a lady to see you, Kate.' Susie stood blocking the doorway to her employer's office, glancing somewhat doubtfully over her shoulder. 'She says it's urgent,' she added. And then, in a stage whisper, 'She says her name's Mrs Muir.'

Mrs Muir!

Kate got abruptly to her feet. 'Um—show her in, Susie,' she said, ignoring the younger woman's efforts to mime her disapproval. 'Go on. She won't bite.'

Susie pulled a resigned face and turned back into the office behind her. 'Mrs Hughes will see you now,' she said, her offhand tone reminiscent of Joanne's. 'Go straight in.'

'Thank you.'

Mrs Muir's gentle brogue was unmistakable, and Kate found herself growing tense despite her confident words to Susie. She couldn't imagine what Alex's housekeeper could want with her.

Mrs Muir came into the office looking almost as nervous as Kate. 'Good morning, Mrs Hughes,' she said, holding out her hand for Kate to shake, just as if she were an ordinary client. 'It's so nice to see you again.'

'Is it?' Kate couldn't help the query, but happily Mrs Muir didn't seem to think it required an answer. Susie was still hovering, so Kate asked her if she'd bring them a tray of tea. 'I'm afraid the coffee is fairly unpalatable,' she added to her visitor as she sat down again.

Mrs Muir had already subsided into the chair opposite, and now she took the time to set her handbag on the floor beside her chair. 'It's a chilly day,' she said. 'Did you have a good Christmas? I expect your daughter enjoyed the celebrations.'

Kate took a deep breath. 'I'm sure you didn't come here to talk about Joanne, Mrs Muir,' she said politely. 'I'd appreciate it if you could tell me what you want.' She rustled the papers on her desk, which were actually bills, but her visitor wasn't to know that. 'I am rather busy…'

'Of course, of course.' Mrs Muir nodded her grey head understandingly. 'I'm sure your success in finding Mrs Sawyer must have brought you a lot of extra business. And I don't want to hold you up. Not at all. But I really felt I had to come and see you and tell you how much I appreciate what you've done for Mr Kellerman.'

Kate expelled the breath she'd hardly been aware she was holding, and then looked up with some relief when Susie came bustling in with the tray. 'I couldn't find any biscuits, Mrs Hughes, so I popped next door and bought a couple of doughnuts.' She pulled a face at Kate's expression. 'I know they're fattening, but you could do with putting on some weight.'

'Yes, you do appear to have lost a little weight, Mrs Hughes.' Mrs Muir took up Susie's comment after the girl had left the room.

'I've—not been feeling very hungry,' said Kate shortly, not wanting to get into personal matters. 'And there was no need for you to come and see me, Mrs Muir. Mr Kellerman's solicitor wrote me a very nice letter of acknowledgement when the police charged Conrad Wyatt with bribery, and conspiracy, and goodness knows what else.'

In fact, as far as Kate was concerned, finding Alicia Sawyer had been something of an anticlimax in the end. The police—especially Inspector Rivers—mightn't have wanted to believe her when she went to them with her suspicions, but Henry Sawyer had proved pathetically eager to co-operate when confronted by the law. It turned out he had worked for Conrad Wyatt years ago and had been dismissed for stealing. It had been a simple matter for Wyatt to remind him of that previous misdemeanour, and threaten him with legal proceedings if Sawyer refused to co-operate with him.

And, of course, he hadn't. Kate didn't know all the details, but somehow Wyatt had convinced both Sawyer and his estranged wife that it would be in their interests to assist him in his plans. She guessed a considerable amount of money must have changed hands. Remembering the two sums Henry Sawyer had given her, she doubted Wyatt would have quibbled over their fee. He'd obviously intended the rumours to spread about Alicia's disappearance just as they had when Pamela had died. Whether he'd ever intended to produce Alicia again was anyone's guess. Kate thought it more likely that when the job was done, and Alex was discredited—yet again—both Alicia and her husband would have been given passports to a more luxurious life overseas.

Kate found the fact that Henry Sawyer had once worked for the Wyatts particularly galling. It had never occurred to her to investigate him, or to connect Alicia's disappearance with Alex's in-laws until she'd examined the photograph again. She was sure an experienced investigator would have seen the connection immediately, particularly after Alex had expressed his suspicions about his father-in-law.

In the event, Conrad's arrest and subsequent charges had proved a nine-day wonder. The local papers had made a big thing of his attempted efforts to destroy his son-in-law's character, but the national papers had barely taken it up. An earthquake in South America and sabre-rattling in the Middle East had driven the story into virtual insignificance, and Kate had thought how unfair it was that nobody had bothered to point out that it had been Conrad Wyatt's allegations at the time of his daughter's death that had caused Alex so much grief.

'His solicitor!' Mrs Muir sounded dismayed now. 'Mr Kellerman had Julian Morris write to you on his behalf?'

'That's right.' Kate sighed and poured the tea. 'But don't look like that. It's not important.' Well, not to him, obviously. 'I wasn't working for Mr Kellerman, after all.'

'All the same...' Mrs Muir was clearly upset by this disclosure. 'I honestly thought he'd been to see you himself.'

'No.' Kate pushed a cup of tea towards Mrs Muir and

gestured towards the doughnuts, which were oozing jam all over the plate. 'Please, help yourself.'

Mrs Muir shook her head. 'The tea is fine,' she said, and Kate agreed with her. The sight of the sticky buns was making her feel sick. But then, most things made her feel sick at the moment, and she hoped when the nausea passed she'd feel more optimistic about the future.

Mrs Muir took a sip of her tea and then replaced the cup on its saucer. Then she bent and lifted her bag into her lap and took a clean white tissue out of a plastic case. She used the tissue to blow her nose before tucking it back into the bag.

The whole operation took several minutes, and Kate had the feeling that it was deliberate. She wondered if Mrs Muir had some other reason for coming here, other than to offer her appreciation of what she'd supposedly done for Alex. Did the housekeeper have a problem? Should she explain that after breaching Henry Sawyer's confidence—however justified it might have been—she intended closing the agency next week?

Mrs Muir took another sip of her tea, and Kate could feel her nerves tightening. It wasn't that she didn't like the little woman, but she wasn't in the mood for social chit-chat today. She was glad that the housekeeper apparently bore her no ill will for deceiving Alex into employing her, but she doubted she was ever likely to see her again.

'Um—' she began, hoping to prompt some kind of action, and Mrs Muir straightened in her seat and pressed her hands together in her lap.

'You'll be wondering what more I could possibly have to say,' she said, as if she could read Kate's mind. 'Well, I thought it was time I told—someone—the truth.'

'The truth?' Kate stared at her, her mind buzzing with half-formed ideas she didn't want to face.

'About Mrs Kellerman's death,' said Mrs Muir. 'It—wasn't an accident. Well, it was,' she hastened on confusingly, 'but that horse was deliberately put into the wrong stall.'

Kate felt the bile rise in the back of her throat. 'You mean, Alex—'

'Alex didn't do it.' Mrs Muir was vehement. 'It was my husband that did it, Mrs Hughes. My Jim.' She groped for the tissue again, and pressed it to her nose in obvious anguish. 'He wanted to hurt Pamela, you see, but he never expected she'd be killed.'

Kate was staggered. 'You mean, all this time—'

'Mr Kellerman wouldn't let Jim take the blame and maybe be arrested. He was ill, you see—Jim, I mean—he'd had a serious heart condition for years. Then when Philip—he was our son—when he committed suicide I think Jim went a little out of his mind.'

Kate hesitated. 'I believe your son was infatuated with Mrs Kellerman,' she ventured, and Mrs Muir didn't seem surprised to hear that she knew that, too.

'He was,' she said bitterly, 'but she was only playing with him. Even when she was expecting his child, she told him to get out of her life.'

Kate breathed deeply. 'And Alex—I mean, Mr Kellerman—told you not to say anything?'

'That's right. Jim confessed what he'd done to Mr Kellerman. Jim and I have worked here all our lives, and we've known Alex since he was a little boy. He and Philip used to play together when they were children. They were such good friends. I think that's why Pamela—Mrs Kellerman—tried to split them up.

'Anyway, as I say, Jim was sick, and we all knew he'd never survive being charged with such a serious offence. That was when Mr Kellerman said that we should say nothing. There was no proof that anyone had done it deliberately and I'm afraid we let Mr Kellerman take the blame.'

'Oh, Mrs Muir!'

'I know.' The housekeeper looked pale and defeated. 'And you're the first person, other than Mr Kellerman, that I've told the story to. At least Jim had several more months of comparative freedom. Though I don't think he ever forgave himself for the abuse Mr Kellerman had to suffer because of what he'd done.'

Or the anguish, thought Kate, with feeling. Alex had lost his wife and had been in danger of losing his livelihood too. Had he thought of Rachel, when he'd made that quixotic decision to shoulder the burden? Had he realised that Conrad Wyatt would use the situation to his own selfish ends?

She thought not. Which probably explained why he'd taken it so badly when the truth hit him. She thought in his position she might have felt like hitting the bottle, too. There'd been no turning back, even though Jim Muir had died only months after the accident. Kate sighed. Poor Alex. No wonder he'd become so bitter. He'd lost his wife and his child for a crime he didn't commit.

Kate shrugged her shoulders now. 'I don't know what to say.'

'Don't say anything.' Mrs Muir put her tissue away again and picked up her bag. 'I just didn't want you to go on believing that Mr Kellerman had killed his wife.'

'I never believed that.' As Kate said the words she realised she meant them.

'You didn't?' Mrs Muir looked confused. 'But I understood you'd told Mrs Sheridan that that was why you took the job.'

'No.' Kate was horrified. Lacey Sheridan had found a way to get her revenge, after all. 'I told Alex Alicia was missing and I agreed to try and find her. I had no preconceptions about how Pamela had died before I came to Jamaica Hill. And—and once I'd met Mr Kellerman I knew instinctively that he'd had nothing to do with his wife's death.'

'Do you mean that?' There were tears shining in Mrs Muir's eyes now, and Kate nodded.

'Of course I mean it. And—and I hope you'll tell Alex what I said. I—I know he and Lacey are very close, and he's

more likely to believe her than me, but I'd like to feel that
he won't think too badly of me when I'm gone.'

'When you're gone?'

Mrs Muir looked puzzled now, and Kate wished she hadn't
spoken so impulsively. 'Yes,' she said at last. 'I'm giving up
the agency and moving to London in a few weeks. I'm hoping to get a chance to work as a solicitor. I have a law degree,
but I've never been able to find a firm in King's Montford
willing to take me on.'

'And—and will your daughter be going with you?'

'Of course.' Kate forced a smile. 'And my mother, too.
She's not very keen at the moment, but it will be good for
Joanne to have a fresh start at a new school. She's been
having some problems at Lady Montford so I don't think
she'll mind.'

'You do know Rachel's living at Jamaica Hill again,' ventured the housekeeper suddenly, and Kate felt a glow of
warmth at the thought that she had played a small part in her
return.

'No, I didn't,' she said. 'But I'm happy for—for both of
them. I suppose Alex feels he's getting his life back together
again.'

'Well, yes.' Mrs Muir looked down at her hands gripping
her bag. 'People have been so sympathetic. I think some of
them have been having second thoughts since Conrad Wyatt
was arrested, and the stables have never been busier. Of
course, there's still to be a hearing about Rachel's future, but
the authorities seem to think that it's just a formality. She
belongs with her father. And Jamaica Hill needs a family
again.'

And it's going to get one, thought Kate, somewhat jeal-
ously. Though she doubted Lacey was the kind of woman to
appreciate having a four-year-old stepchild thrust upon her.
As for Rachel herself—well, Kate supposed she always had
Mrs Muir to turn to. The old housekeeper would always be
there for her, even when her father went away.

Mrs Muir got to her feet. 'I suppose I'd better be going.'

'Yes.' Kate rose, too. 'But thank you for coming, and trusting me with the truth. I'm honoured that you felt you could tell me the whole story. I hope you'll all be very happy in the future.'

Susie came back into Kate's office after showing Mrs Muir out, her eyes wide and curious. 'What did she want?' she asked, and Kate sighed and sank back into her chair.

'She wanted to thank me,' she said. 'For finding Alicia. Now, will you take those revolting doughnuts away before I throw up?'

Susie left for home about five o'clock, as usual. The office was quiet after she'd left, and Kate knew there was no point in her hanging around either. There was only a week to go, a week until she handed over the lease to her landlord. Her mother thought she was crazy, but then, her mother didn't know all the facts.

Nevertheless, she hoped that one of the jobs she'd applied for proved suitable. Even though her father's sister, Aunt Bridget, had said she could stay with her while she was looking for accommodation, money was still going to be tight. Of course, when they sold the flat they'd have a little capital to put down on another property, but Kate had already accepted that it might not be as nice as what they had now.

Which wasn't saying a lot, she thought glumly. When they'd first moved into the flat in Milner Court, they'd all missed the garden they used to have at the house. And now she was expecting her mother to move again, into even less salubrious surroundings. Was she being selfish? Wouldn't it just be easier to speak to Alex and let him play his part?

No!

The idea of asking Alex for anything had evaporated as soon as she'd contemplated Lacey's reaction to what she had to tell him. The thought of Lacey Sheridan making mocking comments about her naïvety was humiliating. She couldn't expose herself to the other woman's pity or contempt.

So—they had to move away from King's Montford. And

as London seemed like the only place where she might be able to pick up her career she had no choice in the matter. It would be good for Joanne, she told herself firmly. Even if the thought of an inner-city comprehensive filled her with dismay.

It was cold in the office, and she turned to close the window. She'd opened it a crack to allow the smell of Susie's perfume to escape, and now the frosty air was chilling the room. But these days anything—strongly smelling food, disinfectants, perfume—they all affected her stomach. She was seriously thinking of going to the doctor for some pills to calm her down.

The door slammed in the outer office, and she turned abruptly, her heart beating rapidly at the thought that someone might have come in. Unless her closing the window had caused a backdraught, she considered hopefully. The office was closed, the sign had been taken down; and, in any case, they'd always closed at five o'clock.

Her heart almost stopped beating altogether when she heard a footstep. Someone was in Susie's office, and she wondered if her assistant had forgotten something and come back to fetch it. 'Susie?' she called faintly, realising she sounded as nervous as she felt. 'Susie, is that you?'

The silhouette in the half-glassed door was definitely not female, and she was horribly reminded of the kind of friends Henry Sawyer might have. He certainly had cause to feel resentful towards her. Because of her evidence, he was facing charges as well.

She stood motionless behind her chair, gripping the back with nervous fingers as her door opened. Then her knees almost gave out on her completely when she saw who it was. 'Alex!' she exclaimed weakly. 'I mean—Mr Kellerman,' she corrected herself. 'Oh, you frightened me.' She struggled to gather her scattered wits. 'I didn't know who was there.'

'And now you do,' said Alex, coming into the office and closing the door. 'So this is where you work.' He looked about him as he unzipped his black leather blouson jacket.

Underneath he was wearing a dark blue silk shirt that complemented his swarthy colouring. 'Or should I say *worked*? Agnes tells me you're leaving town.'

Kate swallowed, averting her eyes from his lean, muscled torso. 'Um—what do you want?' she asked tautly, wishing she'd known it was him before he opened the door. As it was, she had had no time to prepare herself. He looked so good, so disturbing, so just as she remembered him. Did he realise how cruel it was to torment her? No, of course not. Mrs Muir had delivered the news that she was closing the office, and he'd decided she deserved a personal goodbye.

'A loaded question,' he remarked now, lounging into the chair his housekeeper had occupied earlier. He crossed one booted foot across his knee and rested one hand on his thigh. The other curled around the arm of the chair, smoothing the wood almost sensuously. Kate thought of those hands caressing her body. Could she bear the thought that he might never touch her again?

She doubted it.

'Why are you leaving town?' he asked abruptly, when she didn't make any comment. 'Has somebody said something, or done something, to make you feel you can't live here any more?'

Only you...

'If there have been any threats...' he continued, and she realised he'd no idea why she was leaving. 'Kate.' He thrust one hand through his hair in a frustrated gesture. 'For God's sake, answer me, can't you? Don't I at least deserve to know what's going on?'

No...

Kate sighed, and, feeling her way round the chair, almost like an old woman, she sank bonelessly into the seat. 'It's— it's this business,' she said. 'It's going nowhere.' Which was true. 'I've decided to try and put my degree to some use, after all.'

'Where?'

'Does it matter?'

'Humour me,' he said, a muscle jumping in his jaw.

'Well—' Kate paused. 'We're probably going to live in London. I've applied for a couple of vacancies, and I've got an interview for one of them next week.'

'Don't go.'

His request was delivered with clipped intensity, and Kate was glad she was sitting down when she looked into his hard face. 'I don't have any choice,' she said, trying to speak lightly. 'Um—Mrs Muir says you've got Rachel back again. I'm so happy for you both.'

'Are you?'

'Well, of course.' Kate couldn't bear his hostile expression and she hurried on, 'I know nothing can justify what I did in your eyes, but at least the outcome wasn't bad. I should have realised sooner that Conrad Wyatt was involved. If I'd had the sense to look into Henry Sawyer's background, I might have discovered he'd worked for the Wyatts in the past.'

'You didn't know.'

Alex's tone was flat and accepting, but Kate had to make her confession. 'But I should have done,' she said. 'That— that's one of the reasons why I'm giving up the agency. I've discovered I'm not very good at this job. A more experienced investigator would have had their suspicions right from the start.'

'Don't beat yourself up over it.' Alex shrugged indifferently. 'No one could have imagined how devious Conrad would prove to be. Perhaps it was my fault. Perhaps I should have seen how Pam's death had affected him and tried harder to gain his sympathy. My wife's death was a tragic accident. I think he thought that I didn't care.'

'Because you let him believe that you didn't know who'd put the horses in different stalls,' said Kate quietly, and Alex frowned.

'What did you say?' he asked, but she knew he had heard her anyway.

'Mrs Muir told me,' she admitted, feeling the colour warming her pale cheeks. 'She told me about her husband—and her son.'

Alex's nostrils flared. 'Oh, did she?'

'Yes.'

'And what else did she tell you that I should know about? I assume you discussed the case as well.'

'Only briefly.' Kate gripped the edge of the desk. 'I still don't know all the details myself, so I could hardly discuss the case with her.'

'But you know Wyatt was arrested and charged, and released on bail pending the trial? You know it was Sawyer who threw Alicia's suitcases into the skip?'

'No.' Kate tried to stop watching him so greedily. But, God knew, this might be the last chance she'd have to imprint his image in her mind. 'So—so why did they do it? Surely the fact that Alicia was missing was enough.'

'Hardly.' Alex looked as if he would have preferred to talk about other things, but he evidently decided to humour her. 'Things weren't developing fast enough, even though they had gone to the expense of hiring you. You see,' he sighed, 'I think they assumed reporting Alicia's disappearance to the police would promote some kind of investigation. Then they could alert the media to what was going on, and the whole circus would begin again.'

'You mean like—when Pamela died?'

'That's right.' Alex was laconic. 'But people go missing every day, and the police simply don't have the resources to follow up every lead.' He paused. 'I guess that's why they hired you; they hoped you'd be convinced and report your findings to the authorities. But you didn't, so they had to think of something else.'

'Hence the suitcases.' Kate shook her head disbelievingly.

'Well, it was a fairly damning piece of evidence, you have to admit.' Alex grimaced. 'And with Inspector Rivers on my case, desperate to prove he was a better detective than his predecessor, they might have succeeded. Sufficiently so to create doubts in people's minds, at least.'

'And Alicia?'

'What about her?'

'Why did she do it?'

Alex shrugged. 'Who knows? For the money, I suppose.'

'But Henry Sawyer said you'd given her a room at your house.'

'I did.' Alex heaved another sigh. 'She fed me some story that her husband used to beat her, just after she came to work for me. She persuaded me that she was desperate. That she needed somewhere to stay temporarily until she could find a place of her own.'

'I see.'

'I did not have an affair with her, if that's what you're wondering,' he said harshly. 'Despite what you may have heard to the contrary.'

'Not least, from you,' murmured Kate, remembering that awful day at the stables' office, and Alex stared at her with uncomprehending eyes.

'The day—the day you found out who I really was,' she prompted reluctantly, and Alex's expression cleared as he remembered what she meant.

'I was angry that day,' he muttered. 'Bloody angry. I'd thought—well, it doesn't matter what I'd thought now. The fact was, I thought I was in deep trouble and you were a part of it.'

'I wasn't.'

'I know that now. I think I realised it as soon as I saw your face. But I didn't want to let you off too easily. And when that supercilious inspector appeared I'd have said anything to destroy your relief.'

Kate bent her head. 'Well, you certainly did that. I thought you were going to go charging off to see Conrad Wyatt. I worried about it all morning, and then, when I looked at Alicia's picture again…'

'Yeah.' Alex blew out a breath. 'Well, I didn't. And I never thanked you for finding Alicia, when I should have done. But, after what Lacey told me, I guessed you wouldn't want anything from me. That was why I had Julian write that letter.' He grimaced. 'A formal note of thanks for saving my life.'

Kate pressed her hands down on the desk and got to her feet. 'I didn't save your life,' she protested. 'And—and I don't know what Lacey—that is, Mrs Sheridan—told you, but I don't think it was anything I'd said.' She breathed deeply. 'If she told you I only took the job because I was convinced you were guilty of your wife's murder, I have to tell you she was—wasn't telling the truth.'

'You mean, she was lying?'

He looked up at her through narrowed lids, and Kate knew her control was wavering. If he didn't get out of here soon, she had the feeling she was going to start to scream. Why couldn't he just go? Why didn't he see that by staying he was just labouring the situation? She now knew that he and Lacey were together. Wasn't that enough?

Shaking her head, she turned away towards the window. 'Mrs Muir probably got it wrong,' she said. 'Mrs Sheridan doesn't even know me.'

'But she came to see you, didn't she? That day you were leaving?' he queried. 'Sam Guthrie said he saw her leaving the office just after your daughter went in.'

'All right.' Kate couldn't hold out any longer. 'She came to tell me that—that you and she—'

'Had slept together a few times?' suggested Alex flatly, and when she glanced over her shoulder she saw that he had risen to his feet as well.

'That you were lovers,' she amended tightly, turning back to the rain-smeared window. 'It's all right. You don't owe me any explanation—'

'Dammit, it's not all right,' he snarled angrily. She heard him shove the chair he had been sitting on aside, and presently she felt the heat of his body at her back. 'There was no love between Lace and me,' he contradicted. 'Though I'm not denying that she offered me some comfort when I needed it. It's not conceit to say that she got as much out of it as me.'

Kate was shaking her head again. 'Like I said, it's nothing to do with me—'

'And if I want to make it your concern?' he demanded harshly. 'What then?'

'What do you mean?' Much against her better judgement, she turned to face him. 'You don't need my permission for who you take to bed.'

He was close, so close, and the urge to touch him was almost overwhelming. She wondered, if he had any feelings for her, why he didn't touch her. Instead, he just stood looking down at her, at the unmistakable hardening of her nipples. And although she wanted to reach out to him she kept her arms anchored to her sides.

'I took you to bed, remember?' he said at last, huskily, the warm draught of his breath fanning her feathering skin. 'Well, not actually bed, but your sofa was quite comfortable. I'd never had an experience that good before.'

Kate felt as if the air in the room was getting thinner. It was becoming difficult to drag sufficient oxygen into her straining lungs. She couldn't meet his eyes, so she concentrated on his open collar, on the shadow of dark hair she could see outlined beneath his shirt.

'I'm sure you must have,' she said at last, when she could speak coherently. 'And—and now that you've got Rachel back you can think about the future again. I'm sure Mrs Sheridan will learn to love your daughter—'

'God!' He swore then, and his hands fastened on her shoulders. 'Listen to me,' he told her grimly, 'I don't care if Lacey could learn to love Rachel or not.' His thumbs tilted her chin so that she was forced to look up at him. 'Lacey has no part in my future, do you hear me? I may not even have a future if you walk out on me now.'

Kate quivered. 'You don't mean that.'

'And if I do? Would it matter to you then?'

'It matters.' But Kate backed away from his hands, not

daring to believe what she was hearing. 'I just don't know what you want from me. You said—you said that what we had was just—sex.'

'Yeah, I know. I said a lot of things. And I'm not denying that I've fought against admitting what I feel for you.' He groaned. 'But, dammit, when Agnes said you were leaving, I knew I couldn't let you do it. Not without seeing you; not without speaking to you again. Not without giving myself the chance to find out if what Lace had said was true.'

'It's not.' Kate trembled. 'I think she knew how I felt about you—'

'Which is?'

His eyes burned into hers, and she moved her head from side to side, trying to find the words to meet his need. 'Well—that I love you, I suppose,' she said defeatedly, and he made a sound of triumph as he moved towards her.

'You love me,' he said, lifting his hands and smoothing his thumbs over the dark shadows beneath her eyes. 'Is that why you haven't been sleeping properly? Why you've got such an air of fragility?'

Kate found it hard to answer that. 'I suppose so,' she breathed, her words stifled by the brush of his mouth. Her hands curled convulsively about his shoulders. 'Do you love me?'

'Is there any doubt?' he demanded, his voice breaking with emotion. 'Hell, Kate, of course I love you. But I thought— well, that Lace was right. That you had just been playing me along for the sake of your investigations; and besides, what decent woman would want a barely reformed character like me?'

'I would.' Gaining in confidence, Kate wound her arms around his neck. 'Oh, Alex! I don't know what to say. Are you sure about this?'

'As sure as I've ever been in my life,' he muttered fiercely. 'What I can't understand is, why were you going to leave without giving me a chance to make amends?'

EPILOGUE

'I HAVE to admit, it is much more comfortable here,' murmured Alex, some two hours later, rolling onto his side and gazing down possessively at the woman to whom he'd just made slow, sensuous love. Flushed among the tumbled covers of his bed, Kate had never looked more desirable, and he thought how amazing it was that even though he'd taken her twice already he wanted her again.

'Is this really your room?' she asked, deliciously uninhibited in the way she didn't object when he bent to suckle one provocatively swollen breast. 'Mmm, that's nice.' Her breath caught in her throat. 'Oh, Alex, do that again.'

'I intend to,' he said thickly, but then he forced himself to draw back. There was still so much they had to say to one another, and he still nurtured anxieties as to why she would choose to leave King's Montford rather than wait to see if what Lacey had implied was true.

He was not incognizant of the fact that she had avoided any personal questions at her office, choosing instead to indulge in the kind of heavy petting that had left him hard and aching, and mindless with need. Then she'd insisted on calling her mother and explaining that she was spending the evening with him, without ever mentioning the fact that they loved one another.

Why?

His stomach clenched unpleasantly. In God's name, surely she had no doubts about him now?

As if she'd detected his uncertainty, Kate chose that moment to reach up and bestow a lingering kiss at the corner of his mouth, and for a moment Alex allowed his senses to spin wildly out of control. It was so easy to give in to emotion, to forget about tomorrow. But he loved her. He wanted to know what she wasn't telling him.

As it was, he'd had to wait until Rachel was safely tucked in bed before they could be alone together. The little girl had been so excited to see Kate again, and she'd insisted on wringing a promise from her that Kate would bring Joanne to see her tomorrow.

Which was another reason why he wanted to know what Kate was thinking. Rachel had been hurt too many times already. He couldn't take the risk that she might be hurt again.

And although Kate protested when he drew back he wouldn't allow her to sway his mood. 'We have to talk,' he said, sitting up so that he could look down at her. 'It's important.'

'I know.' Despite his fears, there was only tenderness in Kate's eyes, and he was sorely tempted to leave all their talking until later. Much later.

'This room will have to be decorated,' she said, before he could formulate his questions. 'Perhaps green and gold? Do you like green and gold? I do.'

'This isn't the master bedroom,' said Alex mechanically, wondering if he was ever going to get a straight answer from her. 'You can choose which suite we use when you move in here.' He paused. 'I'm assuming you do want to move in here. You and Joanne—and your mother, too, if she's agreeable. There's plenty of room. She could have an apartment all to herself.'

A frown marred Kate's smooth forehead now. 'You're not still having doubts about my feelings?' she asked faintly. She swallowed. 'Or perhaps you're having doubts about your own?'

'Don't be stupid!' Alex was harsh, but he couldn't help it. 'I'm crazy about you, you know that. I want to marry you, for God's sake!' He groaned. 'I just can't get my head round why you were planning on going away.'

Kate hesitated, and then she scrambled up to sit cross-legged beside him. But this time she tucked the quilt beneath her arms, as if she knew how her naked body made him feel. 'What else could I do?' she asked softly. 'I—I'm pregnant. I didn't want you to feel—trapped—because I was having your child.'

Alex stared at her, open-mouthed, trying to make some sense of what she was saying. 'You're pregnant?' he echoed weakly. 'My God, why didn't you tell me before?'

'Before what?' Kate gazed at him gently. 'Before I made arrangements to leave King's Montford, or before I knew you loved me?' She touched his hand with loving fingers. 'Do you mind?'

'God—' Alex cast the covers aside and reached eagerly for her. 'How could I mind? It's as much my doing as yours.' His smile was brilliant. 'And I was thinking that perhaps you thought I was being too impatient. That you needed more time to decide what you really wanted to do.'

'Oh, I know what I want to do,' Kate assured him firmly as he bore her back against the pillows and covered her mouth with his. 'It just seemed like a dream, the kind of dream that could never happen. Loving you, living with you, having your child…'

It was some little time before Alex recovered himself suffi-ciently to talk practicalities. 'Do you think Joanne will object when she hears she's not going to leave Lady Montford after all?'

'What? When she's going to live here with all these horses?' Kate shook her head positively. 'Besides, my mother will be pleased. She always says there's nothing to be gained by running away.'

'Isn't that the truth?' Alex stroked the moist hair back from her forehead. 'What about your mother? Do you think she'll accept me as her son-in-law after all this?'

'My mother's a fairly generous woman. And I know when she hears about the baby she'll be thrilled. As for Joanne, well—she thinks you're pretty terrific. She's probably going to be the least surprised of us all.'

'Smart girl.' Alex grinned. 'So we're going to have three children?'

'To begin with,' said Kate provocatively, putting out her tongue. Then she sobered, running her nail over the beard that was roughening his jawline. 'What about Rachel? Is this going to be very hard for her?'

'Maybe I'm being selfish, but I think it's exactly what Rachel is needing,' declared Alex, grasping her hand and taking her fingers to his mouth. 'A normal home, a normal family, a new baby.' He grimaced. 'I can even find it in my heart to pity Wyatt after this.'

Kate nodded. 'I suppose I feel sorry for him. Well, his wife, anyway. I don't suppose she did anything wrong.'

'Except condone her husband's actions,' said Alex wryly. 'But, knowing Conrad as I do, I doubt she had a choice.'

'Will you let them see Rachel again?'

'Of course. Eventually.' Alex gave a heavy sigh and rolled onto his back. 'And now, I suppose, we ought to go and tell your mother and Joanne.' He grinned. 'I wonder if I'll feel old if Joanne calls me Dad…?'

Innocent Sins

ANNE MATHER

CHAPTER ONE

OLIVER could hear the phone ringing as he vaulted up the steps to the front door. Light shone out through the fan-shaped skylight above, illuminating the crisp piles of snow that he guessed Thomas had cleared earlier in the day. But although he was fairly sure his manservant was at home it seemed obvious that the old man was not going to answer the call.

Which pointed to the fact that he knew who it was. Which, in turn, led Oliver to believe it must be his mother. Only if Stella had been ringing fairly constantly all day would Thomas choose to ignore the summons. He and Stella had never liked one another, and the fact that his mother had expected her son to return yesterday morning would perhaps explain her eagerness to ask him about his trip.

Or not.

Oliver's mouth eased into a wry smile as he inserted his key in the lock. In his experience, Stella was seldom inter-ested in anything that didn't immediately affect her, and if she had been ringing on and off all day there was probably something personal on her mind.

The warmth that accompanied the opening of the door was welcome. Oliver would have preferred not to return to London in the middle of one of the coldest spells of the winter. Particularly since he'd spent the last three weeks sweltering in the extreme heat of the Malaysian jungle.

'Mr Oliver!'

To his relief the phone stopped its shrill bleating at the same moment that Thomas Grayson appeared at the end of the long hallway that ran from front to back of the house. Although Oliver had tried to persuade the old man that such

5

formality wasn't necessary, Thomas insisted on addressing him that way.

Now Oliver hoisted the bag containing his camera equipment inside and, closing the door, leaned back against it for a moment's rest. He didn't often take the time to appreciate the elegant beauty of the narrow, four-storey Georgian house that was his home, but he was always relieved to find that nothing had changed in his absence.

'I expected you back yesterday, Mr Oliver.'

Thomas's tone was almost reproving and Oliver wondered if he considered he was to blame for the delay. 'The plane was late leaving Singapore, and there's been a snowstorm over western Europe for the past twenty-four hours, in case you hadn't noticed,' he responded drily. 'But, hey, don't let that worry you. And it's good to see you, too.'

Thomas, who had been about to wrest his employer's rucksack and garment bag from his hands, straightened abruptly. 'Oh, I'm sorry, Mr Oliver,' he said, with evident sincerity. 'Of course it's good to have you back. But—' He paused. 'I'm afraid there's been something of an emergency while you've been away.'

'What now?'

Oliver was wearily aware that he wasn't in the best mood to suffer another of his mother's crises, if that was what Thomas meant. Resignation replaced his earlier optimism. Where Stella was concerned, there were always emergencies, most recently occasioned by his mother's inability to live within the allowance Griff gave her.

'Your mother's been trying to reach you for the past forty-eight hours,' Thomas continued, and just for a moment Oliver wondered if Laura could be involved. His stepsister used to be a constant thorn in his mother's side, but she'd gone to live in the United States almost seven years ago now. 'I regret to have to tell you that your stepfather died two days ago,' Thomas added gently. 'Mrs Williams has been desperate to get in touch with you ever since.'

Oliver's resignation vanished. 'So that's why you refused to answer the phone?'

'Well, yes.' Thomas was defensive. 'Mrs Williams was getting rather—well, abusive. She accused me of not giving you her messages. She wouldn't believe that I didn't know where you were.'

Oliver pulled a wry face. He knew his mother must have said something upsetting for Thomas to ignore her calls at a time like this. 'If she'd rung the airline, she'd have found out why I was late,' he said wearily. He'd been travelling for the past forty-eight hours and he was tired. He'd been looking forward to nothing more exhausting than taking a hot shower and collapsing into bed. Now he was going to have to deal with his mother, and he could imagine how harrowing that was going to be.

'I'd better give her a ring,' he said, abandoning any hope of getting some rest. He picked up the bag containing his camera equipment and started up the stairs ahead of Thomas. 'Perhaps you'd repack the rucksack with some clean under-wear. If I have to go down to Penmadoc, I might as well be prepared.'

'You're not proposing to drive down to Penmadoc to-night!' Thomas was horrified.

'I'll probably have no choice in the matter,' replied his employer, entering the lamplit room on his left at the top of the stairs. The first floor of the house was given over to this room, which was Oliver's study, the dining room, and a com-fortable sitting room, with his bedroom suite and two guest suites on the second floor. He went straight to the wet bar to help himself to a small shot of whisky. 'I know, I know,' he groaned, when Thomas stood shaking his head in the door-way. 'But I need some fortification. I'll have a sandwich and some coffee before I leave, I promise.'

Thomas's disapproval was apparent, but in the eight years since he'd come to work for Oliver he'd learned when to back off. Leaving his employer to make his call, he continued on his way to the second floor and Oliver heard him opening and closing drawers and sliding hangers about in his dressing room.

The phone seemed to ring for a long time before anyone answered it. Oliver was beginning to wonder if his mother had guessed it was him and was paying him back for not being there when she needed him. It was the sort of thing Stella might do, only not at a time like this, surely.

He could imagine the sound echoing round the draughty old hall, with its beamed ceiling and uneven polished floor. He couldn't ever remember feeling warm at Penmadoc in the winter. Laura used to say the house was haunted and, when he was younger, he'd half believed her.

Laura...

'Penmadoc Hall.'

A voice with a strong Welsh accent interrupted his maundering. 'Oh, hello,' he said, putting the past behind him. 'This is Oliver Kemp. Is my mother there?'

'Oliver.' The tone was familiar to him now, and Eleanor Tenby was surprisingly amiable for once. 'Your mother will be pleased to hear from you. I'll get her for you.'

'Thanks.'

Oliver didn't attempt to detain her, even though it was unusual for Laura's aunt Nell to show any consideration towards either him or his mother. Had it not been for the fact that she was Maggie Williams' sister, and Penmadoc had always been her home, Stella would have got rid of her long ago. But, although Griff had indulged her in most things, where Eleanor was concerned, he wouldn't be moved.

And, ultimately, it had suited his mother to have a ready-made housekeeper, thought Oliver wryly. Because Laura's mother had been ill for several years before her death, Eleanor had taken over the running of the household from her. When Maggie died and Griff married again, Eleanor had retained her position. Stella might have grumbled at first, but she'd never been the kind of woman to enjoy domestic duties.

'Oliver?'

His mother's voice came shrilly over the wires, and although he was used to her dramatics by now Oliver sensed she was more than usually *distrait*. There was a note of hysteria there that he hadn't expected, and he prepared himself to comfort her as best he could.

'Hi, Ma,' he greeted her, with his usual irreverence. Then he said, gently, 'I was so sorry to hear the news about Griff. You must be shattered.'

'Yes. Yes, I am.' Stella's response was taut and uneven. 'Where the hell have you been, Oliver? I've been trying to reach you for days.'

'I know. Thomas told me.'

'Thomas!' His mother fairly spat the old man's name. 'That little weasel had the nerve to tell me that he didn't know how to reach you. As if you'd have gone away without leaving a forwarding address.'

Oliver heaved a deep breath. 'He wasn't lying, Ma. I left Singapore yesterday morning. But the plane was delayed with engine trouble in Bahrain, and then, what with the weather—'

'You could have phoned home.'

'Why?' Oliver could feel his sympathy dissolving into irritation. 'Thomas has eyes. He could see the problem the weather was creating for himself.'

'Is that a dig at me?'

Stella's voice wobbled a little now and Oliver realised that Griff's death had hit her even harder than he'd thought. He was more used to her complaining about the disadvantages of being married to a man considerably older than herself, who apparently didn't understand why she was perpetually short of funds.

'It's not a dig,' he said gently. 'Naturally, if I'd known about Griff—'

'Yes.' To his relief, his mother seemed to have herself in control again. 'Yes, well, I suppose that's a fair point. There didn't appear to be anything wrong with him when you went away, did there? How was any of us to know that in three weeks he'd be dead?' Her voice rose again, but she managed to steady it. 'You're coming down, of course?'

'Of course.' Oliver conceded to himself that there was no way he could avoid it. 'I'll get something to eat and then I'll be on my way.'

'Thank God!' Stella was obviously relieved and Oliver acknowledged the fact that so far as his mother was concerned his feelings counted for little. But then, he'd always known that, hadn't he? 'I'll wait up for you.'

She would have rung off then, but Oliver had to ask. 'Griff?' he said awkwardly. 'I mean—how did it happen?'

'He had a heart attack,' said Stella shortly, clearly not prepared to elaborate on the phone. 'Drive carefully.'

The line went dead and Oliver replaced his receiver with a troubled hand. A heart attack! As far as he knew, Griff had never had any problems with his heart. But what did he know? In the twenty years since Griff had married his mother, they'd hardly become bosom buddies, and although age had brought a certain understanding between them they'd never been really close.

There was still so much he wanted to know. Was Laura coming home for her father's funeral? Of course, she must be. She hadn't come home when her marriage to Conor Neill had foundered, but that was different. Her work was in New York. She'd made a niche for herself there. Why would she come back to England, or, more precisely, Wales, when she had a perfectly good job in the United States?

His lips twisted. Naturally, Stella had been relieved that she hadn't returned to Penmadoc. The last thing she'd wanted was for her stepdaughter to come back and form an alliance with her father against her. Oliver couldn't deny that Stella had always been jealous of the relationship Laura had had with her father. And Laura had never forgiven his mother for replacing Maggie less than a year after her mother's death.

'I've laid out some clean clothes in your bedroom, Mr Oliver.' Thomas spoke somewhat diffidently from the doorway, evidently cognisant of the disturbed expression his employer was wearing. 'I assume you'll be taking a shower before you leave?' he added. 'I'll have some coffee and a light meal ready when you come downstairs.'

Oliver flexed his shoulders. 'Just a sandwich, thanks,' he said wearily. 'I had something to eat on the plane, and I'm not really hungry.' He paused before saying gratefully, 'But the coffee would be welcome. Is there plenty of fuel in the car?'

'I expect you'll use the Jeep?' Thomas arched an enquiring brow and Oliver nodded. He owned a Mercedes, too, but the four-wheel-drive vehicle was obviously the safest choice tonight. It wasn't the weather for breaking the speed limit, and he was likely to run into some really nasty conditions after he crossed the Severn Bridge.

By the time he'd had his shower and dressed again, it was dark. The short winter afternoon had given way to a bitterly cold evening and he wasn't looking forward to the long journey into Wales. Downstairs, Thomas had the promised coffee, and some soup as well as a sandwich, waiting. 'Just to warm you up,' he said apologetically as Oliver came into the kitchen.

Thomas's own apartments were in the basement of the building. Oliver had his darkroom there, too, and on summer evenings Thomas sometimes served his meal in the sheltered charm of the walled garden at the back of the house. Tonight, however, the paved patio was a transparency in black and white, the reflection in the windows of the room behind giving the scene an eerie beauty.

The phone rang again as Oliver was drinking the soup, and this time Thomas had no hesitation about answering it. 'It's Miss Harlowe,' he said, covering the mouthpiece with his fingers. 'Do you want to speak to her, or shall I tell her you've already left?'

'And lie about it?' mocked Oliver drily. Then, taking pity on the old man, he held out his hand. 'I'll speak to her,' he said, deciding he owed Natalie an explanation of where he was likely to be for the next few days. 'Hi, sweetheart. It's good to hear your voice. Have you missed me?'

'Do you care?' Oliver stifled a sigh at the realisation that Natalie was angry with him, as well. 'I've been expecting you to call all afternoon. I rang the airport and they said your plane had been delayed, but—'

'I got back about half an hour ago,' Oliver interrupted her quickly. 'I was going to ring you, but—well, things came up.'

'What things?' Natalie was not placated.

'A phone call from my mother,' said Oliver, taking a bite from his sandwich. Then, chewing rapidly, he added, 'She's been trying to get in touch with me, too.'

'Are you eating?'

Natalie sounded outraged and Oliver swallowed before attempting to speak again. 'Yeah,' he said resignedly. 'I'm just trying to fortify myself for the journey. I've got to drive down to Penmadoc tonight.'

'Penmadoc!' Natalie gasped. 'You're not serious.'

'I'm afraid I am.' Oliver shook his head at Thomas when he mimed making him another sandwich. 'My stepfather had a heart attack two days ago.'

'Oh! Oh, I'm so sorry.' Natalie was all sympathy now. 'How is he? Is it serious?'

'He's dead,' answered Oliver flatly. 'That's why my mother wants me to drive down there tonight. I am her only blood relative. Naturally she wants my support.'

Or did she? Oliver wasn't absolutely sure what his mother wanted. She'd been decidedly strange when he'd spoken to her. Despite the years they'd spent together, he would never have expected Griff's death to affect her so badly.

'Would you like me to come with you?'

Natalie was speaking again, and for a moment Oliver was tempted. But then he remembered Laura and his refusal was automatic. 'I don't think so, sweetheart,' he said. 'Funerals are family occasions, as you know. And I'm not sure what the arrangements are yet.'

'Will your stepsister be there?'

Natalie's enquiry sounded innocent enough, but Oliver sensed her irritation. Ever since he'd mentioned the fact that his stepsister had brains as well as beauty, Natalie had resented her; which was ridiculous really when they'd never even met.

'She may be there,' he said now, evenly. 'But, if she is, I'll be the last person she wants to see.'

'Do you expect me to believe that?' Natalie snorted. 'I haven't forgotten what you told me about her flinging herself at you when she was hardly more than a kid!'

Oliver swore silently then scowled. He must have been drunk if he'd told Natalie about that. 'You didn't believe me, did you?' he scoffed, striving to sound incredulous. 'Come on, baby, I was only kidding. For God's sake, it's been over eight years since Laura and I even met!'

Natalie was silent for a moment, and then she said cautiously, 'So she didn't come to your room and get into bed with you?'

'No!' Oliver stifled a groan. He must have been drunker than he'd thought.

'And your mother didn't find out and threaten the pair of you?'

'I've said no, haven't I?' Oliver knew he could do without this. 'Come on, Natalie, I was only having a bit of fun. You're so gullible sometimes, I can't resist teasing you.'

'You bastard!' Natalie swore now. 'You were so convincing. I thought it was true.'

'So sue me,' he said, desperate to avoid any further revelations. 'Look, sweetheart, I've really got to get going.'

'But what about the Rices' party?' Fortunately, she was easily diverted. 'Couldn't you come back tomorrow? Surely there can't be that much you can do.'

'Except be there for Ma,' suggested Oliver drily. 'I'm sorry, baby, but you're going to have to go on your own.'

'Don't I always,' muttered Natalie, not altogether truthfully. 'Oh, all right. But you will ring me and let me know what's going on?'

'I promise.'

Oliver was relieved to escape so easily, but after he'd hung up the phone the images Natalie's words had evoked were not so effortlessly dispelled. This was not the time to be thinking about Laura, he thought impatiently, or to be remembering what had happened that unforgettable summer night. Or why, instead of taking up his place at university that autumn, he'd left the country, spending a year trekking around Europe, trying to get what had happened out of his system.

'You do realise it's after six, don't you, Mr Oliver?' Thomas's anxious tone interrupted him. 'I'm sure it's not wise to drive down to Wales tonight. There's reduced visibility on the M4 and the motoring organisations are warning people only to travel if it's absolutely necessary. Don't you think your mother would understand if you—?'

'Forget it.' Oliver pushed away from the table. 'As far as Ma's concerned, this is an emergency. Besides, there's always the chance that the weather could worsen. I don't want to find I can't get there tomorrow because they're snowed in.'

Thomas shrugged. 'Well, if you're determined...'

'I am.' Oliver was adamant. 'But don't worry, old man. I won't do anything rash. If I find I'm getting into difficulties, I'll find a motel.'

'You hope.'

Thomas wasn't convinced, and Oliver grimaced at the negative vibes he was giving off. 'Look, I've got to go,' he said.

'Don't you think I've got enough to contend with without you jumping all over me as well?'

Thomas sniffed. 'I'm only thinking of your welfare, Mr Oliver.'

'I know.' Oliver paused to give the old man a rueful look.

'But I must say, this is the first time I've seen you so determined to obey your mother,' he added peevishly, and Oliver's lean face creased into a mocking grin.

'That won't work either,' he said, looping the strap of his rucksack over his shoulder. 'Now, I'll phone you tomorrow, wherever I am, and I'll give Stella your condolences, shall I? I'm sure you don't want her to think you don't care.'

'I've already offered Mrs Williams my condolences,' retorted Thomas indignantly. 'Although I have to say she didn't seem to want any sympathy from me.' And then, because the affection he had for his employer was genuine, he said, 'Do take care, won't you?'

'I will.'

Oliver patted the old man's shoulder in passing, and then, after a regretful thought about the photographs he'd planned to process tomorrow, he picked up his keys and started for the door.

CHAPTER TWO

LAURA shivered.

Despite the heat that was still emanating from the old Aga in the corner, the kitchen at Penmadoc was decidedly chilly tonight. The cold struck up through the soles of her mules and she wondered why Stella hadn't had the stone floor removed and modern tiles installed in their stead. She could guess why, of course. The kitchen was still Aunt Nell's domain and even Stella baulked at locking horns with her. Besides, she doubted if Stella ever entered the kitchen except to issue orders. Domestic duties and cooking had never appealed to her stepmother.

But it was a relief to find that some things at Penmadoc hadn't changed when so much else had. Her father was dead. Impossible to believe, but it was true. Stella was the mistress of the house now. Laura was only here on sufferance.

Was it really only six months since she'd seen her father in London? He'd seemed as hale and hearty as ever, if a little more boisterous than usual. She'd put that down to his usual high spirits at seeing her again, but she wondered now if it had been a screen for something else. Stella had said that she'd known nothing about him having any heart trouble, but he could have been hiding it from her, as well.

Her stomach quivered. If only she'd known. If only she'd had some premonition that all was not as it should be. But although her grandmother had been a little fey, as they said around here, and had occasionally been able to see into the future, Laura never had. Whatever powers she'd possessed had not been passed on to her granddaughter.

According to her stepmother's version of events, her father's attack had been totally unexpected. He'd apparently been out riding earlier in the day. Although he hadn't been a member of the local hunt, he'd always enjoyed following the hounds and, despite the fact that snow had been forecast, he'd ridden out that morning as usual.

Then, also according to Stella, he'd arrived home at three o'clock, or thereabouts, and gone straight to his study. She'd found him there a couple of hours later, she said, slumped across his desk, the glass of whisky he'd been imbibing still clutched in his hand.

Laura expelled a trembling breath. She hoped he hadn't suffered. When she'd spoken to her boss at the publishing house where she worked in New York, he'd said that it was the best way to go. For her father, perhaps, she thought now, but not for the people he'd left behind. Aunt Nell had been devastated. Like Laura herself, she could see the writing on the wall.

She shivered again as tears pricked behind her eyelids, and, dragging the folds of her ratty chenille dressing gown closer about her, she moved nearer to the hearth. Thank heavens they still used an open fire in winter, she thought, hunching her shoulders. There were still a few embers giving out a tenuous warmth.

She sighed and glanced about her. She'd come downstairs to get herself a glass of hot milk because she couldn't get to sleep. She was still on eastern standard time and, although it was after midnight here, it was still early evening in New York. She'd decided a warm drink might help, but the milk was taking so long to boil. Perhaps she should have looked for a hot-water bottle and filled that. At this rate, she'd be frozen before she got back to bed.

She started suddenly as an ember shifted in the hearth. At least, she thought it was an ember. There had definitely been a sound like something falling either in here or outside. She was feeling particularly edgy this evening and she was very aware of being alone downstairs. With the snow falling heavily outside, Penmadoc had an air of expectancy that was hard to ignore.

The milk came to the boil at the exact moment that some-one tried the outer door. The sound was unmistakable, the latch rattling as it had always done when the bolt was still in place. Laura's breath caught in her throat and she was hardly aware that the pan was boiling over until the hob started sizzling and the acrid smell of burnt milk filled the room.

'Oh, God,' she groaned, dragging the pan off the heat. But she was more concerned about who might be trying to get into the house at this time of night. As she listened, she was almost sure a masculine shoulder was applied to the door-frame, and while she stood there, frozen into immobility, an audible curse accompanied another assault on the latch.

Breathing shallowly, Laura left the smoking pan on the Aga and edged towards the long narrow lobby that opened off the kitchen. There was no door between the kitchen and the passage where boots and coats and other outdoor gear occupied a row of pegs. Stella called it the mudroom, but that was just an affectation. It was a lobby, plain and simple, that protected the kitchen from the immediate chill when you opened the outer door.

Breathing shallowly, Laura sneaked a look into the pas-sage. There was definitely someone outside: a man, judging by the muffled oaths she could hear even through the door. But human, she assured herself, despising her timidity. Pushing away from the archway into the kitchen, she stepped nervously into the passage.

'Who's there?' she called sharply, consoling herself with the thought that the door was apparently impregnable.

'Who the hell do you think it is?' the man snapped. 'Didn't you hear the Jeep?'

'The Jeep?' Laura frowned. She hadn't known anyone was expected tonight. 'Do you mind telling me who you are?'

'What?' His incredulity was audible. 'Open the door, Ma, and stop f—mucking about.'

Ma!

Laura's stomach clenched. Oh, no, it couldn't be. Not to-night, not when she was wearing this old dressing gown that she'd found at the back of the closet upstairs. She'd put it on for comfort, because her father had bought it when she was a teenager. But it wasn't particularly clean or flattering, and it clashed wildly with her hair.

'O—Oliver?' she ventured weakly, realising that she'd have to admit him, and he seemed to become aware that she wasn't his mother, after all.

'Laura?' he exclaimed. Then, evidently reorganising his reaction, he said, 'For God's sake, is that you, Laura?' She heard him blow out a breath. 'What are you doing? Waiting up for me?'

Laura fumbled with the bolts at the top and bottom of the door and then, turning the heavy key, she pulled it open. 'Hardly,' she said, keeping her eyes averted as she stepped back to let him in. 'Don't you have a key?'

'Don't tell anyone, but they've yet to invent a key that can open a bolt,' he retorted, and she guessed his sarcasm was an attempt to hide his own surprise at seeing her. He shook himself, dislodging snow from the shoulders of his leather jacket on to the floor of the passage. Then, sniffing expres-sively, he asked, 'What's that awful smell?'

'I burnt some milk,' said Laura defensively, closing and locking the door again before brushing past him into the kitchen. She knew she must look a sight with her hair mussed and her eyes still puffy from weeping. Not the image she'd wanted to present to the stepbrother who hadn't seen her since she married Conor. 'Did your mother know you were coming tonight?'

'I thought so.' Oliver followed her into the kitchen. Then he gestured towards the Aga. 'Oughtn't you to do something about that before anyone starts to think you're trying to burn the old place down?'

'Your mother, you mean?' she asked tersely, plunging the saucepan into cold water before snatching up a dishcloth to mop the stove. Anything to avoid looking at him, she thought, though she was perfectly aware of how attractive he was.

'Possibly,' he said now, and she wished she hadn't jumped so childishly to her own defence. She had told herself that if—*when*—she saw Oliver again she would behave as if the past was another country. She had no wish to go there; no wish to resurrect his memories of the naïve teenager she'd been. He set down his canvas rucksack and draped a garment bag over the back of the old rocking chair that stood on the hearth. 'Anyway, I was sorry to hear about your father. It must have been a terrible shock.'

'Yes. Yes, it was.'

Laura didn't look at him. She merely lifted her shoulders before continuing to scrub the burnt-in stains off the hob.

'It was a shock for me, too,' he added softly. 'Your father and I might not have always seen eye to eye about things, but in recent years I like to think we grew to respect each other's views.'

Laura stiffened her spine and forced herself to glance in his direction. 'In recent years?' she echoed, as her eyes took in the fact that he was broader. But it only served to give his lean frame an added maturity without adding any fat to his long bones. 'I didn't know you spent so much time at Penmadoc.'

'I don't.' He sucked in a breath. 'But you were in the States whereas I was available. He used to come up to London occasionally and, less frequently, I'd come down here.'

Laura tried not to feel any resentment. After all, it wasn't as if her father hadn't wanted her to come home. But, after her marriage to Conor broke up, it had seemed to her that she was a failure. At that, as in everything else, she mused bitterly. And Stella would never have let her forget it.

'He didn't tell me,' she muttered now, turning back to her cleaning, but she was aware of Oliver crossing the room to open the fridge door.

'Why would he?' Oliver asked, peering inside. 'I doubt if he thought you'd be interested.' He heaved a sigh. 'Is there anything to eat around here?'

Laura permitted herself to view his broad shoulders. 'Didn't you have any dinner?' she asked, and he swung the fridge door shut again with an impatient snort.

'Dinner?' His amusement was bitter. 'What dinner?' He gave a grunt. 'I just got back from Singapore late this afternoon. Ma had apparently been ringing for hours, trying to get in touch with me. I only stopped long enough to take a shower before driving down.'

'Singapore?' Laura's curiosity was showing and she quickly changed what she had been about to say. 'Haven't you had anything to eat at all?'

'Soup. And a sandwich.' Oliver glanced into the fridge again. 'Don't people eat any meat these days?'

Laura hesitated. Then she said, 'I expect Aunt Nell has the freezer stocked. She always used to do a weekly shop at the supermarket in Rhosmawr.'

'So she did.' Oliver gave her a sideways glance. 'I guess I'll have to make do with another sandwich.' His mouth took on a humorous twist as he looked at what she was wearing. 'That new?'

Laura held up her head. 'Don't you recognise it?' she asked coldly, and had the dubious satisfaction of seeing a trace of colour enter his lean cheeks. The fact that her own face was red, too, offered little compensation, however. Once again, she'd betrayed what she was thinking and laid herself open to his contempt.

But instead of making some sarcastic comment Oliver merely closed the fridge again and leaned back against it,

arms folded across his chest. 'Okay,' he said quietly. 'Let's
start again, shall we?' His green eyes were narrowed and
glinting with suppressed emotion. 'I don't want to argue with
you, Laura. I know this can't be easy for you—'

'You flatter yourself!'

'I mean losing your father,' he interjected harshly. 'For
God's sake, can't you think of anyone but yourself? I know
you don't like me, Laura, but this is one occasion when I'd
have thought you'd have put other people's feelings before
your own.'

Laura trembled. 'It's late—'

'Yes, it is. But not too late, I hope!' he exclaimed impatiently. 'Look, like I said, let's try and come to some kind of
compromise, shall we? For—well, for your aunt Nell's sake,
if no one else?'

Laura dropped the dishcloth into the sink and tightened the
belt of her robe. 'Very well,' she said, and heard his resigned
intake of breath.

'Very well?' he mimicked drily. He cast his eyes towards
the beamed ceiling. 'Oh, Laura, don't make it easy for me,
will you?'

'I said—'

'I know what you said.' He straightened away from the
door. 'Okay.' He held out his hand towards her. 'Friends?'

Laura moistened her dry lips. She didn't want to touch
him. Dear God, she'd have done just about anything rather
than put her hand into his. But that was stupid! Stupid! Did
she want him to think she was afraid of him, that she hadn't
got over that childish infatuation that had almost ruined her
life?

'Friends,' she got out, almost gagging on the nausea that
had risen into the back of her throat, and his strong brown
fingers closed about her hand.

His fingers were cold but the impact Laura had was one
of heat, a fiery heat that spread up her arm and into her
breasts, making them tingle with an unwelcome awareness.

The warmth of his breath invaded the neckline of her robe and she felt as if she was enveloped by his scent and his masculinity. An image of how he'd looked, lying naked and unashamed on his bed, flashed briefly before her eyes, and she suppressed a groan. But it was all she could do to prevent herself from jerking her hand out of his firm grasp.

'Hey, you're shivering,' he said, and Laura had to bite her lip to silence the instinctive denial. 'I'm sorry. I didn't mean to upset you, you know.'

'You didn't.'

But her voice was high and strained and he seemed to sense it. With an odd expression playing about his mouth, he lifted his hand and stroked the backs of his fingers down her hot cheek, and this time she couldn't prevent her automatic response. With a strangled sound, she jerked back from him, bruising her hip against the corner of the scrubbed pine table that occupied the centre of the floor.

'Laura!'

His irritation was evident, but she suspected neither of them was prepared for his reaction. Instead of letting her go, he went after her, his hand closing on the nape of her neck now, his thumb forcing her face up to his.

'Is this what an unhappy marriage has done to you?' he demanded, and she realised incredulously that he thought she was reacting to some lingering torment from her relationship with Conor. That the panic she was barely controlling was something to do with her ex-husband.

As if!

'I—' She didn't know what to say. Her head was swimming with the emotions his hard fingers were arousing inside her, and blaming Conor for feelings he had never been able to inspire seemed a cruel deceit. But... 'Just let me go, Oliver,' she said weakly. 'I—I'm tired.'

'Yeah, I know.' His thumb was caressing her ear now and she thought how incredible it was that he thought *he* could give her any comfort. 'Poor Laura. Do you have any idea how young you look in that robe?'

Laura felt faint. 'Please,' she said unsteadily. 'Please, Oliver...'

'It's okay. I know.' But just when she thought he was about to release her he changed his mind and, instead of moving aside, he pulled her into his arms. 'You can rely on me, baby,' he said huskily, pressing her face into his throat so that Laura could scarcely breathe. 'I'm here for you. I just want you to know that.'

'What the hell do you think you're doing?'

For a moment, Laura wondered if it was she who'd spoken. It was what she should have said, she knew that, but although the hand that had been stroking her shoulder slid away she sensed Oliver was reacting to a stronger will than hers.

A suspicion that was reinforced when Stella Williams' shrill voice continued, 'For God's sake, Oliver, have you taken leave of your senses? She's not back in this house for five minutes before she's trying to cause trouble between us.'

Laura's jaw dropped. 'I hope you don't think that I—that I—was encouraging him—'

'So what are you doing down here at this time of night?' demanded her stepmother scornfully. She sniffed. 'And what's that awful smell?' Then, turning to her son without waiting for an answer, she said, 'I suppose you got her to let you in. Why didn't you come to the front door? I told you I'd wait up.'

'I did come to the front door,' retorted Oliver shortly, giving Laura a studied look in passing. 'I thought no one was up. There were no lights that I could see.'

Stella pursed her lips. 'I must have fallen asleep for a few moments,' she said peevishly. 'Goodness knows, I've had little enough sleep since Griff passed away.' Her eyes glittered as they turned towards her stepdaughter. 'Just because some people seem perfectly able to forget why they're here—'

'Forget it.' Oliver's voice was harsh as it broke into her provocative tirade. 'Laura couldn't sleep either. She came down to get herself a hot drink and I disturbed her. That's why the milk boiled over. It was my fault. That's what you can smell. Burnt milk. Nothing else.'

'If you say so.' Stella gave Laura a disparaging look. 'Don't you have anything else you could wear?'

Laura shook her head. She had no intention of getting into a discussion about her appearance with her stepmother. 'If you'll excuse me,' she said, not caring whether they did or otherwise, and, putting his mother between her and Oliver, she made for the door. 'I'm going back to bed.'

It was easier than she'd thought. Neither of them offered any objections as she slipped out into the hall. The smouldering embers in the hall grate lit up the door of her father's study, giving her a moment's pause. She was briefly tempted to go in there and try and calm her racing blood.

But the possibility that Stella might decide to show her son where her husband had been found deterred her. Instead, she hurried up the stairs and gained the sanctuary of her room with some relief. Leaning back against the panels, she wondered why she always let Oliver upset her. Whatever he said, whatever he did, he couldn't help getting under her skin.

Straightening, she crossed the floor to the square four-poster she'd occupied when she'd lived here. Although her belongings had been removed and Stella had had the room redecorated, it was still reassuringly familiar to her. But this might be the last time she'd use it, she thought, tears filling her eyes again. Once her father's funeral was over, she'd have no excuse for coming here.

Her reflection in the dressing-table mirror gave her a momentary shudder. For a second, the face that had stared back at her had been her mother's. But she knew that was just because they looked alike. Pale face, pale grey eyes, wild red hair that rioted in an untidy mass about her shoulders. No wonder Stella had looked at her so contemptuously. Compared to her stepmother, she lacked any sophistication.

As for Oliver: well, she preferred not to think about him. She wasn't at all deceived by his attempt at conciliation. She didn't know what game he was playing, but she had no intention of making a fool of herself again.

She sighed now, loosening the belt of her dressing gown and flopping back on to the bed. It was impossible to come here without being assaulted by her memories. And, no matter how she might regret it now, Oliver had been an integral part of her growing-up.

She caught back a tear. She might have hated her stepmother for taking her mother's place, but she had never hated Oliver. At ten years of age to his thirteen, she'd been pathetically eager to be his friend. She'd never had a brother or a sister before and she'd hero-worshipped him. She'd followed him around like a blind disciple, willing to do anything he asked of her, hanging on his every word.

She hadn't been alone. He was a popular boy, and at the comprehensive in Rhosmawr that they'd both attended he'd never been short of companions. For almost six years, she'd deluded herself that the girls who came and went in his life meant nothing to him. Her infatuation had been such that she'd convinced herself he was only killing time until she grew up.

Stella had guessed how she felt, of course. Her stepmother had always had far more experience of life than Laura's father, and to begin with it had amused her that her stepdaughter should have fallen so completely for her son. Stella hadn't done anything about it. Perhaps she'd thought she could leave that to Oliver himself. But she'd got a rude awakening when she'd discovered them together, and despite the fact that Oliver had defended her she'd despised the girl from then on.

Laura groaned now and rolled over on to her stomach,

trying to still the raw emotions that were churning inside her. That was all in the past, she told herself. She'd got over Oliver when she'd married Conor. And she'd grown up long before she took her vows. All right, so the marriage hadn't worked out; but these things happened. Conor had been too young to make the commitment; too willing to leave all responsibility to her.

It was coming back here, she thought abruptly. She hadn't spent any length of time at Penmadoc since she'd left to go to university over ten years ago. Like Oliver himself, she'd left home as soon as her schooldays were over—though he'd deferred continuing his education for a year to go backpacking across Europe instead.

Her lips twisted. It sometimes seemed as if fortune had always smiled on her stepbrother, and it was hard not to feel resentful when her own life had followed such a different course. Although being caught up in the conflict that had ensued after a country's escape from a non-democratic government might not have seemed fortunate at the time, the pictures Oliver had taken and sent back to a London newspaper had ensured him a job in journalism after he'd got his degree. Since then, he'd become famous for his skill in capturing photographic images. Recently, a book of stylised black and white pictures of Alaskan wildlife he'd taken had made the best-seller lists. He worked free-lance these days, accepting commissions as and when it suited him. He also gave lectures: Laura knew because she'd attended one anonymously in New York.

Which was so very different from her own experience, she acknowledged ruefully. After—after what had happened between her and Oliver, she'd found it very hard to trust a man again. Besides which, although she'd got her degree in English, she was no genius. The fact that she'd got a job in publishing was due more to Conor's father's introduction to his brother, who owned the company, than any skill on her part, she was sure.

Conor's parents had been good to her. They were Americans, like their son, and had sent him to England primarily to improve his social skills. He'd told Laura after their marriage that it was her independence and self-sufficiency that had drawn him to her. She'd never told him why she'd had to learn to depend only on herself.

Expelling a weary breath, she cast off the old dressing gown and crawled between the sheets. They were cold now, and she realised she should have filled a hot-water bottle, after all. So what's new? she thought. Her whole life seemed to have been a study in retrospection. With Oliver Kemp the fulcrum at its core.

CHAPTER THREE

OLIVER awakened with a thumping headache.

For a while he lay quite still, trying to work out where he was and how he came to be there. He couldn't understand why his room felt so cold. It didn't get this cold in Malaysia. And if he wasn't there why couldn't he hear the steady hum of the Knightsbridge traffic? Despite double-glazing, he was always aware of the heart of the city, beating away just yards from Mostyn Square.

Then he remembered. Remembered, too, why his head was pounding as if there were a pile driver in his skull. He was in Wales; at Penmadoc, not in London. And it was the fact that he'd consumed the best part of a bottle of Scotch before falling into bed in the early hours that accounted for his hangover.

He groaned. He should have had more sense. But after seeing Laura again and learning why his mother had been so desperate to get in touch with him he'd needed something to fortify his strength.

The will…

Levering himself up on his elbows, he endeavoured to survey the room without feeling sick. But the bed swayed alarmingly, and although he swung his feet on to the floor he had to hold on to the mattress to keep his balance. Dammit, he was too old to be suffering this kind of nonsense. In future, he'd sustain himself with mineral water and nothing else.

Cursing whatever fate had decreed he should return to England at this particular moment in time, he got to his feet. Then, steadying himself on the chest of drawers beside his wardrobe, he shuffled across the room like an old man.

Despite a lengthy exploration, there were no painkillers in

the bathroom cabinet. The light in there was blinding. He
hadn't thought to pull down the blind the night before and
the brilliance of sun on snow was the equivalent of a knife
being driven into his temple. It was the kind of light he usually only saw through a filter, but right now the idea of es-
timating aperture, shutter speeds and distance was quite beyond his capabilities.

'For God's sake,' he muttered, jerking on the cord, only
to have the blind rattle up again at lightning speed. He swore
again, grabbing the cord and repeating the procedure. 'This
is just what I need.'

At least the water was hot and he stepped into the shower
cubicle and ran the spray at a crippling pressure. He hadn't
looked at his watch yet, but he guessed it must be after nine
o'clock. He could have done with a cup of Thomas's strong
black coffee. Instead, he would probably have to make do
with the instant variety which was all Laura's aunt ever had.

Fifteen minutes later, dressed in black trousers and a
chunky Aran sweater, workmanlike boots over thick socks
keeping his feet warm, he left the room. His hair was still
damp and he hadn't shaved, but he doubted anyone would
notice. If his mother was still in the same state she'd been
in the night before, his appearance was the least of his trou-
bles. So long as she felt she could rely on his support in her
conflict with Laura, she'd avoid doing anything to upset him.

Despite the intensive-heating programme his mother had
inaugurated over the years, the corridors and hall at
Penmadoc remained persistently chilly. Why Stella should
want to stay here when she could buy herself a cosy apartment in Carmarthen or Llanelli, he couldn't imagine. He
found it hard to believe that she was so attached to the old
place. There had to be more to it than that.

The stairs creaked as he descended them, but at least the
fire had been lighted in the hall below. Flames crackled up
the blackened chimney, and the logs split and splintered in
the massive grate. Years ago, he supposed, the hall would

have been the focal point of the whole house. According to Griff, parts of Penmadoc dated from the sixteenth century, but so much had been added on to the original structure that its origins were hard to define.

He had paused to warm his hands at the fire when a dark-clad figure emerged from the direction of the kitchen. He saw it was Eleanor Tenby, Laura's aunt. Although he knew she could only be in her fifties, she looked years older, her straight hair almost completely white these days.

An angular woman, she had barely tolerated him as a teen-ager. But, because Laura had been fond of him, she'd treated him more kindly than she had his mother. Then, when the family had broken up, she'd blamed him for Laura's exile, only softening again in recent years when she'd seen how much Griff looked forward to his visits.

'So you're up at last,' she remarked without enthusiasm, proving that, as always, nothing went on at Penmadoc without her knowing about it. 'I offered to bring you up some breakfast, but your mother said to let you sleep. If you're hoping that I'll cook you something now, you're too late.'

'All I want is some coffee,' said Oliver flatly, the thought of grilled bacon and fried eggs turning his stomach. 'Anyway, how are you? This—' He spread his hands expressively. 'It must have been a great shock.'

'It was.' The woman's thin lips compressed into a fine line. 'And you'll not find any consolation in the bottom of a bottle. No one ever improved a situation with alcohol.'

Oliver might have disputed that on another occasion, but this morning he was inclined to agree with her. 'Believe me,' he said, 'I'm regretting it. And I am sorry you had no warning that Griff was ill.'

'Yes, well…' Laura's aunt sniffed deprecatingly, somewhat mollified by Oliver's words. 'You always had more sensitivity than anyone gave you credit for.' She paused. 'I expect you know that Laura's here.'

Oliver nodded, and then regretted the action. His head

thumped and he raised a hand to the back of his neck. 'Do you have any aspirin?' he asked, wincing. 'I've got to do something before my skull splits in two.'

'Come along into the kitchen,' said Aunt Nell tolerantly, and without waiting to see if he was following her she started back the way she'd come. 'What you need is something to eat,' she added, despite the refusal she'd made earlier. 'You'll feel altogether better with a bowl of my oatmeal inside you. You don't want to be poisoning your system by popping pills.'

Aspirin? Oliver grimaced. He'd hate to think what she'd say if she found out he'd been offered cocaine. Thankfully, he'd never been interested in what some people called 'social' substances, but these days they were increasingly hard to avoid.

The kitchen looked much different this morning than it had done the night before. As in the hall, a cheerful fire was burning in the grate and the scent of woodsmoke was not unappealing. There were other smells he was not so keen on, like the many species of herbs that grew in the pots on the windowsills and hung in dried bunches from the beamed ceiling. But there was the smell of freshly baked bread, too, and the crisp crackle of roasting meat from the oven.

Aunt Nell watched him take a seat at the table, and then busied herself pouring milk into a pan. The same pan that Laura had burnt the night before, thought Oliver ruefully. But clean now and sparkling like new.

The idea of drinking some of the thick creamy milk that was farmed locally made him shudder, and he wished he could just help himself to a cup of coffee instead. But there was no welcoming pot simmering on the hob, and he guessed he'd have to make some instant himself if he wanted it.

To distract himself, he glanced out of the window. As he'd noticed when he'd drawn his curtains upstairs, it had stopped snowing for the present and the sun was causing the icicles drooping from the eaves to drip. But it was a white world, only marred by the skeletal shapes of the trees. However, the evergreens that surrounded the vegetable garden outside looked like snowmen with their clinging mantle of snow.

'Have you spoken to Laura?'

Aunt Nell's question was unexpected. 'Don't you know?' he asked, with faint mockery. Then, because her lips had tightened reprovingly, and she was trying to help him, Oliver relented. 'Yeah. She was up last night when I got here.'

'Ah.' Aunt Nell had made a pot of tea and carried it to the table. 'I wondered why she didn't have a lot to say before she went out.'

'Went out?' Oliver glanced at his watch. 'What time did she go out?'

'She said she wanted some air,' replied Aunt Nell evenly. She set a cup and saucer and some milk beside the teapot. 'Go on. Help yourself. It'll do you more good than taking pills.'

Oliver could have argued. He knew where the coffee jar was kept. But his head was still thumping and he couldn't be bothered. There was caffeine in tea, wasn't there? he thought. For the time being, he'd make do with that.

The dish of oatmeal wasn't long in following the tea. Laura's aunt sugared it liberally before passing it over. 'There,' she said, as he put down his cup. 'Get that inside you. I always say that breakfast is the most important meal of the day.'

Oliver was sure he was going to be sick, but he forced himself to swallow several mouthfuls of the oatmeal. He'd eaten worse things in Malaysia, after all. People there ate rice at almost every meal.

'So where has she gone?' he asked at last, reluctantly aware that he was actually feeling much better.

'Into the village,' replied Aunt Nell, tidying the dresser. 'She didn't have a lot to say, as I said.' She turned to give him an appraising look. 'What happened last night? Did you and she have a row?'

'No.' Oliver was indignant.

'I thought your mother was supposed to be waiting up for you,' continued the woman. 'What was Laura doing down here?'

'She'd come down to get a drink,' said Oliver patiently, aware that he was falling back into the old patterns of defensiveness where Eleanor Tenby was concerned. 'Ma had fallen asleep, or so she said. That's why I came round the back.'

'And Laura let you in.'

'Yeah.'

'But I imagine your mother eventually turned up.'

'Yeah.' Oliver regarded her with a wry expression. 'But you know all this, don't you? Laura went to bed as soon as Stella appeared.'

'So she didn't discuss her father's death with you?'

'No.' Oliver was wary. 'What was there to discuss? I already knew how he died. Stella told me when I rang. He had a heart attack. It must have been appalling for her, finding his body. Had he been seeing a doctor, do you know? If he had, he should have warned her.'

'Griff hadn't been seeing the doctor,' replied Aunt Nell firmly. 'When Tenniel Evans came to examine him after—afterwards, he was as shocked as anyone else. Who knows why he died? He's not here to tell us. Perhaps he'd had a shock—or a fall from his horse. It may be that we'll never know.'

Nevertheless Oliver sensed that Laura's aunt had her own opinion. Not that she was likely to confide that opinion to him. But the very fact that she was asking questions was unsettling. For God's sake, surely this was one occasion when she could have given Stella some support.

'Do you know what's in the will?' he asked now, forcing himself to deal with facts, not fantasies, and Laura's aunt lifted her thin shoulders dismissively.

'It's nothing to do with me,' she said, turning away, which

wasn't an answer. But Oliver guessed it was the best he was going to get.

'So—were you here when it happened?' he probed, deciding that in spite of everything he deserved to know the details.

'No.' She glanced over her shoulder. 'I was away for the day visiting a friend in Cardiff. Griff had said he was going out with the hunt, and your mother had arranged to go shopping, or so she said. She told me she'd be eating out and not to bother preparing lunch before I left.' She licked her lips. 'But I did leave Griff a sandwich.' She grimaced. 'He never touched it.'

'I see.' Oliver's headache was definitely easing now and his brain had started functioning again. 'So she was alone in the house when she found him. Poor old Stella. God, she must have been frantic!'

'I dare say.'

Oliver frowned. There was something about the woman's tone that caught him on the raw. 'Do you doubt it?' he exclaimed. 'For God's sake, even you must feel some sympathy for her. There can't be any advantage in finding your husband dead!'

'Did I say there was?'

'No, but—' Oliver broke off abruptly. Then, in a calmer tone, he continued, 'Look, I know you've never liked her, but in these circumstances we've all got to make compromises.'

Aunt Nell shrugged. 'If you say so.' She paused. 'Did your mother tell you she was alone when she found—Griff's body?'

Oliver stared at her shoulder blades, turned to him again now and jutting painfully through the fine wool of the sweater she was wearing over her worsted skirt. Her question disconcerted him. Why did she want to know that?

'Of course she was alone,' he said tersely. 'You know that. You were in Cardiff, as you said earlier.'

'Perhaps you should ask her why it was two hours before she discovered his body,' Aunt Nell remarked, looking at him over her shoulder. 'If she was here, why didn't she hear him come in?'

'Perhaps she did.' Oliver blew out an irritated breath. 'Have you asked her?'

'It's nothing to do with me.'

'Of course it is,' Oliver was impatient and it showed.

'Not according to your mother,' replied the woman smoothly. 'Now, if you'll excuse me, I've got work to do.'

Olivia wanted to question her further. He was angry, and he wanted to know what she meant by making out there was some big secret about Griff's death. There wasn't, he assured himself. Men of Griff's age had heart attacks all the time, and without doing anything as strenuous as riding to hounds.

As Laura's aunt let herself out of the room, he moved to the windows to stare out unseeingly. As always, he never came off best in any encounter with Laura's aunt, and while he knew she wasn't a liar he suspected she'd do anything to cause trouble for his mother.

He scowled, pushing his hands into the waistline pockets of his trousers and forcing the sunlit garden into focus. It was a pretty scene, he thought, considering the frame of poplar trees whose bare branches formed a stark contrast to their surroundings. He would use a colour negative, he mused, to take advantage of the band of sunlight that was presently creating a rainbow of artistry in the thawing icicles. Some of his best work had been done spontaneously, and his fingers itched to capture it on film.

But then his gaze alighted on the line of footsteps that led to the gate and all thought of photographic composition vanished beneath a wave of frustration. Laura was out there somewhere. The footsteps led in only one direction, away from the house, and he wondered what she had thought of what had happened the night before. Was she aware that if his mother hadn't interrupted them he'd been in danger of resurrecting the offence that had driven them apart all those years ago?

Dammit, was he crazy, or what? He hadn't wanted Laura then and he didn't want her now. What had happened had been a reaction to circumstances, that was all, and he ought to be grateful to his mother for preventing him from making an even bigger fool of himself.

And he was. *He was!* But that didn't explain why he'd needed to anaesthetise himself with Scotch before he could get to sleep.

CHAPTER FOUR

LAURA stood in the shadow of a huge snow-covered cypress, warming her gloved hands beneath her arms. She'd been about to enter the garden when she'd seen Oliver standing at the kitchen window and she'd drawn back automatically, his dour expression warning her that he wasn't in the best of moods.

Her heart skipped a beat. Damn, why had he had to be here? All right, perhaps that was unreasonable. His stepfather was dead and naturally his mother wanted her own flesh and blood around her at this time, but if only *she* hadn't had to have anything to do with him.

She'd considered booking into a hotel in Rhosmawr, which was the nearest small town to Penmadoc, but she'd quickly discarded that idea. It wasn't fair to her father—or to Aunt Nell—to behave as if she wasn't the daughter of the house, and just because Penmadoc wasn't her home any more that did not give her an excuse to stay away.

She wondered if Oliver and her father had become closer in recent years. It was possible. There was no doubt that her father regretted her unwillingness to visit Penmadoc, and with the width of the Atlantic between them they'd seen each other much less than he would have liked.

For herself, she'd thought it had been easier for all of them when she went to live in the United States. It had certainly been easier for her—to begin with, at least. In New York, she'd been able to put the past behind her, and, if the wounds she'd thought healed had only been buried beneath a layer of self-deception, by the time she'd realised it, she was able to cope with the pain.

She sighed. She would have to go in soon. It was threat-

ening to snow again and her feet were freezing. She wasn't
used to living in the country in winter. Winter in New York
was a much more civilised affair altogether. The paths were
always cleared; shopping malls were always heated; and her
apartment was always comfortably warm.

Unlike Penmadoc...

She took a deep breath. She shouldn't complain about the
house really. There'd been years when she'd considered it
the most beautiful house in the world. Not that it was beautiful, she conceded honestly. Built of dark Welsh stone, it
sometimes had a rather dour appearance. But its pitched roof
was peppered with half a dozen tall chimneys, and when she
was a child she used to tell everyone that she was lucky
because Santa Claus would have so many to choose from.

She shivered, stamping the snow from her boots and preparing to open the gate into the garden. It was no use putting
it off any longer. She had to go in and face whatever was
required of her. What could happen in a few days, after all?
Her father was dead. His funeral was all she should be thinking of.

And then she felt the breath freeze in her throat. Oliver
was still standing in the window but his face was fading. As
she watched, paralysed by the realisation that she was hal-
lucinating, Oliver's strong face gave way to older, softer features. Hardly breathing, she watched as her father's face
came into focus. He was gazing out at the garden with much
the same expression that Oliver had been wearing—a mixture
of anger and frustration.

Panic gripped her. This couldn't be happening to her. She
wasn't psychic. She'd never been psychic. Her mother, perhaps: her grandmother, definitely. But not her. Never her.

But there it was. Her father was dead. *Dead!* Yet there he
stood, wearing the russet-coloured lambswool cardigan she
had sent him for his last birthday. His hair was grey, greyer
than she thought it had been last summer, but just as neatly
trimmed as ever, his military moustache framing the uncom-

promising curve of his upper lip. There was a thread of hectic colour in his gaunt cheeks and deep pouches beneath his eyes, as if he wasn't sleeping too well. *Sleeping!* Laura stifled the hysterical sob that rose into her throat at the knowledge that her father was *dead*, dammit. You couldn't sleep any sounder than that.

She groaned aloud. Dear God, what was happening to her? This had to be some wild hallucination, brought on by the thoughts she'd been having as she walked back from the village. She'd been thinking about her father and somehow her subconscious had conjured him up. It wasn't as if there was any resemblance between Oliver and Griff Williams.

She blinked and, as if proving the point, magically her father's image had disappeared. Oliver stood there as he had before, a cream Aran sweater hugging his much broader shoulders, his tanned features tough and uncompromising, perhaps, but blessedly normal. With knees that felt decidedly weak now, she opened the gate and trudged into the garden. She wasn't going to think about what had happened, she told herself. It had been an aberration, that was all, brought on by her emotional state.

Oliver saw her immediately and a look of relief crossed his face. And, for once, she was glad to see him. After the experience she'd had, she'd have been glad to see anybody, she thought unsteadily. Even Oliver, she acknowledged. A man towards whom she ought to feel nothing but contempt.

He had the door open by the time she reached the house and she offered him a stiff smile of thanks as she stepped inside. 'I was beginning to get worried about you,' he said, attempting to help her off with her parka, but she shrugged his hand aside and finished the job herself.

'Why?' she asked offhandedly, sitting down on a wooden bench and removing her boots. Her hands were trembling and she prayed he wouldn't notice. She'd hate for him to think that she was afraid of him.

'Because it's going to snow again,' he replied, waiting

until she stood up and walked into the kitchen in her stock-
inged feet. Following, he paused in the doorway, watching
as she extended first one foot and then the other towards the
heat of the fire. 'And you look very pale.'

'I'm cold,' said Laura shortly, aware that the cold she was
feeling came from inside and not out. 'Mmm, that's much
better.'

'Okay.' Oliver was evidently prepared to accept her explanation. His eyes drifted disturbingly over the thigh-length
flannel shirt worn over a black tee shirt and ribbed black
leggings. 'Did you manage to get any sleep?'

Laura tucked the sides of her hair behind her ears before
answering him. 'I slept very well, actually,' she lied. Then,
because it was expected, she asked, 'Did you?'

'No.'

He spoke flatly and, glancing his way, she wondered if
that was true. There was a slight puffiness around his eyes,
but he looked much as she remembered from the night before. Narrow cheekbones angled above an unshaven jawline,
and his thin mouth had a surprisingly sensual curve. He had
never had conventionally handsome features; his face was too
strong for that. But he was the most attractive man she had
ever seen.

'Perhaps your conscience was troubling you,' she said
without thinking, and immediately regretted it. The last thing
she wanted was to dredge up the past again, and she added
quickly, 'I mean, because you weren't here when your
mother needed you.'

Oliver's eyes narrowed. 'What do you know about that?'

'About what?' Laura's eyes strayed compulsively towards
the window. She was half afraid she'd see her father's image
gazing in at her now and a shiver slid uneasily down her
spine.

'About the afternoon your father died,' said Oliver shortly.
And then, noticing her shiver, he added, 'You are cold.
Would you like some coffee?'

Laura was tempted to refuse, but the idea of a hot drink was appealing. More appealing than the isolation of her room at this moment, and she nodded. 'Thanks.'

Oliver filled the kettle and plugged it in before taking a jar and two mugs from the cupboard above the counter. He placed the cups side by side and spooned some of the coffee into each. Then he turned, folding his arms and propping his hips against the unit. 'What did your aunt tell you about— well, about what happened?'

'Not a lot,' murmured Laura, feeling another shiver feather her skin. Glancing round, she saw the rocker beside the fire and curled her long legs beneath her as she settled on to its cushioned seat. 'What your mother told you, I expect.'

'Yeah.' But he didn't sound convinced. 'I thought you might know more about it, seeing that you've been here for a couple of days.'

'I only arrived the day before you did,' protested Laura, frowning. 'Besides, what's there to know? Daddy had a heart attack. Your mother found him.' She swallowed. 'End of story.'

Oliver waited until the kettle had boiled and poured hot water into the mugs before continuing, 'So you don't know what the old lady was talking about?'

Laura blinked. 'I don't know what *you're* talking about,' she said, accepting a mug from him, shaking her head when he offered milk. 'Mmm, this is good.'

Oliver resumed his position against the counter. 'Did your aunt tell you Stella was on her own when it happened?' he asked casually, and Laura stared at him, at last realising that there was more to this than random interest.

'I—yes. Yes, I think so.' She paused, cradling her mug between her hands. 'Why? What has she said to you? That there was someone else here?'

Oliver shook his head. 'You know Aunt Nell. She didn't actually *say* anything.'

'Then—'

'It was just an impression she gave.' He scowled. 'She implied it was odd that Griff had been dead for a couple of hours before Ma found him.'

Laura's eyes widened. 'Was he?'

Oliver pulled a face. 'Surely she told you that?'

'No.' Laura was thoughtful. 'At least, I don't think so. Anyway, why should it be important?'

Oliver shrugged, taking a drink of his coffee. 'No reason.'

But she didn't believe him. 'Do you think your mother was lying?'

'It wouldn't be the first time.' And then, seeing Laura's pained expression, he groaned. 'God, I don't know. Probably not.'

Leaving the stove, he dragged a chair from the table and, swinging it round, he straddled it across the hearth from where she was sitting. Resting one arm across the back, he regarded her consideringly. 'What's wrong?'

His change of topic was unexpected and Laura's eyes were drawn towards the window again before she could stop herself. But, thankfully, her reaction meant nothing to him, and after assuring herself that she had imagined what had happened earlier she shook her head. 'What could be wrong?' she countered, feeling her hair brushing against her shoulders. 'Daddy's dead. What do you think is wrong?'

Oliver sighed. 'Okay. Point taken. But you did look as if you'd seen a ghost when you came in. I wondered if anybody had said anything to upset you.'

'Who?'

Laura resented his perception, and it showed. But, dammit, she was doing her best not to reveal how she was really feeling and having him daunt her at every turn was disturbing to say the least. Despite her best efforts, she was irresistibly aware of the taut seam of his trousers visible between the spokes of the dining chair, and the bulge of his sex evident beneath the soft cloth. His thighs were spread, long-muscled and powerful, his booted feet only a few inches from the legs of her chair.

'I don't know. Someone from the village, perhaps,' he said now. 'So—how long is it since you saw your father?'

Laura moistened her lips. 'Um—about six months, I suppose. I came to London last year. There—there was a conference. Daddy came up to meet me.'

'Was he okay?'

'I thought so.' Laura shifted uncomfortably. 'Does it matter?'

'I guess not.' Oliver paused. 'I'm sure he was pleased to see you.'

'As your mother is always pleased to see you,' retorted Laura, responding to the implied criticism. 'Do you see much of her these days?'

'When I can. Or when she wants something,' commented Oliver drily. 'I've become much more popular since she's proved I'm good for a handout.'

Laura stiffened. 'Why didn't she ask Daddy if she needed money?'

'Oh—' Oliver obviously regretted his careless words. 'You know Ma. She's always short of funds.'

'If that's a dig—'

'It isn't.' Oliver seemed weary now. 'Come on, Laura. All I'm saying is that Stella's always been reckless with money. She's never had enough for her own needs. I should know.'

'Well, it's why she married Daddy, if that's what you mean,' Laura said shortly. 'At least she won't have that problem now.'

'Laura—'

'I mean it. Daddy was very conscientious about paying insurances, that sort of thing. And then there's this house…' Her stomach tightened at the thought of losing Penmadoc. 'She can sell it, if she chooses to do so.'

'I wouldn't bank on that,' said Oliver drily before taking a gulp of his coffee, and Laura wondered what he meant.

'Because she needs somewhere to live?' she probed, but Oliver seemed to think he had said enough on that score.

'Yeah,' he said, before reverting to her earlier topic. 'I wonder why she didn't hear your father come in?'

Laura's brows lifted. 'Do you think she was out?'

'She could have been, I suppose.' Oliver expelled an exasperated breath. 'But if so, why didn't she say so? After all, she'd told the old girl she was going shopping.'

'There you are.' Laura had no particular desire to dwell on the circumstances of her father's death. 'And don't call Aunt Nell "the old girl". She's not that much older than your mother.'

'True.' Oliver conceded the point. Then, with another change of pace, he asked, 'Have you spoken to your father's solicitors yet?'

'No.' Laura felt a twinge of unease. 'Have you?'

'How could I?' Oliver was gazing into the fire now. 'I only learned about—about what happened last night.'

'Hmm.' Laura knew a sudden surge of regret. 'It's a pity Daddy didn't realise your mother was at home when he got back. You never know, there might have been something she could have done.'

Oliver nodded. 'I thought that, too.'

'Or if anyone else had been around,' added Laura, still musing. 'What did your mother tell you last night?'

'Not a lot,' said Oliver briefly, and Laura guessed her stepmother's prime concern had been for herself. Was that why he'd asked if she'd spoken to her father's solicitors? Because Stella didn't want any obstacle to stand in the way of her getting probate?

'I didn't know she'd managed to get in touch with you,' Laura continued when he didn't elaborate. 'I know she phoned your house several times yesterday but that man you live with kept telling her that you weren't there.'

'Thomas is not my partner, he works for me,' stated Oliver, clearly irritated by her description. 'And, as I told you last night, I'd just got back from Singapore that afternoon.'

'Mmm.' Laura refused to be intimidated. 'Whatever. He certainly got under your mother's skin.' She paused, and then asked reluctantly, 'What were you doing in Singapore, anyway? Photographing the Prime Minister or some other dignitary?'

'As a matter of fact, I've been in Malaysia,' replied Oliver mildly. 'I'd been invited to join an expedition going into the Kasong Gorge. You've probably never heard of it, but it's virtually inaccessible except down this narrow defile. I went with a party of naturalists who wanted me to film some of the rare plants and flowers that are found there.'

'And I suppose it will give you enough material for another book,' commented Laura offhandedly, and Oliver gave her a wry smile.

'It sounds as if you're jealous,' he remarked, arousing her indignation. 'Hey, how about if I give Neill and O'Roarke first refusal when the manuscript's ready?'

'That's up to you,' replied Laura carelessly, her initial inclination to refuse tempered by the knowledge that Conor's uncle, who owned the company, would not approve of turning an obvious best-seller down. Besides, she'd never been jealous of Oliver's success, despite everything that had happened. She hadn't advertised the fact that he was her stepbrother, of course, but that had had nothing to do with his work.

'I'm glad you came,' he ventured softly, and Laura wished he'd continued baiting her then; it was easier to deal with. 'I did wonder if you would,' he added. 'The weather's been so atrocious, apparently. What did Ma say when she gave you the news?'

'She didn't,' said Laura swiftly. 'Give me—give me the news, I mean. It was Aunt Nell who phoned.' She refrained from mentioning the fact that she'd wondered if her aunt had called with or without her stepmother's endorsement. Judging from the greeting Stella had given her, she was still *persona non grata* in this house.

'I see.' Oliver's dark brows had drawn together, and she sensed he didn't like his mother's attitude towards her any more than she did. 'Well, you're here now, that's the main thing. Stella will have to get over it.'

'Get over what?'

Laura was confused, but with another of his lightning shifts of mood Oliver changed the subject again. 'You've filled out,' he said, his gaze on her mouth almost palpable in its intimacy. His eyes lowered to her rounded breasts and a kernel of heat ignited inside her. 'Yes, you've definitely changed since I last saw you.'

'If you mean I've put on weight, that's hardly a compliment,' said Laura tightly, using anger to hide the turmoil that was seething inside her. She wasn't sixteen now, she thought resentfully, or even twenty-one, as she'd been at her wedding, which was the last time he'd seen her. 'What gives you the right to make personal remarks?'

'It was supposed to be a compliment,' he protested. 'When you got married, you were as skinny as a rake.'

'Gee, thanks. That makes me feel a whole lot better.'

Oliver blew out a breath. 'I mean it.' His eyes drifted over her again and she had to steel herself not to glance down. But she was sure her peaking nipples were visible despite the serviceable bra she was wearing. 'You look—good,' he continued huskily. 'You're not my little sister any more.'

'I was never your little sister,' retorted Laura. And then, realising she was in danger of saying too much, she forced herself to rein in her emotions. 'Anyway, where's Aunt Nell? It's not like her to let anyone else use her kitchen.'

Oliver shrugged. 'Does it matter?' He pressed down on the bar and got up from the chair as he spoke. 'Tell me about you, about what you've been doing since you got your divorce. I still don't know what happened between you two.' He paused. 'Was there someone else?'

Laura drew back into the rocker, wrapping the folds of her shirt across her breasts. She was half afraid he was going to touch her as he had the night before, and she felt a treacherous moistness between her legs.

'I'm sure you're not interested in me,' she declared, aware that in spite of her efforts her voice was sharp. 'Any more than I'm interested in you and your girlfriends.'

'I don't have any girl*friends*,' responded Oliver, a little impatiently. 'I have one girlfriend. Her name is Natalie Harlowe. You may have heard of her. She's a model.'

'Surprise, surprise!'

Laura couldn't prevent herself from looking up at him, her eyes rolling expressively as she mocked his words. Oliver's face darkened with annoyance, and she quickly returned her attention to the dregs of coffee in her mug, but she was aware of him gazing down at her, and her stomach quivered with remembered pain.

'You'd like her,' he said, after a moment. 'If you got to know her, that is. Or are you so cynical after your own experiences with marriage that you can't face the fact that some couples do succeed?'

Laura's lips trembled. If he only knew, she thought bitterly. It wasn't her marital experiences that had made her cynical, no matter what he thought. She wanted to tell him then, wanted to wipe the smug expression off his face with what was real. But she couldn't. She had never told anyone. And he was the last person she'd confide in, anyway.

'I'm sorry,' she said now, but although she managed a careless glance in his direction there was little apology in her tone. She took a steadying breath. 'But the famous photographer and his model,' she added, trying to make light of it. 'Isn't it just the tiniest bit of a cliché?'

'I don't photograph models,' Oliver countered tightly, and to her relief he strode away to deposit his empty mug in the sink. Then, with his back to her, he continued flatly, 'You and I need to talk, Laura. I think you're still carrying far too much baggage from the past.'

How dared he?

Laura uncoiled her long legs from the chair and stared at his broad shoulders resentfully. Just like that, he thought he could dispose of their history in a few words. If he'd cared about her feelings at all, he'd never have said such a thing to her. What the hell was he implying? That he thought she'd messed up his life?

'I don't think we have anything to talk about,' she retorted, before she could prevent herself. It was all right telling herself she shouldn't stir up all those old feelings, but here, in this house, the past seemed unpleasantly close.

'There you are.' He swung round. 'You are harbouring some kind of grudge against me. For God's sake, Laura, don't you think I've suffered enough over the years?'

'*You've* suffered?' For a moment, for a long, shuddering moment, she was tempted to tell him. As he stood there, staring at her with those cold, accusing eyes, she desperately wanted to tear his shallow world apart. But then common sense—and a dogged sense of pride—came to her rescue, and, shaking her head bemusedly, she said, 'I—don't think anything either of us can say can change how we feel about the past.'

Oliver's shoulders sagged. 'I had hoped you'd have forgiven me. God knows, it's taken me years to forgive myself.'

Laura swallowed. 'I have forgiven you,' she asserted. 'I just don't want to talk about it.' She turned towards the door. 'And now I think I'll go and find Aunt Nell. There may be something I can do to help her.'

'To help her—but not to help me,' said Oliver roughly, coming after her. And, before she could guess his intention, his fingers closed about her arm. 'God, Laura,' he groaned, and she was almost sure he bent his head to inhale the fragrance of her hair. 'Don't do this to me. Last night you said we could be friends.'

Friends!

It was all she could do not to utter a stifled sob of hysteria at his words. The violence of his reaction had shaken what little self-control she had. 'Let me go, Oliver,' she managed unevenly. 'I think you've forgotten why we're here.'

'I've forgotten nothing,' he retorted, and now she was sure he was dangerously close to exposing her charade. His hand slid down her arm, his thumb finding the sensitive inner curve of her wrist. 'Damn you, Laura, it wasn't all my fault.'

CHAPTER FIVE

'SO WHEN is the funeral?'

Natalie was obviously trying to be understanding and Oliver wedged himself more comfortably against the head-board of his bed and switched his mobile phone to his other ear.

'Tuesday, I think,' he said, trying to respond with an equal warmth, but it was difficult to put that scene in the kitchen with Laura out of his mind. It was just as well her aunt had turned up as she had, he thought savagely. God alone knew what stupid stunt he might have pulled if her arrival hadn't interrupted them.

'Tuesday!' Natalie groaned. 'But that's almost the middle of next week.'

'Yeah, I know.' Oliver managed to infuse some sympathy into his voice. He was loath to tell her he didn't actually know what arrangements his mother had made yet. She hadn't got around to telling him.

'But didn't he die on Wednesday?'

'Yes.'

'Then isn't six days rather a long time to...?'

'I believe there had to be a post-mortem,' broke in Oliver reluctantly. 'And the weather's pretty lousy, too.'

'Mmm.' Natalie sighed. 'I suppose so.' She paused, and then added more optimistically, 'But they say a thaw is on the way.'

'Oh, good.'

Oliver knew his voice was lacking in enthusiasm and he was hardly surprised when she picked up on it. 'You don't care, do you?' she accused him indignantly. 'You know I'm leaving for Antigua next Thursday. I had hoped I might be able to persuade you to come with me, but now it sounds as if I'm not even going to see you before I go.'

'I didn't plan it this way, Nat.' But he did feel guilty. He'd forgotten all about the Antigua shoot. 'I'm sorry.'

'Are you?' She didn't sound convinced. There was a pregnant pause. 'I suppose *she's* there.'

'Who?' He knew exactly who she meant, but he needed a few moments to get his thoughts in order.

'You know who!' she exclaimed shortly. 'Laura.' She clicked her tongue. 'How long is she staying?'

Oliver could feel an unpleasant tightening in his stomach. 'Does it matter?' he asked with what he hoped was casual indifference.

'Of course it matters.' Natalie sighed. 'I'd like to meet her. If she's coming up to town when the funeral's over—'

'I neither know nor care what her plans are,' retorted Oliver, with rather less discretion. 'In any case, I doubt if she'll have time to come to London.'

'Why not?'

Why not indeed?

He gritted his teeth. 'Her father's just died, Nat. There'll be—things to do; matters to attend to. Not least, her father's affairs to put in order.'

'But won't your mother be doing that?' asked Natalie in surprise, and Oliver had to acknowledge that it was a reasonable question.

'She—may need some help,' he said, cringing at his own duplicity. 'Look, you know what solicitors are like. These things can be—complicated.'

'In other words, you don't want to ask her.'

'Ask her?' Oliver felt blank. 'Ask her what?'

'To come and stay with you,' replied Natalie impatiently. 'Honestly, Oliver, why couldn't you just come right out and say it? You don't like her, that's obvious. I'm beginning to wonder exactly what did happen all those years ago.'

Oliver stifled a groan. 'Nothing happened!' he exclaimed.

'For God's sake, Nat, stop making a drama out of this.' He took a deep breath. 'All right. If it'll please you, I'll ask her if she wants to come and stay for a few days before she goes back to the States. How about that?'

Natalie sniffed. 'You don't have to sound as if I'm forcing you to do it.'

'For Pete's sake—'

'All right.' She expelled a hurried breath. 'That would be nice. So—so long as you promise we'll have some time alone together after I get back.'

Oliver was tempted to say she couldn't have it both ways, but he had no desire to start another argument so he assured her that he had no plans for leaving town again in the immediate future. Then, desperate to end the conversation before he said something more incriminating, he added, 'I must go, baby. I want to let Thomas know what's going on and there are still arrangements to be made.'

'I know.' Thankfully, Natalie seemed to accept this. Then, just when he thought he was home free, she cried, 'Hey, I've got a marvellous idea. Why don't you invite your mother up to town as well as Laura? It would be a break for her, wouldn't it? It might help her to put the funeral behind her. And you know how much I've wanted to meet your family.'

Oliver's lips twisted. 'I'll—think about it,' he said tightly, aware that Natalie had no idea what she was suggesting. 'Bye, sweetheart. Speak to you soon.'

'See you do.' Natalie suppressed what sounded suspiciously like a sob. 'I love you.'

'Yeah. Me, too.'

Oliver gave the automatic response, but he felt a shameful sense of relief when the call was disconnected. God, he thought grimly, when had his life become so complicated? It didn't use to be. Before he'd left for Malaysia, everything had seemed so simple. He had a job doing something he loved; he owned a house that was the envy of many of his friends; and he was in love with a beautiful woman who, amazingly, loved him in return. He'd thought nothing could change that. Dammit, how wrong he'd been.

Yet, if he was honest with himself, he'd have to admit that nothing had changed. Not outwardly, at least. He still had his work; he still had his house; he still loved Natalie and she loved him. So why the hell was he feeling as if everything he had achieved, everything he'd believed in all these years, was suddenly on shifting sands?

Laura.

He scowled. He didn't have to look far to find the answer. It was the way she'd looked at him earlier that morning, the—what? Pity? Revulsion? Contempt?—in her expression that had cut the ground out from under him. She despised him, that much was obvious, and believing that they might be able to forget the past and start again was as futile as hoping that his mother might have had a change of heart.

But she couldn't put all the blame on to him, dammit. What had happened had been as much her fault as his. If he'd responded to what had proved to be an irresistible provocation, then so be it. But he hadn't initiated that provocation. She had. And the sooner she stopped condemning him for something that had been inevitable from the moment she opened his bedroom door—

His breath caught in his throat as someone knocked at his door. God, he thought, raking back his hair with a slightly unsteady hand. History couldn't be repeating itself. Could it? Did he want it to?

Angry at the sudden quickening of his pulse, he swung his legs to the floor and got to his feet just as his mother put her head round the door. 'You decent?' she asked, and without waiting for a reply she slipped furtively into the room.

Oliver regarded her with a jaundiced eye, aware that it would have been all the same if he'd been stark naked. As always, Stella put her own priorities first, and she offered no excuse for invading his privacy.

'I've been looking for you,' she said, closing the door with what he considered an unnecessary measure of caution. 'What are you doing up here?'

'Do I have to answer that?' Oliver regarded his mother's negligée-clad figure without emotion. He tossed the mobile phone on to the bedside table. 'I was making a call.'

'To Natalie?' For some reason, Stella had decided to endorse their relationship. Probably to ensure that he wouldn't be tempted to make a friend of Laura, decided Oliver cynically. 'You must bring her to meet me some time. She's a very beautiful young woman. As a matter of fact, she reminds me of myself when I was younger.'

'Really?' Oliver gave her a retiring look.

'Yes, really.' Stella huffed a little, and gathered the two sides of her negligée closer together. 'Brr, it's cold in here. I told Griff that these radiators weren't powerful enough. But he always insisted that he couldn't afford to change them.'

'Perhaps he couldn't,' murmured Oliver drily, walking across to the windows and gazing out at the amorphous shapes in the garden. 'This place must eat money.'

'Not that much.' Stella glided over to the bed, seating herself where he had been sitting to make his call. 'Mmm, that's better,' she said, drawing the quilt over her shoulders. 'So—what did Natalie have to say?'

Oliver turned, resting his hips on the ledge behind him. 'Don't pretend you're interested.' He lifted his shoulders in an indifferent gesture. 'Have you decided what you're going to do?'

'No, I haven't.' Stella was abrupt now. 'What time have I had to think about the future? I've been too busy trying to come to terms with the present.'

Oliver blew out a breath. 'So what do you want?'

'Oh, Oliver, don't be so callous. Can't I come and have a private word with my own son without him thinking I want something?'

Oliver's mouth compressed. 'Do you want me to answer that?'

Stella pursed her lips. 'You don't care, do you? I'm your mother and you don't care that I'm about to be thrown out of my home.'

'You don't know that,' replied Oliver flatly. 'You're only guessing what Laura might do.'

'Well, I don't need a crystal ball to see how she's going to react when she finds out,' retorted his mother harshly. 'You've got to help me, Oliver. I'm relying on you for your support.'

Oliver sighed. 'I'll do what I can, of course, but—'

'But what?' Stella was emotional now. 'Are you telling me you won't help me?'

'Of course not.' Oliver groaned. 'I just don't know how you think I can help.'

His mother dabbed her eyes with the corner of her sleeve. 'The will,' she said, as he'd known she would. 'Do you think it's legal?'

Oliver was resigned. 'I don't think that's in question, do you?'

'But I'm—I mean, I *was*—his wife. I thought when a husband died a wife automatically inherited his estate.'

'Only if he hasn't left a will,' amended Oliver flatly. 'And even then things aren't always cut and dried.'

Stella made a sound of distress. 'I didn't even know Griff had made a will,' she protested, shredding the tissue she'd taken from her sleeve between agitated fingers. 'He didn't tell me. Don't you think he should have?'

'Well, it would have been more charitable,' Oliver agreed. 'But, for reasons best known to himself, he decided to keep it from you. Perhaps he thought you wouldn't understand.'

'He got that right.' There was little compassion in Stella's voice at that moment. 'It was a rotten thing to do. Making that little bitch his heir!'

'This house was in Laura's family before her mother married Griff,' pointed out Oliver evenly. 'He probably thought he owed her the chance of deciding what happens to it.'

'But it's my home!'

'It was hers,' Oliver reminded her mildly. 'And Maggie Tenby's before that.'

'So you are on her side. You don't care what happens to me.'

'I'm not on anybody's side,' retorted Oliver, unmoved by his mother's ready tears. He knew Stella could produce tears at the drop of a hat. But he had to give her the benefit of the doubt. 'I just think you should try to be practical about this.'

'Practical!' His mother's voice was shrill now. 'When I'm going to be driven out of my home at any minute.'

Oliver blew out a weary breath. 'As I said before, you don't know that.'

'Don't I?' Stella snorted.

'Well, if you hadn't found the will, you wouldn't be worrying about it. Not yet, at any rate. If there's anything illegal about this, it's the fact that you opened an envelope that wasn't addressed to you. If you'd waited—'

'Until after the funeral, you mean?' His mother sneered. 'I suppose you think I should have let that prig, Marcus Venning, tell me that Griff had done the dirty on me. Oh, yes, he'd have enjoyed that.'

Oliver shook his head. 'You're exaggerating.' He paused. 'How did you find the will, anyway? Was it in Griff's desk?'

'As if.' Stella gave him a sulky look. 'Griff always kept anything of importance in the safe.'

'The safe!' Oliver stared at her aghast. 'I didn't know Griff had given you a key to the safe.'

'He didn't.' Stella shrugged. 'He kept it in his desk drawer.'

Oliver was appalled. 'You mean you riffled his desk before calling the ambulance services?'

'No.' Stella was defensive. 'I've known where it was for ages. I—just thought I ought to know. For—well, for emergencies.'

'Like his sudden death, you mean?' Oliver was scathing.

'Don't be horrid, darling.' Stella pursed her lips. 'I didn't know he was going to have a heart attack, for heaven's sake. He seemed perfectly all right when he left the house on Wednesday morning.'

'You saw him before he left?'

'Well—no.' She sighed at her son's expression. 'You know how early the hunt goes out and what with the weather threatening snow...' She sighed. 'I assume he left about half-past-eight.'

'So how do you know—?'

'How do I know he was all right? Nell said so, of course. She's always up at the crack of dawn.'

Oliver frowned. 'And he hadn't said anything about feeling ill? The night before, for instance?'

'No.' Stella pouted. 'Oh, you might as well know, Griff and I haven't shared a room for the last couple of years. You know what old men are like. They snore, and it was getting me down. I thought it would be easier for both of us if we had separate rooms.'

Oliver shook his head. 'Griff wasn't that ancient.'

'I know that, darling. But lots of couples have separate rooms these days. Besides, it suited Griff as well as me.'

'Did it?'

'What do you mean? You don't think that was why Griff decided to make his will?'

'I'm not sure.' As his mother told him the will had been made quite recently, it was always possible. 'You never know, he might have begun to wonder if you still cared for him.'

'Oliver! How can you say such a thing? I loved Griff.'

'I guess so.'

'You guess so?'

Stella was indignant now, but Oliver couldn't help recalling what she'd said when Griff had first asked her out. The fact that he'd owned Penmadoc and had a thriving veterinary practice besides in Rhosmawr must have dazzled Stella, who had been struggling, as a single mother, to support herself and her son. Stella didn't belong in Rhosmawr. Oliver had been born in London, but soon afterwards Stella had taken up with a Norwegian who had been working on the oil rigs, and followed him to Cardiff. Oliver had never known his own father, and his mother's relationship with the Norwegian hadn't lasted long. When Griff Williams had come on the scene, she'd been working as a waitress, and Oliver guessed she'd seen him as her last chance to make something of herself.

There hadn't been much talk of love in those days, Oliver remembered. He and his mother had been living in a poky one-bedroomed flat, and he'd had to make do with a shake-down on the couch. Which had been something of a handicap to Stella when she'd wanted to bring someone home. And there had been one or two boyfriends before Griff came on the scene, Oliver mused bitterly. Stella had been dangerously close to burn-out before the wealthy widower fell under her spell.

Chance was a strange thing, he acknowledged drily. If Stella hadn't offered to take old Mrs Weaver's cat to the vet, she'd probably never have met Griff. Or realised his potential, Oliver conceded. Stella had always been ambitious. She'd just never had the chance to do anything about it until then.

'Oh, Oliver, what am I going to do?' she groaned, distracting him from his thoughts. She slid off the bed and dropped the mangled tissue into the waste basket that stood just inside the adjoining bathroom door. 'You've got to help me.'

'I'll try.' Oliver sighed. 'But first of all you've got to promise me that you'll forget you ever saw the will.'

'How can I?'

'Just do it,' advised Oliver grimly. 'Remember, this is going to be a shock for Laura, too. And, as she's made a life for herself in New York, what makes you think she'll want to come back here to live?'

Stella's eyes widened. 'Do you think—?'

'I don't *think* anything,' said Oliver heavily. 'I'm just trying to make you see that it might be in your own best interests to behave as if you're in the dark. Laura isn't a monster. She's hurting, too. And she may be prepared to be charitable.'

'Charitable!' It was obvious the word stuck in his mother's throat. 'I don't want her charity. This is my house.'

'No, it's not,' said Oliver levelly. 'You might as well accept it. It isn't as if you're going to be destitute. You're going to be very nicely provided for.'

'Forty thousand a year!' Stella was dismissive. 'How the hell does he think I'm going to manage on forty thousand a year?'

'Forty thousand a year is enough for anyone to live on,' Oliver declared. 'Dammit, most people exist on a hell of a lot less.' He paused. 'We did.'

'That was then; this is now. I'm not used to having to scrape and save for every little thing I want. You know that, Oliver. I thought you of all people would understand.'

'I do understand,' retorted Oliver sharply. 'I understand that you've lived beyond your means for years.'

Stella caught her breath. 'I'll contest it. That's what I'll do,' she declared, ignoring him. 'He won't get away with this.'

'Ma!' Oliver was disgusted. 'You can't do that. You don't have any grounds.'

'I know my rights.'

'No, you don't. A judge, magistrate, whatever, will probably consider you've been more than adequately provided for.'

'With that pittance!'

'Do you know how much money Griff actually left?'

Stella held up her head. 'Not pounds and pence, no. But there's this house, for one thing. It must be worth—I don't know—half a million. And then he had insurances and things.'

Oliver sighed. He was tired of speculating about something his mother had no right to know about. Yet. 'Look,' he said, 'I suggest we leave it for the present. Until the will's been read—'

'But you'll be there for me, won't you?' Stella changed tack now, crossing the room, tucking her hand into his arm and resting her head against his shoulder. 'I don't know what I'd do if I didn't have you.'

Oliver tried not to reject her, but he could feel himself withdrawing, wanting to move away from her, to put some space between them even so. It had always been this way with his mother. She was perfectly willing to forget his existence for months on end, then something would happen, some imagined emergency, and she'd send for him, expecting him to behave as if they had a normal relationship when, in fact, they had never had that.

'Look,' he said. 'We can't do anything until after the funeral's over. Why don't you go and get dressed and then we'll discuss what arrangements still have to be made?'

'I can't think about things like that now,' protested his mother. 'Speak to Nell. She'll discuss things with you. She'll tell you what there's still to do.'

'I don't think so, Ma.'

'And don't call me that. You know I don't like it.'

Oliver shrugged. 'Whatever. I'll be in the study when you're ready to talk.'

'Not the study.'

Stella shivered, and Oliver realised he had spoken unthinkingly. 'The library, then,' he amended. And then, as she moved towards the door, he asked, 'Where were you when Griff had his attack, by the way?'

'Where was I?' Stella paused with her hand on the handle, gazing at him with wary eyes. 'What do you mean, where

was I? You know where I was. I told you. I was here, of
course.'

'In the house, yes. But actually where?'

She looked offended. 'Does it matter?'

'Humour me.'

She frowned. 'I was upstairs, if you must know. Lying
down. I was—tired.'

'After your shopping trip?'

'What—? Oh, yes.' She swallowed quickly. 'Yes, after my
shopping trip.'

'So you didn't hear him come in?'

'I—may have done.'

'But you didn't come down to see how he was, anything
like that?'

'What is this? Some kind of inquisition?' Stella was angry
now. 'Do you think I haven't tortured myself with the knowledge that if I had come down I might have been able to do
something to help? It was terrible, Oliver! Terrible! I never
want to go through anything like that again.'

Oliver hesitated. 'And—you were alone when you found
his—I mean, him?'

'Of course I was alone. What else?' Her eyes narrowed.
'What has Nell Tenby been saying?'

'What could she say?'

Oliver turned the question back on her and with an exasperated toss of her head Stella jerked the door open. 'I suggest you apply that agile mind of yours to finding a solution
to my situation instead of interrogating me about events that
are immutable,' she declared coldly. 'Just remember where
your loyalties should belong.'

The door slammed behind her and Oliver expelled a tired
breath. That was all he needed: for his mother to think he
had turned against her. Knowing how much Nell disliked his
mother, could he really give any credence to anything she
said?

Just the same...

He turned back to the window. The snow had stopped again, but the sky was heavy with the threat of more. He wondered if it would delay the burial, and then remembered that the Tenbys had their own vault in the churchyard here in the village. Griff would be laid to rest there beside his first wife. His worries were over, but Oliver had the unpleasant feeling that his own were just beginning.

CHAPTER SIX

MARCUS VENNING arrived on Monday morning.

Laura had spent the weekend trying to avoid both Oliver and his mother and she was surprised when Aunt Nell came to find her in the drawing room to tell her that the solicitor was waiting in the library.

'I thought you'd prefer to see him in there rather than in your father's study,' the older woman said gently, squeezing her shoulder. 'I think he wants to discuss the arrangements for after the funeral with you.'

Laura gave her a puzzled look. 'With me?' she said. 'Are you sure he doesn't want to speak to Stella?' After all, as her father's widow, she was his next of kin. And, as far as she knew, Oliver had spent most of the weekend dealing with the funeral arrangements. Surely he was better equipped to deal with the situation than she was.

'He wants to speak to you,' insisted Aunt Nell firmly. 'Are you up to it?'

'Oh—well, yes. I'm up to it.' Laura put the newspaper she had been scanning without interest aside and got to her feet. 'Where are the others?'

'She's still in her room,' declared Aunt Nell disparagingly, and Laura knew exactly who she meant. 'As for Oliver—I think he went out after breakfast.'

Laura was tempted to ask where he'd gone, but Oliver's actions were nothing to do with her. Apart from an occasional comment at meals, they hadn't spoken to one another since Saturday morning, and she told herself that that was how she liked it.

She followed Aunt Nell out of the room and then left her to cross the hall to the library. This used to be one of her

favourite rooms, with its tall bookshelves and squashy arm-
chairs, and she paused in the doorway, half expecting to see
her father warming himself before the open fire.

But this thought was quickly suppressed. Thankfully, she
had had no more hallucinatory experiences, and she'd managed to convince herself that she must have imagined the
whole thing. Now the sight of Marcus Venning sitting at the
table in the window, studying some documents he'd taken
from his briefcase as he waited, restored her equilibrium, and
she smiled as she walked towards him, holding out her hand.

'Mr Venning.'

'My dear.' Marcus Venning rose to his feet at her entrance
and came to take her hand between both of his. 'I'm so sorry
about your father. He was a good man. He'll be sadly
missed.'

'Yes, he will.' Laura managed to blink back the tears that
had flooded her eyes at this greeting. 'It's good to see you
again, Mr Venning. It must be—eight years since we last saw
one another.'

'And in much happier circumstances,' he agreed, releasing
her hand to put both of his behind his back. 'Your wedding,'
he added, as if she needed the reminder. 'Is your husband
with you?'

'Um—no.' Laura indicated that he should resume his seat
and took the chair opposite. 'Didn't Daddy tell you? Conor
and I were divorced three years ago.'

'Oh…' He was clearly embarrassed. 'I'm sorry. I wouldn't
have mentioned it if I'd known.'

'It doesn't matter. Really.' That was so true. She hated to
admit it, but since seeing Oliver again she'd realised just how
specious her marriage to Conor had been.

'Well, if you're sure…'

'I am.'

'Then I'm glad.' He grimaced. 'Not that you're divorced,
of course. But that you've obviously found happiness with
someone else.'

Laura coloured now. 'I—wouldn't say that.'

'Oh, but I thought—' He was evidently finding this confusing. 'Aren't you still living in New York?'

'Yes. But that's because my work is there,' she explained, glad that Oliver wasn't around to eavesdrop on this conversation. 'Er—how can I help you?'

'Ah…' The elderly solicitor shuffled the documents he had been looking at earlier into some semblance of order and stuffed them back into his briefcase. 'Well, now, I know this must be very painful for you, my dear, but I just want you to know that—that when the time comes you can rely on my support.'

'Thank you.'

Laura gave a small smile, and acknowledged that it was good of him to come all the way from Rhosmawr to tell her that. And in such conditions. Although the snow had stopped and the thaw had set in, the roads were still treacherous.

'You'll know, of course, that I had a phone call from your stepmother yesterday evening?' he went on after a moment, however, and Laura had to revise her opinion about his reasons for coming.

'I—no,' she admitted, realising she couldn't lie about it. She hesitated. 'Is there a problem?'

'Well, yes.' Venning sighed. 'If Mrs Williams is confined to her bed—'

'Confined to her bed?' Laura couldn't let that go unchallenged. 'I didn't know she was confined to her bed.' She tried to think. When had she last seen Stella downstairs? Saturday evening? Yes, that was it: Saturday evening.

'Well, according to Mrs Williams, the doctor is of the opinion that this has all been too much for her,' continued the solicitor ruefully. 'I fear she may not even be well enough to attend the funeral—'

'No!' Laura was incensed. 'No, that's not true.'

'Well, if your stepmother is prostrate with grief—'

'Prostrate with grief?' Laura hadn't noticed that Stella was prostrate with grief. On the contrary, she'd observed at dinner on Saturday evening that although the rest of them had only picked at their food Stella had eaten everything that was put before her.

'I know you've never been particularly fond of your step-mother, Laura,' the old man put in gently, and she felt a surge of indignation at the thought that so far as the solicitor was concerned it was she who was being unfeeling. 'But in the circumstances, my dear…'

'Stella isn't confined to her bed,' she insisted. 'Why would she say a thing like that?'

'Perhaps she's taken this harder than you think,' drawled an infuriatingly familiar voice, and, glancing over her shoulder, Laura found her stepbrother lounging in the open doorway. The bristle of his overnight beard darkened his jawline and he was apparently still wearing the clothes he'd worn to go out in. His booted feet were crossed and his parka-clad shoulder was propped indolently against the jamb.

'Oliver.' Marcus Venning evidently viewed this intrusion with some relief. 'How are you, my boy?' He got to his feet. 'I'm sorry we have to meet again at such an unhappy time.'

'Yeah.' As if finding his manners, Oliver straightened and came into the room to shake the old man's hand. 'It's good to see you, too, Marcus. You're looking well.'

'Thank you.' While Laura struggled to contain her indig-nation at the casual way Oliver had addressed the solicitor, Venning was visibly flattered by his comment. 'So I don't look as if I'm ready to be put out to grass yet?'

'Never.' Oliver grinned. 'I hope my—sister's been looking after you. As you've heard, Ma's indisposed right now.'

'Your sister—'

'I'm not his sister,' snapped Laura coldly. 'And at least now that Oliver's here he can confirm that his mother's—confinement—is purely voluntary.'

Oliver's dark features tightened. 'As I said before, I think Ma's finding it all very distressing.'

'Do you think I'm not?'

Laura was indignant, but Oliver ignored her outburst. He looked at Venning. 'You understand, don't you, Marcus?'

'What? Oh—I—well, of course.' Marcus nodded, but Laura resented the look that passed between the two men at that moment. It hinted at an accord she couldn't begin to share and she got up from her seat because she couldn't bear to sit still any longer.

'So—was there anything else?' asked Oliver, taking over the conversation, and she stared angrily at him. How dared he behave as if she was too stupid to handle the situation herself?

'Oh, yes.' Marcus looked up from the briefcase he had collected from the table. 'I did wonder if Laura might like to go and see her father before—before tomorrow.' He reached out to pat her hand. 'I'd be happy to accompany you, my dear.'

'If she'd like to go, I'll take her,' declared Oliver at once, earning a look of outrage from his stepsister. But Laura was still trying to come to terms with the fact that Venning had meant her father's *body*, which was lying in the Chapel of Rest at Rhosmawr, and couldn't immediately think of any valid reason why she might refuse his offer. 'I'm sure you've got other commitments, Marcus,' Oliver added, just in case she was tempted. 'There's no need for you to put yourself out when Laura's got family of her own.'

Laura's jaw dropped. The Kemps were not her family, she thought bitterly. But again Marcus Venning chose to accept her stepbrother's offer at face value.

'Well, if you're sure, Oliver,' he began. 'I must admit, I am rather snowed under at the moment, if you'll excuse the pun—'

'I'd prefer to go on my own,' Laura broke in, before he could go any further. She gave Oliver a contemptuous look. 'I'm sure you understand.'

'And how do you propose to get there and back?' he enquired, his pleasant tone masking the glitter in his eyes. 'You don't have a car.'

'Daddy does.'

'You're not planning on taking that old Daimler out in this weather—'

'Why not?'

'Look, there's no need for this.' Belatedly, Venning seemed to realise he had been a little premature in accepting Oliver's suggestion on her behalf. 'Laura can drive back to Rhosmawr with me.'

'And how will she get back again?' Oliver was frustratingly practical. 'It's okay, Marcus. We'll work this out.' He gave Laura a warning look. 'Somehow.'

Accompanying the old solicitor to the door, Laura found she was trembling. It wasn't so much a reaction to what had been said—though she did find Oliver's arrogance unbearable—as much as an increasing feeling of her own alienation here. This wasn't her father's house any more. The pictures, the furnishings, even the books that had been such an integral part of her childhood weren't hers to enjoy any longer. And the car, which she had so blithely said she'd borrow, wasn't hers to appropriate. Everything belonged to her stepmother now; and, by implication, to Oliver. No wonder he felt he could order her about. She was the outsider now, not him.

With the door closed behind the solicitor, Laura would have escaped to her room, but Oliver moved to the foot of the stairs to block her way.

'What are you going to do?'

Laura held up her head. 'That's my business.'

'Do you want to go and see your father?'

Laura's shoulders sagged. 'Look, don't push me, Oliver. I know you feel you have the upper hand here, but if I want to go and see my father I'll make my own arrangements, thank you.'

Oliver groaned. 'Why are you doing this? I've offered to

take you, and I will. But—' he sighed '—if you insist on going on your own, you can borrow my car.'

Laura attempted to move round him. 'No, thanks.'

'Why not?'

'I can get a taxi.'

'Yeah, right.' Oliver regarded her pityingly. 'Do you honestly think you're going to get a taxi driver to come all this way to pick you up, take you in to Rhosmawr and then bring you back again?'

'Why not?' she asked again, and he snorted.

'Get real, Laura. This isn't the States. Have you taken a look outside? The roads are treacherous. You may be lucky and persuade some sap to make the journey, but I wouldn't hold your breath.'

Laura shrugged. 'Then I won't go.'

Oliver swore. 'Can't you at least meet me halfway here? I don't offer the use of my car to just anyone. Take it in the spirit in which it's given.'

Laura hesitated. 'I don't know your car,' she admitted reluctantly. 'And, like you said, it is slippery out there. I'd hate to run it into a tree or something. I've seen your car. It's an expensive vehicle.'

'To hell with the car,' growled Oliver impatiently. 'I'd care more if you damaged yourself.'

Laura's lips twitched. 'Thanks.'

'So what are you going to do?'

Laura bit her lip. 'I suppose you'd better come with me,' she muttered, aware that she really didn't have a choice. She paused. 'If you've got nothing better to do.'

Oliver rolled his eyes. 'And if I do?'

'But you said—'

He shook his head. 'Get your coat,' he said resignedly, and she realised he had only been teasing her. 'I'll go and start the engine.'

Laura collected an ankle-length dark grey cashmere coat from her wardrobe to wear over the warm sweater and woollen trousers she'd put on that morning. Thick-soled Doc Martens ensured that her feet would remain dry and, gathering up her handbag, she hurried back downstairs.

Deciding she ought to let Aunt Nell know what she was doing, she went to the kitchen first. Her aunt was baking, and she looked up expectantly when Laura came into the room. Then, seeing that she was dressed to go out, she said, 'Where are you going?'

'I—er—I'm going into Rhosmawr with Oliver,' replied Laura a little awkwardly. 'Is that all right?'

Her aunt blinked, transferring a smear of flour to her cheek as she brushed a greying hair behind her ear. 'Has Marcus Venning gone?'

'Oh—oh, yes.' Laura had forgotten about the solicitor in her nervousness at going out with Oliver. 'He went a few minutes ago. Sorry.'

'So?' Her aunt looked at her. 'Are you going to tell me what he wanted?'

'Well, yes.' Laura frowned, trying to remember what the solicitor had said. 'He'd apparently had a call from Stella saying that she might not be well enough to attend the funeral—'

'What?'

'That's what I said.' Laura pulled a wry face. 'Apparently she told him that she's confined to her bed.'

'That's the first I've heard of it.'

'I said that, too.' Laura grimaced. 'I think she let Mr Venning think Dr Evans had prescribed total rest.'

Nell said nothing to this. 'Is that the only reason he came?'

'No.' Laura licked her lips. 'I think he wanted to offer his condolences and—and to ask if I intended to go and see Daddy.'

'Ah.' The old woman nodded, and belatedly Laura realised that perhaps her aunt would like to come with them. 'So that's why Oliver is taking you to Rhosmawr.'

'Yes.' Laura hesitated. 'Would you like to come, too?'

'Why would I want to do that?' Nell shook her head. 'Wasn't I here when the poor man was taken away?'

Laura sucked in a breath. 'I never thought.'

'It doesn't matter.' Nell regarded her niece with concerned eyes. 'Are you going to be all right?'

'Why wouldn't I be?' Laura managed an upbeat response. 'Someone has to be. According to Oliver, his mother is finding it hard to come to terms with her loss.'

'Her loss!' Her aunt was scathing. 'That woman has never cared about anyone but herself.'

'Don't say that.' Laura didn't think she could stand any more unpleasantness. Not right now. 'I mean, it must have been awful for her, finding Daddy's—body and all.'

The older woman shrugged. 'If you say so.'

'Oh, Aunt Nell, I know you don't like her—nor do I—but we all have to pull together at a time like this. Don't we?'

'Sounds good to me,' said Oliver, coming into the kitchen as he spoke. 'Are you ready?'

CHAPTER SEVEN

THE sun was shining when they came out of the funeral home.

In Rhosmawr, the thaw was much more pronounced than in Penmadoc with only the occasional pile of slush at the side of the road to remind its residents of the previous week's storms.

Oliver had parked around the corner from the home and he sensed that Laura was glad to feel the warmth of the sun on her head as they walked back to the car. Seeing her father might have given her a sense of closure but he guessed that she wished she hadn't had to do it. The still, almost shrunken figure lying in the coffin had born little resemblance to the vibrant man she remembered, and he thought he saw her shiver as she climbed into the Jeep.

'You okay?'

He glanced her way as he got behind the wheel and Laura nodded. Despite the way she'd objected to his high-handedness earlier, he hoped she had been glad of his company during the ordeal.

'Fine,' she said at last, as if sensing that he was waiting for her to say something. 'Um—thanks for coming with me.'

Oliver's lips twisted. 'Yeah,' he said, not believing her but deciding it wasn't worth arguing over. He started the engine. 'Back to Penmadoc, right?'

'I mean it.' Before he could put the car into gear, Laura drew off her glove and touched his sleeve. 'I am glad I wasn't on my own.'

The impact of those slim fingers gripping his sleeve was electrifying. Although he was sure she wasn't aware of it, he felt as if a magnetic current was penetrating the thickness of the cloth. His pulse quickened; he could hear its clamour ringing in his head, and he stifled a groan of protest. For God's sake, what was happening to him? This was Laura, remember? Whatever immature emotions she had aroused in him were long gone, and the idea that he was having a sexual response now was not only unbelievable, it was insensitive and pathetic.

Something about his attitude, about the way he was staring at her, perhaps, caused Laura to withdraw her hand now, but the heat she'd generated inside him didn't subside. On the contrary, his palms were unpleasantly slick as they gripped the steering wheel and there was a definite feeling of fullness between his legs.

'Don't you believe me?' she asked, and a shudder of relief feathered his spine. At least she hadn't interpreted his behaviour the way he had, he thought with some relief. Her tongue appeared to moisten her lips. 'He looked very— peaceful, didn't he?'

'Yeah.'

Oliver dragged his eyes away from that pink tongue and thrust the Jeep into gear. Then, after checking that the road behind them was clear, he swung out to join the traffic. Thankfully, his actions were automatic and didn't require too much in the way of brainpower. Which was just as well, because his brain felt like mashed banana at that moment.

'I wondered…' She was obviously unaware of his turmoil and didn't even flinch when he went though a set of traffic lights as they were turning red. 'Why don't we have lunch on the way home?'

'Lunch?' His tongue clove to the roof of his mouth. 'Isn't your aunt expecting you back?'

'Maybe.' Laura regarded him out of the corners of her eyes. 'Is that your way of saying you don't want to have lunch with me?'

'It's not that.' Though God knew it was. Oliver took a calming breath. 'Okay. Why not? Where do you want to go?'

'I thought you might know somewhere,' she said quickly, lifting her shoulders. 'But perhaps it's not such a good idea. Your mother is bound to wonder where we are.'

Oliver had no desire to get into what his mother might think about him consorting with the enemy. Well, her enemy as she saw it, he conceded drily. 'Forget it,' he said, before he could change his mind. 'There's bound to be a hotel on the edge of town.'

'If you're sure.'

Her tone was much cooler now, and he sensed a rekindling of the hostility she'd shown towards him up till now. He guessed she was probably regretting making the offer. The feeling of sympathy they'd shared after leaving the funeral home was fast dissipating, and he cursed himself for allowing sex to govern his response. It was only lunch, dammit. Just because he'd become aroused when she'd laid her hand on him that was not her fault.

'I'm sure,' he said now, forcing himself to pay attention to their surroundings. 'Look, there's the Rhosmawr Moat House. Is that okay?'

Laura shrugged and he suspected she was having a hard time recovering her enthusiasm. 'If you like,' she said indifferently, and his mouth compressed. He'd asked for this, he thought irritably. It was his fault that she'd got totally the wrong impression.

They parked the car on the forecourt and picked their way around the pools of melting snow to the conservatory restaurant. Inside, the heat from more than a score of bodies had steamed the glass so it was impossible to see through the windows, but it was light and warm and friendly, and a pretty blonde waitress bustled over immediately to show them to a table in the corner.

'Can I get you anything to drink?' she asked, after they were seated, and Oliver arched an enquiring brow at his companion.

'Um—probably just orange juice,' she said, sliding her

arms out of her coat and draping it over the back of her chair.
'Thank you.'

'Orange juice?' Oliver sounded as exasperated as he felt.
'Wouldn't you prefer a glass of wine?'

'You're driving.'

'That's right. *I'm* driving,' he agreed, giving the waitress
an apologetic look. 'You're not.'

Laura's cheeks had turned a little pink now. 'All right. A
glass of white wine, then,' she said shortly, and he wanted
to groan aloud.

'Fine,' he said instead, forcing a smile for the waitress.
'And I'll have a beer. The non-alcoholic kind. Thanks.'

Laura frowned as the girl walked away and, guessing what
she was thinking, Oliver blew out a breath. 'I don't drink
and drive,' he said, controlling his impatience with an effort.

Her shoulders gave a little bob. 'Oh—good. Nor do I.'

Oliver breathed heavily. 'So, is it okay?'

'It's nothing to do with me what you drink.'

'No, it's not. But that's not what I meant.' Oliver indicated
the conservatory restaurant. 'Do you like this place?'

'It's okay.' Laura barely glanced around her. 'Do you
come here a lot?'

'I've never been here before,' he said, shrugging out of
his parka. Then he asked, suspiciously, 'Did you think I
had?'

Laura toyed with her cutlery. 'I thought you must know
the waitress,' she said offhandedly, and he caught back an
oath.

'Why would you think that?'

'I don't know.' Although she wasn't looking at him, he
could see she was uncomfortable now. 'She seemed very
familiar.'

Oliver gasped. 'She was being friendly, that's all.'

'Mmm.' Laura didn't sound convinced. She picked up the
laminated menu that stood on the middle of the table. 'Do
we choose from this?'

'Why ask me?' Oliver was having a hard time hanging on to his temper. Then, because it wasn't really her fault, he said, 'Yeah. I guess so. Are you hungry?'

'Not very.' Laura scanned the menu without enthusiasm. 'I think I'll just have a tuna sandwich.'

'Right.' Oliver took the menu from her and made his own examination. 'I'll have a sandwich, too.' He breathed a little more easily. 'Here's our drinks.'

The waitress *was* very friendly, he noticed reluctantly. She smiled as she set down his beer and gazed at him with wide blue eyes when he gave their order. 'White or wholemeal?' she asked, after making a note of their selections. 'I suppose you're used to being offered loads of choices. When I was in Florida last year, I was amazed at how many different types of bread there were.'

'We're not Americans,' said Oliver, feeling obliged to answer her, and the girl gave Laura a questioning look.

'But I thought—'

'I've lived in the States for the past eight years but he's very definitely English,' explained Laura tolerantly, and Oliver intercepted the humorous look she cast in his direction. 'What part of Florida did you visit?'

'Oh, Orlando,' said the girl at once, including Laura in the exchange with evident reluctance. 'Disney World. Have you been there?'

'Yeah.' But Oliver didn't want to get into that. He gave a sardonic smile. 'Small world.'

'Isn't it?' she agreed, not getting the pun, and then, noticing that the manager was watching her, she added hurriedly, 'I'll get your order.'

She didn't hurry away, however. She sauntered, hips swaying provocatively towards the kitchens, and Oliver pulled a wry face when Laura arched her brows. 'All right,' he said. 'You were right and I was wrong. But, dammit, can I help it if women find me—?'

He broke off abruptly, belatedly aware of where his words

were taking him, and silently cursing himself for being so crass. As if she didn't already have a low enough opinion of him, he thought grimly, reaching for his beer.

But he saw Laura's eyes were twinkling as she looked at him across the rim of her own glass. 'Irresistible?' she suggested, finishing his sentence. 'Why, no, Mr Kemp, how could it be your fault? We ladies are just bowled over by your southern charm.'

Oliver grimaced. 'I'm sorry. I'm getting used to finding my foot in my mouth.'

'You're too modest.' Laura put down her glass. 'Anyway, I know you too well to be—surprised at your conceit.'

'Ouch.' But Oliver found himself grinning. 'Yeah, I guess you know me pretty well at that.'

'Which isn't to say that I approve of your attitude,' she appended swiftly. 'You always did have an inflated opinion of yourself.'

'Is that so?'

Oliver watched her with indulgent eyes. The tensions he'd felt towards her in the car seemed a million miles away now. Her mouth was curved, her lips had parted in a wide smile, and he realised suddenly how much he'd wanted her to smile at him.

Which was crazy really, remembering their history. Okay, they'd both been a lot younger then, a lot more naïve, he conceded, but those sorts of memories were dangerous now. God knew, he'd been attracted to her that summer she turned sixteen, but that was no excuse. Nor was the fact that it had been bloody hard for him to remember exactly how young she was.

His stomach tightened. He didn't want to think of that. What he'd done had been unforgivable, and she had every right to despise him for it. But, dammit, when she'd come to his room that night he'd been in no state to act sensibly. He should have sent her away. He knew that. If nothing else, the thought of how his mother would react if she found out should have deterred him. But it hadn't. Nothing like that had occurred to him. He'd been caught in the grip of an irresistible compulsion and his sex had governed his response.

In any case, Stella's reasons for resenting the relationship that was developing between her stepdaughter and her son had had little to do with their feelings. She'd been more concerned over what Griff might do if he discovered what was going on. And besides, she hadn't seen the way Laura looked at him, the way her eyes devoured him—or suffered the agony of stifling his arousal every time Laura came into the room.

Afterwards, she'd been furious, of course. And so eager that he should keep what had happened to himself. She didn't care about his morals, or the fact that he'd betrayed Griff's confidence. As far as she was concerned, Laura had started it. She'd deserved everything she'd got.

And because he'd been ashamed of his behaviour he'd let his mother persuade him not to talk about it. He'd taken her advice and kept out of Laura's way from then on. He'd consoled himself with the belief that Laura had regretted it as much as he had and would be grateful for his discretion, but he suspected now that it had been the worst thing he could have done. He'd let her think it had meant nothing to him. He'd let her believe that he didn't care how she felt. And then he'd compounded his guilt by clearing off to Europe, telling himself she'd forget all about him while he was away...

'What do you think your mother will do?'

Laura's voice aroused him from the pit of melancholy he'd made for himself, and he realised they'd been sitting for several minutes not saying anything. Her dark brows were lifted in mild enquiry and he felt a treacherous return of the emotions he'd felt before. Her grey eyes surveyed him, wide and gently appealing, shaded by dark lashes that showed a trace of red at their tips. Pale cheeks, only subtly tinged with colour, were a delicate foil for the wild beauty of her hair. It tumbled about her shoulders, curling riotously, and although it was the last thing he should have been thinking at that moment an erotic image of himself burying his face in its silky coils swept over him.

Oh, Lord, he thought, struggling desperately to remember what she'd said. This was definitely not the time to be picturing himself lying between her pale thighs, delighting in her sweetness, revelling in her innocent sensuality, congratulating himself on arousing such an innocent response...

'Do?' he got out at last, struggling to interpret what she meant. Had Marcus Venning given her any suspicion that the will might not be as straightforward as she'd obviously expected? 'You mean, after the funeral?'

'Well, yes.' Laura frowned, white teeth nibbling at her bottom lip. 'I assume she intends to stay at Penmadoc?'

Oliver took a deep breath. 'I think she'd like to,' he conceded weakly, and she nodded.

'Aunt Nell will be pleased,' she said. 'It's her home, too, you see.'

Oliver hesitated. Evidently she didn't know anything about the will. If she thought his mother would have allowed her aunt to stay on at Penmadoc if she'd inherited the place, though, she was very much mistaken. Despite her usefulness, Eleanor Tenby had crossed his mother too many times for her to expect any favours from her.

'It's your home, too,' he said now, resisting the urge to stretch across the table and capture the hand that was lying beside her glass.

'No.' Laura's expression hardened for a moment. 'No, it's not. It hasn't been my home for over ten years.'

'Just because you don't live there any more doesn't mean it's not your home,' replied Oliver evenly. 'I'm sure you know they still call it the Tenby house in the village.'

'But we know it's not the Tenby house, don't we?' she

pointed out quietly. 'When your mother married my father, it became the Williams house instead.'

'I wouldn't be too sure of that,' said Oliver, before he could prevent himself, but happily the waitress returned at that moment with their food.

'One tuna and one bacon, lettuce and tomato,' she said, depositing the sandwiches with one hand and taking Oliver's empty glass with the other. 'Can I get you another beer?'

'Why not?'

Oliver wished he could have a lager. Right now, he would have preferred something stimulating instead of the non-alcoholic brew. His mother had put him in an impossible position, and he didn't like the thought that Laura was blaming her father for something he hadn't done.

'I'll have another glass of wine, too,' Laura said, before the waitress could move away, and just for a moment she and Oliver shared a teasing glance.

'Oh—right. The waitress took her glass, too, and then, evidently deciding she was fighting a losing battle, she added, 'I'll get your drinks. Enjoy your meal!'

In fact, neither of them was particularly hungry. Oliver watched as Laura picked at her sandwich, wishing there was something he could say to lighten her mood. It was obvious she believed that her father had left Penmadoc Hall to his mother, and that was why she was steeling herself for when the will was read.

'Tell me about New York,' he said, after their second round of drinks had been delivered and they were alone again. 'What do you do at this publishing house of yours?'

'Hardly mine,' she said wryly. 'As a matter of fact, it belongs to Conor's uncle. He gave me a job, you see, when Conor and I first moved to New York.'

'I see.' Oliver squashed a surprising twinge of jealousy. It was nothing to do with him if she chose to continue to work for the Neills. 'But isn't that awkward? You being his brother's ex-daughter-in-law, and all?'

'I thought it might be,' she conceded, sipping her wine in preference to the sandwich. 'But Jeff, that's Conor's father, was really nice about it.' She hesitated, and then said ruefully, 'I think he hoped we might change our minds.'

'About getting divorced?' Oliver knew that it really wasn't any of his business, but he couldn't deny he was curious about the man she'd chosen to marry.

'Mmm.' Laura seemed to realise who she was talking to and a guarded expression came into her eyes. 'But I'm sure you're not interested in me. My career has been singularly unimpressive when compared to yours.'

'I don't see what one has to do with the other,' said Oliver, frowning. 'And I am interested in what you've been doing for the past eight years. What you did after I left for Europe, for that matter. I did wonder if you might write to me. I sent Ma several poste restante addresses, but you obviously didn't want to know.'

Laura gave him an odd look. 'You are joking,' she said disbelievingly, and his frown deepened.

'No.' He paused. 'Why?'

'Oh, come on.' Laura gazed at him incredulously. 'Your mother was unlikely to have given your address to me.' Her face darkened suddenly. 'Besides which, I had nothing to say to you. You destroyed any faith I might have had in you when you ran away.'

'I didn't run away.' But Oliver could feel the heat in his cheeks and he wished they were not sitting in a public restaurant when the guilt he was feeling was on display. 'I'm sorry, but I thought it would make things easier for you,' he said defensively. 'It was going to be damn difficult going on as before.'

'For you.'

'For both of us,' he amended shortly. 'I was nearly nineteen, Laura. What the hell was I supposed to do?'

'What indeed?' She regarded him scathingly. 'I could say you were supposed to be going to Oxford in October, but obviously I was wrong. You wanted to get away, so you decided to delay your education. Backpacking in Europe must have been an inspiration. It enabled you to get away from me, from what I represented, as quickly as you could.'

'It wasn't like that,' he began, but she put up a hand to stop him.

'It doesn't matter any more,' she told him wearily. 'I don't care what your intentions were. As it turned out, you did us both a favour. You got the pictures that ultimately made you famous, and I learned to stand on my own two feet.'

Oliver stared at her impatiently. 'Why do I get the feeling that that's not the whole story?' he muttered harshly. 'For God's sake, Laura, I was hoping we could talk it out.'

'You're too late,' she said, draining her glass and setting it down on the table. 'If you're finished, I think I'd like to go.'

CHAPTER EIGHT

LAURA huddled into her chair beside the library fire. It was late, almost midnight, she thought, but she had little desire to go to bed. This might be the last night she'd spend at Penmadoc, and she wanted to make the most of it.

It was hard to believe that it was all over. Yet the funeral had been a dignified affair, in its own way. The priest who'd led the service had known Griff and that had come through in his eulogy, so that the words Oliver had spoken afterwards had had a poignant echo in what had gone before.

Despite their differences, Laura had been glad of Oliver's support throughout the service. Any sense of unreality had been banished by the presence of the flower-bedecked coffin, and she had found it hard to face the fact that she was now totally alone.

Stella had not attended.

Although Laura had been sure her stepmother would change her mind at the last minute and join the cortège before they left for the church, she hadn't. She'd continued to insist that she was at the mercy of her nerves, that she simply couldn't face the harrowing prospect of interring her husband, and that Griff would understand if he were here.

Actually, Laura rather thought he might. Her father had always been putty in Stella's hands. She'd known that, right from the beginning of their relationship, and although she'd tried to put her resentment aside Stella had never made it easy. She'd always been jealous of their relationship and it had been that, as much as anything, that had persuaded Laura to stay in New York after her divorce.

However, because Stella hadn't left her room all day, the will had not been opened. Which meant that although Laura had intended to leave for London the next morning her plans had had to be delayed. Marcus Venning had been most insistent that Laura should be present when her father's will was read, and despite her belief that her presence was only a formality she felt she owed it to her father to honour his last wishes.

His last wishes...

Her eyes burned. She had thought she was all cried out, but she had only to remember that she would never see her father again for the hot tears to dampen her cheeks. Poor Daddy, she thought, unable to deny her emotions. What a terrible thing it must have been to die alone.

The sound of the door opening behind her startled her. Scrubbing the heels of her hands across her eyes, she glanced across the firelit room. She had thought everyone else was asleep. Her aunt had retired earlier, worn out after greeting the many friends and acquaintances who had come back to the house after the interment to offer their condolences, and as Stella hadn't been available Aunt Nell had stood in her place.

But, to her astonishment, she saw it was Stella who appeared now. She came almost silently into the room, the folds of her dressing gown wrapped closely about her slim form. Laura had been sitting in the firelight, and with her legs coiled beneath her she was virtually invisible. Certainly, her stepmother didn't notice her as she glided across the floor.

Laura didn't know what to do. She didn't want to frighten the woman if she was suffering with her nerves, but at the same time she didn't want to remain unseen and later be accused of eavesdropping.

Goodness knew what Stella was thinking. Perhaps she'd come down to get a drink to settle the very nerves that had kept her from attending her husband's funeral. If so, should Laura speak to her? Was it possible that for once Stella might actually welcome her company?

But, before she could decide what to do, Stella had reached

the desk and picked up the phone. Her long, scarlet-tipped fingers punched out a number she obviously knew very well indeed, and then she put the receiver to her ear, tapping an impatient tattoo on the desk with her fingernail as she waited.

Laura shrank back into the chair. God, this was awful, she thought, stifling a groan. Unless she did something right now, she was going to be the unwilling recipient of her step-mother's confidence and that was the last thing she wanted. If only Stella had switched on the light...

It was too late. Even as it occurred to her that it was strange for Stella to be phoning anyone at this hour, her step-mother spoke. 'Jaz?' she said huskily. 'Jaz, is that you? Oh, thank God! I was afraid someone else might answer the phone.'

There was a pause then while whoever was at the other end of the line said something in their turn and then Stella spoke again. 'I know,' she said urgently. 'I haven't been able to do anything. The house has been full of people all day. I wanted to call you but I was afraid someone might listen in. That's why I'm ringing you from the library now. This way, I can be sure no one else is on the line. Yes, who else? Laura? No, I don't think so. She's far too full of herself to stoop to snooping on my calls.'

Laura could hardly prevent the gasp of indignation that rose into her throat. Who on earth was Stella talking to? Jaz? Who was Jaz? Male or female? And what right did they, whoever they were, have to suggest that she might do some-thing so underhand? Even if...

Stella was still talking. 'No, I'm afraid not,' she murmured, and now there was a defensive note in her voice. 'I can't help that. I really wasn't up to dealing with it all today.'

Laura frowned. All what? What was she talking about? What could she possibly want to know? What could *Jaz* pos-sibly want to know?

'I've no idea,' Stella persisted, suppressing Laura's spec-ulation. 'I mean it. I wasn't looking over his shoulder when

he wrote it.' She broke off and then said fiercely in answer
to whatever she'd heard, 'Well, yes. Yes, I expect so. What
else can I do?'

The will. It had to be the will!

Laura smoothed her trembling palms over the knees of her
woollen trousers, trying not to feel resentful of what was
being said. After all, Stella had no idea she had an audience.
It wasn't fair to judge her when she should have spoken up
before her stepmother started the call.

When the door opened again, without warning, she didn't
know who was the most surprised, herself or Stella. But when
Oliver switched on the light and walked into the room there
was no doubt that his mother's face showed her alarm.

'I've got to go,' she said, cutting the call short and slamming down the receiver. Then, gathering her composure, she
turned to face her son with enviable restraint.

Laura really thought that Oliver had seen her. After all,
the ceiling chandelier was casting light into all the shadowy
corners of the room and her position seemed fatally exposed.
But she'd counted without his very real irritation at finding
his mother—his supposedly grief-stricken mother—recovered enough to come downstairs to make a phone call when
she had a perfectly good connection upstairs. In consequence,
his attention was focussed on her.

'What's going on?' he asked, his voice low and menacing,
and Stella pushed her hands into the wide sleeves of her robe,
as if to hide their reaction from him.

'I don't know what you mean,' she said. 'I should have
thought it was perfectly obvious. I'm making a call, that's
all. Is there anything wrong with that?'

Oliver's lips thinned. 'You tell me.'

'Tell you? Tell you what?' Stella was playing for time and
Laura knew it. 'What can I tell you? I thought you were in
bed.'

'Don't you mean *hoped*?' Oliver wasn't fooled for a moment, but with every passing second Stella was regaining her composure.

'Are you spying on me?' she demanded. 'How long have you been skulking about out there in the hall?'

'Not long.' Oliver regarded her steadily. 'Who were you phoning at this time of night?'

'That's my business.'

'Is it?' He pushed his hands into his trouser pockets. 'So why didn't you make the call upstairs?'

Stella heaved a sigh. 'My phone's crackly, if you must know.' Which wasn't true. 'Might I remind you that until the contents of the will are made public this is still my house? If I choose to phone a friend downstairs, so I don't disturb anybody, it's nothing to do with you.'

So it was the will she had been talking about on the phone. Laura frowned. But what did she mean, 'until the contents of the will are made public'? Surely she didn't suspect that Laura's father had left Penmadoc to someone else?

'I'd still like to know who it was you were calling,' Oliver persisted. 'For someone who only hours ago couldn't leave her bed, you've certainly made a swift recovery.'

Stella caught her breath. 'That's not true.' She pulled a tissue out of her sleeve and blew her nose noisily. 'It's a pity if you can't trust your own mother.'

'Yeah, isn't it?'

Oliver's dark eyes moved assessingly round the room and Laura wanted to curl up and die. Surely there was no way he could fail to notice her and she waited with baited breath for his denunciation.

But it didn't come and Stella was too eager now to escape further questioning to pay attention to anything else. Holding herself stiffly, she moved purposefully towards him. 'May I go now?'

Oliver shrugged without removing his hands from his pockets. He'd apparently shed the jacket of the charcoal suit he'd been wearing elsewhere and the darkness of his skin showed through the thin fabric of his white shirt. Laura was afraid he might not let his mother go until she'd answered his questions, but, as if deciding there was no point in pursuing it, he moved aside.

'Why not?' he said flatly. 'I can always press redial and find out who you were calling for myself.'

Stella's jaw dropped. 'You wouldn't do that!'

'Why? Is it a secret?'

Stella's face contorted. 'You're a beast, Oliver. I don't know why I put up with you.'

'You don't often,' he reminded her drily. Then, shaking his head, he said heavily, 'No, I won't do that.' But when her face lightened considerably he added, 'I'll find out some other way.'

'What other way?' Stella exclaimed warily, and Laura was again assailed with the fear that Oliver was about to expose her.

But all he said was, 'It will come out. These things usually do.' His lips twitched. 'You're not very good at keeping secrets, are you?'

Better than he thought, mused Laura bitterly, but Stella was speaking again.

'All right, all right,' she said, forcing a resigned tone. 'I was talking to Dilys, if you must know. You remember Dilys—Dilys James?'

'I know who Dilys is,' said Oliver, as Laura wished herself any place else but here. But *James*, she wondered tensely. Could that conceivably be the *Jaz* Stella had identified before?

'There you are, then,' Stella declared, brushing past her son. 'Now, if you'll excuse me, I'm going back to bed. I suggest you do the same.'

Oliver inclined his head, but he didn't answer her, and Laura guessed that, whoever she'd been phoning, Stella wouldn't risk making another call tonight. Not with Oliver on the prowl, she thought ruefully. Even Stella had her limitations. She just wished she knew how she was going to get out of the library without him seeing her.

The door closed behind her stepmother and then Oliver said softly, 'Okay. She's gone. Do you want to tell me what you're doing there?'

Laura's breath escaped on a shocked gasp as she uncoiled her legs. 'You—you knew I was here?'

'Not initially,' he admitted honestly, pulling his hands out of his pockets and raking them through his hair. 'I wouldn't have thought it was your scene.'

'My *scene*?'

'Eavesdropping,' said Oliver carelessly, and Laura swung her feet to the floor and stood up.

'You don't imagine I arranged—that?' she asked, flinging a hand towards the phone, and his brows quirked.

'You didn't?'

'No.' Laura was infuriated. 'I was just sitting here, quietly, minding my own business, when your mother came in.'

'In the dark?' he queried sardonically, and she gave him an indignant look.

'Yes, in the dark,' she agreed. 'I was thinking. I didn't know anyone else was up.'

'What were you thinking about?'

'I don't believe that's anything to do with you.' She paused, and then added unwillingly, 'I was reflecting about the funeral if you must know.' She straightened her shoulders. 'I wanted to thank you for your support today. I was grateful you were there.'

'Where else would I be?' Oliver's tone was rueful. 'He was my stepfather, you know.'

'He was your mother's husband, but she wasn't there,' pointed out Laura stiffly. And then, making to step past him, she said, 'I'm going to bed now.'

'Wait.' Oliver blocked her exit without effort. Then, as she gazed up at him with resentful eyes, he asked, 'Do you know who my mother was talking to?'

Laura stared at him. 'She told you.' She waited for him to acknowledge it and when he didn't she added shortly, 'Someone called Dilys, wasn't it? Dilys—James.'

'I know what she said,' said Oliver, scowling. 'I just wonder why she'd feel the need to ring a girlfriend at this time of night.'

Laura's lips parted. 'You don't believe her?'

'Let's say I'm open to suggestions.'

'Well, not from me.' Laura shook her head. She would have stepped past him then, but this time he put out a hand to stop her and she recoiled from the strength of his cool fingers on her wrist. 'Don't.'

'Don't what?'

His eyes were narrowed, but she was disturbed by the dark emotions glittering in their depths. 'Don't touch me,' she said, despising the panic in her voice. 'I can't help you.'

'Perhaps you can; perhaps you can't.' His thumb moved over the sensitive veins that throbbed with the pressure of the blood that was surging through them. 'You're not afraid of me, are you, Laura?'

'Afraid of you?' A squeak of outrage escaped her. 'We're not talking about me, remember?'

'Oh, yeah, I remember,' he told her huskily. 'I remember everything. Like you, I wish I didn't.'

'I think you're giving me too much credit,' she got out nervously, fighting the urge to tear her arm out of his grasp. 'As a matter of fact, I think coming here, meeting you again, has done me some good.' She swallowed a little convulsively. 'It's helped me to get things into perspective. Do you know what I mean?'

'I know what you're saying,' he said huskily. 'But perhaps I don't believe it.' His mouth quirked. 'Do you know what I mean?'

Laura winced. He was making fun of her. Having got no joy out of his mother, he'd turned his attention on her instead and she was a fool to let him get away with it.

'Why aren't you in bed?' she asked, desperately trying to maintain her composure in spite of his provocation. 'Have you—have you been out?'

'Out?' His tone was softly jeering. 'Oh, right. And where would I go?'

'You could have gone down to the village,' she retorted defensively. 'The pub's still there. You used to be quite a regular. And if you were bored—'

'Bored?' He moved closer and it was an effort to simply stand her ground. 'Who said I was bored?'

'You must be if you're reduced to tormenting me,' she replied tartly. 'What's the matter? Are you missing—what was her name?—Natalie?'

Oliver's mouth took on a palm-moistening sensuality. 'If I didn't know better, I'd wonder if there wasn't just a grain of jealousy in those words.'

'But you do know better, right?' exclaimed Laura flatly. 'My God, I sometimes wonder what I ever saw in you.'

It wasn't what she'd intended to say, but his arrogance had caught her on the raw and she was alarmed when he narrowed the space between them. 'Do you want me to remind you?' he asked, his breath fanning her cheek, and she smelt the faint aroma of malt whisky on his breath.

'No!'

He'd been drinking, she realised dully. That was what all this was about. He'd been drinking and, anticipating that she'd be leaving in the morning, he'd decided to amuse himself at her expense.

'Are you sure?'

'I'm sure.' She brought her other hand up to try and prise his fingers from her wrist, catching her breath when he captured that hand as well. 'I think you'd better let me go.'

'And if I don't?'

'I could call for help. I'm sure your mother would be only too eager to come to my rescue.'

'Yeah.' His lips twisted. 'Yeah, I guess she might, at that.'

'And you don't want to fall out with her, do you?' Laura persisted, not sure why she was provoking him. 'Particularly now.'

'Particularly now?' he echoed, and she steeled herself to meet his puzzled eyes.

'Now that she's going to be a wealthy woman at last,' she retorted maliciously, and saw the look of shock that crossed his face.

It had been an unforgivable thing to say and totally unjustified. As far as she knew, Oliver had never profited from his mother's marriage. Oh, he'd gained in small ways, of course. He'd always had plenty to eat, clothes to wear, a decent place to sleep, but any success he'd had he'd achieved through his own efforts and she knew it.

'I—I didn't mean that the way it came out,' she mumbled as he continued to stare at her, but instead of releasing her his fingers slid possessively up her arms.

'Which way did you mean it?' he demanded harshly. 'You as good as accuse me of only being here so that I can benefit from—what would you call it?—my mother's good fortune, perhaps, and I'm supposed to believe you didn't mean it?'

'No—'

'It sounded that way to me.' His lips twisted. 'It's good to know you've got such a great opinion of me. And as you have...' he jerked her towards him '...I might as well take advantage of the fact.'

Her breasts were crushed against his chest. The strong muscles of his thighs pressed against her legs. She wanted to resist him but the memories his hard body evoked were taking over, and she was left with only words to resist his appeal.

'Don't do this,' she pleaded as his hand cupped her nape, turning her face up to his. But resentment, anger—*frustration*?—was driving him on, and she was no match for his grim determination.

His mouth was hard at first, angry, almost bruising in the

way it forced her lips to part to allow the hungry passage of his tongue. It was not the way he'd kissed her all those years ago, but he'd had less experience then, and he hadn't wanted to hurt her as he did now.

Yet, for all that, she could feel his resentment weakening. He'd bound her hands behind her back with one of his, but now, as he sensed her unwilling response, he let them go. His hands shaped the yielding curve of her spine instead, before sliding over her buttocks, pausing to caress the sensitive cleft that was tangible through her clothes. Those caressing fingers tormented her, turning her bones to water, while a feverish heat swept up her thighs to pool wetly between her legs.

He must know how she was feeling, she thought unsteadily as he brought her fully against him. That was why he was letting her know how aroused he was. Despite his anger, he couldn't hide his body's reactions either and his shaft pressed intimately against her stomach.

Laura's body was burning. She'd forgotten what it was like to feel such an abandonment of self. Despite a couple of abortive affairs and a marriage that had been more of a business partnership than a love match, she'd had very little sexual experience. Only with Oliver had she ever lost control of her emotions, and although her head was spinning she knew she mustn't let it happen again.

Yet it was hard, so hard, to hang on to her reason. His mouth was gentler now, softer, his tongue caressing her lips, playing with her tongue, drawing the tip into his mouth and suckling greedily on it. His hand moved from her nape to the waistband of her trousers, lifting the hem of her sweater and exposing her bare skin. His hand spread on her midriff, his palm hot and slick against her ribs.

Laura's stomach plunged. Her heart was racing wildly, trying to restrain the mad rush of blood that filled her veins without success. Every muscle, every sinew in her body was alert to the sensuous brush of his thumb on the underside of her breast, and she had to steel herself not to rub her pelvis against his. But she wanted to; how she wanted to! And although she knew she was playing with fire she couldn't prevent her hands from sliding up his chest and tangling in the damp hair at the back of his neck.

He shuddered then, releasing her mouth to slide his lips along her jawline. 'God help me,' he muttered, pressing hot, hungry kisses against the curve of her throat, and it was the raw anguish in his voice that brought Laura to her senses.

'God won't help you now,' she taunted, somehow injecting a note of mockery into her tone. 'You'd better let me go, Oliver, before we both do something we'll regret.'

'Who says I'll regret it?' he demanded thickly, his strong fingers cupping her breast now, his thumb probing the taut nipple. 'This doesn't feel as if you object.'

'Appearances can be deceptive,' said Laura in a strangled voice. 'As—as you should know very well.' She swallowed on a convulsive sob. 'How about—how about—Natalie? Don't you think you owe any loyalty to her?'

Oliver scowled. 'Don't bring Natalie into this.'

'I didn't.' Laura's voice hardened. 'You did. Or are you as indifferent to her feelings as you were to mine?'

Oliver's fingers dug into her waist for a moment, but to her relief—or so she told herself—she could feel him withdrawing from her, physically as well as mentally. 'Why do you care how Natalie feels?'

'I don't.' To her shame, Laura knew that was true. 'But I hoped it was a way to stifle your libido. Nothing else seems to do it. Not even the fact that I don't want you to touch me. Not now. Not ever.'

And, because he let her, she was able to push him away and walk out of the room with just a semblance of dignity. But it had been a close call. On her part just as much as on his.

CHAPTER NINE

OLIVER slept badly; again. It was getting to be par for the course, he thought bitterly. And the headache he had when he awoke couldn't be blamed on the amount of alcohol he'd drunk either. He'd had a couple of drinks, sure, but he felt he'd deserved them after the day he'd had. And two drinks were not enough to account for the feeling of depression he had when he opened his eyes.

Of course, he wasn't denying that he hadn't expected to have a run-in with either his mother or Laura again the night before. He'd gone for a walk to try and clear his head and it had been pure chance that he'd been crossing the hall when he'd heard his mother's voice. What had she been doing, sneaking about the house making phone calls she could just as easily have made in her room? Had she really been phoning a girlfriend? Somehow, that explanation didn't ring true.

But had Laura believed it? That was what he'd like to know. She'd been in the room the whole time and had obviously heard more of the call than him. Would she tell him if she suspected his mother was lying? After what had happened after Stella had gone to bed, he somehow doubted it. What in God's name had possessed him to kiss her? She was never going to trust him again.

He scowled down at the plate of scrambled eggs Laura's aunt had provided for him. It shouldn't matter what she thought, but it did. Dammit, she'd practically accused him of taking advantage of her father and then imagined that pretending she hadn't meant it would pacify him. The trouble was, the knowledge of the will Stella had found was taking its toll on his nerves, and he'd been so mad that Laura should even *think* such a thing without any evidence, it had shattered his self-control. He'd wanted to punish her, and that was what he'd intended. But when he'd taken her in his arms it hadn't worked out at all the way he'd planned.

To begin with, he'd been angry, but that hadn't lasted long. He'd been in control, too, somehow that had got away from him as well. All his preconceived ideas had taken a beating, but not as much of a beating as he had taken himself.

He expelled an unsteady breath. Imprisoning her hands behind her back had seemed such a good idea, he remembered ruefully. It had made her helpless, vulnerable, susceptible to his every demand. It had also brought her upper body against his, stilling her resistance, but the sensual pressure of her breasts against his chest had aroused an entirely different reaction, after all.

Of course he'd expected her to resist him. He'd wanted her to, if only to prove he had the upper hand. But after those first few moments she'd been as caught up in their lovemaking as he was, and when her lips had parted beneath his he'd been lost.

He'd forgotten how delicious her mouth tasted. Soft, and hot, and so responsive—his blood had pounded like thunder through his veins. His arousal had been instantaneous; there'd been no way he could control that. He'd only buried his tongue inside her, but he'd wanted—how he'd wanted—to do so much more.

He'd let her hands go then, but instead of backing off the way any sane man would have done he'd allowed himself to explore her softness instead. He hadn't been able to resist the urge to bring her fully against him, and there'd been a pleasurable kind of pain in letting her feel his throbbing need.

He felt an unwelcome tightening in his groin at the memory. If she hadn't brought him to his senses then, it would have been too late. In his own mind, he had already stripped her trousers and sweater from her, and he was already imagining how sweet it would be to part those slick petals between her legs...

'Are you going to eat those eggs?'

Aunt Nell's down-to-earth tone caused an immediate re-action. He felt like a schoolboy who'd been caught looking at girlie magazines under the sheets. A faint colour invaded his tanned face, which he hoped she'd put down to the heat of the dining-room fire. He'd hate to think she could detect what was going on in his mind.

'I'm not very hungry,' he said, pushing his plate aside. Which was true. 'Thanks, anyway.'

The woman pulled a disapproving face. 'You need food,' she said. 'I've noticed that your appetite has been sadly lacking all the time you've been here. I can't believe that Griff's death is responsible, and I wouldn't have thought a man like yourself would have any trouble with his weight.'

Oliver gave her a wry look. 'Is that a compliment?'

'It's nothing but the truth,' averred Laura's aunt firmly. She paused. 'Now, do you know if your mother is planning on getting up this morning? Marcus Venning said he'd be back by ten o'clock and it's almost that now.'

'Is it?' Oliver was surprised. He'd spent longer than he'd thought deliberating over the eggs. 'As far as I know, Stella is planning on meeting Marcus this morning.' He forced a casual tone. 'Is Laura up?'

'Laura's been up for hours,' replied Aunt Nell, starting to clear the table. 'She had breakfast in the kitchen with me at seven o'clock.'

'So where is she?' Oliver's voice was sharp, but he couldn't help it. He was half afraid that now that her father was buried she'd decided there was no reason for her to stay.

'How should I know?' Aunt Nell didn't take kindly to being spoken to in that fashion. 'She went out about an hour ago. I didn't ask her where she was going.'

Oliver sighed. 'But you know, don't you?' he said, pushing back his chair and getting up from the table. His mouth compressed. 'Must I remind you that Marcus will want to see her, too?'

Laura's aunt gathered the remaining cutlery on to the tray and then looked up at him defiantly. 'I believe she's gone to the church,' she said. 'She said something about visiting her father before she left.'

'Oh...' Oliver breathed a little more easily. 'Oh, right. So she'll be back soon?'

'Very likely,' said the old woman, heading for the door. 'Oh, and by the way, Beth will be starting on the bedrooms directly. I asked her not to come in yesterday, what with the funeral and all.'

Oliver nodded. Beth Llewellyn came up several times a week from the village. Although Aunt Nell enjoyed running the house herself, she drew the line at doing all the heavy work. In consequence, Beth had been a part of the establishment since before his mother had married Laura's father, and although Stella complained that she was a gossip she wasn't prepared to participate in the housework herself.

Aunt Nell had gone back to the kitchen with the tray and, leaving the dining room, Oliver decided to go and check on the fire in the library. Marcus wouldn't be too happy if the room was chilly. Despite the old man's sprightly appearance Oliver knew he was troubled with arthritis in cold weather.

He also hoped it might serve to exorcise his memories of the night before. In spite of a determined effort to do so, he couldn't get the thought of Laura out of his head. Sitting at the square leather-topped desk, gazing out at the bare trees that were appearing again in the garden as the snow melted, visions of the past engulfed him. He found himself wondering when it was that he'd first noticed that Laura was growing up...

He guessed he must have been about seventeen when he'd realised she wasn't a kid any more. Not that he'd been attracted to her in those days. She'd been more of a nuisance than anything else, always wanting to know where he was going, and with whom; fouling up his relationships, cramping his style.

He'd seemed to spend his days trying to get rid of her, although he'd done his best not to hurt her even then. He'd been aware of the fragility of her confidence. Unlike his mother, he'd never believed that Laura was the brat she claimed.

He supposed he'd been lucky that the summer she turned fifteen, he'd taken a holiday job in Snowdonia. He'd worked at a café near the mountain railway and had spent his free time mixing with hikers and climbers from all parts of the world. That was when he'd first conceived his interest in backpacking, which had proved so advantageous the following year.

He'd begun taking photographs, too. Of his friends, to begin with, and then subsequently of the magnificent scenery in the National Park. Learning how to process the pictures himself had come later, as had the realisation that this was what he wanted to do with his life.

It was during his final year at Rhosmawr Comprehensive that his relationship with his stepsister had altered. At sixteen, Laura had had all the charm and freshness of a young woman, with the added bonus of not knowing exactly how attractive she was. Because she was taller than her peers, she'd walked with a certain diffidence, but Oliver had been fascinated by her slim limbs and long, long legs.

Her hair, of course, had been instantly noticeable. It had been longer then, a riot of fiery curls that fell almost to her waist. She'd said she hated it because people called her a redhead, but even in those days Oliver had known it wasn't red. It was actually strawberry blonde.

In any event, he'd found himself waiting for her, instead of the other way about, sitting with her at lunch break, walking her to the bus. Because her birthday was towards the end of the school year, in June, and his was at the start of the year, in October, there were only two school years between them, and pupils in the fifth year often mixed with pupils in the sixth year, so there was no one to object.

Not at school, at least.

At home, it was very different. His mother objected strongly to the attention he was paying to Laura. She'd warned him that Laura's father would never stand for it, though in all honesty Griff had never voiced any disapproval. On the contrary, he'd seemed pleased that his daughter and his stepfamily seemed finally to have settled their differences. He'd had no idea that his wife was as opposed to his daughter as ever.

The summer before Oliver was due to go to Oxford at the start of the Michaelmas term had been an unseasonably hot one. For weeks the temperature had hovered somewhere in the middle eighties, and he and Laura had spent much of their time trying to keep cool. The River Madoc that meandered through the village widened into a pool near Penmadoc Bridge, and it was a popular meeting spot for all the young people in the village. It was deep enough to swim, and the water was deliciously cold on a hot day.

They'd talked a lot that summer, about anything and everything, sharing their deepest thoughts and dearest wishes. Their relationship hadn't been like the relationships he'd had with other girls his own age. He'd been attracted to her, sure, but it had been her personality that had intrigued him. He'd wanted to be with her, but he hadn't had anything sexual in mind.

Or so he'd told himself.

He scowled now. It had been so easy to delude himself. So easy to pretend that the reason he liked looking at her was because she appealed to the artist in his soul. Her creamy skin, the freckles in her complexion, the provocative upthrust of her small breasts had given a natural sensuality to the photographs he'd taken of her, and he'd fooled himself that his interest was objective, or at least innocent of any prurient intent.

How Laura herself had interpreted his attentions was another story. Or perhaps it was the same one, only he'd been too blind to see where things were heading. During those long summer days, she'd become his soulmate, and he liked to tell himself he'd been unaware of how dangerous her attachment to him had become.

Until the night she'd come uninvited to his room...

The sound of a car's engine interrupted his thoughts. Marcus, he guessed grimly, half relieved at the sudden reprieve. God knew, he didn't want to think about what had happened between him and Laura at this moment. What had nearly happened the night before was still too blatantly vivid in his mind.

The door was pushed open a few moments later and Aunt Nell appeared. 'The solicitor's here,' she said, without ceremony, and stood aside to let Marcus Venning into the room. 'Will I tell your mother or will you?'

'There's no need for anybody to tell me anything,' retorted Stella's sharp voice behind her. 'I'm here.' She flashed her son a defiant look before turning to the solicitor and giving him a thin smile. 'Marcus,' she added, rather less belligerently. 'Punctual as ever, I see.'

The old solicitor huffed a little self-importantly. 'Yes, well, I always like to keep to a schedule,' he said, approaching the desk that Oliver had just vacated. 'I'm glad to see you're feeling much better this morning, Mrs Williams. It was such a pity you couldn't join us yesterday.'

Stella's lip curled. 'I wouldn't call it a pity that I couldn't attend my own husband's funeral. You don't imagine I wanted to let him down—'

'You were devastated, I'm sure,' remarked Venning drily, and Oliver suspected the old man was no more convinced of his mother's incapacity the previous day than he was. He deposited his briefcase on the desk and looked around. 'Where's Laura?'

'She's coming,' said Aunt Nell from the doorway. 'She's just taking off her boots.' She glanced behind her. 'She went to the church earlier.'

'Ah.'

Marcus accepted this explanation with an approving nod and Oliver saw the look of irritation that crossed his mother's face at the realisation that so far as the old solicitor was concerned Laura was still the mistress here. And always would be, he reflected, whether she chose to live here or not.

Laura's appearance a few moments later brought its own tension into the room. Oliver wondered if he was the only one who felt it or whether his mother was as indifferent to Laura's presence as she appeared. Surely she must feel some sympathy for her, he thought uneasily. At a time like this, they should have been able to support one another.

But, as usual, Stella chose to ignore her stepdaughter, and although Laura glanced a little uncertainly at her father's widow she didn't attempt to bridge the gulf that Stella had created between them.

For himself, Oliver had the greatest difficulty in keeping his eyes off Laura. She was wearing a skirt this morning, a pale heathery tweed whose hem ended a good four inches above her knee. He guessed it wasn't deliberate, but it exposed a considerable length of shapely thigh, particularly when she sat down and crossed her legs, and that, along with the vivid glory of her hair, was a potent combination.

'Good morning,' she said, her cheeks flushed from the cold air outdoors. 'I'm sorry if I've kept you waiting. I was talking to Father Lewis and I'm afraid I forgot the time.'

'I'm sure we all understand how that could happen,' Venning assured her warmly, earning another resentful look from Oliver's mother. He looked towards the doorway, where Aunt Nell was still hovering, half in and half out of the room. 'Come and sit down, Miss Tenby. You're a beneficiary, too.'

Laura's aunt looked as if she would have preferred to forego the privilege, but she was obliged to come into the room and take a seat. Then, after assuring himself that Oliver was quite content to remain standing in front of the fire, Venning seated himself at the desk and opened his briefcase.

There was no mistaking the tensions in the room now. Glancing at his mother, Oliver saw the way her knuckles were whitening over the arms of her chair. Even Aunt Nell couldn't hide her own uneasiness, and Oliver wondered if she was anticipating her departure if, as she expected, Griff had left the bulk of his estate to his wife.

If only she knew...

His lips twisted as the old man drew out an envelope. Marcus was enjoying this, he thought. He must know what was in the will and he was deliberately taking his time to prolong the suspense. Or perhaps he didn't know. Perhaps, like Laura and her aunt, he'd been kept in the dark. Perhaps he assumed Griff had left everything of importance to Stella. Maybe this was just his way of showing his disapproval, of dragging out his own moment of power because it might be the last time he performed a duty of this kind.

The documents Venning drew from the envelope crackled ominously and Oliver could fairly feel his mother's agitation. Calm down, old lady, he urged her silently, meeting her distracted gaze with a cool look. It was just as well the others were watching the solicitor, he thought drily, or they might have wondered why Stella was looking so apprehensive.

Venning cleared his throat, quickly scanning the several pages he held in his hand. Then, sonorously, and with all ceremony, he began, '"I, Griffith Henry Williams, being of sound mind—"'

'Must we drag this out?' Stella's nerve snapped at the indication that the solicitor intended to read every word of the will. Then, as if realising how unfeeling she must have sounded, she forced a strained smile. 'I'm sorry. I'm afraid I'm not as strong as I thought I was.'

Venning sniffed and looked round at the rest of them. 'Of course, of course,' he said, though whether that was an answer to her question or a confirmation of her frailty Oliver couldn't be sure. 'If no one else has any objections,' the old man added, 'I see no reason why we shouldn't—what is it they say nowadays?—cut to the chase?' He looked at Oliver. 'Perhaps your mother would like a little brandy.' He shuffled the papers between his gnarled hands. 'None of us minds waiting, I'm sure.'

'I think we'd all prefer it if you got on with it, Mr Venning.' It was Laura who spoke, and for once Stella gave her a grateful glance.

'Yes, please,' she said. 'I'll be all right.' She cast a bitter look towards Oliver. 'I don't usually drink this early in the day.'

'No, but these are exceptional circumstances,' persisted the solicitor, and Oliver found himself expelling an impatient breath.

'Please,' he said, controlling his tone with an effort, 'won't you continue, Marcus? It may be that we'll all need a drink when you're finished.'

'What?' Venning thought for a moment he was serious, and, indeed, Oliver rather thought that he was. But then the old man seemed to sense the irony behind his statement, and, clearing his throat again, he began to speak.

There were one or two small bequests, small sums of money bestowed on colleagues and acquaintances, like the landlord of the pub in the village and the doctor, who'd also been a friend. Oliver wondered if Griff had suspected that his health might be a problem. There was a comfortable legacy for his sister-in-law, too, and Aunt Nell relaxed after her name had been read.

'And now we come to the bulk of the estate,' declared Venning solemnly. 'Naturally, you are all anxious to hear how Mr Williams divided his property, and I don't intend to keep you in suspense any longer than I must. Or course, I must impress upon you that this will is legal and binding and Mr Williams thought long and hard before coming to his decision.'

'Oh, do get on with it.'

Aunt Nell was evidently getting irritated now, and Oliver

realised that the old lady still had a stake in the proceedings. If, as she evidently suspected, Stella had inherited Penmadoc, her own position in the house was hardly secure.

'Very well.' If Venning was offended by her impatience, he hid it well and, clearing his throat for the third time, he began again. '"To my wife, Stella,"' he said, glancing across the desk at her, '"I leave one half share in my house and all my personal possessions, save those articles of jewellery that were given to me by my first wife, Maggie, and which I would like my daughter, Laura, to have as a memento of the love her mother and I shared. I further bestow sufficient funds to enable my wife to continue to live at Penmadoc, if she so wishes, on the understanding that my sister-in-law, Eleanor Tenby, shall always have a home there as well. Should my wife, Stella, choose to marry again, or live elsewhere, the house will revert wholly to my daughter, Laura, as it will, in any event, at my wife's death."'

There was an audible gasp after he'd finished reading this clause of the will, though who had uttered it Oliver wasn't sure. His mother, he suspected, though it would be dangerous for her to show any surprise that this wasn't the same will she had seen. It might even have been Laura. She was certainly paler now than she'd been when she'd entered the library. Like his mother, she must have expected she knew what was in the will.

'Um…shall I go on?'

The solicitor hesitated. Oliver guessed he'd been expecting some kind of outburst from his mother, but Stella seemed too shocked to say a word. It was lucky her reaction could be attributed just as easily to the fact that she hadn't inherited *all* of Penmadoc, he reflected. But what the hell was *he* going to do now?

Realising that Venning was waiting, Oliver gave him a terse look. 'Of course,' he said, his lips tightening in sudden frustration, and the solicitor turned once again to the will.

'"To my daughter, Laura,"' he said, smiling encouragingly at her, ''I bequeath the aforementioned jewellery, as well as all my books and pictures and one half share in the home we shared for many years. Perhaps this shared responsibility will create an understanding between my wife and my daughter that was never evident in my lifetime, and I appoint my stepson, Oliver Kemp, as executor to this effect.''''

CHAPTER TEN

DESPITE Aunt Nell's pleas to the contrary, Laura left Penmadoc that afternoon. She knew there would be things to do, papers to sign, arrangements to be made, but she couldn't bear to stay in the house any longer. She needed time—and space—to come to terms with what had happened, and so long as Oliver was in the same building she knew she'd never have any peace.

Goodness knew, she hadn't had any peace since he'd kissed her. That was why she'd left the house that morning, in the hope of finding some sanctuary in the church which she'd attended as a child. But the church was full of memories, Penmadoc was full of memories, and she'd known then she had no choice but to leave.

Though not in these circumstances, she thought, after the train had deposited her at Euston station and she had hired a cab to take her to a hotel. She'd had no idea that her father might leave Penmadoc to her—or any part of it—and even the knowledge that it was Stella's home for as long as she wanted or needed it, couldn't mar the pride she felt in knowing that the house was going to remain in the family.

Her family.

Aunt Nell's family too, she acknowledged gratefully. It was good to know the old lady's position was secure as well. Although Oliver had reassured her that his mother wanted to stay at Penmadoc, she had had her doubts about Stella's intentions towards her aunt.

Her own position was much more complicated. Apart from the continuing animosity that existed between her and Stella, she didn't see how she could spend any time at Penmadoc when her work was in New York. Besides which, Stella must be furious that Griff had double-crossed her. Laura had few doubts that her stepmother had expected to inherit the house in its entirety.

As for Oliver...

But she didn't want to think about Oliver now. Oliver was still at Penmadoc, consoling his mother, no doubt, reassuring her that Laura was unlikely to make things difficult for her. He knew about her work; he'd cleverly found out all about her while they were having lunch that day. He was in the perfect position to assure his mother that she had nothing to worry about.

It was early evening by the time she'd checked into the hotel and unpacked her belongings. She'd had to choose one of the larger hotels because she didn't know the names of any of the smaller ones. But the one she'd chosen was impersonal and efficient, and she told herself that that was all she needed. After all, this wasn't a social visit. Staying here would give her time to decide what she was going to do.

Room Service provided her with a light supper. She could have gone down to the restaurant, but it was less trouble to eat in her room. Afterwards, she put aside her misgivings and phoned Aunt Nell to let her know where she was, asking her not to broadcast her whereabouts unless some sort of emergency occurred.

'You really ought to have stayed here,' Aunt Nell told her reprovingly. 'This is your house, Laura. Don't let anyone tell you any different.'

'I won't,' Laura assured her, recalling the fact that Stella hadn't said a word to anyone after the solicitor had finished reading the will. Which she might have thought was unusual, she reflected, if she hadn't been so stunned herself.

'Well, you see they don't,' declared her aunt firmly. 'Who knows what that woman will try to do now? She's suffering from shock at the moment, but that won't last. And once she realises you've thwarted her plans she won't be very pleased.'

Laura sighed. 'What plans?' she asked wearily. 'Aunt Nell—'

'Her plans to sell Penmadoc, of course.' Her aunt clicked her tongue. 'Don't tell me you thought that she'd want to stay in the village after Griff had no say in the matter? For pity's sake, girl, she's been hankering after moving to Cardiff or suchlike for years.'

Laura's eyes widened. 'But I thought—'

'Yes? What did you think? That she and your father lived an idyllic life together?'

'Well—'

'Oh, Laura, didn't he tell you? I should have known he'd be too proud to admit it. He and you-know-who haven't shared a bedroom for years.'

Laura sat down abruptly on the side of the bed. She'd had no idea that there was anything wrong between her father and Stella. And yet… She remembered again how unusually cheerful he'd seemed last summer when she'd seen him in London. She'd been wondering whether he'd been hiding the fact that his heart was failing. She'd never dreamt he might have been hiding something else.

'So—what are you implying, Aunt Nell?' she returned at last, not sure where this was heading or even if she wanted to go there. She took a deep breath. 'Was there—is there someone else? Is that what you're saying?'

The old lady seemed to draw back from making such a damning accusation. 'All I'm saying is that you shouldn't take too much for granted,' she said, choosing her words with care. 'Stella will have her own agenda. You can be sure of it. Things aren't always the way they seem, you know.'

Laura stifled a groan. It was obvious her aunt wasn't prepared to make it easy for her. If she wanted to know any more, she would have to find out for herself. It crossed her mind that this might be Aunt Nell's way of getting her back to Penmadoc, but for the next few days she was determined to stay where she was.

She rang Conor's uncle—and her employer—a couple of days later. Matthew Neill was sympathetic about her situation, but it was obvious he wanted her in New York. 'The last time I looked at your desk, I couldn't see it for a mountain of paper,' he remarked drily. 'It's been over a week, Laura. When are you coming back to work?'

'Only just over a week,' Laura pointed out exactly. 'And he was my father, Matt. I need a little time to settle his affairs.'

'Yeah.' She could almost see his scowl. 'And I suppose inheriting this house rather complicates things, doesn't it? Are you planning on selling it? I can't see that it's gonna be of any use to you.'

Laura gave a rueful shake of her head. Where property was concerned, Matt's opinion was that you either lived in it or you sold. He'd handled the sale of the brownstone when she and Conor had split up, thus saving her any heartache, and found her the loft apartment in Greenwich Village which she presently enjoyed.

'It's not mine to sell,' she said now, although that was just a prevarication. Even if Stella was prepared to sell in exchange for half the profits, Laura wouldn't have wanted to get rid of the old house. 'I've told you: my father left half to my stepmother. I couldn't ask her—or my aunt—to find somewhere else to live.'

'Well, you're gonna have to make a decision,' said Matthew flatly. 'I need you here. Like I said before, the work's piling up.' He broke off for a moment. 'There's not something you're not telling me, is there, sweetie? You've not met some man from your past who wants you to stay in England?'

'No!' Laura's response was convincingly vehement, but she couldn't help the unwilling thought that his suspicions weren't that far from the truth. 'I'll be back,' she said. 'Next week at the latest. Until then, you're just going to have to manage without me.'

Nonetheless, Matthew's words had unsettled her. What with Aunt Nell's intimations on the one hand and his insinuations on the other, it was well nigh impossible for her to relax. Was she so transparent, she wondered, that Conor's uncle could actually sense what she was thinking over the wires? Or was she simply attributing him with extra perception because of her own guilt?

Whatever, when she climbed into bed that night, she was hardly surprised when her thoughts drifted back to that fatal evening. The evening when she'd taken her courage into her hands and gone to Oliver's room. Looking back on it now, she didn't know how she'd had the nerve to do it. It was ironic really because she knew she would never have had the courage to do it now.

But then, it was the events that had happened during and after that evening that had made such a difference to her life, she reflected. Without the memories of the past, she wouldn't be the woman she was today. Or feel such a lingering hatred towards Oliver, she told herself, though hatred was not what she'd felt when he'd kissed her the night of her father's funeral. She'd wanted him then; there was no point in denying it; just as much as she'd wanted him fourteen years ago...

It had been a hot day. It had been an unusually hot summer, and the farmers who ran their sheep on the hills around Penmadoc were crying out for rain. But that night, at least, there was the promise of a storm in the offing, and all evening there'd been the rumble of thunder in the distance.

It was the threat of the storm that had made Laura feel restless. Or so she'd told herself. That, and the fact that she'd spent the afternoon watching Oliver training with the school athletics team. She'd felt such pride when he'd returned to her side after every event, flopping down on the grass beside her, to the envy of many of the older girls.

But it wasn't just pride that had caused her to feel so unsettled. It was the lean strength of his long body as he'd lounged beside her that had made her aware of him in a totally physical way. The sweat beading on his forehead, running like raindrops down the smooth skin of his torso had fascinated her, and she'd wanted to press him back into the grass and taste his essence for herself.

Something of what she'd been feeling must have shown in her eyes because Oliver had noticed. 'Hey, don't look at me like that, baby,' he said, 'or you might get more than you bargained for.'

'Could I?' she responded tartly, though her cheeks burned with colour, and Oliver covered her hand where it lay on the grass and pressed his thumb into her palm.

Even that small intimacy set off a series of sensual explosions inside her. Her stomach quivered with an unfamiliar excitement, and she desperately wanted to explore further. She was trembling with the strength of her emotions, and she hoped he might teach her what it meant.

But Oliver was called back to the field at that moment and when he returned Laura had no opportunity to rekindle their earlier intimacy. A group of his fellow athletes came with him and they were keen to go down to the pub to quench their thirst with lemon chasers. Some of the older boys were already eighteen and there was a lot of horseplay about who was going to have a beer and who wasn't. At sixteen, Laura felt very much the outsider, and although she went with them it was the older girls now who held centre stage.

They all walked home together, however, but although she and Oliver covered the last few yards alone all he wanted to talk about was the fact that he hoped to continue with his athletics when he went to university. He was still high from the success he'd had in the last race he'd entered and when they arrived at Penmadoc he went at once to take a shower.

Laura hoped that her father and Stella might be going out that evening. But the prospect of the storm made everybody edgy, and after exchanging words with her husband over the fact that she'd overspent on her allowance again her stepmother announced that she intended to take a bath and didn't

want to be disturbed. Oliver disappeared up to his room as
Laura and Aunt Nell were doing the dishes, and as her father
always retired to his study when he was upset she spent the
rest of the evening on her own.

She went to bed at eleven o'clock and spent the next hour
trying to make sense of the Margaret Atwood novel that had
previously held her interest. But the words all ran together
and, after turning several pages without having the faintest
idea what she'd read, she put the book aside.

She couldn't stop thinking about Oliver. She didn't know
why exactly, but somehow that afternoon their relationship
had taken a more serious turn and she badly wanted to talk
to him about it. She wanted to know if he felt the same, if
he'd experienced any of the feelings that had troubled her
since he'd touched her, or whether she'd only imagined the
sudden intimacy between them.

She might be only sixteen, she thought, but she wasn't
naïve. She knew what went on between a man and a woman,
and she'd had first-hand knowledge of how strong that attraction could be. Surely her father could never have become
involved with Stella so soon after her mother's death if he
hadn't been irresistibly attracted to her. Although she still
found that hard to stomach, Laura had learned to be philosophical about something she couldn't change.

Even so, she couldn't believe that the way she felt about
Oliver bore any resemblance to what went on between her
father and Stella. They were so much older, for one thing.
She wasn't even sure if they did 'it' any more.

She'd learned what 'it' was when she was about thirteen,
and since then it had become a regular topic of conversation
among her contemporaries at the comprehensive. Some of
the girls even claimed to have done 'it' themselves, but Laura
doubted that many of them had actually taken the risk. Even
in this age of sexual freedom, most girls would fight shy of
inviting an unwanted pregnancy and all that it would mean.

Nevertheless, the idea of making love with Oliver was a

captivating thought. Remembering his lean brown torso and the way his stomach muscles rippled beneath his taut skin caused a shiver to feather down her spine. He was hairy, too; not a lot, just a light sprinkling on his chest and over his arms and legs that deepened his tan. But it was the place where it arrowed down below his navel that fascinated her. She was curious to know if he had hair between his legs.

Her thoughts troubled her. She'd always felt a certain contempt towards girls who talked constantly about sex and what it meant to them. Although she'd loved Oliver for years, she'd never imagined herself falling *in love* with him. Yet there didn't seem to be any other reason for the way she was feeling. Or for the tingling awareness that was prickling her skin.

It was upsetting, but it was also exciting, and she knew she would never get to sleep if she didn't share her feelings with someone else. She'd never had a really close girlfriend, and there was no way she could discuss it with her father. As for Stella, well, she knew exactly how her stepmother would react if she confessed her feelings to her.

There was only one solution: late as it was, she would have to hope that Oliver wasn't asleep. He had a computer in his room, and she knew he sometimes played games on it for hours. So much so that his mother had threatened to deduct the cost of the electricity he was using from his allowance.

It was rather daunting to leave her bedroom. She entertained the nightmare of what she would do if someone saw her going into Oliver's room. As well as her stepmother's disapproval, she doubted it would find much sympathy with her father. As far as Griff Williams was concerned, she was still his little girl.

Despite the fact that she was wearing her dressing gown, the corridors were cold and just a little spooky. Although she used to tease Oliver that Penmadoc was haunted, she'd never really believed it herself. Until tonight. Her feet were bare and she shivered uneasily. It was so easy to imagine she wasn't alone.

It was quite a relief to reach Oliver's room. There was no sign of a light under the door, but he didn't always use the light when he was working on his computer, for obvious reasons. However, when she took her courage in both hands and opened the door, the sight that met her startled eyes caused a sudden constriction in her throat.

Oliver was there, all right, but he wasn't working on his computer. He was in bed, asleep, the sheet which was all that had covered him kicked down around his ankles. He'd once teased Laura that he wore nothing to sleep in. She'd never dreamed she'd find out that it was true.

Hardly knowing what she was doing, Laura stepped into the room, allowing the door to close behind her. Somehow her hand found the handle and prevented any sound from escaping into the corridor, and then she sank back against the panels, gazing open-mouthed at her stepbrother's reclining form.

The curtains were open, and moonlight streamed down on to his naked body. In the silvery light, his skin had an unearthly sheen, like the pelt of a selkie, that mythical creature that was said to haunt the waters around Scotland and which assumed human form to seduce a woman. And seeing him, like this, seduced Laura's sensibilities, so that instead of getting out of there as she knew she should she pushed herself away from the door and approached the bed.

She stood for several minutes, just looking down at him, and then the temptation to touch got the better of her, and, sinking down on to her knees, she stretched out her hand and ran her fingers over the smooth curve of his hip.

'What the hell—?'

Oliver came awake with a start, frightening Laura so much that for a moment she couldn't move. She froze there, her eyes wide, like a rabbit caught in the headlights of a car, and gazed at him in total panic.

'Laura!' Although Oliver must have been as startled to find her there as she was at being caught, he recovered more rapidly, dragging the sheet up around his hips with one hand as he pushed himself up with the other. 'For God's sake, what's wrong?'

Laura's mouth was dry. 'I—I—nothing's wrong,' she protested, shocked by the awareness that his arousal had manifested itself first in a different part of his body. 'I—well, I wanted to talk to you.'

Oliver blinked and glanced at the clock on his bedside table. 'At half-past twelve?' he exclaimed disbelievingly. 'For pity's sake, what was so important that it couldn't wait until morning?'

'I—nothing.' Suddenly, Laura was convinced she had made a terrible mistake. Contrary to her beliefs, Oliver hadn't been affected by what had happened that afternoon. And why should he have been, for goodness' sake? It wasn't as if he hadn't had other girlfriends, other relationships. He'd only squeezed her hand. She'd blown what had been a purely friendly gesture right out of proportion. 'It was nothing.' She scrambled to her feet. 'I'm sorry I disturbed you.'

'Laura…'

His tone was frustrated, but she had heard enough. She'd made a total fool of herself, and she'd be lucky if he didn't tell all his friends what an idiot she was. All she wanted to do was get back to her room as quickly as possible and try and forget what she'd done.

She was fumbling for the handle of the door when his hand came over her shoulder and flattened against the panels. 'Wait,' he said huskily, his breath warm against the nape of her neck. 'Tell me why you really came to my room. I want to know.'

Laura took a deep breath. God, she thought unsteadily, he was right behind her. She could feel the heat of his body reaching out to her, enveloping her, wrapping her in the same intimacy she had felt that afternoon.

'You don't want to know,' she said in a muffled voice, but of course he did. He wouldn't have left his bed and come after her if he hadn't wanted to know exactly why she'd felt compelled to do something so out of character, so dangerous. And suddenly she knew she was in danger. But not from him; from herself.

'Tell me,' he said, his lips brushing her ear, and her stomach turned over at the unexpected tingle that caused. 'Come on, baby.' His hand left the door to curl across her throat and grip her shoulder. It took a very little pressure to bring her back against his chest. 'Talk to me.'

Laura's heart was pounding. Being close to him like this was more thrilling than she could ever have imagined, and the awareness that only the man's tee shirt she used to sleep in and her thin dressing gown were all that was between them caused a fluttering sensation in the pit of her stomach.

'Laura…' His voice had thickened, and his free hand came around her waist. Whether by accident or design—she was too bemused to decide which—his fingers slid beneath the opening of her robe, gripping her hip and pulling her even closer. 'Dammit, Laura, talk to me. Tell me you didn't come here because of what I said this afternoon. I was a fool. I shouldn't have—teased you like that. It wasn't fair.'

Laura swallowed the lump that rose in her throat at his words. Her excitement dissolved into quivering humiliation, but when she would have dragged herself away from him he muttered an oath and held on to her.

'Don't,' he groaned, his hand sliding possessively across her abdomen, and as he held her there against him she felt the unmistakable hardening of his sex against her bottom.

Then, when she was half afraid her shaking legs were going to give out on her, he turned her round and brought her fully against him. Laura's eyes were wide with wonder when she looked up into his face, and as if some lingering twinge of conscience still troubled him Oliver lifted one hand to cup her cheek. 'You know this is crazy, don't you?' he said unsteadily, and she realised that what he'd said before hadn't been the truth. He hadn't been teasing her that afternoon. He'd been as aroused by what had happened as she had and he'd only said what he had to try and influence a situation that was rapidly moving out of control. He uttered a harsh sound. 'Tell me to stop.'

'Why should I?' she asked, her hands sliding up his chest to grip the dark hair that tangled at his nape. The power she sensed she had over him was tantalising. 'That's not what you really want to hear.'

'You don't know what I really want,' he replied thickly, his fingers tightening on her chin, causing her mouth to open and emit laboured panting breaths.

'Don't I?' Somehow, she pulled her face free of his hand. 'I'm not a child, Oliver.'

'I wonder.' He gritted his teeth, but his hand moved almost compulsively to the back of her neck, tilting her face up to his. 'I wonder,' he muttered again, and this time he couldn't stop himself. With the tumult of his emotions darkening his eyes, he bent his head and covered her mouth with his.

Laura's knees buckled and she clutched his shoulders to prevent herself from slipping to the floor. There was such a wealth of emotion in his kiss and although she was by no means experienced when it came to making out with boys she instantly recognised the difference between Oliver's love-making and the amateurish fumblings she'd known before. For one thing, Oliver knew exactly what he was doing and, for another, for the first time in her life she wasn't repulsed by it.

'God, Laura,' he said hoarsely, when he released her mouth to seek the sweetly scented skin of her shoulder. His fingers peeled back the layers of cloth to expose her creamy flesh, brushing aside the tendrils of red-gold hair that had escaped from the braid she'd worn to sleep in and kneading her quivering skin. 'I want you. You know that. But not like this. It isn't right.'

Laura's confidence wavered for only a moment. 'It is for me,' she told him fiercely, winding her arms around his neck and lifting one leg to caress his calf with her heel. She'd seen that done in a play she'd watched on television and she was amazed to find it stimulated her just as much as it apparently stimulated him. 'I want you. How can that be wrong?'

'God knows,' he groaned, his hands sliding down her back to cup her bottom and lift her against him. 'Perhaps it isn't,' he added, as if trying to convince himself, and then, because she wrapped her legs around him, he gave up the unequal struggle and carried her to the bed.

For a moment after he'd pushed off her dressing gown and peeled her tee shirt over her head, Laura knew a moment's panic. His sheets were cool at her back and they caused a brief spasm of sanity to chill her blood. But it didn't last long. When Oliver knelt beside her and bent to take one erect nipple into his mouth, she thought she was in heaven. She was half afraid she would die from the pleasure his darting tongue evoked.

Time was suspended as he ran his hands over her body. She had always thought she was too tall and too lean, but evidently he didn't agree with her. There was genuine satisfaction in the eyes that met and mated with hers, and she found herself moving instinctively with him, arching her body and spreading her legs in a way that at any other time would have mortified her soul.

But there was no shame with Oliver, no inhibitions when he straddled her and invited her to touch him. His shaft was hot and hard and incredibly smooth, like steel beneath soft velvet. But, in spite of his eagerness to share his excitement with her, when her slim fingers closed around him, he moaned aloud.

'I can't—I can't wait,' he said in a strangled voice, and with a groan of anguish he came into her, slowly at first and then with an unrestrained eagerness he couldn't deny. Her muscles froze at first and then expanded to accommodate him. She felt as if it was never going to end, and she stifled a cry.

She'd been prepared for it to hurt, but what she'd not been prepared for was that after that initial agony she would begin to enjoy it. The girls at school, who had been so keen to share their experiences with her, had evidently never had a lover like Oliver. His skill and consideration soon had her moving with him. Moving willingly, instinctively, reaching for the seemingly unattainable release of the emotions he was building inside her. His lean body quickened, stroking in and out of hers with an ease and slickness that had her clinging to him helplessly. Her nails dug into his shoulders, and she wrapped her legs around him, little breathless cries issuing from her throat.

And then what had seemed to be impossible happened. Almost simultaneously, he came into her with such force that she thought she might not be able to take him after all. But she could; she did; his groan of satisfaction proved it, mingling with the cry she uttered as a devastating wave of pleasure spread throughout her body.

She wanted to weep. What had happened had been so—so beautiful, and Oliver's still shuddering body lying on top of hers gave her a feeling of real contentment. She was a woman now; in every way. She loved Oliver, and he loved her. Nothing anyone said or did could change their feelings for one another.

She'd been so wrong. Laura acknowledged that now with a shiver of distaste. What had happened afterwards had been so awful, so ugly. She couldn't even think of it without feeling a surge of nausea in her throat.

Predictably, it was Stella who had ruined everything for them. No, not for *them*, she amended bitterly. For her. The way Oliver had behaved after that night had seemed to confirm everything his mother had claimed. But when her stepmother had burst into the room and found them Laura had been too bemused to think coherently, blinking into the harsh electric light like a mole that had just been dug out of its hole.

And that was how she felt: shocked and ashamed that Stella should have been the one to find them. Her contorted face had destroyed the sweet intimacy she and Oliver had shared, and how she'd kept from screaming her outrage Laura never knew.

Of course, Stella had had some justification for her anger. This was her home and they had abused the trust she'd put in them. Laura acknowledged that, acknowledged that her stepmother must hate the fact that it was she who had been responsible for Oliver abusing that trust. But what she couldn't forgive was the fact that Oliver had conspired with his mother to keep what had happened between themselves.

The threatening storm had apparently kept Stella awake, too. The heat and humidity had made her restless, and she'd been on her way downstairs to get herself a drink when she'd heard Laura's faint cries.

At the time, Laura remembered, she'd been only too glad that it hadn't been her father who'd found them. As she scrambled out of Oliver's bed, dragging the folds of her dressing gown over her nakedness, behaving like the frightened mouse she must have appeared, Stella had had an easy target. It wasn't until later that she'd discovered that her stepmother's reasons for not betraying her to her father had had less to do with saving her from certain punishment than with stopping her son from making what she'd seen as the biggest mistake of his life.

God knew what she'd said to Oliver after Laura had left the room. Laura had thought she was making things easier by getting out of there. It was only afterwards that she'd realised that by giving in to Stella's demands then she had created a precedent that had never been reversed.

It had been comparatively easy for her stepmother to see that Laura had no further opportunity to be alone with Oliver before he left for Europe. As Laura hadn't even known he

was thinking of going, she'd been prepared to wait and bide
her time, sure that sooner or later Oliver himself would arrange for them to be together.

But it hadn't happened. She'd awakened one morning to
be told that Oliver had left for Dover the night before.
There'd been no farewell, not even a message to say how
sorry he was that things had turned out as they had, and
because her father had known nothing about what had happened there'd been no way she could share her feelings with
him.

Laura turned and punched her pillow now, wishing it was
Oliver's head. How could she have allowed him to kiss her
just a few days ago? she wondered painfully. How could she
have let him get close enough to her to even think that she'd
welcome his treacherous caress? He hadn't changed. He was
just as two-faced now as he'd been then, only now it was
some other girl who was being deceived.

Poor fool!

Laura sniffed and settled down again, but her mind
wouldn't let her rest. Not yet. Oliver's leaving for Europe
hadn't been the end of the story, as she knew only too well.
A few weeks later, when her period was late, she had had
another reason to regret her recklessness.

For over a month, she'd been in a state of panic, not knowing what to do, where to turn. The idea of confiding her secret
to a stranger didn't bear thinking about, and Dr Evans was
a friend of her father's. How could she tell him?

And then it was all over. One day, as she was cleaning
out her room, trying to imagine what she'd do if her father
disowned her, she'd felt a cramping pain in her stomach. It
had been worse than any of the monthly cramps she'd had
before, and she'd barely made it to the bathroom before she'd
felt a gushing wetness between her legs.

The ugliest part of it all was that Stella had found out about
that, too. Her stepmother had come looking for her and found
Laura trying to erase any trace of what had happened from

the bathroom floor. She'd been so pitiful, Laura remembered bitterly. She'd actually been crying over losing the baby, when what she should have been doing was jumping for joy.

But at least Stella's finding out had enabled her to handle the situation without involving Dr Evans. Her stepmother, now she came to think of it, had been amazingly knowledgeable about the miscarriage, reassuring her she had nothing to worry about, helping her to cope with her loss. In fact, Laura belatedly wondered whether Stella herself hadn't lost a baby. It did seem unusual, that having had Oliver when she was just a teenager, she should have gone—what? Thirty years?—without getting pregnant again.

But Laura didn't want to think of the connotations of that suspicion. And at the time she'd been so eager to put it all behind her, she hadn't looked beyond her own mistake. Even Stella's warning that if she told anyone else about it she would tell her father had seemed justifiable recompense for her stepmother's silence. She hadn't thought that her father might have blamed someone else.

Of course, in the weeks that followed, she'd realised why Stella had been so helpful, why she'd been so willing to hush it up. She hadn't wanted her precious son to hear about it. As always, she'd been protecting Oliver, making sure he didn't get bogged down in unwanted guilt.

Unfortunately, it had always been there between her and her stepmother, and she supposed it always would. That was why their relationship had never changed. She knew her father had hoped that as she grew older they'd have more in common. But Laura had never been able to put the past behind her and Stella had never let her forget.

That was why she'd refused to come back to Penmadoc after her university days were over, why she'd jumped at the chance to marry Conor Neill, even though she'd known that she didn't love him as she should. She'd wanted to get away, as far away as possible, and with the width of the Atlantic between her and Oliver she had hoped to find a better life.

And she had, she assured herself fiercely. All right, her marriage hadn't worked out, but that had been as much Conor's fault as hers. They'd wanted different things from the relationship, and she'd been unable to give him the understanding he deserved.

All the same, seeing Oliver again had been a daunting experience. She had thought she would be able to handle it better than she had. She hated the thought that he might think he'd got to her—even if he had...

CHAPTER ELEVEN

'ARE you all right, Mr Oliver?'

Thomas Grayson paused in the action of removing Oliver's plate, looking down at the half-eaten pasta with some concern. Since his employer had returned from Wales two days ago, he'd barely touched his food and the old man was getting worried abut him.

'Yeah, I'm fine.' Oliver lay back in his chair and looked up at Thomas with resigned complacence. 'I guess I'm still adjusting to the change of circumstances. I'm not used to sitting around all day, doing nothing. Going down into that ravine was pretty exhausting, I can tell you. Nothing like working in a comfortable studio, with every technological advantage at your fingertips.'

Thomas settled the plates on his arm and then pulled a wry face. 'It's been almost three weeks since you got back from Malaysia, Mr Oliver. You can't still be suffering from jet lag. I don't buy that.'

'Buy?' Oliver arched his dark brows humorously. 'Since when have you been using language like that?'

'Don't try to dodge the issue, Mr Oliver.' Thomas pressed his thin lips together. 'There is something wrong, isn't there?' He took a breath. 'Should I know about it?'

'If you mean, am I suffering from some fatal disease that I'm not telling you about, then forget it. I'm as fit as a flea, as far as I know.'

'Then why—'

'I'm not hungry, right?' Oliver was getting impatient now. 'I—had a burger at lunchtime. End of story.'

'That was at least six hours ago—'

'Thomas, enough. I know you mean well, but I do know when I'm hungry and when I'm not. And right now I'm not.'

'Very well.'

Barely concealing his disapproval, Thomas left the room and, stifling an oath, Oliver got to his feet and followed him. Entering his study, he went straight to the wet bar and poured himself a generous measure of Scotch, not feeling any release of tension until the single malt had invaded his bloodstream. Then, as its heat eased the grinding stiffness in his bones, he breathed a weary sigh.

But, dammit, it was a bad job if he was admitting that he needed alcohol just to function normally. What the hell was the matter with him? Thomas was right. He was different. But how different he had yet to find out.

Thomas appeared in the doorway as he was finishing the Scotch. 'Will you be wanting pudding, Mr Oliver?' he asked stiffly, his tone still showing his disapproval, and Oliver set down his empty glass and shook his head.

'Not right now,' he said, injecting a note of apology into his voice. 'I—I think I'll go out. I promised Guy McKenna I'd show him the rough proofs as soon as they were available. And a lot of them are done.'

But that was another source of frustration to him. Although he'd been back from Wales for over two days, he'd done very little work. Most of the film he'd shot in the Kasong Gorge hadn't even been processed, and if he did intend to see Guy McKenna it would be to apologise for the delay.

Of course, he knew McKenna would understand. It wasn't every day that there was a death in the family. And if his restlessness owed less to the actual bereavement and more to the knowledge of the will his mother had taken from Griff's safe, McKenna wasn't to know about it.

But he had yet to decide what he was going to do about it. He didn't even know if the will was legal, though it had been signed and witnessed by two people who, even though their names were unfamiliar to him, were obviously people Griff had trusted.

His mother had demanded he destroy it. And it would be a simple matter to do so. No one appeared to know about the second will; certainly not Laura, who had left Penmadoc the same afternoon the will was read without even saying goodbye. She clearly didn't want to live at Penmadoc, not immediately, at least, and it would come to her automatically if his mother married again.

Or died, he added, with rather less indifference. The idea of Stella shuffling off this mortal coil was not quite so easy to face. She was his mother, dammit. Whatever she'd done, whatever secrets she'd kept from him, she had been Griff's wife. Didn't he owe it to her to let her live in the home they'd shared for the past twenty years?

But for some reason Griff had changed his will, and Oliver could only wonder at the feelings that had caused such a change of heart. What had Stella done? What lie had Griff caught her out in? What betrayal had been so bad that the old man had decided she didn't deserve to stay at Penmadoc?

In the days following Laura's departure, he'd found no answers. His mother had said and done nothing to arouse his suspicions, and Aunt Nell had been as predictably reticent about her feelings as she was about Laura's whereabouts. If she knew where her niece was, she wasn't saying, and Oliver had wondered if the kindest thing of all wouldn't be to leave the situation as it was. Goodness knew, he didn't want to be the one to drive his mother out of Penmadoc. But he also knew he'd be betraying everything he'd ever believed in if he allowed her to have her way, and until the situation was resolved he supposed he'd go on having sleepless nights.

That was why he'd brought the will back to London with him, along with the key to the safe. Although his mother had assured him that she wouldn't attempt to tamper with her husband's papers again, Oliver was of the opinion that it was wise not to put temptation in her way.

Which was much the same thing as not trusting her, he
acknowledged drily, thinking of the will locked securely in
the drawer of his desk. But one way or another it was down
to him, and until he'd had a chance to tell Laura he was
making no promises he couldn't keep.

'If you say so, Mr Oliver.'

Thomas's disapproving response brought him to an abrupt
awareness of where he was. Clearly, the man was not in the
mood to be placated by a few words and Oliver wondered
when he'd started down this track. When Griff died, he reminded himself grimly, refusing to admit that meeting Laura
again had done more to upset the comfortable little niche
he'd made for himself than anyone—or anything—else.

However, before either of them could say anything more,
the phone rang. Thomas arched a brow, a silent enquiry as
to whether he should answer it, but on the off chance that it
could be important Oliver crossed to the desk and picked up
the receiver himself. He needed the diversion, he thought.
There wasn't a cat in hell's chance that it might be Laura.

'Oliver!' Natalie's voice sounded shrill and unfamiliar.
'Oliver, it's me! Guess where I am?' Then, without waiting
for an answer, she pressed on. 'I'm here, at Heathrow. The
shoot's been cut short because two of the girls were taken ill
so I'm back earlier than I expected. Isn't that great? Have
you missed me?'

'I— Sure.' Oliver raised his eyes to Thomas's and gave
an imperceptible shrug of his shoulders. 'That's—wonderful,
Natalie.' He struggled to inject a more positive note into his
voice, which was difficult when he'd barely thought of his
girlfriend for the past three weeks. 'You—just caught me,
actually. I was on my way out when you rang.'

'Out?' Natalie sounded less than cordial now. 'I tell you
I've just flown more than four thousand miles to be with you
and all you can say is that you're on your way out. Come
on, Oliver. You can't be serious.'

'I'm afraid I am.' Oliver stifled a sigh, reflecting with some irony that he was in danger of alienating all the people he cared about in his life. He'd already had a blazing row with his mother when she'd discovered he'd taken the safe key with him. Did he really need any more aggravation? He strove for an upbeat response. 'It's good to hear your voice again, Nat. Did you have a good trip?'

'Do you care?' Natalie didn't attempt to hide her irritation. 'I was going to suggest you might like to come out to the airport to pick me up, but I suppose you're too busy. I'll have you know we left the island at dawn just so we could connect with this morning's Concorde from New York. I'm cold and I'm tired. I just want to go home and have a shower. I had thought I might have it with you.'

Oliver groaned. 'Look, Nat—'

'Don't try to humour me, Oliver. Not when you can't even put off whatever it is you were going to do to see the woman you're supposed to love. Do you realise it's been almost a month since we were together?'

Well, near enough, thought Oliver, knowing better than to show surprise. 'Yeah, I know, but—'

'But you're not going to change your mind, are you? I sometimes wonder if you care about me at all.'

Oliver had been wondering that, too, and it didn't help when Thomas, who had been pottering about the room as he spoke, turned to give him an enquiring look. 'Okay,' he said heavily, grimacing at Thomas's expression, 'forget what I said, right? I'll come. Yeah, yeah, right away. Tell me where you are.'

'Another change of plan?' asked Thomas primly as his employer put down the phone, and Oliver blew out a weary breath.

'You might say that.'

'Would you like some coffee before you leave?'

'No.' Oliver scowled. 'I'll get something at the airport.'

'The airport?' Thomas pretended not to understand.

'Yeah, the airport,' agreed Oliver, refusing to be provoked. 'Natalie's back. I'm going to pick her up.'

It was after midnight by the time Oliver left Natalie's apartment. The formalities at the airport had taken longer than he'd expected and then Oliver had had to pay a fine to rescue his Mercedes from the compound where it had been sequestered for being parked illegally. He knew he hadn't been in the best of moods as he'd driven back to town and his irritation had only been aggravated when they'd arrived at Natalie's apartment and she couldn't find her key. She'd eventually found it at the bottom of the vanity case she'd carried on to the plane, but not before Oliver had searched the car from end to end because Natalie had been convinced it had been in her handbag when she left the airport.

His refusal to accept her invitation to come in had provoked another argument but by then Oliver had been too tired to humour her. He'd promised to ring the next morning instead, climbing back into the Mercedes with a definite—and disturbing—feeling of relief.

There was a message on the pad beside the phone when he got home. Half expecting it to be from Natalie, checking that he'd gone straight home, he gave it only a cursory glance. If Thomas answered the phone while he was out, he usually left a handwritten message for his employer to read and Oliver assumed it wasn't important.

But, as he was turning away, Eleanor Tenby's name jumped out at him. Thomas always printed names in block letters, and curiosity as to why Laura's aunt might be ringing him had him reaching for the pad.

Thomas's message was short and to the point. There'd apparently been a break-in at Penmadoc that evening while Miss Tenby and his mother had both been out. As she'd been sure Laura would be upset at the news, she wanted him to get in touch with her and tell her what had happened.

The address of Laura's hotel followed and Oliver thought how ironic it was that suddenly he was permitted information

that up to now had been denied him. He ought to ring her
back and tell the old woman to find someone else to be her
messenger boy, he thought grimly, but then the wider connotations of what had happened occurred to him and he
wished Thomas had thought to ask what, if anything, had
been stolen. He refused to acknowledge the treacherous suspicion that Stella might be involved.

He frowned, tearing the note off the pad and screwing it
up before dropping it into the waste basket. If only he hadn't
had to go out this evening, he might have been able to do
something about it tonight. He wondered what time the old
lady had rung. He might at least have been able to get in
touch with Laura and find out what—if anything—she intended to do now.

He glanced at his watch. Whatever he was going to do
would have to wait until morning. If he got to her hotel early
enough, he should be able to catch her before she went out—
if she was going out, that was. He had no idea how she was
filling her time or indeed why she'd felt the need to leave
Penmadoc as she had. He didn't flatter himself it was because
of anything he'd done, although his own guilt wouldn't go
away. She probably had friends in London, he assured himself firmly. Her publisher had an office here. She was probably catching up with her colleagues.

But what colleagues? he brooded, as he climbed the stairs
to his second-floor suite. Male or female? And what the hell
did it matter to him anyway?

Despite the assurances he'd made to himself that Laura
was unlikely to leave her hotel before nine o'clock, Oliver
was up and dressed by seven o'clock the next day. Surprising
Thomas browsing through the morning newspapers as he
sipped his first cup of tea of the day, Oliver took the opportunity to question him about the call he'd taken the night
before.

'What time did she ring?' he asked, refusing the man's
offer to make him coffee and pouring himself a cup of tea

instead. 'Did she say if the intruder had been caught? What
was taken? Your note didn't give any details.'

'Miss Tenby didn't give any details,' replied Thomas, folding the newspaper and putting it aside. 'I don't think she
wanted to talk to me. All she said was that there'd been a
break-in and would I ask you to deliver the news to Mrs
Neill. I suppose she thought you could always ring her back
if you wanted to. But my impression was that she wanted to
keep the call as brief as possible.'

Oliver wondered why. Did his mother know she'd called?
And, if not, why not? Why hadn't his mother rung him herself? The temptation to call Stella and ask her what was going
on was appealing, but he squashed it. He preferred to see his
mother's face when he was talking to her, and if that was a
shameful admission—on his part—then so be it.

But that didn't stop him from ringing Laura's aunt, and,
going on the supposition that his mother was unlikely to be
up so early, he made the call while Thomas made him some
toast.

To his relief, Aunt Nell answered the phone herself and
she didn't seem surprised to learn that it was him. 'What's
all this about a break-in?' he asked, deciding that she would
prefer him to get straight to the point. 'What happened?'

'Have you seen Laura?' countered the old lady, not answering him, and Oliver breathed an exasperated sigh.

'Not yet,' he said flatly. 'I was hoping you might be able
to give me a few more details. What was stolen?'

Aunt Nell hesitated. 'I'd rather not discuss that over the
phone,' she said, after a few minutes. Then, because she
seemed to realise that something more was expected of her,
she added, 'I'm not sure what was taken. We—we're still
checking.'

Oliver suppressed his impatience. 'But it was a robbery?'
he persisted, and he heard her give a little tut of offended
dignity.

'I'd rather talk to Laura, if you don't mind,' she said, and

Oliver knew a moment's impulse to ask why the devil she hadn't phoned her, then. But he supposed he could understand the old lady's reticence to discuss anything with him. Whatever had happened, it was Laura who was really involved.

'Will you be going down to Wales again?' Thomas asked, as his employer spread butter and marmalade on a slice of toast and attempted to shovel it into his mouth. 'I assume you will be going to see Mrs Neill after breakfast.'

'Right now,' said Oliver, around a mouthful of the delicious concoction. He grimaced. 'Sorry.' He swallowed the dregs of his tea. 'That was great.'

'Don't you want any more?' Thomas was dismayed.

'I'll get something later,' Oliver promised. 'Oh, and if Miss Harlowe calls—'

'I'll tell her you've had a family emergency,' said Thomas drily, and Oliver gave him a grateful grin.

'I owe you one,' he said, heading down the hall. 'I'll let you know what's going on when I know myself.'

CHAPTER TWELVE

A UNIFORMED commissionaire eyed Oliver's arrival at the West End hotel with doubtful eyes. But he was evidently used to seeing all-night partygoers arriving back at breakfast time and Oliver, in his black turtleneck sweater, black jeans and black leather jerkin, looked the part. Particularly as he hadn't taken the time to shave and the dark stubble of his beard gave him a disreputable elegance.

He supposed he should have phoned before turning up out of the blue. Crossing the marble reception hall, he approached the desk with some misgivings, but he hadn't wanted to give her the chance to ring Penmadoc to find out if anything was wrong and for his mother to exaggerate the situation. Stella would have few qualms about upsetting Laura, and until he'd spoken to her and gauged her reaction to the news he preferred to keep the reason for his visit to himself.

The receptionist was very accommodating. It helped that she recognised him, and his assertion that he'd just got back from abroad and was hoping to give his stepsister a surprise elicited the number of Laura's room without too much effort. Oliver took the lift to the sixth floor, aware that his heart was beating much faster than it should, and when he knocked at Laura's door he felt the unpleasant dampness of his palms.

Dammit, what was happening to him? he wondered irritably. He wasn't a schoolboy any longer and he'd never felt like this when he was going to meet Natalie. When he was going to meet any woman, for that matter, he conceded grimly. And Laura wasn't just any woman, she was his stepsister.

There was no response to his first knock and, gritting his

teeth, he knocked again. There didn't even seem to be any movement beyond the heavy panels, and he wondered if she was still asleep. She could be. Unlike him, she didn't appear to have suffered any after-effects from their encounter at Penmadoc, and he was half inclined to go away again and tell Aunt Nell that he hadn't been able to reach her.

The security peephole in the middle of the door mocked him. What if he was mistaken? What if she was standing at the other side of the door right now, watching him? He scowled. He didn't like the idea that he was providing entertainment for anyone. Least of all her.

He was getting paranoid, he thought impatiently. And, as he was weighing his options, he realised he could hear something beyond the wooden door. It was the sound of water running, and he guessed Laura was taking a shower. That was why she hadn't answered his knock. She hadn't heard him.

But, as the sound of the water was abruptly cut off, another thought occurred to him. He was probably being monitored on one of the hotel's security cameras. The rest of the corridor was deserted and there was no doubt that his presence was suspicious.

He sighed. He'd give it one last try. If she didn't open the door this time, he was going to go downstairs and find a courtesy phone. The last thing he needed was to be arrested for loitering with possible intent.

He felt self-conscious as he knocked again. Being aware of the camera made everything that much harder and he breathed a sigh of relief when he heard movement in the room beyond. There was a nerveracking moment when he thought she'd looked through the peephole and decided not to let him in, but then the lock clicked and the door opened.

She didn't immediately say anything at all. She just stood there, wrapped in one of those chunky towelling bathrobes that hotels provided for their guests, a towel attempting to hold the red-gold tangle of her wet hair in check. It wasn't succeeding. Curling strands clung damply to her flushed cheeks and were a vivid contrast to the white collar of her robe.

'Hi,' he said, when she said nothing, still aware of those security cameras. 'May I come in?'

'Why?'

Wrong answer.

Oliver heaved a sigh and glanced up and down the corridor again. 'Because our conversation is being monitored,' he said evenly. 'I've been banging on this door for the past five minutes and the management is becoming suspicious.'

'I was in the—'

'Shower. Yeah. I can see that.' He couldn't prevent his eyes from seeking their own appraisal and his lips took on a sardonic slant. 'Well? Are you going to risk being responsible for one of your closest relatives getting arrested?'

Laura's lips had tightened at the searching penetration of his gaze but she didn't contradict his interpretation of their relationship. 'I suppose you'd better come in, then,' she said, stepping aside, and Oliver moved gratefully beyond anyone's analysis but hers.

Laura waited until his shoulder had taken the weight of the door and then scooted quickly back into the bathroom. By the time Oliver had closed the outer door, the bathroom door was closed, too, and he expelled an aggravated breath. What now?

'I want to talk to you, you know,' he said, putting his face close to the panels. 'You can't stay in there for ever.'

Silence greeted this announcement, and he was just about to demand that she stop behaving like an idiot and come out of there when the door opened and Laura's face appeared.

'What do you want to talk to me about?'

'Come out and I'll tell you,' said Oliver, annoyed to find that, far from being angry with her, he was fighting a totally different kind of emotion. He walked determinedly into the room beyond the dressing area and turned to face her. 'Have you heard from your aunt?'

For once, he must have said the right thing. Wrapping the folds of the bathrobe closer about her, Laura left the comparative safety of the bathroom and came further into the bedroom. She was barefoot, he noticed, and that didn't help his rampant libido. Nor did the fact that the curtains were still drawn against the dull twilight of early morning, and the only illumination came from the lamps beside the queen-size bed.

'Why would I have heard from Aunt Nell?' she asked, obviously still wary of him, and Oliver scowled.

'Well—she rang me last night.'

'You?' Evidently, that surprised her.

'Yes, me.' Oliver endeavoured not to feel affronted by her reaction. 'There are obviously times when I have my uses.'

Laura rolled her lips inward. 'Go on.'

'Well…' There was no easy way to say it. 'Penmadoc was broken into yesterday evening.'

'No!' Laura's face paled. 'Oh, God—what was taken?'

'I've no idea,' replied Oliver. 'The old lady didn't want to discuss it with me. She just wanted me to break the news to you. I suppose she thought you'd be upset.'

But had that been her only motivation? Oliver couldn't help thinking that Laura was not some frail blossom, after all. All right, she had just lost her father, but was that a good enough reason for Aunt Nell to involve him?

Laura shook her head. 'I can't believe it,' she said. 'Why would anyone want to break into Penmadoc?'

'Why does anyone want to break in anywhere?' asked Oliver a little drily. 'People die and unwittingly draw attention to themselves. Perhaps the thief, whoever he was, wanted to see what was on offer.'

But he didn't truly believe that. With its forbidding stone walls and long narrow windows, Penmadoc didn't invite intruders. On top of that, anyone watching the house would know that there was usually someone at home, and for the robbery—if it was a robbery—to take place on the very evening that both his mother and Eleanor Tenby were out was quite a coincidence.

'And Aunt Nell didn't tell you anything more than that?'

'No.' Oliver regarded her with rueful eyes. 'So…' He drew a breath. 'What are you going to do about it?'

'Well, I suppose I'd better give her a ring.'

Oliver frowned. 'Is that wise? I wouldn't have thought you'd want to discuss anything with my mother.'

'Your mother?' Laura looked confused. 'I thought you said Aunt Nell rang you.'

'She did.' Oliver sighed. 'But if you ring the house, can you be sure Aunt Nell will answer?'

Of course she couldn't, and Laura made a *moue* with her lips. 'So what do you think I should do?' she asked, with some reluctance.

'Well, I think the old lady expects you to go down there,' Oliver declared evenly.

'Do you think so?'

Laura looked thoughtful, holding the lapels of her robe together with a nervous hand. The action forcibly reminded Oliver that she was probably naked underneath, her skin as flushed and creamy as the delicate flesh of her throat.

'I think so,' he muttered now, feigning interest in the toes of his boots. He rocked back on his heels and then forward again. 'Well—if you want a lift, let me know.'

'A lift?'

She looked doubtful and he cursed himself for getting involved again. 'Yeah,' he said flatly. 'I guess I ought to go and see how Ma's taking it.' Among other things.

'Oh, I see.' She took an involuntary backward step as if he'd actually invaded her space. 'You're going, too.' She swallowed. 'Well, I'll probably be leaving after you.'

'Will you?' Oliver allowed himself to look at her now, stoking the anger he felt at the casual way she'd dismissed his offer in an effort to stem the flare of desire her slender frame evoked. 'How do you know when I'll be leaving? Did I say?'

'No.' The colour in her cheeks deepened a little. 'But— well, I'm sure you have better things to do than wait for me.'

'What you mean is, you'd rather not come with me,' retorted Oliver tersely, not knowing why he was making such a thing of it. 'Why don't you come right out and say it? What's the matter, Laura? Are you scared of being alone with me? Are you afraid you won't be able to trust yourself?'

Laura's jaw dropped. 'In your dreams,' she muttered in a muffled voice, turning away, and although he knew he was being all kinds of a fool for prolonging this Oliver reached out and grasped her shoulder.

'I used to be,' he reminded her, swinging her round to face him, and although he felt a pang of self-reproach when she flinched he didn't let her go.

'In my nightmares, maybe,' said Laura harshly, and he gazed at her disbelievingly as his reckless action caused the towel to tumble from her hair.

The vivid tangle of red-gold curls fell about her shoulders, and his throat constricted at the sight. She looked so young, so vulnerable, so much like the girl who'd come to his bedroom all those years ago, that he felt a familiar tightening in his groin. He'd wanted her then, and he wanted her now, no matter how stupid that might be. He wanted to take her in his arms and make love to her. Not as he'd done then, but now with all the skill and experience he'd learned over years of searching for something that he was now afraid he might have had—and lost. Only he had been too young—too arrogant—to realise it.

'Laura.' He said her name hoarsely, and, as if realising the whole tenor of the conversation had changed, she moved her head slowly from side to side.

'No,' she said, and he could hear the quiver in her voice.

'Don't say anything else. I don't want to hear it. Do you hear? I don't want to hear it.'

'Why not?' It was crazy but he couldn't stop himself. Moving closer, he let his hand slide to the back of her neck, under the warm folds of her robe. Her hair clung damply to his wrist, but he scarcely noticed. He was too intent on watching her, on watching the way her eyes widened and darkened until they looked more black than grey. 'You are afraid of me.' His thumb massaged the skin below her ear. 'You have no reason to be.'

'Don't I?'

There was a curious note in her voice but he refused to acknowledge it. 'No,' he said huskily, bending to bestow a warm kiss on the curve of her jaw. 'I only want us to be— to be—'

'Friends?' she demanded breathily, and he decided he liked the heat of her breath moistening his cheek.

'Lovers, maybe?' he offered unsteadily, hardly aware of what he was saying with the knowledge of her robe brushing the sensitive swelling between his legs. God, he was hard, he realised; hard, and aching with a need he'd never experienced before. His free hand moved to loosen the cord that held her robe in place, and when the two sides parted he caught his breath at the naked beauty he'd exposed. 'Oh, baby, you're beautiful!'

Her breasts were fuller than he remembered, two rounded globes that begged for him to weigh them in his hands. Pointed nipples drew his attention to their rose-coloured areolas, the skin fine and smooth, and as soft as silk. A narrow waist, deliciously curving hips, long, long legs that were crowned with a triangle of curls as vivid as her hair. She was perfect, he thought incredulously. How could he ever have thought otherwise?

'Satisfied now?'

The words were bitter, but they were tempered by the quaver in her voice and Oliver was not deceived. Sliding his hands beneath her robe, he slipped it off her shoulders. It pooled about their feet as he drew her towards him and he felt an exultant satisfaction as her closeness went some way to easing his aching need. 'Not nearly,' he said, rubbing his hips against her, and was gratified when her mouth parted to admit his searching tongue. 'Not nearly,' he said again against her lips. 'God, Laura, we can't let this get away from us again.'

He kissed her once more, then trailed his tongue along her jawline before dipping to press hot wet kisses on the creamy slope of her breast. He licked one swollen nipple before taking it into his mouth and sucking strongly on the tip. She jerked when he bit her and he knew she was as sensitive to his touch as he was to hers.

His hands brushed the undersides of her breasts before curving over her hips to find the provocative swell of her bottom. She couldn't prevent herself from arching towards him when his thumbs skimmed the responsive cleft that marked the nub of her spine, and he heard her catch her breath when he parted her legs and found the pulsing petals between.

'You're wet,' he said, his voice thick and triumphant, and, picking her up, he carried her to the bed.

He knew a momentary uncertainty when he saw that her eyes were open and watching him with an odd expression in their depths as he attempted to kick off his boots and un-buckle his belt all at the same time. There was a disturbing lack of emotion in her gaze, but he convinced himself that he was imagining it. She was just as aroused as he was. He'd proved that for himself.

Achieving his objective, he flung himself beside her, but as he was reaching for her she spoke. 'Are we going to have sex now?' she asked in a low voice, and his breath gushed out of his lungs in a crippling rush.

'No,' he said, when he was able to speak again. 'We're going to make love.'

'Love?' Her voice broke as she echoed his reply. 'You don't know the meaning of the word.'

Oliver's arousal subsided as quickly as it had stiffened earlier. 'What the hell—?'

'Is that why you came?' she asked, propping herself up on her elbows, seemingly indifferent to the fact that she was naked as the day she was born. 'Has there really been a break-in at Penmadoc, or was that just a way of getting in here?'

Oliver swallowed, feeling sick to his stomach. She didn't even sound like the Laura he knew any more, and he stared at her as if he couldn't believe his eyes. 'Don't be so ridiculous,' he muttered, rolling away from her so she couldn't see his flaccid sex. 'Of course there's been a break-in. Would I lie to you about something like that?'

'I don't know.' She paused. 'Would you?'

'No, I wouldn't,' he snapped, getting off the bed and keeping his back to her as he hauled on his trousers. 'Don't be stupid.'

'But is it stupid?' She spoke consideringly and he hated the way she was weighing his words before she answered. 'I suppose it begs the question of what you would lie to me about, doesn't it?' She took a breath. 'Have you lied to me, Oliver? Since I got back, I mean? I'd like to know.'

'I don't want to have this conversation,' he said heavily, wondering if he had ever felt this bad before. He didn't think so. He zipped up his trousers and fastened his belt. Then, forcing himself to turn back to her, he added, 'I've given you the message. What you choose to do about it is your decision, not mine.' He picked up his jerkin off the floor where he'd dropped it, deliberately keeping his eyes away from her still too delectable body, and started towards the door. 'I'm out of here.'

'Wait!'

Her cry arrested him, and although he desperately needed to put some space between himself and the pathetic mistake he'd just made he halted. But he didn't look back; didn't do anything except wait for her to tell him what she wanted, and he heard her scramble off the bed and the frantic tussle she had to put her bathrobe back on.

'What time are you leaving?' she asked, and now he did cast a disbelieving glance over his shoulder.

'What's it to you?'

Laura shrugged, but the deepening of colour in her cheeks showed that she was no longer as immune to any emotion as she'd appeared. 'Because—because I'd like to accept your offer of a lift, if it's still available,' she said awkwardly. 'If—if you don't want to take me, I'll understand.'

Oliver's fists clenched now. 'Oh, will you?' he said, angry that she could still stir his emotions without any apparent effort on her part. But he had to get a hold of himself, he thought. He couldn't let her see how badly he'd been affected. 'Shall we say a little over an hour?' he asked, playing her at her own game. 'I'll pick you up outside the hotel at nine o'clock.'

'All right.' Laura's tongue appeared to moisten her lips and he had to drag his gaze away from its provocative assault on his senses. She paused, and then, as he completed his journey to the door, she added, 'I'm sorry if you think I've treated you badly. I—just don't like being mauled, you see.'

CHAPTER THIRTEEN

OH, GOD, why had she said that?

As she phoned Room Service for fresh orange juice and coffee, she groaned aloud at her own stupidity. Why had she attempted to make any kind of an apology to him? He certainly didn't deserve it. Aunt Nell might have asked him to tell her what had happened—she had to accept that—but she knew her aunt wouldn't expect him to turn up at her hotel at half-past seven in the morning. He'd probably anticipated that she'd still be in bed. Had he come here with the express intention of joining her?

She paced restlessly about the room. The nerve of the man! And then to aggravate the offence by pretending he wanted to 'make love' with her. Did he think she was a total fool? Well, yes, of course he must. Why else would he have suggested such a thing? He didn't care about her; he didn't even care about his girlfriend. No, the only person he cared about was himself.

So why had she taken him up on his offer of a lift? The train timetable was lying in the drawer of the bureau so she didn't even have the excuse of not knowing what time the trains to Swansea ran. She should have let him go. Proved to him, once and for all, that she didn't need anything from him. So why hadn't she?

She sighed. The truth was, she didn't know why she had asked him to take her to Penmadoc. Unless, contrary to her vain posturings, she did still care about him. It was crazy, particularly after the way he'd treated her, but no matter what she said, what she did, she had never found the happiness with any man that she'd once known with Oliver.

Not that she intended to tell him that, she thought bitterly

145

as she hurriedly doffed the bathrobe and rummaged in the drawer for her underwear. She didn't spend a lot of time on her hair. It was still damp when she twisted it into a French braid, tendrils falling in bright curls against her pale cheeks. She wore the trouser suit she'd worn to her father's funeral, a dark blue woollen velour, teamed with a cream silk shell to highlight the neckline.

She was fastening thick-soled boots when her breakfast arrived, and she drank the orange juice and two cups of coffee while she packed a few personal items into her backpack. She only intended to take sufficient clothes to last a couple of days. The time Matthew Neill had given her was running out and unless she intended to run the risk of losing her job she had to leave for New York before the end of the week. It was not a prospect she faced with any degree of enthusiasm at the moment, but she was not naïve enough to think that she really had any alternative.

She was downstairs, informing the receptionist that she was going away for a couple of days but that she was leaving most of her belongings in her room, when Oliver came through the lobby doors. He was now wearing a black parka in place of the leather jacket and she couldn't help the unwilling thought that dark colours always drew attention to the vivid green of his eyes. He still hadn't shaved, she noticed grudgingly. But then, why should he? He didn't care what she thought of him.

'Are you ready?' he asked, crossing the floor in lithe, easy strides, and against her will Laura felt her stomach tighten in unwelcome anticipation of the journey ahead of them.

'Almost,' she said, turning back to the receptionist, but now the girl was looking at Oliver with warm, approving eyes.

'Hello again,' she said. 'Did you surprise her?' Then, glancing awkwardly at Laura, she said, 'Oh, of course, you must have. That's why Mrs Neill is checking out, I suppose.'

'I'm not checking out—'

'No, well—'

'Bethany—' Oliver had scanned the name-tag pinned to the receptionist's jacket and used the girl's name with a confidence Laura could only envy. 'Bethany very kindly gave me your room number,' he said, his eyes warning Laura not to make an argument of it. 'I told her I wanted to surprise you.' His eyes darkened. 'I guess I did.'

Her lips thinned, but she didn't contradict him. There wasn't much point, and at least it explained how he'd known where to find her. She didn't remember giving Aunt Nell the number of her room and she had wondered how he'd found out. But it had been a fleeting thing, and she'd had so much else on her mind at the time that it hadn't lingered.

'Going somewhere nice?' asked Bethany conversationally, but Laura discovered there was a limit to how much she could take.

'No,' she said abruptly, and, collecting her handbag from the desk and the backpack off the floor, she turned away.

Oliver's Jeep was parked outside. She could see it through the swing glass doors, and as she walked towards them she heard him thanking the girl for her help. She ground her teeth together in frustration, but there was nothing she could do about it. However, when he came after her and attempted to take the canvas bag from her, she held on.

'I can manage,' she said coldly, and his lips twisted in weary resignation.

'Of course you can,' he said, holding the door open for her. 'You've made that perfectly clear.'

'Well, what did you expect?' she snapped, incapable of remaining silent now that they were outside. 'I suppose you'd prefer it if I was as easy to charm as—as Bethany!'

Oliver grimaced. 'Well, now you come to mention it—'

'You—beast!'

'Hey…' He opened the passenger door for her to get into the vehicle. 'Can I help it if you're jealous?'

'Jealous!' Laura's jaw dropped as he slammed the door

behind her. Then, after he'd circled the car and got in beside her, she exclaimed, 'I'm not jealous! I—I despise you.'

'Yeah, I know.' Oliver closed his own door and adjusted the rear-view mirror. 'I just wish I knew why.'

Laura turned to stare at him, but he wasn't looking at her. He was concentrating on pulling out into the stream of traffic that made Park Lane such a busy thoroughfare, and she eventually returned her attention to the tight ball she'd made of her hands in her lap.

In fact, they didn't talk again until they'd joined the M4 heading west. At this hour of the morning the roads around the capital were busy, but once they reached the motorway the pressure was eased and traffic moved quickly along the three-lane highway. A lot of the vehicles heading towards Wales and the west were of a commercial nature, and Oliver drove almost constantly in the overtaking lane.

'All right?' he said at last, when Laura was beginning to wonder if he intended to cover the whole distance without saying a word, and she pressed her lips together and shrugged.

'Why wouldn't I be?' she countered, and this time he turned to give her an impatient look.

'Why, indeed?' he agreed, turning back to the road. 'Tell me, do you get pleasure out of being unpleasant to people in general, or is it only me who brings out the worst in you?'

Laura caught her breath. 'What did you expect?' she demanded. 'You don't exactly treat me with respect.'

'No?'

'No.'

He frowned. 'So what are we talking about here? The mistake I made in thinking you wanted me to make love to you a couple of hours ago, or am I right in thinking you're still bearing a grudge because of what happened fifteen years ago?'

'Fourteen years ago,' Laura corrected him quickly, and

then wished she hadn't when his eyes darkened with sudden understanding.

'Damn, that is what this is all about!' he exclaimed incredulously. 'My God, you said you'd got over it. That you'd forgiven me. What the hell did I do to make you hate me so much?'

Laura turned her head towards the window. 'Nothing.'

'Don't give me that.' Oliver was getting angry now; she could sense it. 'Talk to me, dammit. We used to be able to tell each other anything.'

'When we were kids,' said Laura disparagingly. 'That was a long time ago, Oliver.'

'Don't I know it? Which only makes this conversation even more incredible. I've said I'm sorry, for God's sake. I am. If I'd known it was going to foul up our relationship—' He broke off, and then added flatly, 'Hell, Laura, if it hadn't been me, it would have been someone else.'

'Someone else?' She arched a haughty brow. 'Someone else, what?'

'Don't make me spell it out,' he said harshly. 'You know exactly what I mean. That summer—you were growing up, Laura. I wasn't the only guy who couldn't take his eyes off you. You were hot. A ripe, luscious peach just waiting to be picked.'

'You bastard!'

Laura's fist connected with his midriff with more force than she guessed he would have given her credit for. It knocked the wind out of him and for a few seconds the Jeep veered dangerously out of control. But somehow he managed to hang on to the wheel, and when he could get his breath he swore angrily.

'Crazy bitch,' he choked, using the car's indicators to signal that he was leaving the motorway at the next exit. Moving into the nearside lane, he swung up the ramp into a service area and, finding a parking space, he rammed on his brakes.

Laura was already feeling some remorse for attacking him

as she had, and she knew Oliver had every right to be angry when she'd recklessly endangered both their lives. But shame, and a certain stubbornness, kept her silent, and it was left to Oliver to turn in his seat and stare at her with grim, accusing eyes.

'What the hell was that for?' he demanded, rubbing his midriff with a defensive hand. 'Can't you have a conversation without resorting to violence?'

'Not with you, no.'

Oliver blew out a frustrated breath. 'Why not?'

'I don't want to talk about it.'

'Well, I do.' Oliver was not prepared to be conciliatory. 'You either tell me what this is all about now, or you can find your own way to Penmadoc.'

Laura's lips parted. 'You wouldn't!'

'Try me,' he said flatly. 'Go ahead. Push me far enough and you'll find out.'

Laura held up her head. 'You can't threaten me.'

'I'm not threatening you.' Oliver groaned. 'Well, I am, I suppose, but not in the way you mean. I want some answers, Laura, and you're going to give them to me.'

She stiffened. 'I don't know what you're talking about.'

'Yes, you do. I'm talking about you; me; us. I want to know what happened to turn us from—from friends into enemies.' He sighed. 'I'd hazard a guess that this has something to do with my mother. What the hell did she tell you to turn you against me? She swore you'd understood, that you were eager to put what had happened behind you, not just for your own sake but for your father's.'

Laura's lips twisted. 'How convenient for you.'

'What's that supposed to mean?' Oliver's fist clenched on the wheel. 'Wasn't it true? Are you saying you blamed me for what happened?'

Laura bent her head. 'Not exactly.' This was getting too deep and she didn't want to go on with it. At least he'd explained why he'd never attempted to get in touch with her.

Knowing Stella as she did, she was fairly sure that she'd have conveyed an entirely contrary message to her son. 'Look, let's just say your mother and I never did see—eye to eye.'

'So you did blame me?' Oliver shook his head. 'I wish you'd written and told me.'

'Told you what?'

'How you felt, of course. I may have been pretty arrogant in those days, but I would never have hurt your feelings. God, surely you know that?'

Laura's gaze flickered towards him and back again. 'And what would you have done?' She paused. 'Come home?'

'Maybe. If you'd wanted me to.'

'Oh, right.'

'It's true.' Oliver groaned. 'I guess I'd have done most anything for you at that time. That was half the trouble. I was crazy about you. You know that.'

'Do I?'

'You should.' Oliver scowled. 'But, dammit, Laura, I knew you were too young. When Ma suggested the kindest thing might be to give you some space to grow up a little, I—well, I believed her.'

Laura took a trembling breath. 'Am I supposed to believe this?'

Oliver balled his fist and hit the wheel impatiently. 'Okay,' he said. 'I guess I wanted to believe her. That's true, too. I knew we couldn't go on seeing one another without—well, being together, and we both know where that might have led.'

'Do we?'

'Stop pretending you don't know what I'm talking about.' He sighed. 'If you'd got pregnant and had to give up school— What? What?' He saw the disbelief in her eyes. 'It could have happened. Don't look at me like that, Laura. We were lucky we got away with it as we did. Just imagine how your father would have felt if he'd found out about us that way.'

Laura expelled an unsteady breath. 'Just imagine,' she said bitterly. 'We were lucky, weren't we?'

'That's what I'm saying,' went on Oliver eagerly. But although she said nothing to contradict him, he seemed to sense her withdrawal. 'Hey,' he protested. 'Hey, are you listening to me, Laura?'

'Of course.'

But Laura wouldn't look at him now and he was forced to go on. 'I guess this means you weren't as happy about me leaving as Ma said,' he muttered, revising his opinion. 'I suppose I knew that.'

'Did you? You hid it well.'

'Yeah, well—' He raked back his hair with an impatient hand. 'I guess I was hoping I was wrong.' He shook his head. 'But of course I wasn't. I mean, you practically ignored me when I came home, and then you went off to college and married that—jerk, Neill.' His jaw compressed. 'God, you have no idea how much I hated that supercilious bastard!'

Laura sniffed. 'Conor wasn't a supercilious bastard.'

'Wasn't he?' Oliver rubbed his chin against his fist. 'He seemed that way to me. But then, I was pretty peeved with you, too. You wouldn't even talk to me. I knew you were making a mistake marrying that—marrying him,' he amended harshly. 'I wanted to tell you, I wanted a chance to make amends for what I'd done, I guess. But you just cut me dead. I wasn't proud of myself, Laura. I'd have told you that, if you'd let me. When I lost you, I lost the most precious thing in my life.'

Laura turned burning eyes in his direction. 'Oh, please—'

'I mean it.' His mouth tightened. 'You know, sometimes I've wished that you had got pregnant, after all. Yeah—' this as she gave him an incredulous look '—crazy, eh? Selfish, too. But we'd have still been together. And I missed you so much.'

'Don't say that.' Her voice broke on the words, and, realising she couldn't take much more of this without breaking down completely, she turned her head away. 'I think we'd better go.'

'Not yet.' Oliver's knuckles brushed her cheek and she realised when he sucked in his breath that he had discovered the dampness she hadn't had time to scrub away. 'You're crying,' he said, his tone deepening with concern. 'Don't cry, sweetheart. That was then. This is now. Whatever happened in the past, we can start again.'

'Can we?' She sniffed again and pushed his hand away. 'I'm afraid I don't want to.'

'I don't think you believe that any more than I do,' Oliver told her huskily. 'If we were indifferent to one another, we wouldn't be having this conversation.' He caught her chin in his hand and turned her face to his. 'Tell me I'm wrong.'

'You're wrong,' she answered fiercely, twisting away from him. 'Aunt Nell told me your girlfriend is away on some kind of photographic shoot at the moment, so I suppose you're feeling horny. Well, tough. I won't let you use me as a substitute for her.'

Oliver stared at her. 'Is that what you think I'm doing? Do you honestly believe that this whole thing is just the ravings of a sick libido?' His lips twisted. 'God, you don't pull your punches, do you?'

Laura quivered. 'Do you deny it?'

'Yes, I deny it,' he snarled. 'Natalie's back, if you must know. I picked her up from the airport last night. And if I'd been as desperate as you say I've had—what?—more than twelve hours to get it on.'

Laura moistened her lips. 'If you say so.'

'I do say so,' he grated, turning back to the wheel. 'I don't know why I'm bothering to try and justify myself to you. You're never going to believe me. You never did.'

'That's not true.'

The words were torn from her, and his fingers stilled on the ignition key. 'Yeah, right.'

'I mean it.' Now she was aware of a reluctant need to justify herself. 'For—for years I believed everything you said.'

Oliver turned his head to look at her. 'So why don't you believe me now?'

Laura let out a breath. 'Because...'

'Because what? Because fourteen years ago I did something any normal red-blooded male would have done? I'm not a saint, Laura. I have all the usual flaws and deficiencies. And when something you want is—offered to you—you don't stop to think of the consequences.'

'I know that.'

'So?'

Laura bent her head. 'You don't understand.'

'No, I bloody don't,' he said savagely. 'So why don't you enlighten me?'

'I can't.'

'Why not?'

'I just can't, that's why.' She licked her lips. 'I'm sorry.'

'You're sorry?' His eyes were tormented, and before she could anticipate what he was going to do he turned and looped a hand behind her neck, bringing her towards him. 'I'd like to make you sorry,' he muttered, and then his mouth was on hers, and there was no time to govern her response.

She melted against him, her limbs softening into helpless pliancy as his tongue plundered her mouth. Fire, hot and purifying, spread from his lips to hers, and when his hand slipped beneath her jacket she couldn't prevent the instinctive need to arch her body against his. Her silk shell was easily freed from her waistband and when his thumb brushed the swollen tip of her nipple she felt a groan of pleasure rising in her throat.

Wherever he touched, her skin came alive, heating to a feverish pitch that no amount of reasoning could deny. What had begun as a punishment became a subtle assault on her senses and she was no more capable of stopping him now than she had been all those years ago.

She didn't try. Lifting her arms, she gripped his neck to hold him closer, sliding her hands into his hair, feeling its strength and virility curling about her fingers. The roughness of his jawline abraded her skin, but she didn't care. She was totally absorbed with what he was doing to her and even breathing had become of less importance than the need to sustain that hungry kiss. His warmth, his maleness, his distinctive scent were all she cared about, and the heat that had started when he touched her spiralled down into her thighs.

She briefly acknowledged the risks she'd taken that morning when he'd attempted to make love to her at the hotel. When she'd taunted him, she'd thought she'd been in control; but she'd been wrong. If he'd ignored what she'd said, if he'd pinned her to the bed with his hard, muscled body as he was pinning her to her seat now, it would have been a different story. She couldn't control herself now and they were on a public car park, in full view of anyone who chose to walk by.

But, ultimately, it wasn't the fear of discovery that brought that passionate embrace to an end. It was the gear console between them that prevented Oliver from lifting her into his lap. It was an unrelenting barrier, and he swore as he was forced to accept defeat. And, as the world swam back into focus, Laura realised that once again she had had a lucky escape.

'We'll continue this later,' Oliver said darkly, but Laura was already regretting her own impulsive nature.

'Continue what?' she countered a little breathlessly, and felt a measure of satisfaction when Oliver jarred the gear as he started the car.

'Don't,' he warned her sharply, and she told herself it was only apprehension that caused the unfamiliar frisson of excitement in her stomach.

CHAPTER FOURTEEN

OLIVER stopped at another service area at lunchtime. He made a half-hearted attempt to swallow a ham sandwich and a can of soda while Laura tackled a tuna salad, but his stomach refused to accept the food, and, pushing his plate aside, he went and got himself another cola. He drank it, staring broodingly out of the diner's window at the traffic passing by on the road beneath them. He'd promised himself he wouldn't reopen his argument with Laura until he could be sure they wouldn't be interrupted, and he confined himself to comments about the weather—which was worsening—and the merits or otherwise of motorway food.

Laura answered him in monosyllables, but at least she said something, which was some relief. He'd been half afraid she'd revert to her earlier mood of outright opposition and ignore him completely.

It was dark by the time they crossed the Severn Bridge. A dull day had given way to an even duller late afternoon, and the rain spattering the windscreen was gaining in strength. Fortunately, they'd made good time to Port Talbot. The traffic had been light, but when they turned on to the road to Rhosmawr they hit the evening's rush hour. In consequence, it was almost seven o'clock when they reached the village.

He was aware that Laura was tenser now than she'd been for most of the journey, and he guessed that, like him, she was apprehensive about what they were going to find. The possibility that the thief—thieves?—might have vandalised the place was not appealing, although Oliver was sure Aunt Nell would have warned him if that had been the case. Whatever, as on the occasion when Griff had died, they were

156

both returning here in less than happy circumstances and Oliver, for one, would be glad when he knew the worst.

There was a car blocking the lane that led to the house and Oliver was forced to park behind it. It wasn't familiar, but that meant little. He didn't spend enough time at Penmadoc to recognise anyone's vehicle, but he did wonder if his mother had had another of her breakdowns and the doctor had had to be called out.

But that was uncharitable, he decided, aware of the irony in the thought. Being robbed was an unpleasant business, and Stella was unlikely to react to it any differently than anyone else. Besides, despite the incident of the phone call—which had acquired rather different connotations in his mind in any case—he had no real reason for doubting Stella's sincerity. Despite everything, surely even she would fight shy of actually shunning her own husband's funeral?

Or not.

'Your mother has visitors.'

Oliver grimaced. It was typical that the first words Laura had volunteered without encouragement should concern her stepmother.

He shrugged. 'Or your aunt does,' he countered, and felt her eyes flicker briefly in his direction.

'Oh, right,' she said, preparing to get out of the Jeep. 'Aunt Nell is a regular party animal.'

'One car does not constitute a party,' retorted Oliver, getting annoyed in spite of himself. He didn't want any reinforcement of his own doubts and his jaw compressed. Then, taking possession of the backpack, which she had stowed behind her seat, he pushed open his door. 'Wait here. I'll get an umbrella from the house.'

'I'm not made of sugar,' replied Laura, surrendering the backpack to him with evident reluctance. 'I won't melt.'

'Ain't that the truth,' muttered Oliver drily, but although he spoke in a barely audible tone he could tell by the way she glared at him that she'd heard what he'd said.

It had obviously been raining for some time because the ground underfoot was soft and muddy. It was an effort to keep his balance, and he felt a small smile curve his lips when he felt Laura clutch his coat to save herself. But he didn't say anything, and nor did she.

They tramped round to the back to save treading mud all through the house, and this time the outer door was unlocked. They both paused in the passage to remove their boots. It was easier for Oliver. He kicked off his without much effort. But Laura had to sit down on one of the wooden benches to unfasten her laces.

'Let me,' he said resignedly, brushing her cold hands aside, and although she would have obviously preferred to do it herself she didn't argue.

Oliver had half expected Aunt Nell to be waiting for them. But when they entered the kitchen the room was empty. Even the fire in the grate was in danger of dying, and Oliver used the iron poker to riddle the ash before adding a couple of logs to its smouldering embers.

'It's not like Aunt Nell to forget about it,' murmured Laura, clearly of the same mind as himself, and he nodded.

'Perhaps she's not feeling well,' he offered. 'It's possible that the shock of the break-in could have upset her and she's gone to bed.'

'Leaving the back door unlocked?' Laura arched her brows disbelievingly. 'I don't think so.'

'Then what's your solution?'

She shook her head. 'I don't have one.'

'Good. Nor do I.' Oliver gestured towards the door into the hall. 'Let's find Ma.'

'If she's here,' said Laura tightly, and Oliver gave her a retiring look.

'She's here,' he said, and somehow he knew that she was. Though why he was so sure, he didn't care to think.

The hall, too, offered no answers as to the whereabouts of the occupants of the house, and Oliver disliked the decidedly ominous feeling he was getting. Where the hell were they? he wondered impatiently. And why the devil didn't he just call his mother's name and let her tell him where she was?

There was no one in the dining room, the drawing room, or the library, but there was a light on in the study, and Oliver approached it with a feeling of apprehension. So far he'd seen no evidence of the break-in and he had the uneasy feeling that he was about to find out why. Laura was behind him as he pushed open the door and he sensed she was apprehensive, too, but once again the room was empty.

The picture which covered the door of the safe was in place, and Oliver swore. 'Dammit!' he exclaimed, stepping back into the hall and looking up the stairs. 'Is everyone in bed?'

Laura's lips parted. 'Are you sure it was Aunt Nell who phoned you last night?' she asked in a doubtful voice. 'I can't see that anything has been—'

'Disturbed?' Oliver's lips twisted. 'Yeah, I know. But it was Nell. I spoke to her this morning and she confirmed it.'

'So…' Laura shrugged. 'What should we do?'

'Find Ma,' said Oliver flatly, and without any more hesitation he started up the stairs.

Laura followed him. Even without looking, he was aware of her presence behind him, and the urge to tell her to stay downstairs was almost overwhelming. He didn't know what he was going to find, but something told him it wasn't going to be good.

But before they could reach the top of the stairs they heard voices. A man's voice at first, and then a woman's. Stella's.

'I tell you I did hear something,' the man insisted, and Oliver came to an abrupt halt.

'You're imagining things, Jaz.'

Stella sounded drowsy, and Oliver's heart skipped a beat.

'I don't think so. I heard voices,' the man asserted, and the increasing volume of his voice indicated that he had come out of the room. 'After what happened with Griff, we don't want to risk getting caught again. God, Stell, it could be that old woman. Perhaps she's brought someone back with her.'

Oliver didn't look at Laura but he knew exactly how she must be feeling and he uttered an inward groan for the death of his own hopes and expectations. Despite what had happened on the way here, he knew she wasn't indifferent to him, but after this... He closed his eyes for a moment in utter despair. She was never going to listen to him now.

'Nell's in Cardiff, I tell you.'

Stella had evidently come to join the man and Oliver heard the sound of their footsteps approaching along the corridor that led from his mother's room. There was a moment when he considered going back down the stairs before they reached the landing and discovered him, but although he knew Laura wouldn't have stopped him he couldn't do it. He was fairly sure it was for this reason that Nell had brought them here, and while she couldn't have been sure that they'd come together she must have had a fairly good idea that they would.

'D'you want to leave this to me?' he asked in a low voice, but Laura was staring white-faced down into the hall and he wasn't sure that she'd even heard him. 'Laura,' he whispered, lifting a hand and touching her cheek, wondering if this would be the last time he'd ever lay a hand on her, and he felt the effort it took for her to turn her head and look at him.

'Daddy,' she breathed, through dry lips. A wavering finger pointed towards her father's study. 'I—I saw Daddy. He was there.' She swallowed. 'In the doorway. Do you think he turned on the light?'

The hairs rose on the back of Oliver's neck, and although his common sense was telling him that she couldn't possibly have seen her father something had evidently drained every scrap of colour from her face.

'I—Laura—' he began helplessly, and then his mother started to scream. The shrill sound was enough to banish any intruder, ghostly or otherwise, and he saw, with some relief, that Laura, too, was distracted by the sound.

'God!' It was the man, Jaz, who spoke first, and Oliver could even find it in his heart to feel sorry for him. Confronting his—what? Lover's?—son in only a pair of cotton boxers, while she shrieked like a banshee beside him, must be humiliating to say the least. 'I knew I'd heard something. Oh, hell—Stell, stop that horrible caterwauling, for God's sake.'

'Laura—Laura said she saw Griff,' she stammered, gathering a satin wrap around her, trying to get a hold on herself. 'In—in the doorway of the study. Oh, God, Jaz, do you think he was there?'

'Of course not.' Jaz gazed at her with impatient eyes. 'She's upset, that's all.' He grimaced. 'And who can blame her? I told you it was too soon to—to—'

'To what?' broke in Oliver coldly. 'To continue with your affair? God, Ma, you disgust me! And to think I believed that you were sincere.'

Stella pouted. 'What are you two doing here anyway?' She came down the stairs towards them. 'Don't be angry, Oliver. I've always needed affection, you know that.'

'Affection?' Oliver scoffed. 'This isn't affection!'

'Oh, and you'd know, of course.' His mother soon recovered her self-possession. 'You're so pure and untainted by sexual lusts yourself.'

'I'm disgusted because you were obviously conducting this affair right under Griff's nose,' snarled Oliver. 'I heard what your boyfriend said just now. You were here the afternoon Griff came back from hunting. He must have found you together. Was that why he had his heart attack?'

'No! No!' Stella was horrified. 'It wasn't like that.'

'What was it like, then?' Laura intervened, and Stella blinked rapidly before focussing on the younger woman. 'You phoned—*him*—' she indicated the older man '—the same night after you'd sworn you weren't fit enough to attend Daddy's funeral.'

Stella was taken aback. 'How do you know that?'

'She was there,' said Oliver flatly. 'Go on. I'm waiting to hear what happened the afternoon Griff died.'

Stella shook her head, clearly puzzled as to how Laura could have heard her call, but her son's expression forced her to continue. 'I—' She looked at her companion. 'I'm not sure what happened.'

'Oh, come on.' Oliver could feel his control slipping. 'You're not going to pretend that Griff didn't see you?'

'I don't know what he saw,' muttered Stella, wrapping her arms around herself.

'But he must have seen you,' said Laura unsteadily, and Jaz seemed to take pity on her.

'I heard something,' he admitted reluctantly. 'I told Stell we should have checked it out, but she said I was only imagining it.' He shrugged. 'She was obviously wrong.'

'*We* were wrong,' put in Stella, evidently not prepared to shoulder all the blame. She turned to her son. 'I tried to tell you how it was before the funeral. I'm a passionate woman, Oliver. I need—love.'

'What you need is sex,' Laura said tremulously, before Oliver could respond. 'Don't pretend Daddy didn't love you. He did. I only wish he'd never set eyes on you.'

'That's enough!' Stella was furious now. 'Don't you dare to talk to me in that holier-than-thou tone, because it won't wash, young lady.' A trembling finger was pointed at Laura. 'I know too much about you. I always have. That was why you took every chance you could to tell tales about me to your father; why you poisoned Griff's mind against me—'

'That's not true!' Laura's voice was trembling, but Stella didn't seem to care.

'How do you think your precious father would have felt if he'd known what you were really like?' she demanded contemptuously. 'He thought you were such a good little girl. That butter wouldn't melt in your mouth.'

'For God's sake, Ma—'

'No, why shouldn't I defend myself?' Stella exclaimed,

shaking off her son's attempt to restrain her. 'She was eager
enough to tell me what she thought of me.'

'For pity's sake, Stella—'

Jaz appealed to her, but she ignored him. 'I've waited a
long time to say this, Oliver,' she declared. 'I won't let her
get away with it.'

'This isn't going to change anything, Ma—'

'Isn't it? Isn't it?' She held up her head. 'You don't know
the half of it. You don't know why she really came to your
room, what she'd planned—'

'Planned?' Oliver was frankly scathing. 'For God's sake,
Ma, stop while you've still got a shred of decency left.'

'You don't understand.' Swallowing convulsively, Stella
pressed a trembling hand to his chest. 'You think I'm just
making these things up to defend myself, but it's not true.
She wanted you, Oliver, and she was prepared to do anything
to get you.'

'No—'

Laura's cry almost went unnoticed, but Oliver had heard
it, and, putting his hands on his mother's shoulders, he said
flatly, 'Let's leave Laura out of this, shall we? I know you've
never liked her. You've made that plain enough, God knows.'
He glanced at Laura's white face. 'But it's been fourteen
years since that night. We've got over it. We've moved on—'

'She hasn't.' Stella turned to point at her stepdaughter once
again. 'She still hates me. She always has.'

Oliver groaned. 'You're not going to get away with this,
Ma.' He took a deep breath. 'Now, I think we've established
that Griff saw or heard—something when he got back that
afternoon. I assume that accounts for the fact that it was two
hours before you found—found him?'

'That's right.' Jaz nodded. 'Stell was nearly frantic when
she found the body. But it was too late. There was nothing
we could do.'

'Except hide what had really happened,' said Oliver bitterly. 'My God, Ma, how could you live with yourself?'

'Don't preach to me about living with myself,' retorted his mother savagely. 'At least I've never had to get myself pregnant to try and hold on to a man.'

There was absolute silence after this revelation. Even the house was still, as if even inanimate objects sensed that any sound would be a desecration. Oliver didn't move. He couldn't. For a few moments the actual portent of his mother's words had him stunned and frozen to the spot.

Then, with an anguished sound, Laura broke the death-like stillness. Whirling, she turned and ran back down the stairs, and as Oliver watched her go so many things suddenly made sense to him. God, he thought, his brain stumbling slowly back into gear. She had been pregnant when he went away. She had been expecting his baby, and he'd known nothing about it.

But before he could go after her Stella seemed to realise she'd made a fatal mistake. In her efforts to discredit Laura, she had inadvertently told her son something that it was not in her best interests to reveal.

'Oh, Oliver,' she said, reaching for his arm. 'I'm so sorry. You were never meant to hear about this. Especially not from me.'

Oliver shook her off, dragging his eyes away from the stairs down which Laura had just vanished with an effort. 'What?'

'The fact that she was pregnant,' Stella prompted him urgently. 'That's what she'd intended all along. Don't you see? It was her way of getting back at me—at both of us—for my marrying her father. Thank heavens nothing came of it. It would have ruined your life—all our lives.'

Oliver stared at her disbelievingly. 'You're crazy!' He blinked. 'And what did you mean? Nothing came of it?' His blood chilled. 'Did she have the child?'

'Of course not.' Stella was impatient.

'So she—what? Miscarried?' Right now, Oliver didn't know which was worse.

'Yes, she lost it,' said his mother irritably. 'Honestly, Oliver, I would have thought—'

'That's the trouble,' said Oliver heavily. 'You don't think. You never have.'

'The safe's been opened.'

Laura spoke from the foot of the stairs, successfully putting an end to their discussion, and Stella started to protest behind him.

'How does she know?' she cried, but Oliver wasn't listening to her.

'I'm coming,' he said instead, and hurried down the stairs to where Laura was waiting. 'Perhaps there has been a robbery, after all.'

'A robbery?'

His mother hurried after him, and he wondered if she was as much in the dark as he was himself. 'The break-in,' he said, as he reached Laura. 'Aunt Nell phoned me last night. She said someone had attempted to break in.'

Stella's eyes flashed. 'There was no break-in!' she exclaimed, but she was forced to follow her son and her stepdaughter across the hall and into the study, however unwilling she might have been. She stared mutinously at the open safe that Laura must have found when she'd removed the picture. 'If Nell told you there was a break-in, she was trying to cause trouble, by the sound of it.' She scowled. 'I opened the safe.'

'You opened it?' Oliver's lips tightened. 'How? You didn't have a key.'

Stella coloured. 'If you must know, I had a copy of the key made before Griff died. It's hardly Fort Knox. A child could have opened it.'

Oliver looked at Laura. She had no idea what he was thinking, and he knew the time had come when he had to climb down from the fence. 'So what did you find?' he asked, knowing full well his mother would know what he was saying. He crossed to the safe and removed the handful of papers and documents he found there. 'There's nothing much here. Just a few old bank statements—' He paused, and then drew an envelope from his pocket. 'I wonder—were you looking for this?'

It was the will and Stella's consternation was plain. 'I knew you had to have it with you when it wasn't there, but you can't—you can't—'

Stella was almost beside herself, but it was Laura who was looking puzzled now. 'A will?' she exclaimed blankly. 'Did Daddy keep a copy of his will in the safe?'

'Not this will,' Oliver told her heavily. 'This isn't the will he'd deposited with Marcus Venning, I'm afraid. This is his new will. It was made fairly recently. My mother found it before the funeral, you see.'

Laura blinked. 'Then why didn't she—?'

'She naturally assumed it was the same will that Marcus had witnessed. It wasn't until the will was read that she realised her mistake. And by then she didn't want to admit she'd found it, particularly as the old will was so much more favourable to her.'

Laura hesitated. 'The terms of the new will are different?' she asked faintly, and Oliver realised she still didn't understand what it might mean.

'They are,' he said gently. 'Penmadoc is left to you entirely. My mother—' He gave Stella a scathing glance. 'My mother is quite adequately taken care of, but your father obviously wanted you to have the house.'

'And you've had this will all along?'

Laura was evidently making sense of what he'd said, and Oliver felt his spirits sink to the floor. 'Since I went back to London, yes,' he said, ignoring Stella's scowling face. 'I took the safe key, too. I had no idea my mother had a copy.'

'You had no right to take the will,' began Stella angrily, but this time Jaz, who had halted in the doorway, chose to intervene.

'Leave it, Stell,' he said. 'Laura knows about it now, so

there's no good in labouring the point. I told you that Oliver would never stand for it, but you wouldn't listen to me.'

'Well, I'll never forgive him for this,' choked Stella tearfully, but Oliver sensed they were tears of anger, not of distress. He'd never forgive himself, but for an entirely different reason. In even listening to his mother, he had probably destroyed any chance of Laura's trusting in him again.

'I can't believe it.' Laura was shaking. 'So that's why Stella didn't want to attend Daddy's funeral. She was putting off the reading of the will—why? Because she thought I'd put her out of the house?'

'Yeah.' Oliver nodded. 'And I didn't say anything, even when Marcus read the old will,' he added, condemning himself completely. 'I wanted to talk to you first, but you disappeared before I got the chance. Then this morning—' But he didn't want to go into that, not in this company. 'She is my mother, for my sins. I guess I didn't want to be responsible for driving her out of her home.'

'I—I can understand that.' Laura was more charitable than he would have given her credit for. But Stella wanted nothing from her.

'Just listen to her,' she said. 'Miss Prim and Proper! You weren't so prim and proper when you were crawling into my son's bed!'

Laura blanched, and Oliver had heard enough. 'Shut it, Ma!' he exclaimed savagely. 'I still don't think you have any idea what you've done. Without you, Laura and I might still have been together. You ruined my life. You've ruined all our lives. I'll never forgive you for that.'

CHAPTER FIFTEEN

LAURA sat at the window of her apartment in Greenwich Village, gazing out at the plane trees in the park across the street. It was early evening and the park was practically deserted now, the children and their carers who had occupied the swings and fed the ducks on the ornamental pond were long gone, and twilight crept like a violet wraith across the grass.

Laura sipped at the cup of coffee in her hand. Despite its beauty, this was the time of day she liked least. Evening heralded the night and she was still sleeping badly. She often spent the early hours of the morning reading some would-be author's manuscript, and she'd threatened Matt that she was going to bill him for all those extra hours.

Of course, she wouldn't. Since her return from Wales almost four months ago, her employer had been particularly nice to her, and although she suspected it was because he didn't want to lose her it was good to feel needed.

By someone.

She took a deep breath and fought back the wave of anxiety that swept over her. She had nothing to be anxious about. Not really. It wasn't as if she hadn't been in this situation before, and she'd coped then. She could cope now. What had changed, after all? Nothing. And she'd been a fool to even imagine that it might.

All the same, the knowledge of the phone call she'd made three days ago weighed heavily on her conscience. She'd known at the time she was dialling Oliver's number that she was probably making another stupid mistake, but that hadn't stopped her from going through with it. She'd needed to speak to him; she'd needed closure, she'd told herself, if that

was what it achieved. She couldn't go on living in this vac-
uum of emotion, not knowing what, if anything, she might
have rescued from the wreck she'd made of her life.

Predictably, perhaps, Oliver hadn't been at home when
she'd rung. His man, Thomas, had explained that he was in
Spain taking pictures of bulls and bullrings for an exhibition
of Spanish culture that was to be shown in London later in
the year. When he'd asked her if she had any message she
would like him to pass along, she'd demurred. 'It wasn't
important,' she'd assured him firmly, and then burst into tears
as soon as she'd put down the phone.

Which seemed to prove that she hadn't got over Oliver,
after all. And that was the real reason she was feeling so
anxious now. How long was it going to take for her to start
feeling in control again? How long before she stopped scanning every newspaper, North American and English, for
some word of him? How long before her life resumed its
normal pattern and she could start feeling whole again?

For ever?

She expelled a rueful breath. Of course, if she hadn't been
scanning the papers so avidly, she might have missed the
article about Natalie, she consoled herself. At least now she
didn't have to picture him and the beautiful model together.
They had apparently split and Natalie was now engaged to
be married to a Greek shipping tycoon. It must have been a
whirlwind courtship, Laura reflected, unless Oliver and
Natalie had broken up as soon as she'd returned to the States.

It was possible, she supposed. After the things Oliver had
said, it would have been hypocritical of him to pretend that
he and Natalie had a future together. But then, he had said a
lot of things, most of which had gone over her head, and in
the aftermath of learning of Stella's betrayal Laura had found
it difficult to take anything in.

That night—the night the truth had come out—didn't seem
quite real now. Stella's affair with Dilys James's husband—
that was who she'd been phoning after the funeral, not

Dilys—her father's death; the duplicity over the second will; —it all seemed totally remote from her life here in New York. It was as if it had all happened to someone else and even now, four months on, she couldn't quite believe it.

Perhaps that was why she'd been so willing to take the easy way out and return to the United States. Life was so much less complicated here and certainly Matt had been glad to see her back. He wasn't interested in what her stepmother had done, or who owned Penmadoc. As far as he was concerned, she had a job to do, and if she didn't want to do it he'd find someone who would.

Not that anyone else had attempted to change her mind. Apart from informing Marcus Venning that a new will had been found—and Oliver had done that—her contribution to events had been minimal. Despite his offer to take responsibility for what had happened, Laura had had no desire to take legal proceedings against either Oliver or his mother, and a story had been concocted as to why the will hadn't been discovered before now. The fact that it had involved a missing key was something of an irony; but Marcus Venning was more concerned that her father should have felt the need to approach some obscure firm of solicitors in London, rather than admitting his personal grief to him, and hadn't probed too deeply into their explanation.

Stella had left Penmadoc the morning after the scene in the study. With Jaz James's help, she'd moved into a flat in Rhosmawr and, as far as Laura was aware, she was still there. Whether the affair would survive recent events was anyone's guess. Stella had expected to inherit Penmadoc and with the sale of the house behind her she would have been a very wealthy woman. As it was, she was just another widow, living on a pension, and if that pension was rather more generous than most it was still considerably less than Jaz must have anticipated.

Laura's lips flattened against her teeth. Her heart ached for what her father must have suffered in the months before he died. He'd obviously known Stella was being unfaithful to him, ergo the new will, but finding her with another man in his own house must have been the last straw.

Of course, it was always possible that his heart attack would have happened anyway. In her more charitable moments, Laura hoped that this was so. It made it a little easier to try and forgive her stepmother—although she knew she would never forget.

As far as her own psychic experiences were concerned, she was rather less certain. Although she thought she knew what she'd seen, she had to accept that she'd been in a particularly receptive mood, and the mind could play tricks on the eye. Of course, if she'd still been alive, her grandmother would have believed her, but the old lady had always been looking for evidence of second sight in her offspring. Whatever, Laura was sure she hadn't imagined the change of atmosphere in the house after Stella had departed. Maybe there were such things as restless spirits, after all.

It had been agreed that Aunt Nell should continue to live at Penmadoc. Laura had given her aunt power of attorney to act in her absence, which meant the old lady wouldn't have to apply to her for funds for the day-to-day running of the house. It suited Laura that way. Much as she loved the place, it would be a long time before she'd be able to face the thought of living there again.

Oliver had left for London as soon as the formalities had been dealt with. To get back to Natalie, she'd assumed, though subsequent events had cast doubt on that supposition. Whatever, he hadn't seemed inclined to offer any explanation, and she'd left for New York without speaking to him privately again.

She had wondered if he might try to get in touch with her. Aunt Nell had her address and she'd left instructions that, should he ask for it, her aunt should feel free to pass it on. But she'd been back for almost four months now and it seemed that, as far as Oliver was concerned, she might as well have dropped off the roof of the world.

Then she'd read the article about Natalie.

At first, she'd decided it was nothing to do with her. As far as she knew, Oliver could be heartbroken over the severing of his relationship with the fashion model and any intervention on her part might be construed as interference. But then she'd started remembering the things he'd said to his mother that night in her father's study and her spirits had taken a distinctly upward turn.

After all, it was possible that Oliver thought she didn't want to talk to him. She'd given him very little encouragement to believe she'd be willing to listen to anything he had to say. After that scene in her hotel room and what had happened on the journey to Penmadoc, he must have felt he was fighting a losing battle with the past.

That was why she'd made that phone call. Straight away, so that she'd had no time to have second thoughts. But— Oliver hadn't been available. He'd been too busy getting on with his life, and if she had any sense she'd do the same.

A cab cruised along the street below her. It was moving slowly as if the driver—or his passenger—was scanning the numbers on the buildings, looking for a particular address. It slowed outside the warehouse, above which she had her loft apartment, and then moved on down the street. The momentary thrill she'd felt at the prospect of a visitor quickly dissipated. Who was likely to come and see her? She blew out a tired breath. She really would have to get herself a life.

The cab was coming back. Laura guessed the driver had unloaded his passenger and was hoping to pick up another fare to take back to Manhattan. But, to her astonishment, the cab stopped right outside her building and the rear door was thrust open to allow a man to get out.

Oliver!

Laura scrambled up from the banquette, almost spilling her coffee in her efforts to get away from the window. That was all she needed: for him to see her sitting there like some sad waif waiting for someone to notice her. She was supposed to be living the good life in New York. What was he going to think if he found her spending a lonely evening dwelling on the events of the past?

Did she care?

She inched back towards the window, using the silk drapes as a screen between her and what was going on outside. Oliver had evidently paid the driver because the cab was some distance away now, and she drew a sharp breath when she thought for a moment that Oliver had gone with him. But then he stepped back from under the overhang and looked up at her windows, and she realised he was probably trying to gauge if she was at home.

She could pretend to be out.

Drawing back, she gave the thought only a momentary consideration. What would be the point of that? she asked herself scornfully. Was her pride so great she was prepared to gamble on the chance of him coming back?

No!

As the doorbell rang, she was already hastening across the wide expanse of the living area, depositing her coffee cup on the breakfast bar, opening the door that led to the stairs. A steep flight led down to the outer door which, in common with most doors in New York, was fairly heavily secured.

For once, she didn't attempt to identify her caller before opening the door, and she took an involuntary gulp of air when she pulled it inwards and found Oliver waiting outside. He looked so beloved, so familiar. It took an actual effort to merely stand aside and invite him to come in.

'Hi,' he said, evidently feeling some greeting was necessary, and Laura managed a faint smile as she closed the door behind him.

'Hi,' she said a little huskily. 'Do you want to come up?'

Oliver took a deep breath. 'Why not?' he said, stepping back and indicating the stairs. 'After you.'

Laura would have preferred to follow him. In dark trousers and a matching V-necked sweater, he looked good from any angle, while she was acutely conscious of the definite drawbacks of short dungarees and bare feet.

But being bashful now wasn't going to get her anywhere, and, taking her courage in both hands, she hastened up the stairs in front of him.

He paused in the doorway to her apartment and looked around. The huge space had been divided into areas for living and cooking and sleeping, with the bathroom concealed behind opaque glass walls. Laura was quite proud of the way she'd furnished it, and the overall effect was one of lightness and comfort. Despite its size, underfloor heating could cope with the lowest temperatures, but this evening the windows were open and the breeze that rippled the rose-pink curtains brought the scent of the flowers that grew in the park across the way into the room.

Laura halted in the middle of the Chinese rug that defined the living area. Her knees felt decidedly shaky, and she would have liked nothing better than to curl up on the ivory velvet sofa, but until she knew why Oliver was here she knew she'd never be able to sit still.

'Impressive,' he said at last, coming into the apartment and closing the door. He glanced up at the wide skylight. 'This would be a great place to have a studio.'

'I suppose it would.' Laura wondered if he was as nervous as she was, and then decided he couldn't be. If he were, he wouldn't be wasting time talking about her apartment. Or would he? 'You'd know more about that than me.'

'Yeah.' Oliver's lips tightened for a moment. 'Yeah, I guess that's one thing I do know about.'

Laura forced a smile. 'You're too modest.'

'Am I?' He shrugged. 'I wouldn't put money on it.'

Laura asked, 'Can I—can I get you anything? Some coffee? A drink?'

'Do you have anything alcoholic?'

'I think so.' Moving round him, Laura hurried into the small kitchen and opened the fridge. 'Is a German beer okay?'

'Anything,' said Oliver, crossing the rug to the window. 'Nice view.'

'I like it.' Laura hesitated over whether to offer him a glass and then decided she was being too formal. She came out of the kitchen again and held out the bottle. 'There you go.'

'Thanks.'

He came away from the window to take the bottle from her and their fingers touched. Laura drew her hand away immediately but she couldn't stop her gaze from darting to his face. It was the first time she'd looked into his eyes since he'd come into the apartment and her breath caught at the instant awareness that leapt between them. It was as if something hot and heavy had entered the air and for a moment it was difficult to breathe.

'Why did you phone?'

He spoke roughly, as if the words had been dragged out of him, and Laura wished she'd thought to pick up her cup of coffee in passing, to give her hands something to do.

'Why—why did I phone?' she echoed, her fingers opening and closing below the denim hems of her dungarees. She turned the question back on him. 'Why—why do you think I phoned?'

'Oh, no.' Oliver swallowed a mouthful of his beer before regarding her impatiently. 'I asked first.' He took a deep breath. 'Is something wrong?'

Laura's jaw was in danger of dropping, but she managed to control it. 'What could be wrong?' she countered. 'Did—did Thomas tell you I'd said that something was wrong?'

Oliver closed his eyes for a moment and then opened them again to give her a weary look. 'Why are you doing this, Laura?' he asked. 'It's a simple question. I want to know why you rang. What's the matter? Do you wish you hadn't?'

'No!' She swallowed. 'No, of course not.'

'Then why did you ring?' he persisted. 'I—have to know. I *need* to know.' He heaved a sigh. 'Can't you tell me if I've made another stupid mistake by coming here?'

Laura's tongue circled her upper lip. 'You haven't,' she said swiftly. Then, before she could lose her nerve, she added, 'I—I'm glad you came.'

'Are you?'

He didn't sound as if he believed her and she hurried to reassure him. 'Yes. Yes, I am. I wanted to see you.' She paused, half afraid that she was presuming too much. 'I—I wanted to tell you how sorry I was when I read about—about you and Natalie.'

Incredulity entered his features now. 'Me and Natalie?' he echoed disbelievingly. 'You're not serious.'

'Why not?' Laura endeavoured to sound convincing. 'I read about her engagement to some Greek ship owner in the newspaper.' She lifted her shoulders. 'You split up.'

Oliver stared at her for a long moment and then raised the bottle to his lips again. She watched the strong muscles of his throat work as he drank the cold beer and then flinched when he lowered the bottle and turned a contemptuous gaze on her.

'You phoned to commiserate with me about Natalie?' he said harshly. 'Gee, thanks.'

Laura quivered. 'Don't speak to me like that. I didn't know how you'd feel about it.'

'Didn't you? Didn't you?' He almost sounded as if he blamed her for the break-up. 'Get real, Laura. You knew exactly how I'd feel about it.'

'But I don't.' The words were wrung from her, and she thrust her hands into the pockets of her dungarees to hide their agitation from him. 'I don't know anything.'

Oliver's mouth compressed and he turned, very slowly, and deposited the bottle on the window seat behind him. Then, turning back, he said flatly, 'I'm supposed to believe that?'

'Yes. Yes.'

'Well, what the hell do you think I'm doing here?' he demanded, and she realised that although she'd thought he looked much the same as usual there were distinct hollows beneath his eyes.

But she couldn't mention them, not when he was waiting for an answer, and, curling her fists into balls, she said, 'I don't know, do I? Maybe you've got an assignment in New York. Maybe you thought you'd just—look me up.'

'Oh, right.' Oliver shook his head. 'That would have been convenient, wouldn't it? An assignment in New York turning up just three days after your call?'

'It could have happened,' she protested, and he gave her a disparaging look.

'No, it couldn't,' he said harshly. 'I was in Seville—should still be in Seville, if everybody had their rights. But I'm not.'

Laura stared at him. 'You—you came back—for me?'

'Yes, I came back for you,' he said impatiently. 'For God's sake, Laura, I thought something must have happened—' He broke off wearily. 'I thought you needed me.'

'Oh, I do.'

Laura's cry was heartfelt, and Oliver gazed at her with tormented eyes. 'Do you mean that?' he asked hoarsely, and she knew she couldn't prevaricate any longer.

'Yes. Yes, I mean it,' she said huskily, reaching for him, and with a muffled oath Oliver captured her hands with his.

'God, Laura,' he said, taking her hands behind his back, bringing her close to his lean, muscled body. 'Do you like putting me through this kind of torture?' His mouth nuzzled her cheek. 'Don't you think I've suffered enough?'

Laura couldn't speak. For so long she'd accepted that anything there might have been between her and Oliver had been destroyed by his mother's treachery. Even knowing that he'd wanted to make love to her when they were in London hadn't been enough to breach all those years of pain and humiliation when she'd believed that the love they'd shared had meant as little to him as his mother had said. But, suddenly, anything was possible, and when his mouth first nudged and then took possession of hers she had no hesitation in arching against him and parting her lips for his kiss.

When his hands came to cradle her neck, hers slipped beneath his sweater, finding the warm curve of his spine. His skin, smooth and warm, seemed to welcome her caress, and the sound he made against her mouth convinced her that this time she was doing something right.

Meanwhile, his kiss was melting any remaining inhibitions. It hardly seemed possible that just a few minutes ago she had been despairing of the emptiness of her life. His tongue, his lips, the sensual pressure she could feel against her stomach were pouring heat and colour into her soul. She felt dazed; enchanted; blessed; granted the second chance she'd never dreamed might be hers.

'I was scared, you know,' he muttered, releasing her mouth to seek the scented hollow of her throat. 'All the way over on the plane, I kept telling myself I was taking one hell of a chance, that I had no real proof that you wanted to see me, that you might not simply have wanted to talk…'

'To talk?' Laura's voice was scratchy. 'What about?'

'You tell me.' Oliver's hands curved over her shoulders, sliding the straps of her dungarees aside. The cropped top she was wearing underneath exposed a satisfying width of her midriff, and she felt the loose denim sliding down her legs. 'How about Natalie?' he suggested, his breathing unmistakably quickening. 'Do you need me to tell you that from the minute I saw you again there was no room in my life for anyone else?'

Laura's nod was shaky. 'Yes,' she said definitely. 'Yes, I need you to tell me that.'

'Okay.' Oliver's fingers insinuated themselves into the top of her bikini briefs. 'So I've told you.' He caught his breath as his hands cupped her bare bottom. 'Anything else?'

Laura trembled. 'Did—did you mean what you said that night at Penmadoc?'

Oliver groaned. 'Yes, I meant it,' he muttered, parting his legs to bring her even closer against him. 'I meant everything I've ever said to you, baby. I love you. I guess I always have. I was just too stupid to do anything about it before now.'

For the first time, Laura appreciated the advantage of her bed being just at the other side of the loft. A colonial four-poster, it was easily big enough to accommodate Oliver's greater length, and after he'd deposited her on the rose satin coverlet she took great pleasure in watching him strip off his clothes.

It had been almost fifteen years since they'd first made love, but Oliver had hardly changed at all, she thought, hugging herself. He was still strong and muscular, and if the years had added maturity that was only to be expected. His chest was broader than she remembered, perhaps, and his stomach was flatter, but the powerful thickness of his manhood still rose proudly from its nest of coarse dark hair.

She'd watched him that day at the hotel, of course. But then she'd believed his only intention was to humiliate her, and that was why she'd done her best to humiliate him. She hadn't succeeded. She'd only succeeded in embarrassing herself; in proving once and for all that where Oliver was concerned she had no real resistance at all.

'Hey.' Oliver saw her watching him. 'Am I the only one getting naked around here?'

Laura caught her breath. 'No,' she conceded, using her crossed arms to haul her cotton top over her head. But when it came to loosening her bra her hands stilled.

'Don't be shy with me,' he said gently, coming down on to the bed beside her and moving her hands aside. With enviable skill, he released the front fastening of the lacy garment, and then sucked in a breath. 'There: that's better.'

Laura's face flamed with colour as he bore her back against the pillows, and panic, plain and simple, made her tremble as if this were her first time. And it was, in a way, she thought unsteadily, as his fingers hooked the hem of her briefs and tugged them off. Her experiences with Conor had hardly been earth-shattering, and towards the end of their marriage they'd barely spoken, let alone anything else.

She was half afraid she wouldn't know what to do, what to say, how to please him, but she needn't have worried. With Oliver, everything had always been instinctive somehow, and his hands and lips made a nonsense of her fears. With only a touch, he was able to arouse her deepest needs, her deepest feelings, and she gave up worrying about anything but the pleasure he was so effortlessly bestowing.

His hands skimmed her breasts, teasing the taut peaks with his palms, before replacing one of his hands with his tongue. He rolled the swollen nipple between his tongue and his teeth, and then dragged it into his mouth to suckle on the tip.

Both breasts received this sensuous attention before he trailed kisses over her stomach and midriff, exploring the dark hollow of her navel, nudging the red-gold curls that hid her femininity. One long finger discovered her moist readiness, and although she didn't want to expose her eagerness she couldn't help arching up against that sensual invasion.

'Oh, baby,' he said thickly, 'me, too.' And, easing himself between her splayed legs, he joined his body to hers.

'God, you have no idea how much I've wanted this,' he added as she reached for him. 'How much I've wanted to be buried deep inside you, so deep that we don't know where you end and I begin.'

'I love you, Oliver,' she breathed, her chest constricted by the ache of emotion that seemed to be filling her. 'Oh, Oliver, I love you so much.'

Some time later, Laura opened her eyes, to find Oliver propped on one elbow beside her, watching her. For a moment, she was too embarrassed to say anything, and, as if sensing her confusion, Oliver bent his head to kiss her lips.

'Mmm, you taste as sweet as you look—and I should

know,' he murmured, reminding her that he hadn't been satisfied with making love with her just once. There'd been a second time, when he'd brought her to the brink of fulfilment with his tongue, before his own needs had demanded a fuller demonstration of his love for her.

'You shouldn't say things like that,' she said now, her cheeks brimming with becoming colour. 'Isn't it enough that you've reduced me to a trembling supplicant at your hands?'

'Well, hell, lady, join the club,' he teased her softly. 'And I reckon I've earned the right to tell you I love you any way I choose, don't you?'

Laura pressed her lips together. 'I—I suppose so.'

'You suppose so?'

'All right.' She dimpled. 'All right, yes. So long as I can do the same.'

'Hey, you can say what you like to me,' he assured her. 'So long as you're prepared to take the consequences.'

'What consequences?'

A trailing hand cupped her breast. 'Do you want me to show you?'

'I—no.' With some regret, Laura declined. 'I—I think we should talk about the consequences of—of what—this means first.'

Oliver sighed. 'You mean us?' He gave her a wary look. 'I should have thought that was obvious.'

'Is it?' Laura was nervous.

'I hope so.' His eyes darkened. 'I assumed—I hoped—it meant that we were going to be together from now on. I mean,' he hastened on, 'I'm not suggesting you should give up your life here if that's what you want. I'm quite prepared to relocate, if that would please you.'

'Please me?' Laura felt the tears sliding down her cheeks but she couldn't help it. 'You please me,' she said, lifting her hand to cup his face. 'So—so very much.'

Oliver's eyes softened. 'Well, then—'

'There are other—other things we have to talk about.'

'What other things?' He closed his eyes for a moment. 'Oh, you mean the baby.' He groaned. 'Dear God, if I'd known—'

'I don't mean the baby,' she told him softly. 'Losing it was terrible, but, believe me, it was nothing compared to losing you.'

'Oh, sweetheart—'

'No, let me finish. I want you to know I don't blame you for anything any more. We were both too young, I realise that now. In that, at least, your mother was right—'

'My mother—'

'Yes, your mother,' agreed Laura huskily. 'She's not going to be pleased about—about us.'

'And that worries you?'

Laura nodded. 'A little.'

'Well, don't let it.' Oliver drew her closer. 'If and when my mother decides she has anything more to say to me, she'll say it in my time, not hers, and she knows that.' He paused. 'She and I have come to an understanding since you left Penmadoc. She doesn't interfere in my life and I don't interfere in hers.' His lips twisted. 'Of course, she was sure you would never speak to me again, and until Thomas rang me in Spain and told me about your call I'm afraid I was inclined to believe her.'

'Oh, Oliver…'

She reached up and bestowed a warm kiss at the corner of his mouth and he pulled a wry face. 'It's true. I guess I've been as guilty of listening to her lies as anyone. But, I have to admit, in this instance, I thought she'd got it right.'

'How could you think that?'

Laura was appalled, and Oliver hastened to explain. 'I was sure you'd try to see me again before you left for the States. This assignment I was on in Spain is already way behind schedule because I hung about for so long, waiting for you to contact me.'

'But you left Penmadoc,' protested Laura. 'As soon as

you'd arranged things with Mr Venning, you cleared off back to London. To Natalie, I assumed. Why else?'

'Try imagining how I was feeling,' Oliver said simply. 'Between us—my mother and I—we'd really mucked up your life. I was sure you'd never believe anything I had to say again.'

Laura shook her head. 'And I thought you were only using me to prove to yourself that I'd never got over you.'

'I wish.'

'Do you?' She looked up at him with guarded eyes.

'That you'd never got over me?' said Oliver ruefully. 'Of course I do. I'm only human.'

Laura caught her lower lip between her teeth. 'I wish I'd known.'

'Why?' He gazed intently at her. 'I thought you hated me—for a while, at least.'

'I never hated you,' said Laura honestly. 'I resented you; I resented the way you could hurt me. But I never hated you.'

Oliver frowned. 'But when you married Neill—'

'I should never have married Conor.' She sighed. 'I knew that when you came home for the wedding. I guess I was hoping I could get you out from under my skin. Trying to prove to myself that I didn't care you'd made a success of your life without me.'

'Hey...' Oliver's knuckles brushed the dampness from her cheeks. 'Being good at what I do doesn't mean I've made a success of my life.' He grimaced. 'These last few months I've realised that I've spent all these years searching for something I had and lost. You. Everything else is unimportant.'

'You don't mean that.'

'Don't I?' His thumb skimmed her breast. 'Well, I suppose I am proud of some of my work, but it means very little if you've no one to share it with.' He nuzzled her throat. 'I want to share it with you, Laura. Only you.' He drew back to look at her. 'Will you marry me?'

'Marry you?' Laura's lips parted. 'Oh, Oliver—'

'No, wait.' He seemed to think she was about to refuse, and he hurried on, 'I know your job's important to you—

'Oliver—'

'—and, as I said before, if you'd prefer to stay in New York, I'm quite prepared to live here.'

'Oliver, listen to me—'

'I don't know how Thomas will take it, of course. But we can face that hurdle when we come to it. So long as we're together—'

'Yes, so long as we're together,' broke in Laura breathlessly. 'Darling Oliver, of course I'll marry you, and I'll live any place you like.'

He looked stunned. 'You will?' he exclaimed, and then pulled her into his arms and buried his mouth on hers. Hot passion flared between them once again, but on this occasion he tried to keep his head. 'And—and your work?'

'I've thought about it,' admitted Laura softly. 'I've already discussed working at home with Conor's uncle Matt because I fully intended to return to my roots one day. I had thought I'd stay with Aunt Nell at Penmadoc, but I'd much prefer to stay in London with you.' She smiled. 'We could even keep this place as an extra studio. It might be nice to come here sometimes and remember tonight.'

'You mean it?'

Oliver was delighted and Laura wound her arms around his neck. 'Well, one day we might go back to Penmadoc. I want to have your baby, and the air there is much better than in the town.'

'As long as we're together,' he echoed softly. 'I never want to risk losing you again.'

It's a world of Gucci and gossip and suddenly everyone is talking about the steamy antics at the Cannes Film Festival.

HOLLYWOOD LIFE OR ROYAL WIFE? by Fiona Hood-Stewart

When scandal threatens to engulf Hollywood sensation Victoria Woodward, Prince Rodolfo sweeps her off to his Mediterranean kingdom. But despite her dreams of a royal wedding, it seems Rodolfo's princess must be chosen for her blue blood, not her red carpet reputation…

MARRIAGE SCANDAL, SHOWBIZ BABY! by Sharon Kendrick

The world's most glamorous couple, Jennifer Warren and Matteo D'Arezzo, are on the red carpet at their latest premiere – despite having just split up! Only, watching their steamy movie together sparks unstoppable passion…with life-changing consequences.

SEX, LIES AND A SECURITY TAPE by Jackie Braun

Rumour has it former film star Colin McKinnon's got serious political ambition. No wonder he can't afford to be seen with infamous Tempest Herriman. Too bad he's been caught on CCTV in flagrante with the wild child!

On sale 19th May 2006

Available at WHSmith, Tesco, ASDA, Borders, Eason, Sainsbury's and all good paperback bookshops

www.millsandboon.co.uk